CASSANDRA PAGE

www.cassandrapage.com

Cassandra Page
www.cassandrapage.com

Cataloguing-in-Publication data available from
the National Library of Australia www.nla.gov.au

ISBN: 9780648130246

Cover and paperback design by KILA Designs
www.kiladesigns.com.au
Cover image: © Shutterstock / Dm_Cherry

For storytellers everywhere

CHAPTER ONE

"The ships. They're in the harbour!"

Rheia's younger brother brushed past her, sandals slapping against the flagstones in the central courtyard as he darted for the villa's outer door. Scowling, she steadied the heavy jar of oil in her arms and glared after him. Then his words sank in. *Father.* "Aias, wait. I'll come with you!"

The door slammed and he was gone.

Cursing, she hurried into the kitchen and set the jar down on a shelf next to its almost-empty twin.

"Watch your language." Rheia's grandmother, Charis, sat by the stove, basking in the warmth from a log whose heart glowed cherry red as it slowly turned to cinders. Her hands worked busily, grinding barley into powder to make bread. "You sound like a soldier with that mouth. Or a sailor."

"Perhaps because I'm the daughter of a soldier-turned-sailor?" Rheia suggested with a grin, rubbing her nose with the back of her hand. A thin plume of smoke from the fire was drawn out the narrow window set high in the wall, but it still tickled her sinuses.

"Cheeky." Charis's dark eyes crinkled in a smile, undermining her reprimand.

"Sorry, *Tethe*," Rheia said, bobbing her head in an apology. "But Aias said the ships are returning and then left without me."

"Oh, he did, did he?" Charis sat up straight, brightening at the news.

"Would you like to come to the harbour?" Charis nodded, and Rheia's eyes widened. Her grandmother rarely left the villa these days, not even to go to the *agora*, the city's teeming marketplace. Instead she was content to stay at home, cook the family's meals, and grumble about the produce selected by her son's wife, her grandchildren, and the serving girl who came every morning except on holy days to help with the chores.

Rheia's delight faded to impatience as she waited for the old woman to fetch her shawl from upstairs. To hide her desire to run as Aias had, she busied herself with fastening her loose scarf, pinning it so the fabric covered the dark fall of her hair. Rheia loved her hair, the way the sunlight picked out a chestnut brown in the ebony locks—but that was something she only got to see when the sunlight angled just so through her bedroom window, or when it slanted down into the courtyard. When she went out in public, her hair must be covered, for propriety's sake—and, as a girl of marriageable age, she could never go out alone.

Sometimes she envied Aias. Although he was only nine, he was allowed the run of the city. And his *chiton* only came to his knees, which would be much more

comfortable in the hot summer air than the ankle-length garment Rheia wore.

Charis finally descended the stairs, dressed in defiance of the season in her heavy woollen *chiton* and a shawl dyed scarlet. She saw Rheia's incredulous look and pursed her lips. "Just wait until you are old and your bones feel the cold as mine do."

"No veil, *Tethe*?" Rheia asked, taking her grandmother's extended arm. Her glance flew to her grandmother's exposed hair. The old woman's locks were iron grey and flowed down her back in an intricate braid.

"I don't have time for that nonsense anymore."

Rheia raised her eyebrows but said nothing, her feet dancing with impatience at her grandmother's side as they left the villa, turning down the hill towards the harbour.

The ocean gleamed a vivid blue so bright it almost hurt the eyes to look at it; the sun's reflection shimmered in a streak of white-hot fire where it struck the water's surface. Closer in to the harbour, with its long stone pier and sandy shore, the water lightened to the same shade as the turquoise bead at Rheia's throat.

Oars striking the water in perfect unison and white sails billowing, four triremes sailed into the harbour. Each trailed a column of dark smoke as its engine worked to drive the three banks of oars propelling it along. The sight filled Rheia with awe, but her grandmother wrinkled her nose as she stared at the dark pillars. "Not so long ago the men would have been rowing, not standing around like a gaggle of gossipy serving girls, looking pretty."

"They don't seem to be gossiping," Rheia said, peering at the distant decks of the ships. The soldiers—around one hundred on each ship—all stood to attention, probably aware of the city's eyes on them.

"Still, it's a wonder they are able to keep fit enough to do their duty," Charis said, feet shuffling along the dusty road. People flowed around them. The streets were growing crowded—the wealthy residents of Rheia's neighbourhood mingled with servants and the occasional slave who'd been captured on some distant shore. "All that rowing used to keep them strong."

"They do still train, *Tethe*," Rheia murmured. She'd caught glimpses of their training when she was a small girl and her mother, Antheia, had taken her to see her father at the barracks. She still remembered the bronzed warriors fighting in the dusty field, naked to the waist, before her mother had gasped and covered Rheia's staring eyes.

Her grandmother clicked her tongue before falling silent, allowing Rheia to watch as the triremes slowed like lazy gulls coming in to land at the pier, tired and with bellies full of fish. Or, in this case, treasure—offerings in recognition of the great and powerful army of the island of Oreareus, home of Areus, god of war and holy fire.

By the time the pair reached the docks, the triremes had lowered their gang planks. Rheia struggled to see over the many-headed crowd, most of them taller than she was, but her grandmother tugged her hand, pulling her over to a stack of crates. "Up here, girl," the old woman said with a glint in her eye as she lifted the hem of her *chiton* to step up onto the small platform. A trader scowled at them but, taking in the fine-dyed linen of their clothes, said nothing.

From her perch beside Charis, Rheia's eyes picked out

the figurehead of her father's trireme—at least, the one he captained. Like all the others, its figurehead was a carved wooden sculpture of mighty Areus, but on her father's ship the god's armour had been clad with iron, the rarest of the metals. His curly hair and beard were gilded with gold, and where his eyes should have been were set two fiery gems that glinted scarlet in the afternoon light.

Even at this distance, those blank, staring eyes chilled Rheia. Hugging herself, she tore her gaze away from them to watch as half the ship's complement of soldiers rattled down the gang plank, forming an honour guard. Sunlight glinted off the buckles on their leather armour, bright flecks of honey gold against the dark brown.

Fearless of the peril of wearing a bronze breastplate at sea, her father, Loukios, gleamed like the sun god made flesh as he strode down the gang plank on worn sandals. His helmet covered his ears and cheeks, while a long nose guard reached down to his stern lips. The horsehair crest on top of the helmet stood stiff and proud, carefully dyed a fresh scarlet by Antheia before his departure. At his hip a precious iron sword hung in its scabbard, and his bronze-clad shield was slung across his back. On his other hip, strapped into a bronze-plated leather holster, his fire-thrower hung—the latest weapon divine Areus had gifted his armies. Loukios looked like the great Orearean trierarch he was, and the crowd's cheer soared into the sky when they saw him.

The cheer waned to a reverent murmur as the *helot thysies*—the human offerings of the *helot* people from across the sea—stepped into view.

The four young people trailed in her father's wake down to the pier, their hands bound behind their backs.

5

The eldest looked no older than Rheia, who was now in her sixteenth summer, and all were dressed in pure white *chitons* with uncovered hair. The two boys held their heads high, jaws clenched and grim as they stared around them. Rheia could see the whites of their eyes; they were like wild stallions on a lunge rope for the first time, wishing they could break free. Did they know their fate? She supposed they must—the details of the arrangement were part of the treaty between Oreareus and the *helot* people. The treaty had ended the long war, freeing the *helots* from the fear of raids by Orearean triremes and soldiers with god-given arms they could never hope to defeat.

One of the two girl *thysies* hung her head, her long, dark locks—so like Rheia's—hiding her face. The other's posture mirrored that of the boys, chin lifted as she regarded the soldiers and the crowd beyond, her grey eyes narrowed with contempt. Rheia saw the stiffening shoulders and clenching fists as the Oreareans around her took offence.

Perhaps sensing the shift in mood, Rheia's father glanced back. His lips moved as he said something. A warning? The second girl lowered her gaze, veiling her disdain as efficiently as Rheia had veiled her hair.

"Isn't it great?" Aias said, squeezing up onto the crate between Rheia and Charis. "Father is home. I wonder what treasures he brings us."

"Aias," Rheia's mother chided softly, coming to stand before her children. She looked beautiful in a grass-green *chiton*, with a light shawl the colour of yellow flowers over her hair. "The treasures are for the people and the temple. You should not say otherwise, or people might think your father greedy."

"Yes, *Mammidon*," Aias replied, grinning. "But when I said us, I meant the city." He spread his arms wide, nearly knocking Rheia from her perch.

"If you say so," Antheia replied with narrowed eyes and an edge to her tone. Rheia suspected her mother didn't believe him, but—conscious of nearby, attentive ears—was choosing not to argue and cause a scene. As they turned back to drink in the spectacle, Rheia reached behind Aias's back and pinched his arm. He yelped. She feigned innocence.

The soldiers escorting their father and the *thysies* passed close by where the four of them waited, but if Loukios saw them he did not pause. Nor did Rheia expect him to, not when he was guarding such a prize—but she did feel a little surge of disappointment as the entourage moved on and up the hill towards the *agora* and the temple of Areus.

"That was magnificent," Aias breathed as the last of the armed men moved out of sight. His eyes gleamed as he turned to look at his family. "One day I will be a soldier, and I'll have my own trireme and bring back iron and spices and *thysies* for the Beast. You'll see."

Rheia felt a shiver of cold at the mention of the Beast. She couldn't think of anything worse than being in that monster's service ... and yet, her father did it.

"We would be so proud," their mother murmured, cupping his cheek in her palm.

"I'm not a baby." Aias stiffened and brushed her hand away, glancing around as if to see whether anyone had noticed.

Antheia smiled faintly and looked in the direction in which her husband had departed. "We should head to the villa and prepare a fine meal for when he arrives home. By the time he has delivered the *thysies*, it will be sundown."

"But *Mammidon*, I wanted to stay and watch them unload the treasure," Aias wailed, rather like the baby he'd just claimed he wasn't. His eyes drifted back to the busy pier. The other three triremes, which did not have a precious cargo of *thysies* like Rheia's father's had, were now covered with scrambling men in the fiery orange linen of temple servants. The other captains directed the men as though the unloading was a military operation—which, given the value of the cargo, Rheia supposed it was.

"I need you to come home," Antheia told Aias. "Water must be drawn for your father's bath when he returns, and the fire stoked to heat it."

"The girl can do it." Aias folded his arms, clenched his jaw and avoided his mother's gaze. His hair curled on his smooth forehead, lighter than Rheia's: a warm brown only a few shades darker than his tanned skin.

"She doesn't work after midday." Antheia's voice was tight, stretched almost to breaking. Aias knew their serving girl wouldn't be home—he just didn't care.

"Why can't we buy some Arean fire from the temple? Then we wouldn't need logs for a boring old fire anymore."

Rheia rolled her eyes at her brother. The holy fire of Areus was expensive; even her father's captain billet wasn't enough to pay for it. And although Arean fire powered his fire-thrower, it was sealed in glass, part of the weapon. To use it improperly to heat bathwater or cook their meal would be sacrilege. Their best chance to get some was to earn the temple's goodwill. Then they might receive the fire as a gift.

Aias opened his mouth to argue, and Rheia's hands curled in the front of her *chiton*. "I can stoke the fire," she said, turning to her mother. Her brother's mouth snapped shut and his eyes widened. "But perhaps Aias could pick up some honeyed dates for dessert?"

"Loukios does love them, Antheia," Charis pointed out to Rheia's mother, a glint in her eye as she studied her granddaughter's bland expression.

"Please?" Aias begged. "I will be home well before dinner."

"Very well." Antheia sighed. Before her son could cheer, she added sternly, "But you will buy honeyed dates, a wheel of cheese and a bag of grapes. And you will be home in time to wash and change."

Aias drooped. "Yes, *Mammidon*."

Rheia hid a smile behind her hands as her mother handed the boy a couple of silver coins. The three women walked back to the villa, Rheia and Antheia slowing to keep pace with the older woman's tired shuffle as they climbed the hill.

Rheia swept the courtyard while her mother and grandmother began preparing dinner. Although it was mid-afternoon, the sun beat down and—her scarf placed carefully to one side—Rheia's hair grew hot with its kiss, a physical reminder that it was only half a moon until midsummer and the Festival of Areus. Still, she sighed with relief when the white disc sunk down below the villa's roofline, blanketing the paving stones in cool shade. Once the courtyard was clean enough that the family could eat their meal off it if they wished, Rheia placed a stack of cut wood beside the baths. Then she donned her veil and collected a bucket from the storeroom. "I'm fetching the water now."

Antheia opened her mouth to speak, probably to protest her daughter leaving the villa unescorted, but Charis put a hand on the younger woman's arm. "I will move to the stoop. I can shell these nuts as easily there as I can here, and the bench will be warm from the afternoon sun."

Antheia nodded and returned her gaze to the fish she was descaling.

"Don't think I don't know what your plan was, suggesting honeyed dates," Charis said to her granddaughter as they crossed the courtyard.

"I don't know what you mean," Rheia protested, eyes downcast.

"That Galen, the attractive young man from the marketplace. Isn't his father the one who imports dates from the east?"

Rheia held the outer door open for her grandmother. "Yes...?"

"They are a good family." Charis eased herself down onto the bench against the villa's white wall with a serene smile and didn't elaborate any further—but she didn't need to.

Rheia felt the older woman's eyes on her back as she walked over to the fountain in the adjacent plaza to fill her bucket. The centre of the fountain was shaped like a dolphin, spouting water from its smiling beak.

The third time she placed the bucket under the splashing water, Rheia's heart leapt into her throat. *There he is.* Galen strode up the hill, a cloth-wrapped package tucked under one arm. His eyes were as bright as the sky, and his smile was even brighter, as he saw her and approached. She placed the half-full bucket down at her

side before she spilled it on herself, and brushed her work-reddened hands together. They had spoken many times over the last year, conversations at the marketplace under her family's watchful eye, but this was the first time they would have a little privacy—from listening ears, if not from watching eyes.

"Fair Rheia, daughter of Loukios," Galen greeted her with a flourish, his voice almost as musical as the fountain's tinkling. Her grandmother was right—he was handsome, with his strong jaw and straight nose. "Why is such a lovely maiden doing a slave's work?"

"We have no slave. My father doesn't approve of them." The fact was the cause of some astonishment among the other wealthy houses, but Loukios was proud of his decision so Rheia refused to be ashamed. Galen's brow furrowed and he opened his mouth, probably to ask why, but she spoke first, lifting her chin. "Why are *you*?"

"I wanted to deliver the dates myself. They are some of the sweetest we've made yet, and I was concerned your younger brother may not give them the … appropriate care." Galen offered the bundle and she took it. His warm fingers brushed her palm during the exchange, and a shiver ran up her spine. His gaze was warm on her eyes, her lips, as he spoke in a lowered voice. "Also, I was hoping to see you."

Warmth heated her cheeks. "My father will be pleased. About the dates, I mean. He has a sweet tooth."

"That is good to know," Galen said, hesitating before adding, "since I wish to earn his favour."

Rheia's eyes widened and her heart leapt. Was he suggesting what she thought he was? Presumably reading her expression, he nodded, a hesitant smile at the corner of his mouth. Slowly she smiled back, and his expression transformed into a grin.

"Rheia," Charis called from behind them. Bitter disappointment burned in Rheia's chest at her grandmother's awful—and possibly deliberate—timing. "Are you finished? Your mother needs our help."

"I will see you another time," Galen said and, greatly daring, placed a quick kiss on the back of her hand. She gasped, clutching the bundle of dates, as he turned back towards the *agora* and the setting sun.

CHAPTER TWO

With dark, grey-speckled hair still damp from his bath, Loukios sat at the head of the table, dressed in a simple *chiton*. It had been only two months since Rheia last saw him, but he looked older, the lines on his forehead and around his mouth and eyes deeper. *He is weary; that is all*, she reassured herself. The ships had no doubt been sailing since dawn, and it had been after dark by the time he returned from delivering the four *thysies*—late enough that Charis had already retired. They ate now by the light of a round clay lamp, flax wicks trailing from its two nozzles.

Antheia had also washed and was dressed for dinner in a fine blue *chiton* and a necklace of beaten gold whose pieces curled like autumn leaves at her throat. She wrinkled her nose as she nibbled the fish, which was dry from overcooking. Her husband brushed the back of her hand with his fingertips. "I had to deliver the *thysies* from Areus's temple to the House of the Beast after they were sanctified," he said. "There was ... an incident."

"What was it?" Aias said, speaking around a mouthful of food. He didn't seem troubled by the cooking, chewing enthusiastically. "The incident?"

Loukios hesitated a moment, lifting the cup of watered wine and sipping, before he answered. "One of the girls tried to escape." Rheia's mind flashed back to the proud girl with the grey eyes who'd regarded the Oreareans with such disdain. "I had to make sure they were safely in the Broken Ones' care before I departed."

"Doesn't the temple have guards for that?" Antheia's eyes were fixed on her husband's face as he spoke, her gaze almost hungry after so long an absence. Rheia wondered whether she too would gaze adoringly at her future husband after being so long married. The thought of staring across a table at Galen made her pulse race.

"It was those same temple guards that the girl managed to slip by. If we hadn't still been there, she would have been down the hill and vanished into the city." Loukios scowled into his wine for a moment and then straightened, smiling at his children. "But never mind. The *thysies* are safe in the arms of the Broken Ones and are no longer my problem."

Safe is an interesting choice of word. The leather-covered cushion of Rheia's stool creaked as she shifted. The idea of the Broken Ones had frightened her since she had first heard of them when she was a child; they were the deformed servants of the Beast itself. And where had the girl imagined she'd go, if she had escaped? There wasn't a single citizen of Oreareus who would shelter her, not given the consequences.

Aias interrogated Loukios about the *helot* lands, and whether he'd had to do any fighting, repress any rebellions.

Their father shook his head, his eyes shadowed as he studied his plate. "They don't resist us, not since the war. The only time we had to draw our weapons other than for show was when one of the soldiers startled a wild boar while he was, ah—" he glanced at Antheia and then at Rheia, "—relieving himself."

"Did you use your fire-thrower?" Aias took a sip from his cup. Like Rheia's, his wine was well watered, diluted even more than what the adults drank.

"No."

The boy chortled. "If you had, your dinner would have already been cooked."

"Perhaps," Loukios agreed. "But the boar was close to my man, and the fire-throwers are an indiscriminate weapon with a sensitive triggering mechanism. In close quarters, a short sword is always preferable."

Aias's eyes widened. "You killed a boar with a short sword?"

The rest of the mealtime conversation was consumed by talk of wrestling boars, and the various ports the triremes had visited while collecting the *helot* peace offer-ings. Rheia only half listened, eating her food mechanically as her thoughts returned to Galen's comment at the fountain. Had he truly been suggesting he intended to ask her father if they could wed? Or had she imagined it, a combination of wishful thinking and the hot sun? But no, she was sure that was what he'd been hinting at. When would he do it? Sixteen was not too young for her to marry—she knew other girls her age who had already moved in with their new husbands. Not many, but some. One girl's belly already swelled with child.

When the meals were done, Rheia and Antheia gathered

the dishes and took them to the kitchen, brushing the food scraps into a bucket and setting the plates aside for their serving girl to wash tomorrow morning. Since Charis came out in an itchy red rash if she touched a dog, the family didn't have one to gobble their scraps. But their girl's parents kept pigs outside the city, so she would take the leftovers away when she went home at midday. Once a year, Loukios bought one of the fattened pigs, for the feast in honour of Eidoneus.

Not many worshipped Eidoneus anymore, not with Areus ascendant, but Loukios said a soldier needed to keep the god of the underworld onside, and so paid Eidoneus his due. Rheia liked the god's little green and white statue, which she occasionally glimpsed on a shelf in the *andron*, the men's room. Unlike Areus, whose carved face always regarded the world with either fury or contempt, Eidoneus was calm—despite the long dagger held defensively in one hand. In his other hand was an open scroll, the deeds of each dead soul inscribed upon it. Sometimes, after Rheia spied the statue while bringing an *amphora* of wine or a plate of food to her father and his guests, she would dream of Eidoneus, not of stone but of flesh. The god would kiss her forehead in benediction.

The memory of the dream god's warm lips on her skin made Rheia think of Galen, and the way his lips had brushed her hand like feathers. What would those lips feel like, pressing against hers?

"*Mammidon,*" she said slowly as she covered the tops of several open jars with thick leather squares and wound them around with cord to discourage rodents. "What does Father think of Phidias?"

Antheia blinked, turning to study her daughter in the dusty orange light from the dying fire. "Who?"

"The trader."

"Oh." Understanding dawned on her mother's face. "The trader with the handsome son who delivers honeyed dates to select customers?"

"*Tethe* told you, did she?" Despite her burning cheeks, Rheia kept winding the cord, determined to keep her hands busy.

"Of course she did." Antheia sounded amused. "I'm not sure whether your father has an opinion either way about either Phidias or Galen. But, to my mind, theirs is a good family. Would you like me to speak to him?"

Rheia bit her lip. Did she? "I don't want father to think I am being forward, or to presume anything of Galen's motivations."

"But you think the boy is interested? Not just flirting with a pretty girl?"

"I do." Rheia's voice cracked.

Her mother stroked Rheia's hair back from her face, smiling softly. "Then I shall talk to your father. Now, help me put these jars away."

Perhaps conjured by her thoughts of him, that night Rheia dreamed of Eidoneus—a mixed-up nightmare in which she fled a wall of flame roaring down the mountainside, her hand tucked in the god's. He had dropped his scroll somewhere so he could hurry her along, his fingers cool on her palm despite the wash of heat. She woke feeling muddle-headed, eyes filled with grit as though she had run through clouds of smoke so thick she could barely see. Splashing water on her face helped with the grit, but not with the sense of unease, which lingered past breakfast.

Her mother, perhaps assuming her daughter was unsettled by a certain boy, smiled and sent her and Aias down to the *agora* to purchase milk and a bag of fennel seeds. Phidias didn't sell either of those things at his market stall, but Antheia remarked that the best fennel was sold by the herbalist on the corner near the temple of Areus. Her eyes twinkled, telling Rheia she knew as well as her daughter did that Phidias's stall was beside the herbalist's.

Their ears ringing with Antheia's admonition that they *stay together or your father will hear of it*, the pair headed down the hill towards the market, Aias swinging the empty basket as though it were a sword as he fought imaginary foes.

The Orearean *agora* was in the centre of the city, halfway between the harbour and the mountain's foothills. All the wealthier families lived uphill of the marketplace: officers, experienced soldiers, traders, nobles and courtiers. From Rheia's family home, a walk up the slope would show the villas growing larger the closer they were to the king's palace. The palace itself towered above everything, even the House of the Beast, which sprawled behind a white wall covered in carvings of a huge bull's head, a ring through its nose.

The homes closest to the *agora* were less grand than the two-storey villa Loukios owned, but the neighbour-hood was still clean, kept that way by the slaves who

swept up each day, shovelling animal droppings into carts and taking them beyond the city walls. Guards in burnished bronze stood at each corner of the marketplace, watching the teeming customers with a bored eye that drew a frown of disapproval from Aias. "Father wouldn't stand for that sort of sloppiness," he declared, his high voice carrying even amidst the cries of the hawkers. "I bet he'd have those men flogged."

Rheia shushed him as they hurried past a pair of slaves haggling with a woman selling embossed leather and around the corner to the herbalist's. The air was heavy with the mingled scent of dried herbs in baskets, growing hot and aromatic in the sun; her nose picked out mint, dill, thyme and the fennel they were there for. Rheia looked over the herbs, her expression feigning boredom as she glanced to her right, her gaze seeking out Phidias's stall. Disappointment weighed on her heart when she saw Galen wasn't there; instead his father, red-faced in the heat, watched as a dark-skinned *helot* slave unloaded a basket of imported jewellery, positioning each glittering item on a piece of fine linen spread across the table.

Aias didn't seem to be feigning his boredom; he sighed and scowled as Rheia negotiated with the herbalist, an older woman with wrinkly brown skin like a nut. She was bundling the fennel seeds in a strip of cloth when Aias nudged Rheia in the ribs with a pointed elbow and said, "Look there!"

She turned, following the direction of his gaze to the temple of Areus. The building wasn't quite as intimidating as the palace or the House of the Beast high above them at the mountain's foot, but it was more magnificent. The stone statue of the god at the temple's pillared entrance still stood taller than any of the adjacent buildings, its gaze fixed on the horizon out beyond the harbour. Its features were weathered by decades of sun and rain. Fluted pillars ran around the looming brick building, each one gleaming white. The edge of the sloping, tiled roof was carved with images of war: spears, triremes, chariots, fire. In the orange-tinted gloom within the temple, Rheia saw hurried movement as acolytes scurried to and fro. She frowned. What could be causing them such consternation? She turned to Aias, mouth open to speak, and gasped. He'd slipped away from her side, weaving through a herd of goats and past their startled goatherd towards the temple.

Rheia waited, fidgeting, until the herbalist finished tying off the bundle of fennel and counting out her change. Then she tucked the herbs into her basket and followed her brother, head down so as not to attract attention: an unwed, unaccompanied woman. She would *kill* Aias if his running off resulted in any slight against her name. Thankfully, Phidias was too busy to notice … assuming he even knew who she was. Would Galen have mentioned his interest to his father? She swallowed and adjusted her veil, making sure her hair was completely covered.

She found Aias standing in the deep shadows beneath the statue. He couldn't see into the temple from there, wedged as he was between one huge sandalled foot and an outer pillar, adjacent to the shadowed porch, but his head was cocked as he listened, eyes wide as wine cups. "You just wait until I tell *Mammidon* about this," she hissed.

"Shh," Aias whispered, raking her with a contemptuous gaze. "I'm listening."

"And if the priests see you out here, lurking like a thief, what will they say?" She grabbed his arm and tried to pull him away, but he eeled from her grip and stepped closer to the entrance. If she tried to grab him again, he might stumble backward, out into the bright sunshine where he would be much more obvious. Grinding her jaw with frustration, she glared at him.

He glared back, head tilted upward to meet her gaze. "Rheia, something is going on. They are stirred up like an ants' nest. Don't you want to know why?"

"No," she whispered, shaking her head emphatically. And she didn't. She wanted to browse the trinkets at Phidias's stall, see if he knew her name, see whether Galen was lurking out the back somewhere and might come over to see her.

But she couldn't do so without Aias. "All right," she said with a sigh, crossing her arms and looking away towards the harbour as though she was merely taking a moment to shade herself from the hot sun. "One minute."

Resolved not to listen to the voices inside the great building, Rheia studied the mason's mark hidden at the statue's heel as though it were the most interesting thing in the world. She had heard of Myron, even though he'd died when her grandmother was a baby; the huge statue had been his last great work. But a babble of raised voices as they passed close by the inside doorway caught her ear: the words *thysia* and *offering* louder than the rest, as the speaker emphasised a point. They fell away, and she wondered what had happened to cause such consternation. Had the *helot* girl tried to escape again? Had she been successful this time? There would be a city-wide manhunt to find her if it were true. A surge of sympathy for the girl made her purse her lips. How awful it would be, to know you would be dead when next the moon was full.

Aias's fingers digging into Rheia's arm brought her back to herself. "Rheia," he whispered, the sound sharp with fear. "Let's go."

"Finally," she muttered, glancing up and down the street for watching eyes before hurrying him away from the temple, her hand at the small of his back so he couldn't dart off again. But when she tried to stop at the goatherder's stall to buy a pottery jar of milk, he dragged her on, out of the *agora*. "Aias, stop! Wait!"

"You heard what they said." He shook his head, curls bouncing emphatically as he hauled her along the street, almost at a run. "We have to get home. Father will know more."

Rheia's heart felt strange in her chest, anxiety making it flutter. "More about what? I was trying not to listen. As you should have been."

Her little brother stopped, staring up at her with his mouth ajar. Then he pulled her by the hand into a quiet alley, away from the bustling traffic of the main street. "One of the *helots* is dead," he whispered, eyes glittering with excitement. "One of the girls. Suicide, they say."

Rheia's eyes widened as she stared at her brother. The flutter in her chest expanded to swallow her belly. "But what will happen now? It's only two weeks until the festival. The offering!"

"That's what they were arguing about. One of the priests thought the triremes would be sent back out, while the other said it was too late. Father will know; if the ships are to be sent, he will captain the fleet. Come

on. Before he leaves!"

Rheia let Aias drag her up the hill towards their villa, her mind whirling with the implications. The Broken Ones were meant to have the *thysies* for a full ten days before the ritual. Something about cleansing rituals. But that would only give the triremes three days to get to the *helot* lands and back again. Would it be enough?

And if not, what was the alternative?

CHAPTER THREE

Loukios was gone when his two children ran into the villa, panting and out of breath. Antheia gathered them to her, hugging them until Aias wriggled and danced away. Her mother was worried; Rheia could read it in the tense line of her jaw, the way she avoided her daughter's gaze, the fact that she didn't chide her children for failing to buy the milk. When Aias tried to press her with questions, she shushed him. He continued and she sent him out to split logs for the fire, her words blistering his ears as she chased him out into the courtyard.

Rheia retreated to the *gynaikon*, the women's room—the only place in the house she was guaranteed some peace from her brother. Charis was already there, the older woman sitting at a low, flat table, measuring out a length of sumptuous grey fabric the colour of a dove's wing. The older woman's skin was faintly sheened with perspiration; the top floor of the villa was hotter than the bottom one, where the *andron* was. She glanced up as Rheia sat in the other chair. "What has got you all

aflutter, girl?"

Rheia recounted what Aias had overheard, fidgeting with the folds of her *chiton* until her grandmother snapped at her to hold the grey fabric steady while she cut it with a pair of bronze shears. The blades were sharp enough to draw blood; Rheia remained silent until the cutting was done and the unwanted fabric set aside. Then she leaned forward. "*Tethe*, how long have we been making the sacrifices at the Festival of Areus?"

Charis wrinkled her brow and stared up at the rectangle of blue sky in the window for a moment as she considered. "At least a hundred years—or so the story goes." The corners of her eyes crinkled. "I am old, but not so old that I remember for myself."

"And we only went to war with the *helots* twenty years ago," Rheia said. Charis nodded, and her granddaughter took a deep breath, asking the question that had been bothering her. "So what did we do before the *thysies* and the war prisoners? Who was sacrificed to keep the demon bound? You must remember that."

"I do." Charis's tone indicated she wished she didn't. She set down her shears and leaned back. "We were. Oreareans. Some people were able to substitute slaves, prisoners of past wars or their descendants, but not many."

"Why not? Who wouldn't choose to give up a slave to save a loved one?"

"Back then not every household had a slave—they weren't so common before the war. And the sacrifice must be a virgin." The old woman grimaced as though she had tasted something bitter. "It is a sad truth of a slave's life that not many can say that for themselves.

At least, not for long. That is the real reason the *thysies* are given into the Broken Ones' care. They keep them pure until it is time."

"So if they can't get a new *thysia* to replace the one who died—"

"Oh, hush. They will. Your father will make sure of it."

"But *if* they can't, how would the replacement be decided?"

Charis shrugged, folding the fabric in half with sharp, precise gestures and smoothing it flat as though it had offended her.

"Well, how was it decided *before* the war?"

"Lottery," Charis admitted. "The names of all the city's children, from babes in arms to unwed boys and girls your age, were written on *ostras* and put into a huge jar." Short messages were often scratched into *ostras*, the abundant shards of broken pottery, when more expensive parchment wasn't available. "The high priest of Areus would draw out the names, two boys and two girls. Because balance is pleasing to the god." She muttered this last part with a frown, looking away as though she realised how strange it sounded. As if there could be balance in death.

"Even babies?" Rheia gasped, a chill creeping over her. Even though she knew the story, that Areus had defeated a demon and required the blood of four innocents each year to renew the binding and keep it imprisoned, the thought still horrified her.

Charis nodded. "Yes. But what was the alternative? The demon would destroy us all with fire, or so the priests say."

Rheia remembered her nightmare from the night before, the heat in the *gynaikon* growing suffocating as

she imagined what such a demon might look like. "And they say the sacrifices, even the *helot thysies*, sit at Areus's right hand in the afterlife," Charis added. "He showers them with perfumes and gold, and the finest foods, to thank them for what they surrendered."

The cold, greedy eyes of the statue outside the temple didn't seem to belong to a benevolent god. Rheia doubted the god of war and fire would be so generous. Also, how many right hands could he possibly use? But she kept the thoughts to herself.

Loukios hadn't returned home by sunset, and Rheia's unease grew as she changed into a simple shift, a light *chiton*. Surely, if her father had been sent off to sea already, he'd have sent a message to Antheia? What if he hadn't been given time? Wishing she could go down to the harbour and see for herself whether the triremes still clustered there, Rheia settled onto the cushions of her bed, covered herself with a thin sheet, and tried to sleep. A cool breeze off the ocean blew past the hanging fabric in her window, sometimes mustering the strength to puff the material out like a pennant before dying back and letting it drop with a dull slap against the bricks. The air tickled the outside of her arm, up to her shoulder, doing what it could to reduce the evening heat. Still she tossed and turned, the woven base of the bed creaking beneath the cushions as she shifted, longing for winter. Then, once the fire was banked, the house would grow frigid, but she could pile her bed with blankets and burrow under them.

The sound of footsteps on the road outside their home carried clearly in the quiet night air, as did the creak of the door as her father let himself into the villa. Her mother's soft voice greeted him. He replied with a murmur. The bar thunked into its bracket, securing the door, and then footsteps ascended the stairs as they crept up to their own bedroom. It was next to Rheia's, with Aias's on the other side, closest to the stairs. Although they drew a heavy cloth across their door, she still caught snatches of their conversation over the sounds of her father removing his sandals and dropping them in the corner.

The word *lottery* caught her ear and, before she could question the wisdom of it, she rolled out of bed and padded to her door on bare feet, pulling her own hanging cloth aside so she could better hear what they were saying.

"I told them that," Loukios was saying in a tired voice. "I could've had my crew ready and at the dock with the tide at dawn. But the priests argued against it and the king listened to them, not me."

"What reason did they give?" Antheia's voice was tight.

"They said it would mean renewed war with the *helots*, who would claim they had already given the required number of *thysies* this year. If we Oreareans are too careless to keep them alive, that is our problem." His words were bitter.

"For followers of the god of war, the priests have taken a remarkably cowardly position," Antheia said acerbically. Rheia covered her mouth to muffle her gasp. She had never heard her mother speak ill of a priest before.

Loukios grunted an agreement, before adding reluctantly, "But they are right. And more citizens would die in a new war than would die in this single lottery."

"Why then could the king not buy a young slave girl, provide the *thysia* himself?"

There was a long pause. When Rheia's father spoke,

28

his voice was low, reluctant. "Honestly? I think the temple sees this as an opportunity. A lottery would remind the city of the god's power—of the *temple's* power. And it would silence dissent about the need for continued subjugation of the *helots.*"

"But ... a lottery? They were awful. I never wanted our children subjected to that." Antheia's voice sounded hoarse, as though she spoke around tears. "When will it be?"

"Tomorrow. They don't want to give people a chance to hide their daughters, or to marry them off." Rheia's heart leapt into her throat at the word. *Daughters.* Of course they'd need a girl to replace a girl. As Charis had said, the god liked balance. But hearing her father say it in such tones of distress drove the reality home.

Across from her, on the other side of her parents' doorway, Aias's startled gaze stared back at her from a crack in the fabric at his own bedroom door.

"Loukios, should we...?"

"We can't. Draconaidas is already looking for an excuse to call for my exile. We must be above reproach."

Draconaidas was Areus's high priest. Rheia bit her lip, wondering briefly what her father had done to earn his displeasure, but her thoughts skittered away from the question like a fish on a line, drawn back to the bigger issue. *A lottery.*

"But Rheia—" Antheia said.

"—will be fine. There will be hundreds of names in the lottery. Thousands, even." Loukios's voice was soothing.

Rheia's fingers fluttered to her forehead as she remembered the kiss of benediction in her dreams, and her nightmare the night before. The kiss from Eidoneus, God of the Underworld. Even as the recollection surfaced, she saw his face in her mind's eye, watching her with kind eyes and a sad smile. The conviction that hers would be the *ostra* drawn tomorrow crept over her. With tears burning her eyes, she looked at her younger brother. His expression was stricken; he stared at her as though she were already dead.

CHAPTER FOUR

Rheia's eyelids scraped against her dry eyes every time she blinked, and her face felt taut and hot from crying. After returning to bed, she'd spent half the night praying to Eidoneus not to take her, to stay Areus's hand in the lottery. When she'd finally tumbled into sleep, exhausted beyond measure, she'd dreamed of the god of the underworld: his face was proud as he cupped her cheek and shook his head. His eyes were filled with sorrow.

When she woke in the morning, she knew. Groaning, she covered her face with the sheet and wished she could sink through the ground into Gaea's cool, damp earth, or fly away with the gulls.

Dawn was just beginning to lighten Rheia's window when Charis came into the room with a bowl of water. Rheia peeked out from under the covers, and Charis regarded her granddaughter's puffy face with solemn eyes. "Have you been weeping?"

"Yes," Rheia admitted.

Charis put the bowl down on top of the only other

furniture in the room: a chest that held Rheia's clothes and jewellery. "What is troubling you?"

"I ... I heard Father and *Mammidon* speaking last night. There is to be a lottery. Today," Rheia whispered, sitting up on her bed and clutching the sheet to her chin as though that would save her from the Broken Ones.

"I know. Antheia told me," Charis said, her voice subdued. Then she squared her shoulders and smiled brightly, tugging the sheet from Rheia's hands and placing it at the end of the bed, beyond her reach. "Well, cheer up. You are very unlikely to be chosen today. The lottery is meant to be random, but..." She chewed her lip for a moment, as though wondering whether to continue. "I've been to dozens, and I noticed they *happen* to choose children from less influential families. Coincidentally, I'm sure." Her voice was heavy with irony. "I doubt the temple would want to earn your father's wrath."

"Father said the high priest doesn't like him." Rheia put her feet on the floor but didn't stand, instead looking up at her grandmother.

"He did, did he? Well, even so. The odds are good. Get up, girl. We need you to look your best for the city." Charis turned to the bowl of water, dipping a corner of cloth into it and turning back to Rheia. "Think of all the boys whose eye you could catch. Not just your trader's son. The princes will be there!"

The idea of trying to find herself a husband at a gathering where one of the girls would be chosen to die would have made Rheia uncomfortable under normal circumstances, and these weren't normal circumstances. She had to make her grandmother understand "*Tethe*, listen to me." The seriousness of her tone brought Charis up

short. Avoiding the old woman's gaze, Rheia continued, "Last night Eidoneus came to me in my dream. My name will be drawn today."

Charis's lips pressed together, turning as pale as Rheia felt. "Are you sure it wasn't just your mind, playing tricks on you?"

Rheia nodded, her vision of her grandmother blurring into fragments as tears burned her eyes yet again. "I will be the fourth *thysia*," she sobbed.

"Ah, hush." Charis wrapped her in a hug that smelled of scented oil and woodsmoke. "Ah, my poor girl." She made soothing sounds, as she had done when Rheia was a small child and had grazed her knee, patting her back until the sobs subsided into little hiccoughing breaths.

"Please don't tell Mother and Father," Rheia whispered, wiping her eyes on the back of one hand. Charis batted it away and used the damp cloth, patting at the tears. "They'll find out soon enough." Rheia didn't think she could handle their mournful stares across the dining table.

"If that's what you wish," Charis said, her expression grim. "Here, hold this cloth over your eyes for a couple of minutes. I'll be back."

Rheia lay back on her cushions, draping the cloth across her face. It was cool, leeching the angry heat out of her skin. A droplet of water from the fabric ran down past her ear and into her hairline. She took deep breaths, willing herself to calmness. If today was the last time she'd see her parents, she wanted them to remember her as being strong.

Charis returned, a small phial of scented oil in one hand, and the dove grey cloth folded over her other. "Here," she said, holding out the oil to Rheia, "use some of this."

Rheia uncorked the phial and the sweet scent of attar of roses, like musk and fresh tea, reached her nostrils. The aroma was lovely, even despite her sinuses being partially blocked by her weeping fit.

"It's too expensive," she protested. It took buckets of rose petals to produce even one small phial of oil; who knew how her grandmother had come by it.

"Nonsense," Charis said briskly, touching the oil to her finger and dabbing it at Rheia's throat and wrists. "I was saving this for your wedding day, but today seems as good a day as any." Her voice grew husky with unshed tears but Charis did not let them fall. Instead, she berated Rheia into rising and removing her shift, her expression as solemn as if she were going to war. Charis washed her all over with that damp cloth as though Rheia were a child or a princess being tended by a slave, and combed her hair until it fell down her back in a glossy, dark wave. "I have a new *chiton* for you." Charis picked up the rectangle of soft grey fabric she'd cut the day before, wrapping it around Rheia's body and fastening it at her shoulder and down her upper arms with small gold brooches. The excess fabric she'd cut off yesterday she bound around Rheia's waist as a belt, shortening the full length of the skirt—which was so long it dragged on the ground—by pulling the excess material up so it ruffled at her waist. Finally, Charis drew around Rheia's eyes with charcoal and slipped bronze bracelets over each of her wrists; they coiled like snakes around her forearms.

"There. You are ready," Charis said, standing back to regard her granddaughter. "Now, remember to breathe."

Breakfast passed in a blur. Rheia wasn't hungry, but nibbled dutifully at a piece of bread as she listened to

her parents talk. After telling her about the lottery, they avoided discussing it further, intent on discussing trivial matters. Even her stoic father joined in the conversation, overly animated, as he tried to distract his daughter and wife from what was to come. Aias remained silent. Whenever he looked at Rheia, his eyes were wide. At least he didn't regard her as though she was a walking corpse anymore.

As the family left for the *agora* and the lottery, Aias finally said what he was thinking. "You look beautiful, Sister." His expression was solemn as he slipped his small hand into hers.

"Thank you," Rheia said. She wore an opaque veil that hung down her back to cover her hair but left her face visible. Her eyes ached in the bright sunlight.

People crowded the road, all heading the same way. Not all of the families had girl children. Those who did clustered around them, even as Rheia's did around her. Mothers carried toddlers or babies in their arms with expressions that said the temple would have to pry their daughters from their hands if the worst were to happen. Staring at the dark golden curls on the head of a girl too young to have her hair veiled, Rheia consoled herself with the thought that at least she was sparing that child from having her life cut short by the Beast's blade.

Those members of the crowd who didn't have girls peered at their neighbours with either pity or a sort of gleeful curiosity that made Rheia's skin crawl, as though they were enjoying the excitement and melodrama of the moment. Still, she met each inquisitive gaze directed her way with a prideful tilt of her chin. Let them see how brave she was. Let them remember.

The market stalls had been cleared away from the *agora*, which was already crowded with people even though it wasn't yet time for the lottery. Enterprising traders had rigged up portable stalls that they wore like battle harnesses, and wove through the crowd selling light foods and watered wine. The wine sold more swiftly than the food; the square was already hot and growing hotter as more people poured into it. But the crowd recognised and parted for Loukios, the famous trireme captain. He led his family to a place near the temple where they found some scant shade from the sun—not far from where she and Aias had hidden the day before and heard the news of the dead *thysia* girl.

The eyes of the towering stone Areus still glared out to sea, but they cast a pall over Rheia. She couldn't help but feel as if the god was leering down at her, waiting for her *ostra* to be drawn so he could tear her away from her family, her life. Her hands began to shake. She hid them in the folds of her *chiton*.

Galen stood nearby with his father and mother. He was the tallest of several solemn children—he had one sister, she noted—and when she saw him, her heart trembled in her chest, not with joy or anticipation as it had in the past, but with grief. There didn't seem to be any point in imagining a future with him. Not now.

Galen saw her staring and smiled, leaning over to say something to his mother, a large woman with a kind face. She watched with a tolerant smile as Galen wove through the crowd towards Rheia's family, clearly approving of the potential family connection.

Loukios was distracted, talking to one of the city guards near the temple; Antheia was half listening to

her husband and half keeping a careful eye on her son, lest he disappear into the crowd to wreak mayhem. But Charis watched Galen as he bowed from the waist to Rheia. "You look beautiful," he murmured, echoing Aias.

Despite everything, a blush heated Rheia's cheeks. "Thank you. It was my *tethe*'s idea."

"I can see why. The whole city is here."

She looked around the *agora*, but couldn't see far over the crowd of heads, some veiled, some wearing helmets, many bare: men, boys, and girl children not old enough to have reached puberty yet, as well as a handful of elderly women such as her grandmother, who no longer worried about what the city thought of their virtue. A few girls were veiled so completely that even their faces were covered. Rheia's eyes lingered on the young, bare faces of the children nearest her: so sweet, so worried. When she looked back, she saw Galen's gaze hadn't left her.

A mad, wild thought seized her, and she stepped forward so she could murmur into his ear without being overheard. Charis's hearing wasn't as sharp as it had once been. She wouldn't be able to catch Rheia's words over the crowd's low rumble. "Galen, do you mean to wed me?"

"I ... what?" His mouth fell open.

She grabbed one of his hands, clutching it as though it were a lifeline and she a drowning sailor. "Do you see me as your wife one day?"

His blue eyes dropped to his sandalled feet and it was his turn to blush. "I have thought about it, yes."

"If you wish to marry me, there is something you must do for me. Right now." She smiled shyly. "I think you may not mind so much."

"What is that?" He glanced up, saw her expression, and stared.

"Take my maidenhead." Her voice came out a whisper; that she even suggested it would bring shame to her father, her mother. But better that than death.

Galen's eyes widened, and he glanced down again, this time to the front of her *chiton*. His hands clenched around hers, engulfing them. They were calloused, she noticed. Calloused with work, not swordplay: a merchant's hands. "Why would you offer this to me?"

"Because if you will become my husband there is no dishonour in it. Not really. And it will save me from the lottery."

"Wait," he squeaked. "You want me to take your maidenhead *now*?"

"We can run off," she said, her voice low and urgent. "If we run down there, beside the temple—" she nodded to an alley beyond the statue "—we could easily lose any pursuit in the maze of buildings behind the *agora*. Then we can find somewhere, um, somewhere and you can..." Her eyes wanted to slide away from his face, so ashamed were they at what she was saying, but she couldn't let them. So much depended on this.

Galen considered it. She could tell he did, by the way his gaze lingered on her face, drifted down to the bare expanse of her throat as though he was entertaining ideas about kissing her there. For a moment her heart soared. Then he shook himself, like a hound after it splashed from the waves. "I can't go now. My sister's name is in the lottery. But afterwards," he leaned in and whispered in her ear, "I'd be happy to meet you outside

your villa. I could find somewhere truly nice for us to go. I could show you what manner of husband I can be."

Seeing she was losing him, she clutched his hands until he looked down at them, eyes widening. "This isn't an offer I'll be making again," she said with absolute sincerity. "It is now, before the lottery, or never."

"Rheia, I *can't*." He pulled his hands free and stepped back, his expression regretful. "But we can talk about this again when we next meet."

With tears in her eyes, she shook her head and turned from him. After a few breaths, she heard his footsteps retreat as he walked back to his family.

Charis slipped an arm, still strong from decades of household work, around Rheia's waist, drawing her back to her parents' side. Rheia glanced at her grandmother's face and saw the understanding in her eyes. She knew what Rheia had done, had tried to do, and didn't judge her for it. The compassion was nearly Rheia's undoing. She choked back a sob, and her grandmother hugged her briefly. "The boy is a fool, turning down an offer like that," Charis murmured, pinching her cheek lightly. "But you know he had to. If your dream is true and Eidoneus and Areus have chosen you for this, then Galen could never have said yes. The gods would have struck him down, or rendered him unable to perform."

"I had to try," Rheia whispered. "I had to."

Charis nodded sadly. "I know."

CHAPTER FIVE

T he high priest of Areus must have already been outside
the temple, because Rheia didn't see him exit the huge
building. The first she knew of the lottery's commence-
ment was a flash of movement on the raised platform
dominating the *agora*'s western edge. She glanced up
from her grandmother's shoulder and saw two acolytes,
barefooted boys dressed in knee-length *chitons* dyed
carmine, the colour of dry blood. They pushed a heavy
clay jar that squatted on a wheeled platform between
them, their muscles straining even as they struggled to
keep neutral expressions. The jar's sides were a glossy
black, covered in burnt umber images of Areus—the god
stared out at the crowd, naked except for a helm and a
heavy pendant, and holding a spear aloft in his right
hand as though about to cast it at an enemy.

"That jar contains the *ostras*." The sound of Charis's
voice startled Rheia, so lost had she been in her own
terrified thoughts. The wheels rumbled along the platform
like distant thunder—but the silence that followed was

even more ominous. Rheia tensed.

The high priest, Draconaidas, strode onto the stage, the impact of his ornate sandals juddering timber beams. The acolytes drew back, hands at their sides, leaving their master alone before the crowd.

The priest's *chiton* was scarlet, fresh blood rather than dry, and was woven through with golden thread that stitched out a pattern across his chest and hips, tracing the outline of an invisible breastplate and sword belt. Despite this, he was unarmed, and the only armour he wore was an ornate iron helm. Rheia felt her father stiffen, probably at the sight of the precious metal. Was he thinking it was wasted on a man of the gods when it could be reforged into swords for soldiers? Rheia wondered whether the helm would even be of use in battle, despite the precious metal it was made from: two great, sweeping horns rose from the protective shell, one from each temple, like those of an oxen or a bull. Surely they would channel a sword stroke to the centre of the skull rather than sending it skittering off like her father's round-topped helm would, even with its horsehair crest?

The helm's face plate was open instead of sweeping in to protect the nose and cheeks, and revealed Draconaidas's stern face. His jaw was strong despite the weight of years that sketched lines across his brow and down the sides of his mouth; his skin was the colour of polished yew wood; his eyes were narrowed and dark as he scanned the crowd.

Whatever he was looking for—signs of dissent, perhaps—he didn't find it, and a faint smile plucked at his lips. Rheia knew her neighbours, and even her parents, must resent the temple for threatening their daughters, but fear kept their mouths closed. Fear and also hope, she realised—hope that, if they didn't displease Areus, he'd direct his priest's hand to another family, another child. One less pious than theirs.

Draconaidas rested one hand on the lottery jar, raking the crowd with a final glance before he began to speak, his voice booming out to reach every corner of the *agora*. "One hundred and twelve years ago, a demon called Typhein came to the island of Cretea. The demon was wreathed in fire and wielded twin swords with flaming blades that sheared through armour like flesh. The swords were called *Miaiphonos* and *Thouros*, Murderous and Furious, and well did they deserve their names." Draconaidas paused, eyes blazing, and Rheia gritted her teeth at his theatrics. Everyone knew the story, but he didn't seem able to pass up the chance to preach. "Typhein stood three times the height of a man and had a snake's heavy coils instead of legs. But, despite his size, he moved like a wildcat.

"When the armies of Cretea marched forth to meet him, the demon cut them down like grain in the field, leaving them to spill their lifeblood into the earth." Draconaidas paused, as though savouring the mental image this invoked. Rheia looked down at her feet, not wanting to see the priest's satisfaction. The press of bodies close around made the already-hot courtyard seem hotter than before, and the air stank of sweat and spilled wine. Her head swam with dizziness.

"The people turned to their gods, begging for aid," Draconaidas continued. "Arean augurs slew a white bull and read its entrails to divine the god's will. Areus would, they saw, help the tattered remnants of Cretea's once-strong army, but asked for something in return.

A sacrifice was made in his name, a priestess willingly giving her life to appease the god and strengthen him with her passing. Areus was much pleased, and in return lent his strong arm to the warriors. With his aid, they were able to bring the demon low." The sound of Draconaidas's fist thumping down on the lip of the jar made Rheia jump, and she glanced up. The priest's eyes were afire with enthusiasm.

"But Typhein was not slain, for he was a true immortal. Instead, he was bound in stone with the blood of four innocents—for innocent blood is pure, and is anathema to demon-kind. And so the demon slumbered.

"To give thanks, the Creteans became known as Oreareans, and changed the name of their island city to Oreareus, the mountain of Areus. There, they raised Areus high, making him their most-favoured god. And he gave them gifts of fiery weapons and engines so theirs became the strongest army in the world, that all others might fear the sight of their white sails on the horizon. All Areus required in return from his people for this great beneficence was the blood of four innocents at sunset on midsummer day, during the Festival of Areus— although this was not for his own glory, but to renew the demon's bonds.

"So his people didn't have to sully themselves with the task of sacrificing the innocents, Areus plucked a child from his mighty thigh, an avatar beast that dwells in the depths beneath the House of the Beast, where the Broken Ones dwell. This beast only emerges from its house on the night of the festival, to do its divine duty."

Rheia shuddered when she recalled her last glimpse of the Beast: she had been twelve, and had begged her father to let her go to see the *helot thysies'* sacrifice. Marpessa, a sometimes friend of Rheia's, had spoken of going and Rheia hadn't wanted to seem ignorant—just as Loukios did not keep slaves, he didn't take his family to see the sacrifice, instead preferring to enjoy the less-bloody parts of the festival. Seeing the curiosity in her eyes, he'd relented, and Rheia had gone, accompanied by Charis, to stand outside the walls of the House of the Beast and watch the spectacle on the raised dais.

Afterwards, she'd wished she hadn't; it had been months before her nightmares of the strangely compelling silhouette, with its huge, horned head and the body of a man, had left her dreams. Months before she could shake the image of the *thysies'* bodies, their throats bloody gashes, crumpling to the ground like broken dolls.

The memory returned now, and she shuddered so violently that not only Charis but also Antheia, standing further away, noticed. "This lecture is almost done. It won't be long now and we can go home," Antheia breathed in her daughter's ear. "Be still."

I wish that were true. Rheia inhaled deeply, trying to ease the wave of giddiness that threatened to undo her. Somewhere a baby wailed, quickly hushed. *I wish he'd just get on with it.*

"The bindings on the monster Typhein require two males and two females, for balance: the male side to bind the demon's good right arm, and the female to bind its sinister left," Draconaidas continued. Beside Rheia, Charis sniffed. "As most of you will now be aware, one of the female *thysies* was found dead in the House of the Beast yesterday. There is no time for us to send for a new *thysia*, and an augury has revealed that Areus will bless

a lottery. So, with a heavy but pious heart, the king has ordered a lottery be held. Those of you whose names are in this jar—" he patted the vessel fondly "—are too young to have had your *ostras* in there before. But this is a sacrifice your parents and grandparents know well, and perhaps it is fitting to remind the newest citizens of Oreareus of the price of our safety and prosperity."

As he finished speaking, Draconaidas's gaze once more roamed the crowd, and this time he spotted Loukios and his family. His dark eyes were like balls of coal as he looked from her father to her mother, and then to her. His lips curved in a smile and she knew what he was thinking: *Here is the girl whose name I will draw.* His hand reached into the jar to find her *ostra*, and Rheia caught her mother's hand in her own. "I love you, *Mammidon*," she murmured in Antheia's ear. "You and Father both. Remember me once I'm gone, and keep Aias out of trouble." Her voice broke on the last word, and she lifted her chin lest more tears spill down her cheeks. She was sick of crying.

Antheia turned to stare at Rheia with eyes so wide her daughter could see the realisation dawning in them. "Oh, no..."

"Rheia, daughter of Loukios," Draconaidas boomed from the stage. A pottery shard was clutched aloft in his hand, writing turned outwards so that those closest to him might be able to read the name and verify his words. A ripple of surprise ran over the crowd. Everyone knew who Loukios was, if not his daughter.

"*No*," Antheia gasped, turning to her husband. "You can't let them!" Loukios's face was pale as he stared back at his wife.

"It's alright, Father," Rheia said, voice trembling as

hot hands grasped her elbows, pulling her from the protection of Charis's arms. Loukios turned a stricken gaze on her, but nodded, apparently accepting her words. She turned to see four burly, orange-clad servants of the temple standing there, expressions grim as they prepared to haul her away. Their eyes flicked from her to her father as though expecting an attack. One had his hand on the hilt of a sword, his jaw clenched. But Loukios stood still, gaze cast downwards, ignoring Antheia's urgings.

He would not fight for Rheia.

Even though that was what she'd wanted, disappointment stung like ocean water in a cut, bitter and sharp. Would he have fought if it had been Aias? Sons were worth more than daughters. The thought shamed her, and she rounded on the guards who jostled her, her eyes narrowed with indignation. "Release me!" she snarled. "I will walk."

Surprise widening their eyes, they did as she demanded. For a fleeting second she toyed with the idea of running. But what was the point? She would find no shelter on the island. The Oreareans needed her to die. If she didn't, one of their daughters would perish in her place. No one would help her.

Still, the sight of Galen turning his back on her as she followed the servants into the temple of Areus tore at her heart.

CHAPTER SIX

Rheia blinked as she entered the temple for the first time since she was a small girl, passing from the small, semi-protected porch into the main room, the *cella*. After the noisy brightness of the *agora*, the temple's interior was all grey shadows and the muted sounds of shuffling feet, lit only by a handful of fat oil lamps nestled in brackets on the walls. Beneath each sconce, sitting in a pool of light, were the city's offerings: baskets of fruits and spices, small leather bags bulging with coins, loaves of bread and rolls of fine cloth. The air smelled of sandalwood incense, imported from across the sea. The Oreareans had been most generous to their god—and his priests—in the lead-up to the lottery. Rheia's lips twisted downwards as she wondered whether her name would have been drawn if Loukios had come to the temple during the night and left some treasure for Areus and his priests.

But no. Rheia suspected from her father's words that the decision to choose her name had been political. How had the high priest done it? Had he placed her *ostra* on the top of the pile in the jar beforehand? Chosen a distinctively shaped shard so he knew which one he grasped? Or had her name been on all the topmost shards, so it didn't matter which one he chose?

As her eyes adjusted to the dimness, the tall shadow at the other end of the long room resolved into a finely carved statue of pale stone. As with his depiction on the side of the *ostra* jar, here too Areus was almost entirely naked, one leg bent as though ready to lunge forward, displaying his carved nethers to the worshippers. His only garments were a golden helm and a glowing pendant that sat heavily on his chest. The helmet was shaped much like the one his priest had worn: open-faced, with sweeping horns that almost brushed the high ceiling. The pendant was carved in the shape of a sun, and at its heart was a glass sphere containing Arean fire. The light pulsed, growing and diminishing like flame guttering in a breeze. Like a heartbeat. The god leaned on a gold-plated spear with one arm, while the other was twined around by a snake all the colour of malachite except for its eyes, which were glittering orange chips.

An acolyte, a golden-haired young man not much older than Rheia, came forward to greet her. The flickering lamplight deepened his features, but his slender face wore a kind smile that softened his demeanour, seeming ill-suited to a priest of a war god. "Thank you, daughter of Oreareus, for your sacrifice," he said, placing a cool hand on each of her cheeks and leaning forward to kiss her forehead. He didn't wait for her to reply. What might she have said if he had? Nothing gracious. "The first thing to happen now is the judging and cleansing. Remove

your sandals and make yourself comfortable." The acolyte gestured to a cushion that had been set before the statue.

Grimacing, Rheia slid her shoes off and placed them beside her. Then she knelt on the cushion, brushing her *chiton* smooth over her thighs. At least they hadn't demanded she kneel on the hard stone floor.

The orange-clad servants—they were also guards, Rheia realised, seeing the way the muscles in their arms bulged—withdrew, leaving her alone with the acolyte who had spoken to her. Under any other circumstance, her being unattended with a young man would have brought great shame to her family.

Sighing, Rheia let her gaze wander up to Areus's face, so far above her. Unlike on the huge statue outside the temple, here he'd been depicted with a furrowed brow and a downturned mouth, as though the sight of his worshippers made him angry.

She wasn't exactly pleased with him right now, either.

The acolyte started chanting, and Rheia lowered her eyes to study her hands, flat against the grey fabric of her lap. She shifted as pins and needles danced along her calves. How long would this go on? What exactly did judging and cleansing involve, anyway?

After a time, the chanting fell silent, and a hint of movement near the foot of the statue tugged at the periphery of her vision. Rheia looked up and her eyes widened. A viper's head poked out from between Areus's feet, examining her with slitted eyes the colour of moonstone in a snub-nosed face. It seemed to take the meeting of their gazes as an invitation, for it slithered out of the god's shadow towards her. She froze, cold fear creeping over her at the gentle scraping of its belly on stone. The snake resembled the venomous vipers she'd sometimes encountered in the fields around the city, but it was much larger: at least as long as her extended leg. Its body was thick, covered with pale grey scales the colour of hearth ashes. A darker pattern zigzagged down its spine, outlined in black.

No wonder everyone else had left the *cella*.

With her mouth dry, Rheia glanced at the acolyte. He stood to one side of the room, hands clasped, his smile replaced by a tightness that made her think he was holding his breath. The high priest stood beside him. Draconaidas had been so silent when he entered that she hadn't realised he was there. Seeing her wide-eyed regard, the acolyte nodded reassuringly, while Draconaidas smiled. The expression didn't reach his eyes, which glittered as cold as the viper's. "The venomous snake is blessed of Areus," the high priest rumbled. "The god will test your purity to determine your suitability for the sacrifice. You need not fear. Only the impure feel the sting of his fangs."

Rheia's gaze pivoted back to the viper, which had paused before her, its head raised to examine her. Her fingers, resting on her thighs, wanted to crawl away from it; she wanted to flee screaming from its cool stare. But if she startled it, it might strike. So instead she pressed her eyes closed, trying to slow her panicked breathing, and said a prayer to Eidoneus. Surely the god of death didn't intend to take her so soon? *If you do take me, Lord, please make it quick.*

The snake's weight pressed against her thigh as it glided onto her lap, the scales on its belly shifting against the backs of her hands as its muscles bunched and contracted, propelling it forward. It was lighter than she'd expected. Something so deadly should weigh more.

I am pure, she told the viper silently, eyes still closed. *I have never known the caress of a lover. Now leave me be.* Although … she had tried to give herself to Galen not an hour before, her futile attempt to thwart the god. Would Areus condemn her for that? Cold sweat broke out on her forehead, the back of her neck. Death by viper venom usually took hours, contorting the body with spasms that left its victim shrieking.

When something pushed against her belly, Rheia's eyes flew open and she bit her lip to stop from screaming. The viper's head was pressed against her, its tongue flickering out as though to taste her flesh through the fabric of her *chiton*.

A soft sound caused her to flick a glance at Draconaidas. The high priest's gaze was hungry. His eyes were wide and dark, no longer cold, and he rubbed his hands together slowly, his palms gliding against one another in a rhythmic way. His tongue flickered out like the snake's, wetting parted lips.

Rheia swallowed hard and resumed staring at the viper. Its inhuman regard horrified her less than Draconaidas's clear arousal.

The creature stared out of eyes gone orange with reflected lamplight and turned around on itself, coiling between her hands like a lap dog as it stared at Draconaidas. She held her breath and, after a time, it lowered its head to the back of her hand, radiating an air of satisfaction.

"Congratulations," the acolyte said in his soothing voice. "Areus has judged you worthy."

Relief flooded Rheia but she didn't dare reply, not wanting to disturb the creature. Its breath puffed out of slitted nostrils, two thin streams tickling her wrist.

Chanting once more, the acolyte lifted a clay bowl, tucking it into the crook of one arm. He knelt before her, dipping his fingers into water whose surface glistened with aromatic oils. He dabbed them against her temples and at her throat, under each side of her jaw, before swiping a finger across her upper lip. Then he wiped his hand thoroughly on the hem of his *chiton*.

The water was cool on her skin, and smelled of unnamed spices, like fire and blood and snow on the mountain. They mingled with the rose perfume she wore, a heady blend. The scents flooded her, filling her skull until it seemed to detach, to float above her body. Her fear leeched away under the effects of the spice drug, leaving numb acceptance, and she stared for a time at the dull scales of the viper resting on her lap. Its eyes seemed normal now, no longer filled with sinister orange light. It was beautiful. Why had she been afraid of it?

Well, they could've done this sooner, she thought dully. But no. Draconaidas had enjoyed her fear too much. When she dragged her gaze upwards to see if the high priest still looked aroused now she was deadened to the terror, she saw he was gone, as though he'd never been there. Was he an apparition, then? A hallucination of her frightened mind?

She sighed when the viper was lifted from her lap, and the acolyte took her hands, coaxing her to stand. He unfastened the brooches along her shoulders and arms, and her *chiton* puddled around her feet. The bracelets were slid free and placed on top of the grey fabric. She stood, naked and passive, as he anointed her with the scented water on the inside of each wrist, between her breasts, inside her thighs, at the back of her knees and

on the top of each foot. His touch was gentle, reminding her of her grandmother's loving ministrations that morning, and part of her knew she should be horrified at this turn of events. But his expression was calm. His eyes did not fill her with dread as Draconaidas's heavy-lidded gaze did. At least the high priest had left before she was stripped bare by his acolyte. Only Areus watched, his dead eyes frowning down at her.

Soft white cloth was wrapped around her and fastened with golden brooches—but not the same ones she had entered the temple with. These were small discs, each embossed with a curving shape like a bull's horns. The veil was removed from her hair, which flowed freely down her back. Rheia looked at the pile of discarded clothes and something stirred within her. "My things," she said, whispering through lips gone numb. "Can you return them to my family? Please?"

The acolyte regarded her for a long moment before nodding. When he replied, his voice was as quiet as hers. "I will do this for you, daughter of Loukios, if you do not speak of it to anyone."

"I won't," she promised.

"Thank you." The acolyte leaned in until his face filled her vision, and placed a quick kiss on her lips. Her heart fluttered in her chest, but her limbs remained still, under the sway of whatever drug permeated the anointing water. His nostrils flared as he inhaled the scent of her, and he ran a pink tongue along his lips, his eyes shifting towards the statue of Areus as though he expected to be chastised for what he'd done. But there was no one there but the stone god: even the viper had vanished.

He stepped back, and a pang of regret stabbed her

heart. He was comely, and he had gentle hands for the servant of a warrior god. For a fleeting moment she'd wondered if he would free her from her fate the same way she'd begged Galen to.

"From here, you will be escorted to the House of the Beast. There you will be kept like royalty. Until mid-summer."

"Until the Beast arises," she replied.

"Yes. Until the Beast arises."

CHAPTER SEVEN

emple servants surrounded Rheia, escorting her out
to a carriage. She squinted, surprised to discover it
was only mid-afternoon. Her time in the temple had seemed
to last an eternity. Perhaps an entire day and night had
passed? But no, wouldn't she be hungry? A strong arm
was proffered, a silent offer to assist her into the carriage.
Part of her wanted to refuse, but her legs felt strangely
weak, so she leaned on it and clambered up. The guard
checked to make sure she was seated on the thin cushion
before tugging a curtain across the window, blocking her
tired eyes from the sun's harsh glare.

Her body tingled, growing increasingly numb, and
she let her head loll to one side as she waited for the
carriage to move. A familiar, gravelly voice spoke outside,
although she couldn't distinguish individual words.
Draconaidas? She knew she should be afraid, but couldn't
muster the energy to care.

By the time the carriage lurched into motion, drawn
by slaves up the road to the House of the Beast, her eyes

had drifted closed. The smell of the dusty streets wormed its way through the gaps in the curtain, itching her nose, and her mind wandered like an untended goat. Had her parents gone home after the guards took her into Areus's temple? Continued about their day? Charis had planned bean and onion soup in fish bone broth for dinner. Now her mother and grandmother didn't have Rheia to help prepare the food, would Aias do it? Or would they pay their servant girl to work longer hours? Perhaps Rheia's father would have to get a slave after all.

If he'd had a slave girl, a virgin, would Rheia be at home right now, the slave girl sitting in this lurching carriage in her place?

Her thoughts chased themselves around and around until she fell into a numb sleep-like state. Only when her ears picked up the muffled sounds of arguing voices did she begin to come back to herself.

"Areus save us, how much nightsleep did you give her?" a somewhat husky female voice demanded. Who was it? She sounded appalled and far away.

"Mind your tone, woman." That voice Rheia knew. Draconaidas. He sounded closer than the woman, although she didn't hear the sound of movement. Instead it was like Rheia was drifting closer to the pair, back to her own body. "After that last *thysia* tried to escape from the temple, we didn't want to risk this one. She is chosen by Areus himself."

"Not to mention that if she escapes there'll be a riot before the city allows another lottery," the woman muttered. "Still, if she dies before her time, it's the same end result as if she escapes, no?"

"So don't let her die." There was a threat in the high

priest's tone. Even Rheia, eyes closed and floating detached above the conversation, could hear it.

Someone lifted Rheia's arm, and cool fingers prodded her wrist. She felt limp and wrung out, like washing spread out in the sun to dry. Her head seemed pleasantly wrapped in wool and her body lay flat, on soft cushions. She wasn't in the carriage anymore.

An astringent smell crawled up her nostrils, plucking the wool away and setting her skull to throbbing. Rheia groaned, pressing her eyes more tightly closed as though to deny the headache admission to her skull. It was like trying to close the port when the invading army was already sacking your harbour. Nearby—close, she realised—somebody exhaled with relief.

"Good," Draconaidas grunted. "I will leave you to get her settled in. Ensure you keep her well-guarded."

"We will," the woman replied, her tone stiff. A heavy tread retreated, and the woman's voice was softer when she spoke again. "Are you alright, girl?"

It took Rheia two goes to force any sound out, and when she did, her voice was hoarse. "Head," she managed, before a cough tore from her throat. She wasn't sure what hurt more: the cough, or the blades that seemed to pierce each of her temples simultaneously. A tear of pain leaked from beneath her closed eyelid.

"Those priests are idiots," the woman muttered, supporting Rheia's head until the spasm passed. Then she bustled away, leaving Rheia alone for a time, in silence except for the pounding of her pulse.

When the woman returned, she spoke softly. "Can you sit?"

Rheia finally forced her eyes open, squinting at the

blurry oval above her. A few blinks helped it to resolve into a round face, wrinkled across the brow and framed by silver hair. The face's eyes were wide with concern. Waiting for an answer. Rheia nodded faintly, afraid of setting off the booming fire-thrower newly installed inside her skull. The woman slid an arm under her back and helped Rheia to sit, manoeuvring a cushion behind her. The girl reclined against it with a sigh.

The woman turned away, returning with an elegant clay cup whose glazed exterior glistened with condensation. A reed poked out the top. "Here, sip this," she said, nudging the reed to Rheia's lips.

The girl sucked tentatively. The reed was hollow, and a sweet, syrupy liquid filled her mouth: strained grape juice thickened with honey. The drink soothed her dry throat and refreshed her parched tongue so it no longer cleaved to the roof of her mouth.

Finally, when the cup was empty, Rheia dared to speak. "Thank you," she said, pushing the reed away from her mouth with a sigh. Her headache began to ease, the clamps loosening around her skull. "What did they do to me?"

"The oil they anointed you with contained a powerful herb called nightsleep," the woman said, her expression so intent on Rheia's face that it was somewhat unnerving. The girl felt certain the old woman would notice every flutter of her eyelids, every twitch of her muscles, with such intense scrutiny. "It numbs the mind and eases the spirit, but too much of it is dangerous. It can cause the heart to stop beating. And, even at lower doses, clearing it out of your system the way I did can cause pain."

"I noticed." Rheia grimaced. She recalled the delightful

numbness that had crept over her in the temple, and then, with faintly flushing cheeks, the acolyte's daring kiss. At the time, she had been unconcerned—even a little fascinated. He'd been attractive and kind. But she realised now, with growing horror, that she'd have let him do anything while under the nightsleep's effects. She didn't think of herself as one to let a pretty face and a few gentle words turn her head. Losing herself so entirely due to the effects of a plant frightened her, the hair standing up on the back of her arms despite the summer heat pouring in the open window behind her head. She was just grateful that the acolyte's respect for her—or perhaps fear of his god or high priest—had stayed his hand. "I thought I knew all the herbs," Rheia said, her voice wavering. "But I haven't heard of nightsleep."

"I am not surprised. Any citizen of Oreareus who is found with it outside the temple or the Beast's house faces a death sentence. There have been times in our city's past when addiction to nightsleep has become a plague, and the king's grandfather enacted stern laws to prevent it happening again," the woman said, standing up straight. Her dark-eyed gaze remained on Rheia's face, a frown between her eyes. "It is only grown on the high slopes of the mountain, and only the Beast's caregivers are permitted to pick it."

The Beast's caregivers? Rheia had never heard the phrase before, and she looked more closely at the woman, realising now her head was clearing that the woman was missing the fingers on her left hand. She held the cup in her right. "You're a Broken One," Rheia gasped, her eyes widening as her heart gave a little flip in her chest. The woman's lips pursed as though she'd bitten into a piece of unripe fruit, and a blush seared Rheia's cheeks. "I'm sorry. That was rude."

The woman shrugged. "It is understandable, though that is not what we call ourselves." She held up her left hand so Rheia could see that it was free of scars; the skin grew smooth over small stumps. "I am not broken. The gods took my fingers when I was still in my mother's womb. My parents gave me into the keeping of the caregivers when I was born, and I was raised here in the Beast's service. I've been inside these walls my entire life. All his servants are in some way misshapen, most of us from birth, but some after physical injury. There is no shame in it."

Rheia's mind whirled. Why had the Beast chosen to surround himself with deformed people? Was it a reflection of his own twisted spirit? But the thought seemed unkind, given how gently the woman had tended her. Shame grew into a nauseous lump in Rheia's stomach, driving away her apprehension. She hung her head. "Please forgive me."

"There is nothing to forgive, child. You repeat what everyone in the city says. We know what they call us, how we are regarded. But we have been chosen for our duty by some god, so we endure."

"Some god? Not Areus?" Rheia glanced up, surprised.

"Who knows? He has not deigned to tell me himself," the woman said brusquely, setting the empty cup on a nearby table.

Rheia nodded. Belief in gods other than Areus was generally a private matter, and she didn't want to offend this woman any more than she already had. The woman's hair, Rheia saw now, fell in a heavy braid down her back, and a simple gold circlet sat on her head. A mark

of authority?

"My name is Besadora, by the by. You may call me Dora if you wish. Now, as I was about to say, we offer nightsleep to the *thysies*, although in smaller doses than what you were given. Some prefer the numbness to the—" she paused, seemingly considering her words "—knowledge of what is to come."

What is to come. Rheia's throat cut by a descending sword, the bellow of the Beast, the roar of the crowd. A lump of ice settled in Rheia's chest where her heart used to be. "Do many take up that offer?"

"Most," Dora admitted.

"I ... don't think I will." Rheia rubbed her temples, which ached only a little after the syrup. A tangled lock of hair caught around her hand and she grimaced. Her hair was a mess, as though she had tossed her head all night in a fitful, sweat-soaked sleep. "I did not enjoy the aftereffects, or being so vulnerable."

"There would be a consistent supply, so there wouldn't be aftereffects," Dora said. "As for vulnerability, there are few safer places in Oreareus than the House of the Beast." Again, Rheia saw that sour twist of the lip. "The palace is divided into four: the *andron* wing for the male *thysies*; the *gynaikon* wing for the females; the caregivers' quarters; and the Beast's home beneath us. The *thysia* wings in particular are well guarded. You will be safe."

Rheia had always felt safest inside her home's *gynaikon*, and something inside her unknotted at the idea that there might be such a refuge here. And yet, her fresh fear of that numbed state outweighed her dread of what was to come. "Still, I would rather not have any more nightsleep."

"Very well. If you change your mind, let any of us

know and we will take care of it for you." Dora smiled, seeming satisfied as she helped Rheia from the bed. Her bare arms were corded with muscle. "Let's get you cleaned up, shall we?"

Dora led Rheia out of the healing chamber, moving slowly. Rheia was grateful; her limbs were stiff and sluggish, aching with each step. Still, the exertion was worth it when Dora brought her to a bathhouse the likes of which the girl had never seen. Two square pools sat end to end, forming a rectangle, one raised a foot above the other. Water trickled over the higher one's lip and into the lower pool. Steam wavered in the air over the raised pool, and Rheia's eyes widened as she realised it was a huge bath. But, unlike the one at home, it wasn't raised from the ground to allow a fire to be stoked underneath. Instead, both baths were set into a floor covered with pale blue tiles.

Dora smiled, probably at her stunned reaction. "Yes, it is magnificent. The biggest bath in Oreareus except for the one at the king's palace, or so I'm told. There is a room beneath us where the fire is fed and tended. The water is changed daily."

"I would have thought you'd have holy fire here," Rheia said, reaching to undo the brooches at her shoulders, to free herself of the white *chiton* and the stink of anointing oil.

"No." Dora stepped forward to help, seeming to understand Rheia's haste.

"Then that must be backbreaking work," Rheia said. "Do you have slaves here?"

"No, we don't keep slaves. By the laws of the city, we *are* slaves, given to the Beast as we are. Certainly we're

not free to seek employment elsewhere. But it is a good life for one who would otherwise find the outside world … difficult." Dora removed the last brooch and helped Rheia step out of the fabric and up to the hot pool. "Let's wash off the dregs of that oil, so your body can be free of the last remnants of nightsleep."

Rheia eased herself into the water, which was hot on her feet after the cool tiles. Still, once she submerged herself in it, her body quickly adjusted to the temperature, and she leaned back against the edge with a sigh. Dora fetched a basket from the wall, its handle hanging from her left arm, and pulled a herb-speckled soap from it with her whole-fingered right hand.

"If you don't mind me saying, you're deft with your movements despite your misfortune," Rheia said, closing her eyes as Dora rubbed the soap against each of her temples, building up a lather. The air filled with the sweet, cleansing aroma of dill. "I'm sure you could find work elsewhere, if you wished."

"It is not my ability to find work that concerns me, but the reception I would get from the city. Before the Beast started taking us for his servants, malformed babies like me were often left outside the city walls for predators." Dora's tone was matter-of-fact, but Rheia's eyes flew open with horror.

"How awful!"

"Yes. But most families find it hard to care for a child that may not be able to contribute to the family. And who would agree to marry their own child to a lad or lass who might struggle to provide for or tend their new spouse? So you can see why we don't mind living here, even though we are slaves. Besides—" amusement filled

Dora's voice "—the house isn't so bad."

"You must have seen a lot of *thysies* come through here," Rheia murmured. Even though she was one of the sacrifices, she still felt some sympathy for this woman and her ilk, who'd seen so many come here to be slain by the Beast. Also, tending the monster himself had to be awful. She shivered.

"Yes. The babies were the worst," Dora said in a subdued voice.

"Babies?" Rheia stared up at the older woman. Her grandmother had said the same thing, but she hadn't wanted to believe it.

"We haven't many babies since the *helots* started providing *thysia*. One or two deformed little things that would have been caregivers if they were Orearean. Before that, when the lottery was common, we'd have one every two or three years." Her voice dropped to a whisper. "Once, the lottery drew out three babies and a toddler, a girl no more than three. That was a grim year."

Rheia's mouth fell open. Dora sounded so *matter-of-fact* about it. The woman saw her expression and shook herself, as though recalling who she was speaking to. She pressed the soap into Rheia's hand. "Here, you will need to wash the rest of the oil from your body. If I lean forward any further, I'll be joining you in the water."

Jaw clenched, Rheia took the soap in a grip so tight she left divots in its soft surface. She scrubbed her skin as she tried not to think of Dora, handing a squalling baby to the ravenous Beast. *How could she do it?* Rheia couldn't imagine how callous and hardened the caregivers would have had to become. Dora seemed kind, but how could she be, knowing her job was to ensure Rheia put

her own throat on the butcher's block when the time came?

She couldn't look at the caregiver when she stepped out of the pool, her hair dripping. Perhaps the woman truly was as broken as the epithet suggested.

CHAPTER EIGHT

Dressed in a clean *chiton* the colour of honey and a pair of soft leather sandals that fit so well they could have been made for her, Rheia followed Dora out of the bathhouse. She felt more alert now, her limbs freed up by the hot water and a soak in the cooler pool below. The pair strode down a wide corridor lined with gleaming timber statues, each set on a stone pedestal. Mercifully, none of the carvings were of Areus; Rheia wasn't sure she could stomach the god staring at her as though she were a goat waiting for slaughter. Instead, the sculptures were of various inanimate objects, lovingly carved. Some were breathtaking in their intricacy, such as a *kithara*, each of the instrument's strings so thin she thought they were thread until she peered closer and realised they too were timber. Others seemed simple, such as a bowl of dried figs—but when she examined them she noticed the wood grain on each piece of fruit ran the same way as the wrinkles in a real fig's skin would. She felt she could split one open and spill seeds into her palm.

There had to be two dozen carvings, each so well executed they could have sat on the king's table—and not a god or man among them. Carvings and sculptures were common in the houses of Oreareus, but carvings of inanimate things were rare. Perhaps one of the Broken Ones had a talent for sculpture, now or in the past, and a disdain for things that drew breath.

Dora noted Rheia's careful inspection of the sculptures. "Lovely, aren't they?"

"Yes." Rheia glanced at the woman, wondering if she was the artist. But no, she doubted a woman with one good hand could manage work this fine. "I would've thought bulls would be more in evidence than they are, in honour of your master below." Her voice was flat.

"There are places within the house where that's the case," Dora admitted, "but not in the *thysies'* wings. We like to maintain an air of serenity as much as possible."

So we forget why we are here? Rheia hugged her arms to try and hide the shudder that rippled through her.

Dora blinked, but didn't say anything except, "Please, this way."

The corridor ended in a pair of heavy doors banded with bronze. One door had a post affixed to its lip; a bolt attached to the other door had its end buried deep into the post. Dora pulled a jingling bundle from a pouch at her waist, selecting a thin shaft of jagged-edged metal and fitting it into an opening on the bolt. Something clicked, and she slid the bolt sideways, swinging the door open. Rheia had heard of locks, a new gift from holy Areus to his priests, but had never seen one before. Usually, doors were simply barred from the inside.

She saw, as she followed Dora through the door, that

there was no way to open the door without a key, regardless of which side you were on. It was a prison. "How do the female *thysies* get to the bathhouse, locked in as they—we— are?"

"The bathhouse is shared by all within these walls," Dora said in a gentle voice. "We take the female *thysies* there after lunch each day, and the male *thysies* after the evening meal."

"You keep us separated, so we can't, what? Conspire to lose our purity in an act of defiance?" What better way for the *thysies* to avoid the blade?

Dora sighed but didn't answer.

Rheia's bitter thoughts were stunned into silence as she emerged into a lush green courtyard, growing cooler now the sun had dipped below the roofline. Still, even during the middle of the day, the courtyard would be pleasantly shaded by the tall date-plum tree whose glossy leaves were interspersed with clusters of soft pink flowers. Beneath it, a stone fountain in the shape of a sea nymph trickled water from a tipped vase into a stone pool. Elegant benches crouched on either side of the tree, large enough to seat two but each separate from the other to allow for quiet contemplation as well. Grass sprung underfoot as Dora led Rheia across to a covered walkway on the far side, past a caregiver woman who hunched over, carefully tending a low bush. Pillars ran along the walkway's outside edge, while the inner wall opened onto several rooms.

One of them was closed off by a heavy curtain. "That is the other *thysia's* room," Dora said, nodding at it. "Her name is Parthenia. I am sure you will meet her at the evening meal." Rheia recalled the proud, grey-eyed *thysia* she'd seen on the docks, the one who'd regarded the

crowd with such contempt. Her stomach fluttered nervously at the idea of meeting the girl. "And this room is yours," Dora continued.

The chamber was at least five times as large as Rheia's bedroom at home. Its stone floor was covered with rich brown furs, and the bed was big enough for three, the cushions fat with downy feathers. The clothes chest was huge, its lid open so she could see folded fabric in an array of colours; a small shelf above it bore neatly arranged brooches to pin the *chitons*. Other chests sat around the room, lids closed. The inner walls were covered with tapestries: one, a rolling hillside covered with flowers; another, a herd of goats grazing peacefully, watched over by a small girl.

The windows were blocked by wooden panels carved with flower-shaped holes each the size of Rheia's fist— large enough to allow her to see out and to admit a breeze, but small enough that she couldn't escape through them. That, more than anything, drove home the lock's lesson. Her stomach swooped as she saw the room for what it was: an elaborate cage.

"Is this the same room the dead *thysia* slept in?" Rheia blinked, realising she'd spoken the question aloud when Dora's expression filled with pity. That was all the answer she was going to get, but she knew what it meant. Of *course* it was the same room. There were only two female *thysies* at any one time. Why maintain lavish rooms for more?

"The evening meal is in an hour. Why don't you rest? I'll fetch you when we're ready."

Dora slipped away, leaving Rheia truly alone for the first time since her *ostra* had been drawn. She hurried over to the window, hoping she'd be able to catch a glimpse of something familiar through the holes: the *agora*, the harbour, or—if she was lucky—the orange-tiled roof of her parents' villa. But all that met her gaze was the sheer side of Oreareus Mountain, grey and bleak where the shadow of the house fell upon it. The sight was a punch in the gut, winding her. She sank down onto the furs, lowering her head into her hands. Her throat was tight with tears but, although a black despair hung over her, she refused to cry. Instead she blinked rapidly, taking deep breaths until the hot sting faded.

"So you're the Orearean sacrifice," an accented voice said.

Rheia looked up, expecting to meet the gaze of the grey-eyed *thysia*. Her eyes widened with surprise when she saw an unfamiliar face, no older than her own. Wide-set, pale brown eyes regarded her above a strong nose and generous lips, now thinned into a hard line.

Rheia examined the girl for signs of deformity but, except for a general slackness of limb, she saw nothing obvious. And the girl's hair was as thick and dark as Rheia's own. She recalled that the second female *thysia* had hidden her face from the crowds behind a fall of hair. "Parthenia?" she guessed.

The girl nodded. "You seem surprised." Her voice was musical.

"I am," Rheia admitted. The grey-eyed girl had seemed so proud, so determined. When she'd heard the rumour that one of the *thysies* had killed herself, she'd assumed it would be the one who'd tried to hide herself away—Parthenia. Had the other girl already planned her suicide, that day on the docks? Had her contemptuous glare indicated her

intent to rob the Oreareans of her blood, forcing them to kill one of their own daughters? *If so, it worked.*

Rheia swallowed her bitterness. "My name is Rheia," she said instead. "I'm a *thysia*, like you. Would you like to sit?"

"You are *not* a *thysia*," Parthenia said, staying in the open doorway. Her tone was dismissive, contemptuous. A gold bracelet jingled on her arm as she brushed her hair back from her face.

"My *ostra* was drawn from the jar today." Rheia's eyes narrowed.

"So? *Thysies* are part of the peace treaty between your people and mine, an offering to slake the thirst of your angry god so our people may live in peace. You are Orearean. You are not a *thysia*."

"But I am to be sacrificed," Rheia protested, before realising how absurd the words sounded—as though she were defending some privilege. Cheeks burning, she stood, not liking the way this girl looked down on her. The fur was so thick it tickled the sides of her feet through the straps of the sandals. She was of a height with Parthenia, she realised.

The other sacrifice shrugged, her top lip curling. "That may be. But you are not Carmean."

"Carmean?"

"That is what we call ourselves. The name of our people." Parthenia lifted her chin. "You call us *helot*. Slave."

"Does it matter?" Rheia sighed, her shoulders slumping.

"That you call us slave?" Parthenia's eyebrows shot up. "Of course it matters."

"No, not that. Whether I am called a *thysia* or a sacrifice. Either way, my blood will end up on the Beast's blade and

I will die."

Parthenia's eyes widened and her skin paled. Her nostrils flared as she took a deep breath and regrouped. "You aren't fit to walk in her shoes," she spat, her eyes shimmering with sudden tears. Then she turned and fled, the hard leather soles of her sandals slapping on the tiles in the corridor.

Frowning, Rheia stepped forward to untie the curtain bundled to one side of the doorway, letting it swing closed over the entrance to the room. *What a strange girl.* Rheia bit her lip as she realised she'd been hoping to find some comfort in the company of her fellow sacrifice. They had their dire fate in common, after all. But the *helot*—no, the *Carmean*—resented her for being Orearean. Rheia could understand that, but why did she get the sense Parthenia also resented her for trying to take the other girl's place?

Like it was my idea. Rheia snorted. Still, if she wanted company she'd have to befriend the Beast's caregivers. It was a sobering idea—Dora had been kind, but she didn't trust these people. Perhaps it would be better to remain alone, until her time was done. *Twelve days until the Festival of Areus. Twelve days until I meet the Beast.*

Desperate for a distraction, Rheia approached the closed chests, opening them with trembling fingers. Panels along the outside of each bore ornate carvings, though not done with as much skill as the sculptures in the hall outside the *gynaikon*. A small one contained jewellery— bracelets, necklaces and hairpieces, glittering with gold and gemstones. The idea of sporting adornments worn by girls now dead churned her stomach and she slammed the lid shut. A larger chest contained several rolled papyrus

scrolls with brightly coloured parchment covers, and her eyes widened at the rare treasures. She spent some time admiring the painted illustrations, but the poetry, although beautiful, was mostly about love—something she would never know. Not now. Biting her bottom lip so the tears wouldn't spill in defiance of her vow, she re-rolled the scrolls and returned them to their chest.

When she discovered the pan flute, a smile split her face. It was more elegant than the simple one at home, each of the fat, hollow reeds carved with leaves and berries, and stoppered at one end with beeswax. The reeds were strapped together in a row, from shortest to largest, and when she blew a gentle breath across the top of each one, she found they'd been perfectly tuned.

It had been more than a year since she'd played. She'd been distracted by more adult concerns—mainly Galen, if she were honest. Still, it came back to her quickly, and by the time Dora arrived to invite her to dinner, she was playing a complex lullaby her mother had sung when she was a girl.

"How beautiful," Dora said, a smile splitting her face as she watched Rheia play. "We'd love to have you play for us after the meal, if you would?"

"Not today," Rheia said, avoiding eye contact with the woman. "I'm still reminding myself how to do so."

"Very well. Perhaps in a few days, when you're more comfortable." Dora held the curtain aside so that Rheia might exit. The smell of cooking meat reached her nose—pork, if she was not mistaken. Her mouth began to water at the notion of such a treat. She might be dead in less than two weeks, but it seemed they would feed her well in the interim. She hadn't had pork since the last feast of Eidoneus, in the dead of winter.

"Will Parthenia be joining us?" Rheia asked, noticing the curtain to the other sacrifice's room was still drawn.

"Not tonight." Dora shook her head. "She is feeling unwell and asked to eat in her room."

Despite her own predicament, Rheia felt a surge of sympathy for Parthenia. She'd boarded that trireme knowing she was going to die, but at least she'd had a sister from her homeland to keep her company. She must feel bereft now she was alone among the people she regarded—correctly—as her enemy.

Rheia kept her gaze on the closed curtain until it was out of sight.

CHAPTER NINE

Exhausted and still recovering from the effects of the nightsleep, Rheia slept dreamlessly and late into the morning. A sound nearby finally woke her where distant birdsong had not: gentle footsteps inside her chamber, followed by a soft wooden click. Rheia stirred, her eyes fluttering open, and then felt the weight of despair settle on her chest as she recalled she wasn't in her bed at home. She was in the *gynaikon*, where she would be pampered until she was sacrificed like the pig whose flesh had filled her belly the night before.

Something moved at the corner of her eye, and she bit the inside of her lip to keep back a cry of surprise. One of the caregivers, Yalee, had placed a bowl of water on the chest beside the bed. The surface of the water, crystal clear, still wavered.

Yalee was a graceful girl not much older than Aias, long of limb and already starting to come into her womanhood. Her dark golden hair was a thing of great beauty, but her place as a caregiver was assured by the fact her top lip was split in the middle, revealing her teeth and lending her a feline cast. Dora had introduced them the night before at dinner, explaining Yalee had been born with the split lip, and had lost her hearing after a fever the previous summer.

Even having been served by Yalee at dinner, Rheia found it hard to look into the girl's face. Yalee's shoulders slumped, and Rheia chided herself. This was just a child. Not a monster. Not a cold-blooded killer. Steeling herself, she met Yalee's eyes, which were wide-set and kind. "Good morning, Yalee," she said, speaking slowly in the hope the girl would get her meaning even if she couldn't hear the words.

Yalee smiled brightly, hazel eyes crinkling with pleasure. It made her lovely, and Rheia found herself smiling back, her unease forgotten. The girl nodded at the water, and then gestured to Rheia. "Do you want me to help you?" she said, her words loud and slurred, like a man who'd had too much wine. Still, that she could speak without hearing what she said amazed the older girl.

Rheia shook her head, sitting up on the cushions and drawing her sheet up to her chin. "I can do it myself," she said with what she hoped was a grateful smile, before sliding from her bed and walking to the bowl. Embarrassed, she kept her back to the room as she washed, trying to ignore the girl bustling around, laying out a *chiton* and brushing specks of dirt off Rheia's sandals. She'd been waited on like nobility since her *ostra* had been drawn—and even before, with Charis helping her dress for the lottery— but in the clear light of day, awake and drug-free, she found this attention from strangers harder to deal with.

At least she can't listen to me washing up, I suppose.

Rheia splashed her face and scooped up the chosen *chiton*, winding it around herself and taking each brooch from Yalee's outstretched hand to pin the material over each of her shoulders. Once she was done, she felt less uneasy about the girl's presence, as though the clothes were forged bronze rather than mere fabric.

"Do you want me to brush your hair?" Yalee said. Rheia started to shake her head and the girl's face fell, so she changed the gesture to a nod, sitting on the fur. Yalee knelt behind her, her movements deft as she wielded a comb pulled from a pouch at her belt. After Rheia's hair had been brushed until it crackled, Yalee indicated the door with an expansive gesture.

The dining room was opposite the sacrifices' rooms, open-sided to look onto the central courtyard. Outside, Rheia saw one woman, belly round with child, fishing fallen leaves from the fountain, while another swept the pavers. Normal, homely activities. Neither woman wore the gold circlet Dora did, confirming Rheia's suspicion that the headpiece was a mark of position.

Niches in the dining room's remaining three walls bore more of those elegant wooden sculptures, interspersed with sconces, unlit at this time of day. The room would be cold in winter, that great empty wall allowing heat to escape and offering no protection against the icy wind. *But then,* Rheia realised, *it is only used in summer.* A low table filled the centre of the room, with lounges on either side of it. Parthenia reclined in one, eating sliced plums from a plate on the cushion beside her. Dora stood by the table, her silver braid hanging over her shoulder and down the front of her body in a glimmering rope.

The old woman smiled as Rheia entered, Yalee at her

heels. "Please, sit," she said, indicating the other lounge. "Would you like porridge?"

Rheia's stomach rumbled. "Yes. Please." She watched with interest as Dora spooned the food into a shallow bowl. The grains glistened with honey, and were mixed through with raisins gone fat with soaking, and with soft whey cheese. Not so dissimilar to the porridge she'd have made at home, although her family's stock of raisins had been exhausted months ago. Dora added a handful of plump blackberries; they dimpled the surface of the porridge.

Rheia's stomach fluttered as it struck her that she wouldn't be able to go picking grapes later in the season. Autumn was her favourite time of year. She loved roaming the skirt of the mountain, basket filled with fruit. Would her mother take Aias alone this year? Charis wasn't able to manage the foothills any longer, and Loukios was too busy with his duties.

"Rheia?"

She snapped back to herself, realising Dora stood beside her, the bowl extended. The berries were gone, stirred through.

"Are you well?"

Rheia ignored the question. "Thank you." She took the food with a half-hearted smile, not sure she wanted it anymore. Still, Yalee watched her expectantly, and she took a mouthful. The porridge was delicious, sweet and warm.

Parthenia rolled her eyes to peer at Rheia, contempt written into her narrowed gaze and the tightness of her lips as she watched the other girl eat. That stare robbed the food of some of its flavour, and Rheia looked back at

her, swallowing. Irritation surged. "Is there something you'd like to say?"

"I was just thinking, once a slaver, always a slaver," Parthenia said, her tone flat.

"I'm not a slaver," Rheia said, her eyes widening. "My family doesn't even have a house slave." An unwelcome thought intruded: her father's position as a trierarch— the one who had brought the *thysies* to Oreareus, no less—would make Rheia the daughter of a slaver in Parthenia's eyes.

"Well," the other girl said, "you seem to be adapting to being waited on well enough." Unaware of her poor timing, Yalee stepped forward, holding an elegant *amphora*, to refill Parthenia's cup. The Carmean girl slapped her hand away, and the young caregiver stepped back, eyes lowered, mouth turned down at the corners. Her fingers, where they curled around the handles at the neck of the *amphora*, were white.

Rheia scowled. "I am well-bred enough to remember my manners," she snapped, anger dancing on her tongue, bitter after the taste of honey. "These people are no more at fault for your captivity than they are for mine," she spat, realising the truth of it. "They do as they have been tasked. You seem determined to make their lives unpleasant when they aren't the source of your troubles. Are all Carmeans so rude, or is it just you? Is that why they chose you to be *thysia*?"

Parthenia stared at her, face pale. Then she stood, fleeing the room, bare feet thudding on the pavers outside. The plate of half-eaten fruit teetered on the edge of the cushion before toppling to the tiles. It shattered, the plums splattering wetly.

Dora gave Rheia an appraising look, opening her mouth to speak. Then she looked after Parthenia and closed it again, sighing. "Excuse me," she said. "Yalee will see to your needs." She hurried after the Carmean girl.

To make sure she doesn't harm herself? Rheia wondered, guilt settling onto her chest as she watched Yalee bend to pick up the shards of broken pottery. Why had she spoken so cruelly? "Here, let me help you," she said, putting her food on the table and kneeling.

Yalee startled at Rheia's actions, shaking her head. "Finish your meal," she said, gesturing to the couch with a plum-stained *ostra*. "This is for me to do. Please."

Parthenia's words still stung, and Rheia felt like she was taking advantage of the girl. But she didn't want to cause a scene by insisting. Instead, she finished her food quickly, leaving the plate for Yalee to clean up, and returned to her room to fetch the pan flute. *Better to remain alone,* Rheia reminded herself. She sat on the cool grass underneath the date-plum tree, her back against its trunk. The caregivers who'd been sweeping up earlier had gone, although a young woman stood idle near the entrance to the *gynaikon* as though waiting for something.

Rheia slipped her sandals off and buried her toes in the green blades. At this time of year, the lawn should be a sere brown, but instead it was thick and damp; the caregivers must water it. The tree branches stirred overhead in a gentle breeze, and the fountain sang. Sighing, she began to play, warming up by going through all the songs she'd been taught as a child.

Once she had exhausted her repertoire, Rheia attempted to teach herself a simple old hymn her grandmother used to sing, a paean to the goddesses Kloe and Despoina. The

tune was sweet and sad. By the time she had the way of it and was able to play it through without hesitation, the sun had crested its arc and was sliding down the sky towards dusk, and her heart was melancholy.

When the tune wound to a close, Rheia was surprised to see Parthenia, sitting on one of the benches. The Carmean girl watched her, a frown between her brows and her hands curled in her lap. Rheia set the pan flute down and met Parthenia's gaze. "What do you want now?" she said, tired. Her cheeks ached from playing, her heart with the strangeness of this place. "I came out here to seek peace, not to provoke a fight."

"I ... don't wish to argue with you," Parthenia said, her voice soft. Rheia could barely hear her over the whispering treetops. "I heard you play that song and wondered where you learned it?" There was a question in her voice.

"My *tethe* used to sing it. The words tell the story of two of our goddesses, Kloe and Despoina, and of Kloe's grief at being parted from her daughter for three months of each year. That is when Despoina goes to be with her husband, Eidoneus, and the world mourns."

"We have these goddesses also, and that god," Parthenia said, her frown deepening.

"Then what troubles you?"

"Don't Oreareans only worship Areus?"

"Areus is ascendant because of the favour he grants us." Rheia arched her back in a stretch, curling her shoulder blades towards one another. The bones of her spine popped. The tree wasn't the most comfortable seat, but despite her melancholy she felt calmer here, as though divine Kloe reached out through the plants to steady her.

"But there are shrines to all the old gods, if you know where to find them."

"Is their worship forbidden, then?"

"Not ... exactly." Rheia thought of her father's statue of Eidoneus in his *andron*. Not secret, but not on public display either. "But Areus is our patron god, and his priests are powerful. It is them that bear the responsibility of ensuring the demon remains bound, and that the *thysies* are gathered." She remembered Parthenia's objection to Rheia appropriating the word and hastily clarified, "The sacrifices, I mean."

"Oh."

"Do your people worship Areus?"

"Not anymore," Parthenia muttered. She turned her head to the side, and Rheia saw that her temple glistened with a sheen of oil. Nightsleep, Rheia was sure of it. Dora's doing. Still, who was she to judge if the other *thysia* wished to dull her own fear, her own anger at the injustice of her situation? Wasn't that why Rheia sat where she did and played?

Guilt stirred her to speak. "I'm sorry." Rheia sat the pan flute aside. "For what I said before."

"No, you were right to chastise me. That girl with the curled lip—"

"Yalee."

"Yes, Yalee. She didn't do anything to deserve my rudeness. She didn't captain the ship that brought me here."

Rheia winced, then hid it by picking a blade of grass, twirling it between her fingers. If Parthenia noticed Rheia's expression, she didn't say anything.

"My parents *did* raise me better than that," the Carmean girl said with a sigh.

"Still, I can understand why you'd regard us all as enemies, man, woman and child." Rheia stared up at the canopy of the tree as she tried to find the right words. "I confess, until yesterday, I hadn't given much thought to the *thysies*. I knew what fate they faced, and found it ... distasteful. *Distasteful*." Her fingers crushed into fists, her nails biting her palms. The blade of grass was smeared to green mush. "I should have been horrified. Should have urged my father to insist the temple seek another way to keep the demon bound than this slaughter of innocents. I am just as complicit as Dora in the sacrifice of b-babies." The truth of it, hot and heavy, forced tears from her eyes. They spilled down her cheeks, and she didn't fight them this time—they were the mark of her shame and regret. *Now* she realised, and it was too late for her to do anything about it. She hung her head. "This—my name being drawn—it's the gods' justice."

A hand, soft and tentative, wrapped itself around Rheia's fist. Parthenia's. Someone else approached, asked a soft question, and the Carmean girl sent them away with a word. She didn't speak again until the well of Rheia's tears had dried up like a spring in drought.

"I know something of complacence," Parthenia said at last. Wiping away her tears, Rheia looked up. "I came from a poor village on the ocean, a fishing village. My parents owned the land all around, and those villagers who didn't fish worked it in exchange for a share of the crops." She hesitated. "A small share." She spoke softly, as though ashamed. "Last winter, two-faced Appelon sent a plague across Carmea. Do you have Appelon here?"

"He's our god of sickness and healing. Yours too?" Parthenia nodded, and Rheia grimaced, wiping her cheeks with the hem of her *chiton*. The crying had numbed her grief almost as effectively as nightsleep.

"Many died. Including my parents and both of my brothers. When the Carmean lords declared our village would take a turn in providing one of the *thysies* ... the villagers gave them me."

Rheia stared at Parthenia. "You don't have the lottery there?"

"What is a lottery?"

Rheia explained how it worked—the drawing of a name at random by the high priests. "The temple says the lottery lets Areus choose through his *most holy* servants," she added bitterly, "but I suspect the god's hand plays less of a part than the priests themselves."

"You don't believe you were chosen at random."

Rheia shook her head. "My father is—" She considered telling Parthenia of his part in bringing the girl here, but loneliness and fear stopped the words in her throat. After swallowing them down, she continued, "Well, he's an important man who has earned the wrath of Draconaidas, the high priest. I think Draconaidas took advantage of the situation, the other *thysia's* suicide, and—"

"Suicide?" Parthenia gasped, regarding Rheia with a frown, her lip curled with disgust. "Is that what they say? That she *killed* herself?"

"Well ... yes. Is it not true?"

"No, of course not. Aglaia would never have killed herself. She was *murdered!*"

CHAPTER TEN

*M*urdered.

The world dropped out from under Rheia. Dizziness overcame her and she felt as though she was falling. Nausea churned, coating her tongue with bitterness. A gust of wind blew, shaking the date-plum. Blossoms rained around her and Parthenia in a shower of pink.

"Rheia, are you well? *Rheia*?" There was the sound of running feet leaving her side, but Rheia felt detached from it. *Murdered?* But that meant...

The implications slammed into her, leaving her breathless. If the grey-eyed girl had been murdered, then Draconaidas hadn't been taking advantage of random chance to get to a political enemy. He'd manufactured the opportunity, Rheia was sure of it. He'd murdered Aglaia *with the intent of offering Rheia to the Beast.*

Rage drove her to her feet. Her heart pounded, and her tongue tasted strangely metallic in her mouth. She stared around, her nostrils flaring. The scent of flowers and crushed grass almost overwhelmed her. Dora approached, sunlight glinting like a spark of fire off her circlet. Parthenia strode at her heels.

"Rheia, what is it?" the old woman said, voice low and calm, hands spread and held low, as though she were trying to soothe a wild animal.

"He means to see me dead!" Rheia shouted.

"Sweet girl." Sadness and compassion widened Dora's eyes and softened her lips. "Would you like some night-sleep?" She reached into a pouch at her belt, retrieving a small clay pot. It was painted with a stylised leaf.

She thinks I'm hysterical. "I told you no," Rheia said, taking a step back. Her hands shook as she held them before herself. "No drugs. I'll be even more vulnerable then."

"Vulnerable to what?"

"To being murdered! Like that other *thysia* girl." Now Dora's moment of unease when she'd described the house as safe for the *thysies* made sense. It *wasn't* safe. Not always. Those locks on the outside of the *gynaikon* door wouldn't stop a temple assassin slinking in under the cover of night.

"No one is going to murder you." Dora took a step forward, off the pavers and into the tree's shade. The clay pot was still in her hand. It loomed in Rheia's vision as though it were a dagger that Dora wielded, instead of simple herb-infused oil.

"But Draconaidas murdered her to bring me here. I'm sure of it!"

"Let's say for a moment that's true," Dora said, her voice still low and calm. How many times had she had to practice this art of soothing upset *thysies*? Dozens? Hundreds? "If he meant to kill you, he wouldn't have bothered to bring you here. He'd have had you knifed in

the street on the way to the *agora*. No, Rheia, you are safe here."

"For eleven more days," Parthenia added. Dora speared her with a glare. "Don't look at me like that," the girl said with a shrug. "It's true. If this priest has orchestrated Rheia's presence, it's to see her slain by the Beast you love so much, Besadora. It is a strange kind of safety you offer."

Dora froze for a long moment, her wide eyes on Parthenia, before nodding stiffly. "I cannot dispute that. But it is safety, nonetheless. After … well, after Aglaia was killed, we increased the number of guards on the outer wall, and added internal bars to the gates rather than relying on the locks the temple installed for us. Strange as it may seem, Parthenia, the caregivers take the *thysies*' safety seriously, and always have. What happened to Aglaia brought shame on us all. We won't let it happen again."

Rheia looked around and saw several other caregivers—all female, of course—watching them from the edges of the courtyard. Their faces were familiar; she'd seen them sweeping, tending the garden, serving and cleaning up after meals. But now, looking with fresh eyes, she noted their watchful gazes, the way each of them held something that could be used as an improvised weapon— a broom, a mop, a pair of bronze shears. Even the pregnant woman was there, a kitchen knife sheathed at her rounded hip.

Her father, with his sword and fire-thrower, would make short work of such a ramshackle defence, she was sure. She wondered whether the caregivers' increased vigilance would be enough to deter the temple from striking again, and then shook her head. Dora was right. The lottery had cost the temple, not financially but in good will from the city. Draconaidas wouldn't kill her now, not after all that.

He'd let the Beast do it for him.

Her panicked breathing eased as the anger ebbed, leaving grim determination in its wake: rocks bared by the retreating tide. "I need to get word to my family," she said, hands on her hips as she stared at Dora.

"Why?"

"My father needs to know. Draconaidas interfered with the lottery. I'm not meant to be here."

Parthenia barked a laugh, the sound hard with bitterness.

"The *thysies* aren't permitted contact with their families once they enter these walls," Dora said. But there was a thread of uncertainty in her voice.

"But I'm not a *thysia*, am I?" Rheia pointed out. "I'm Orearean, not Carmean." She barely noticed as Parthenia turned and stalked from the courtyard, her bare feet thumping against the pavers. "Look, Dora, is there a rule against it? Or is it just that for the last twenty years it hasn't been an option because the *thysies'* families have been too far away?" *And because they were* helots*, so no one cared enough to let them send a letter.*

"I don't..." The caregiver woman's shoulders slumped and Rheia knew she'd won. "No, there's not a rule."

"Good. May I have something to write on?"

While Dora fetched the requested supplies, Rheia paced under the tree. The grass poked and tickled the arches of her feet, but she ignored it, biting her lip as she considered what to write. Her first instinct was to write everything down, spill out her suspicions and fears across the parchment like tears, begging for her father's

aid. But that was a bad idea. The caregivers couldn't leave the house to deliver her message themselves. It would be entrusted to a messenger boy, easy for the temple to intercept.

And that was assuming the caregivers themselves weren't corrupt. Dora seemed earnest. She was sure the woman was dedicated to the task she'd had for a lifetime—but what was it Parthenia had said about her *loving* the Beast? Surely not. And there were dozens of other caregivers Rheia didn't know, hadn't met.

So, putting the truth in the letter was out. Rheia would need to see someone in her family face to face. Her father? They would never let him into the *gynaikon*, and she wasn't sure she wanted to see him anyway. The memory of his stunned acceptance as Rheia had been carted away, a calf to be slaughtered, wasn't one she cared to haul up from the bottom of the mental well to which she'd consigned it.

When Dora returned, the girl was sitting at one of the benches, plucking fallen blossoms from her long hair. She smiled at the older woman and indicated the space beside her.

Eyes narrowing, Dora sat.

"I want to write to my grandmother, ask her to come visit me," Rheia said bluntly. "To speak with her in person."

"Absolutely not."

"Why not? She's a frail old woman." That was why Rheia had decided to request her grandmother rather than her mother. "She won't be any threat to the *thysies* or the caregivers."

"Only caregivers can come into the house."

"But you know that's untrue, Dora," Rheia said. She was guessing, but was confident of her assumptions. "You can't go out to the marketplace to buy your food or supplies. There must be deliveries that come within these walls. And Draconaidas was here only yesterday. He's not a caregiver."

Dora blinked. "Still, this is the house's most holy time, a time for care and contemplation. We don't often take deliveries during the four weeks before the Festival of Areus."

"Not often, but sometimes?"

Dora's lips twitched for a moment before she settled her expression to stillness. Still, Rheia's heart soared when she saw the tic. "Yes, sometimes," Dora admitted.

Rheia leaned forward to clutch one of the woman's hands. Dora's skin was loose and thin on the back of her hand, as though the supporting bones and flesh had shrunk with age. "I just want to talk to her. I won't try anything. And it's not like she could sneak a man in under the folds of her skirt. Or would, even if she could." She paused, letting the tears well in her eyes. "*Please. Just let me have a chance to say g-goodbye.*"

"We both know that's not your true motivation, Rheia," Dora chided, but her eyes crinkled with open amusement now. "Look, the best I can promise is that I will ask for permission. It isn't my decision, but I will make your case to the master of the house and see what he says."

The master of the house? She doesn't mean ... the Beast? Rheia swallowed, but nodded. "I'll wait to see what he says, then," she said, collecting the well-scraped piece of parchment and the pot of ink Dora had brought and taking them to her room. There, she lay on her bed

and stared at the ceiling, turning over in her mind what she would say in the letter, how she would try and convey what she believed had happened to her in a subtle way that wouldn't attract the temple's ire, if the *master of the house* said no to her request.

The idea of the Beast—if the master was the Beast—knowing her name filled her with dread. She knew the reaction didn't make sense. The creature was going to kill her anyway. It didn't matter whether it thought she was impudent. But still, goosebumps prickled her flesh whenever she considered the idea of it turning its mind to her, as though it were a spirit that walked the halls, and might pre-emptively strangle her in her bed. For all she knew, it could. It was the offspring of Areus, after all.

Not wanting to look Parthenia in the eye after she'd so clearly highlighted the difference in their statuses, Rheia took her evening meal in her room. That was where Dora found her, sitting by the carved window panel as the sun set and the light faded. The shadows were already long outside Rheia's window, and she wished again that her room faced the harbour so she might watch the sunset rather than staring at grey gloom.

"You might consider putting a garden out there," Rheia said, her throat tight as the old woman pushed aside the curtain over the door. She forced herself to keep her tone even, not to reveal the bone-deep grief at the reminder of how fleeting her remaining time was. "There is a patch of grass before the mountain's edge where the soil might be good. And it would lift the spirit of the next girl to use this room."

"That's a kind thought," Dora said. Rheia watched as the old woman used a taper to light the wick hanging out of the oil lamp on a shelf by the door. "You shouldn't sit in the dark, child." She hurried across the room, sheltering the tiny flame with her fingerless hand, and lit the lamp by the bed. Then she blew out the taper with a sharp puff of breath.

"It wasn't dark until a little while ago," Rheia murmured, turning back to look out the window. With the light behind her, the night seemed darker. She could barely see the faint wall of grey beyond the grass, where the cliff loomed impossibly high.

"He has agreed to your request," Dora said, cushions shifting as she sat beside Rheia at the end of her bed. The girl clasped her hands together with delight, and the woman continued in a warning voice. "He requires, though, that your grandmother dress herself as a merchant woman and conceal her face with a shawl. Some might recognise Loukios's mother, and decide the House of the Beast is meddling where it shouldn't."

Rheia swallowed. "Dora, is the master of the house a caregiver? Or is he...?" Her words faltered.

"Is he the Beast?" Dora supplied. Rheia nodded, pressing her lips together, and Dora examined her expression with that piercing gaze. Then she nodded once. "Yes, he is."

Butterflies tickled Rheia's stomach, the back of her throat, but all she said was, "Oh."

"You don't seem surprised."

"Should I be? It is the House of the Beast. I would assume he is the master of that house, in the same way my father is the master of *his* house."

"Most assume the Beast is a dumb animal, like the bull whose head he bears," Dora replied in a soft voice. She looked away, and Rheia couldn't see her expression.

"He has the body of a man, though, and is the child of a god. Also," she added with a bitter smile, "I have never seen a bull wield a sword. If the Beast gouged the *thysies* with a horn, or trampled them underfoot, I might think it—he—was a beast in truth. But animals don't use weapons."

Silence settled. The corner of Dora's lip was caught between her teeth as she studied Rheia, her expression contemplative. Finally, the discomfort grew to be too much, and Rheia stood, crossing to where the ink and parchment lay on top of her jewellery chest. "I will write the letter now, and ask my grandmother to dress as the Beast has requested. Her name is Charis, and she lives with my parents."

Once the letter was written onto the hide and the ink blown dry, Rheia rolled it and handed it to Dora.

"I will have this delivered in the morning. Sleep well, Rheia."

"And you," the girl replied politely. But she doubted she would sleep at all.

CHAPTER ELEVEN

Rheia's silent prediction proved true: she lay awake for hours. The evening before, the nightsleep remaining in her system had claimed her. There was no drug within her now, and she refused to ask for it. Her mind ran in circles like a wild animal in a trap, wearing a well-worn path from one thought to the next, and then back again: that tomorrow she might see her grandmother; that when she woke, she would only have ten days left to live. At times she seethed at the injustice of it all. How dare Draconaidas kill another *thysia* and put her in their place, all to spite her father? As if *she* had anything to do with city politics! At other times remorse overcame her, as she realised the injustice occupying her mind was the smaller one, when a much greater injustice loomed. Was Typhein so terrible that his remaining trapped was worth all the lives the binding had consumed? The dead sacrifices alone must number close to five hundred, and she didn't even like to think about the number of Carmeans who had died during the Orearean war to secure the *thysies*.

Was Typhein so fierce that the improved weapons the Orearean army wielded now couldn't take him down?

The idea made her sit up on her bed, mind working as her eyes stared, unseeing, at the heavy shadows coating her room. Her pulse raced in her ears. The fire-throwers and iron weapons, and the great cannons that protected the harbour, which could shoot huge bronze balls at enemy ships—the Orearean army had had none of those back when it had faced Typhein more than a century ago. And the city had the Beast himself, a god-borne creature who wielded a great sword. Could they … fight back?

The moon was halfway to its bed when exhaustion finally claimed Rheia. The nightmares claimed her soon after.

Again, Rheia dreamed she was fleeing a huge wall of flame roaring down the mountainside. A sharp crack sounded once, twice. She glanced over her shoulder and saw an olive tree explode as fire engulfed it with a greedy hand. The wave of heat battered her skin and dried her eyes in an instant. She looked forward again, face burning with pain. If she didn't run faster, her hair might catch alight. Her *chiton*. Her skin.

A hand in hers urged her to run faster, willed her to do it, and she found her sandals flying even more swiftly down the mountainside. She glanced over, expecting to see the familiar face of Eidoneus, the god who'd haunted her dreams since childhood, silent and smiling...

The huge, horned head of the Beast stared back at her. Its teeth were bared as it panted for breath.

She screamed. Something tangled her legs and she struggled, terrified she would fall and the fire would sweep over her. The Beast, swordless, would tear her limb from limb...

"Rheia. Rheia!"

The sound of her name drew her back to herself, to her room. A hunched figure loomed by the window. Rheia recoiled—or tried to, but her limbs were still bound together. Still fogged with sleep, she opened her mouth to call for help, certain the temple had sent an assassin despite Dora's reassurances. But, as the dream fog lifted, she saw the figure was one of the caregivers: the woman with a misshapen back, whom Rheia had seen tending the plants in the courtyard. Heart still thundering in her ears, Rheia realised her blankets were wrapped around her legs. She kicked them off savagely.

"Bad dream?" The woman shuffled across the room to Rheia's clothes chest. The wan light of the morning sun, blocked as it was by the shadow of the mountain, shone through the holes before the window, faintly illuminating the room.

Rheia nodded, sitting up to study at the woman. Her brain still felt fuzzy with lack of sleep, and the spectres of the Beast, the fire, lurked in her mind, lurching forward every time she closed her eyes. "Why did you wake me?" she mumbled. Judging by the scant light seeping in the window, it wasn't far past dawn. What good was being a sacrifice if she couldn't at least sleep in a little?

"Dora asked me to." The chest lid thudded against the wall as the woman opened it, pursing her lips as she selected a neatly folded square of fabric in a bluish purple the same colour as the twilight sky.

Rheia's heart leapt into her throat. "My letter...?" she said, her voice breathy with anxiety.

"It was delivered at first light. A boy has just delivered

a reply to the gate," the woman said. Her tone was flat, but Rheia barely noticed. Had it been her little brother who had run the reply back to the gates?

"What—what did it say?"

"I'm to get you dressed. You are to receive a visitor."

The news leant Rheia's feet wings. She leapt from the bed, not even complaining when the caregiver set herself to the task of preparing Rheia for the day, stripping her with a brusque professionalism that spoke of either boredom or dislike. Maybe she just didn't like any business that took her away from her garden. Rheia bore it in silence, her mind fixed on her visitor, even when the woman brushed her hair so roughly it hurt.

Once Rheia was ready, the woman led her out the door.

"Thank you for attending me," Rheia said meekly as they walked down the corridor towards the open-sided dining room. "Forgive me, but I don't even know your name."

"Erika," the woman grunted.

"Well, thank you, Erika."

The woman regarded her with raised eyebrows before bowing her into the dining room.

Rheia had been bracing herself for an encounter with Parthenia. But the *thysia* wasn't there; her side of the table was empty. Had the caregivers let her sleep, or was she angry at Rheia? A pang of sympathy made Rheia hang her head. She wished there was something she could do for the Carmean girl. Still, if Rheia's mad ideas in the middle of the night went anywhere, perhaps she could save them both. She'd just have to convince her grandmother to convince her father to convince the king that they should free the demon so they could kill it.

That should be easy, right?

The size of the task didn't depress her spirits and she ate quickly and well, smiling at Erika and praising the lushness of the garden until the dour caregiver smiled back. Feeling as though she'd won a great victory, Rheia hummed to herself as she went to sit under the date-plum when directed, arranging her skirts around her, and waited. "It shouldn't be long," Erika said, before leaving.

The sun inched up the sky and out from behind the mountain; the tree's shadow shortened and deepened as the summer heat grew. Sweat beaded Rheia's brow. Still she waited. And waited.

Has something gone wrong? Rheia shifted on the hard bench. Her bottom was starting to go numb. Had no one come after all? She gave a pleading look to Yalee, the only caregiver to pass through the courtyard, but the mute girl shrugged her lack of understanding, her arms full of linen, and hurried on.

When the double doors to the house's main chambers opened at last, Rheia almost burst into tears. Her stooped grandmother, Charis, shuffled in, Dora at her side. Rheia leapt to her feet and rushed across the grass to fling herself into the old woman's arms.

"*Tethe*, you came," she sobbed into her grandmother's shoulder. "I was worried."

"Of course I came," Charis soothed, patting Rheia's back and stroking her hair.

"Then what took so long?" Her voice came out in a wail, like a child's, and she bit her lip, feeling her cheeks burn with shame. "Sorry."

"Don't apologise. The delay arose from a bit of a disagreement," Charis said, an edge to her voice. Rheia looked

at her sharply, wiping the tears from her eyes. "Still, it is no matter. Come, let us sit. What a lovely garden!"

Rheia took a deep breath, swallowing her distress. "Isn't it?" Smiling brightly, she showed her grandmother around the courtyard, pausing as Charis splashed water on her face from the cascading fountain before sitting beside her on the bench. She slipped her hand into her grandmother's and clung to it, not wanting to let go. "So, what was the disagreement?"

"It was nothing," Charis said quickly. Rheia raised her eyebrows, disbelieving, and the old woman shrugged. "They insisted on searching me," she grumbled. "As though I had a fire-thrower in my basket, or a great dagger concealed along my spine. And then they kept the basket outside anyway." Charis was dressed in a rough *chiton*, nothing like her usual elegant fabrics. A poor woman's disguise, Rheia realised.

"Did you wear the shawl they requested?" she asked anxiously.

"Yes, child. I left it in the basket. Along with a stack of honeyed dates I picked up this morning at the market for you. They wouldn't let me bring them in."

"From Galen?" Rheia gasped.

"I bought them from Galen's father," Charis said, looking at a cluster of sweet-smelling herbs growing near her sandalled foot like it was the most interesting things in the world. Rheia slumped. Of course Galen hadn't sent her sweets. He'd given up on her the second her name was called—she could read that in her grand-mother's hunched shoulders.

"Oh. Well, don't take offence, *Tethe*," she said, squaring her own shoulders and trying to hide her disappointment.

"The caregivers spoil us here. And they are very conscious of security." Dora stood by the door, giving them the illusion of privacy, but watched them both carefully. Still, Rheia lowered her voice. "In fact, that's why I wanted to see you."

"Oh?"

"The other *thysia*, the girl who died? She was *murdered*."

Charis paled, her face turning the colour of fireside ashes as the blood fled her cheeks. Rheia rushed on, clutching her grandmother's fingers like they were a tether preventing her from being lost in a storm at sea. "I'm sure the temple did it so there'd be a lottery. Draconaidas means to punish Father."

"After your name was drawn, we wondered if that might be the case." Charis's voice came out in a whisper.

"It's true, I'm sure of it. You have to tell Father. Maybe— maybe he can use this to save me." Rheia's voice broke on the last two words, and Charis's eyes flooded with sympathy. She shook her head, and Rheia's heart sank to her stomach, churning it until she felt sick.

It sank even farther when her grandmother replied, "What do you think he can do?"

"Tell the king! If he knows Draconaidas is rigging a holy ritual for his own personal gain—well, that's blasphemy!"

"Blasphemy is a matter for the temple to decide, not the king," her grandmother said gently. "And Draconaidas is the highest authority in the temple ... other than Areus himself."

"Well, then Father could take it to the *agora*." Rheia's voice grew loud, but she didn't care. "Tell the people what Draconaidas has done! Surely they would prefer Typhein be freed than see this injustice take place?" Charis's lips tightened, and Rheia felt panic flutter in her chest where

her heart used to be, a trapped bird. "Our armies are much stronger than they were before, when the demon was last free. We could slay it. The fire-throwers, the—"

"Hush," Charis said, putting a finger to Rheia's lips. "Think about what you are suggesting, child. That we free a monster who slew many hundreds of us—maybe thousands, if some of the stories are to be believed. That we risk those deaths again for the chance to save one. I wish our fellow Oreareans were so self-sacrificing but..." She sighed heavily. Rheia hung her head, her hands falling into her lap, and her grandmother hurried to add, "That is not to say it wouldn't work, my sweet child. But we would require proof."

And we have only ten days to find it. Rheia heard the words her grandmother didn't say. The girl's head drooped and she stared at her hands as they fell limply into her lap. "Oh."

"We will look for it, of course," Charis said more briskly. "I will find Loukios straight away and tell him your suspicions and your plan. If anyone can make it happen, it's your father."

Rheia knew her grandmother was trying to lift her spirits, and she forced herself to smile even though her heart wasn't in it. It was unlikely that Dora could be persuaded to let the old woman visit again, and Rheia wanted Charis to remember her as brave, not desperate, if this was the last time they'd see each other.

The last time before the day of the sacrifice, of course.

When Charis left, promising to pass on Rheia's love to her parents and even to her pesky little brother, the girl shuffled back to her room as though asleep. There, she lay on the bed, curled on her side. She felt numb all over, as though she'd submerged herself in a winter sea until the icy chill stole away all sensation from her skin. Her breath came fast and shallow, and the room seemed darker at the edges of her vision, despite the midday sun beating down outside her window.

After a time, Dora came, again offering nightsleep with gentle words. When Rheia clenched her jaw shut and scowled, the woman retreated. Soon after, Yalee arrived, bearing a fat clay pot with a hollow in its belly and a hole in the top. The girl set a candle within it, and then poured glistening liquid into a shallow bowl. This she set above the flame, so its belly nestled in the hole. The gentle, sweet scents of chamomile and lavender eased into the room; Rheia's nose catalogued them even as her mind refused to function. Yalee sat in the corner of the room, silent as a statue of the gods, and studied the golden patch of sunlight near the window as though she wasn't there to watch over Rheia.

The patch of sunlight had crept quite a way along the floor when Parthenia arrived. Rheia still felt numb, but the soothing herbs had loosened her limbs, drained the knots from her jaw.

Still, they couldn't drain the ice of despair from her heart.

The *thysia* sat on the edge of Rheia's bed. Instead of scolding Rheia for her Orearean arrogance and privilege, Parthenia began to comb Rheia's hair with gentle fingers. "Last night I was overcome with jealousy," the girl said,

her accent thicker than usual. "I blamed you for my inability to see my own family again before I die. But now I think perhaps I am the lucky one. It would burn my heart like fire to know my parents and brothers were outside that wall, so close and yet out of reach."

Rheia felt something then; her throat burned as it tightened with grief.

"Still," Parthenia continued, "I know they are all waiting for me in Eidoneus's halls. Ten more days and I will be with them. They are free of Appelon's sickness and I will be free of Areus's doom, and we will all be happy together once more."

"My family are still alive." Rheia had never known her other grandmother, or either of her grandfathers. There had only ever been her mother, her father, Charis and Aias.

"Then you'll have to prepare the way for them," Parthenia said, "since you will be the one waiting on the far side of that bridge."

"But I'm too young to die," Rheia whispered.

"So am I."

CHAPTER TWELVE

Parthenia was still there when Rheia fell into an exhausted sleep just as the sun set. When she awoke the next morning, a still-warm depression in the blankets beside her suggested someone had stayed the night in Rheia's room. Had the other sacrifice fallen asleep herself?

Sighing, Rheia slipped from her bed and padded over to the clean bowl of water that had already been left out for her. Yalee was gone too, and the candle in her clay pot had long since burned out. The scent of sweet, soothing herbs was as faint as a dream.

The comparison brought a frown to Rheia's forehead as she splashed water on her face, lifting her hair to wet the back of her neck. She didn't recall any troubling nightmares last night. Maybe Parthenia's closeness had kept them away. It reminded Rheia of the way her mother had soothed her to sleep when she was small, singing and patting her back. She bit her lip, wondering whether to be embarrassed that Parthenia had seen her in such a vulnerable state.

But no. Both girls had struggled during the past two days—and before that, Parthenia had lost the other Carmean girl, Aglaia. If there was no way out of this for Rheia, there was no sense in being embarrassed at showing grief and despair to one similarly stricken. Why waste what time she had left worrying about social niceties?

As for the caregivers ... Rheia wrinkled her nose. They had seen it all before.

She washed and dressed herself, glad to be able to perform the simple morning ritual alone for a change, and went in search of food and a quiet place to sit. Her emotions felt hollowed out after yesterday's disappointments. A numbness had settled in her lungs, stopping her from taking a full, clean breath, when she'd realised there was nothing her family could do to help her. Still, she didn't want to risk an argument—with anyone—dislodging that numbness.

If it did leave her, she mused as she raided the dining room for the food set out there, perhaps she should accept that offer of nightsleep after all. The idea felt like giving in, and part of her still resisted it, but she wasn't sure she could handle nine more days of the gut-wrenching grief and panic that had crippled her the afternoon before. She wasn't that strong.

When Dora came looking for her, she was in the courtyard, sitting on the edge of the fountain and nibbling at a honey and sesame cake. The morning had grown hot while Rheia slept, but a playful breeze seized handfuls of spray from the descending water, throwing it at her and cooling her skin. The droplets glittered like jewels and speckled her reflection in the fountain's pool.

The caregiver woman bowed and sat on a bench in

the shade, out of the water's reach. She smiled—but the expression didn't reach her eyes, which were once again full of that speculative look Rheia had noticed before.

The girl swallowed a mouthful of cake, deciding to take the bull by the horns. Here in the House of the Beast, it seemed appropriate. "Why do you stare at me so?" she asked in a quiet voice.

Dora blinked, taken aback. "What do you mean?"

"Sometimes I feel as though you think I'm a puzzle box to be unlocked."

"I..." The woman wiped her forehead with her good hand, leaning back on the other as though weary. "Not a puzzle box, no. But it's been a long time since we've had a sacrifice come through with such spirit. Aglaia was such a one, but usually the Carmeans—both male and female—are more subdued."

Rheia shrugged, looking back at the fountain's spray, which glowed purest white in the sun. "Perhaps that's because they've had more time to adjust to the idea than I have. They already know they could be offered as a *thysia* and then, once they are, they have the journey here to accept their fate." Although the journey from the Carmean coast to Oreareus was only a day's sail, Rheia understood from conversations with her father that many of the *thysies* were shipped overland to the coast before being surrendered.

"That may be part of it," Dora murmured, her tone huskier than usual. Rheia glanced back at her, tipping her head to the side and raising her eyebrows in a questioning expression. The old woman stared at her for several heartbeats before blurting, "Would you like to meet the master of the house?"

Rheia's mouth fell open. She had misheard, surely. "I'm sorry, did you say...?"

"I asked if you would like to meet him. A—the Beast."

The world seemed to withdraw and fade before Rheia's eyes; even the fountain grew quiet, its shushing and gurgling replaced by a ringing that filled her ears and echoed inside her skull. She closed her eyes to gather herself before the dizziness overcame her. When she opened them, Dora was waiting, eyes bright with expectation.

"You mean before the sacrifice, I assume?" the girl croaked.

"Yes. Today."

"I'm not ready to die." Rheia's voice was a whisper. She'd crushed the last mouthful of her sesame cake in her fingers, but she couldn't force open her fists to shake off the sticky crumbs.

Dora shook her head. "He wouldn't kill you, child. The timing of the sacrifice is important. But you misunderstand my purpose. Sometimes, back when I was younger and the sacrifices were all Orearean, it helped them accept their situation to meet the hand of their fate. It reduced their fear of the sacrifice itself, because the Beast wasn't an unknown monster anymore."

No, he'd be a known one. Is that any better? Rheia took several long breaths to calm herself. Gradually, her thundering heart slowed to a canter rather than its careening gallop down the mountainside. A thought occurred to her. "Would you have offered this to Aglaia? If she'd survived?"

"I'm not sure. Probably not. Oreareans can at least see the benefit of Typhein's imprisonment and Areus's favour. I expect most Carmeans would be glad if the demon got free and slew us all. I couldn't be sure a Carmean *thysia* wouldn't try to kill the Beast if given the chance—*especially* one with spirit. And if the Beast dies, the demon escapes."

Rheia frowned. "The way Draconaidas tells it, the Beast only exists to stop us from having to kill our own people. To keep Orearean hands clean. Is that not true?"

Dora shook her head. "I can't speak to Areus's motivation, but I know the Beast is a part of the binding ritual. The spell is quite specific. It must be him who spills the blood at the festival, or the binding will unravel. Besides," she added flatly, "it's not as though our hands are free of blood, given the number of Carmeans who died during the war to secure the flow of *thysies* and the treasure that comes with them. We have become quite adept at slaughter in our own right." A shadow seemed to pass before the sun at the caregiver's words.

"No wonder they'd prefer to see us dead," Rheia murmured, finally able to open her fist enough to wash her sticky fingers in the pool beneath the fountain. She bit her lip, watching the crumbs grow fat as they soaked up the water before swirling away on a gentle current. "Why would Draconaidas not want people to know about the Beast being part of the binding?"

"He himself may not know," Dora said, her tone conveying her indifference. "It has been more than a century." Unspoken was the fact that Dora was in a position to hear it from the only one who'd been alive since the day Typhein was bound: the Beast himself.

Rheia looked up at her, her fingers still trailing in the water. "You haven't told him?"

"Why should I? Draconaidas has earned no favours

from me."

"But you both serve Areus!" Rheia's eyes widened with shock. She'd known there was no love lost between Dora and the high priest, but she hadn't thought it went so far that the caregiver might actively resist him. Although it should have occurred to her, she realised now. Why else would Dora have agreed to request that Charis be invited to visit? The woman had known from the start that Rheia planned to accuse Draconaidas.

"As I told you once before, Areus has never made his will known to me. I serve my master and therefore the sacrifices," Dora pointed out. "It is he who insists we keep you in safety and comfort. The temple wouldn't care if we threw you in a dungeon, so long as we kept you pure for the ritual."

Rheia's eyes widened and her hand stilled at this revelation. She'd already known the Beast wasn't a mind-less animal, but this second hint that he was a creature with compassion stunned her. "Oh."

"So," the caregiver went on, "do you want to meet him? Would it help you?"

Rheia tried to stop her mind's frantic whirling and consider the question from all angles. Did she want to meet the Beast? The creature from her nightmares?

Would a nightmare creature care if she was kept in comfort rather than in a dank cell filled with rats? Whether she got to speak to her grandmother one last time?

"Yes. Please." Rheia blinked in surprise as she realised the words had tumbled from her lips, almost as if someone else had spoken. Her heart kicked so hard in her chest that her hand flew to cover it, afraid it might pound its way free of her ribs like an unruly mountain goat.

"Excellent," Dora said, standing. Her smile—genuine this time—lit up her face, making her look twenty years younger. "I will come for you after the evening meal." She swept away, the braid at her back gleaming as it swayed.

Rheia opened her mouth to call the old woman back, to say she'd changed her mind—but then she caught sight of Parthenia, peering from the dark shadow of her room. A blush heated Rheia's cheeks, as though she'd been caught admiring the young men, bare from the waist up, who sometimes cooled themselves at the fountain near her home. While she wasn't the one who had chosen to exclude Parthenia from the offer to visit the Beast, she still felt bad for the Carmean girl.

Even if it wasn't an offer Rheia was pleased about accepting.

Once the double doors to the *gynaikon* thumped closed, Parthenia slipped out of the shadows and drifted across to where Rheia sat. "May I?" she said, indicating the grass by Rheia's feet. When the Orearean girl nodded, Parthenia settled herself there, leaning her back against the edge of the fountain. Her hair grew darker as the fine mist settled on it. "I didn't mean to eavesdrop, but I heard Aglaia's name."

"Forgive me," Rheia said, her cheeks still burning. "Dora mentioned she and I are ... were ... alike." Her voice wavered, and she swallowed.

Parthenia tipped her head to the side, her eyebrows raised as she looked up at Rheia. "She certainly had your determination." Her shoulders drooped and she fell silent, her gaze sliding away to stare into the distance. Rheia wondered if she was seeing the other *thysia* standing there.

"Were you friends with her?" Rheia asked, speaking

quietly. She didn't want to drive Parthenia away. Being alone with her thoughts had lost its appeal.

"I only knew her for three days." Parthenia brought her knees up to her chest and curled her long fingers around them. "I met her the day we boarded the ship to come here. I tripped coming up the gang plank, and two of the soldiers laughed, called me a clumsy *helot* whore. She caught my arm to steady me, and then blistered their ears with her rebuke." A bitter smile twisted her lips. "Told them that if I were a *helot* whore, I wouldn't be on their stinking tub of a ship to be sacrificed as a virgin."

"What did the ship's captain do?" Rheia wanted to sound casual, but her voice was tight. Surely her father wouldn't have condoned that sort of behaviour?

Thankfully, Parthenia didn't seem to notice her apprehension. "We *thysies* were secured in two rooms below decks, one for the boys and one for Aglaia and I, so I didn't see. But the next day, when we were escorted above decks for some fresh air and exercise, we saw the men had stripes on their shoulders from a whipping. They glowered at Aglaia and me, but never spoke to us again."

"Oh. Good." Rheia grimaced. "Still, I'm sorry that happened to you."

"It's fine." Parthenia shrugged. The dark skin of her upper arms glistened, bare on either side of the brooches holding her *chiton* in place. The ends of her long hair curled with apparent delight at the fountain's moisture. "Anyway, after that, Aglaia was very protective of me, and she consoled me after I ... I tried to escape. She was a year older than I am, so it was a bit like having a big sister must be." Parthenia sighed wistfully.

"How old are you?" Rheia asked.

"Fifteen."

"Then Aglaia was the same age as me."

"Yes." Parthenia sounded distracted, though, her mind elsewhere. Rheia waited, and eventually the other girl spoke, her voice so soft she could barely be heard over the fountain's song. "She volunteered, you know."

"For what?"

Parthenia rested her forehead on her knees; the fabric of her *chiton* muffled her voice when she spoke. "To come here. Her family is powerful. She wouldn't have had to come, but she volunteered."

What? Rheia slid off the edge of the fountain to sit on the damp grass beside the other girl. "Why on earth would she do that? Did she want to die?"

"Not exactly," Parthenia murmured, leaning towards Rheia to rest her head on the Orearean girl's shoulder. Her lips were close to Rheia's ear. "If I tell you, do you promise to keep it a secret?"

"I promise," Rheia said, her mouth gone suddenly dry.

"There was a prophecy. The temple in her town foretold the same thing again and again, seeing it in the storms and the birth of a misshapen sheep. Her parents sacrificed a bull, hoping for a different answer, but it came back the same. If Aglaia came here to Oreareus, her death would mean our freedom. The end of Orearean oppression." Parthenia began to cry quietly, tears running from the corners of her eyes to soak Rheia's *chiton* and mingle with the fountain's spray. "That must be why Areus sent his priests to murder her," the Carmean girl sobbed. "He found out, somehow, and warned them. They wanted to stop her fulfilling the prophecy."

Rheia felt cold all over, as though she sat on a bed of

winter frost. Aglaia had come here, as foretold—and she had died, which had brought Rheia to the house. Was it possible Rheia was actually the gods' instrument in the Oreareans' downfall? In *her own people's* downfall?

It took her two tries before she was able to speak. "Which god's priests made the prophecy?" she croaked, clutching her arms around her belly as she shivered.

"Eidoneus."

CHAPTER THIRTEEN

Rheia followed Dora through the *gynaikon*, her hands clenched under the heavy folds of her *himation* to stop them from shaking. Dora had suggested Rheia wear the outer cloak over her *chiton*, assuring her she would need the extra warmth, but for now she sweltered in the loose, charcoal-dark fabric. The summer heat clung to the city, reluctant to release it and give way to night, and Rheia ached to feel the ocean breeze on her face.

She'd decided to go through with the visit to the Beast after Parthenia's revelation. Maybe there was a way to free the Carmeans that didn't involve Typhein laying waste to the entire island. Perhaps she could ask the Beast to tell Areus about how Draconaidas had killed Aglaia and rigged the lottery. Or maybe she could learn something from the Beast that would help her figure out what Eidoneus wanted from her. Surely the god wouldn't ask her to destroy her own people to free another?

Perhaps the prophecy had already been foiled, as Parthenia believed. Either way, a spark of curiosity

glimmered amidst the swarming clouds of dread in Rheia's heart.

She was going to see the Beast, and she was terrified.

The heavy bolt shot home as Dora locked the *gynaikon* doors. The sound was loud, echoing in Rheia's mind with a dreadful finality. She barely saw the magnificent carvings as she followed the caregiver, who strode down the corridor and turned left at the end. They passed another caregiver, a silver-haired man who lit hanging lanterns with a long taper. The man peered at them from the corner of his eye but didn't speak, keeping his head bowed as they passed. Ignoring him, Dora made another turn, this time into a short hallway ribbed with pillars of reddish limestone. A carved bull's head loomed over a heavy stone door, its horns spread so wide they brushed the walls on either side.

Dora stopped beneath the bull's head, turning to face Rheia. "This is it," she said needlessly. "Beyond this door, a flight of stairs will take you down to the Beast's home."

"You—you're not coming with me?" Rheia squeaked. The caregiver shook her head. Rheia waited for her to elaborate, but the older woman remained silent. "Why not?"

"I have other tasks that need attending to." But Dora's gaze slid from Rheia's to study the empty corridor.

"You're lying." Rheia jutted out her jaw and scowled.

Dora's eyes widened for a moment, and then she grimaced, her cheeks colouring a dusky pink. "Not precisely. I do have tasks, but they can wait. The Beast asked me to remain above."

Rheia's insides turned to water, her organs slushing together as panic shuddered through her. "Why would he do that?"

Dora shrugged, crossing her arms in front of her chest and shifting from foot to foot. The action reminded Rheia of Aias, and she stared in astonishment. She'd never imagined the self-assured caregiver could look so uneasy. "He's wroth with me," Dora admitted finally. "He banished me from his presence."

"So it's not about me?"

"No." Dora turned, her *chiton* swirling around her ankles, and reached for the handle with her good hand. The muscles in her arm strained as she heaved. The door was neither barred nor locked from either side; it scraped against the tiles as it swung along its arc, the sound setting Rheia's teeth on edge. Beyond, a dark rectangle loomed. "But I'll wait at the top of the stairs for you. You'll be fine."

Trembling, Rheia inched forward, peering down the flagstone staircase. As her eyes adjusted, she realised the stairs weren't as dark as she'd first thought; in the distance a lantern hung, gleaming yellow like a distant star. With huge eyes, she looked back at Dora. The caregiver's expression softened with sympathy as she said, "Don't be afraid. He's not what you expect."

"Even though he's angry at you?"

"Even though." Her voice was thick with feeling, and her eyes shone with devotion. *Parthenia is right,* Rheia realised. *Dora loves the Beast.*

"And you'll stay right here?" Rheia hated the begging note in her voice, but she couldn't shake it. The notion of walking down a flight of stairs that would take her below the ground was unnerving enough; Rheia knew the palace had rooms below ground, and had heard the same of some of the biggest houses in the city, but her

parents' villa and those of her friends did not, and she had never been underground before. The knowledge that a creature from her nightmares waited at the bottom transformed her discomfort into something that made her want to cling to Dora's skirts and wail like a child.

"I'll stay here," the old woman said, reaching out to brush a strand of hair back from Rheia's face. "Call if you need me," she added.

Squaring her shoulders, Rheia turned back to the staircase. Afraid of tripping, she lifted the hem of her *chiton*, the blue fabric swirling around her foot as she stepped down onto the first stair. And then the next. Soon, her cautious pace brought her even with the lantern, which hung from a sconce set high on the plain stone wall, illuminating a small landing. The staircase doubled back on itself. Below, another lantern glimmered above another landing. *How many of these must I pass before I reach the bottom?*

She turned and looked back up the stairs. The pale shape of the caregiver waiting in the open doorway reassured her a little, although once Rheia started down the second flight of stairs she'd be gone from Dora's sight and the tenuous protection that offered. She gave the caregiver a tentative wave, waiting until the gesture was returned. Then she started down the next flight of stairs.

The answer to Rheia's question was three: three lanterns above three landings. By the time she reached the third, the bare skin of her forearms prickled with goosebumps as the air grew cool and damp. She hugged the *himation* around her, exhaling with relief when she saw that the stairs ended—after another, shorter flight— in an open room. Rheia's mind skittered away from contemplating the weight of the rock and earth above her head as she forced her legs to move once more, starting down the last set of stairs.

The room at the bottom of the long staircase was wide and narrow, forming a foyer. Plain stone pillars stood close by one another, supporting the ceiling; between them were tables, each holding one of those beautiful timber carvings. A feather, each barb ornately detailed. A trireme, complete with tiny oars, but missing its smokestack. A scroll case so realistic her fingers itched to pop the cap off and see what treasure furled inside.

With her heart racing, Rheia crept through the foyer, emerging into a broad-ceilinged room that reminded her of her father's *andron*, except there was only one reclining couch—empty—beside the low table. The fabric on the couch cushions was plain, nothing like the ornately patterned fabric in the *gynaikon*. By way of contrast, the top of the table was magnificent, carved in a repeating pattern of flowers. One side wall was hung with a simple, heavy tapestry, probably in an attempt to reduce the chill. Opposite it, framed by an arch that drew the eye, was a life-sized statue of a man, formed of white stone. No, not a man. A god. Appelon wore a circlet of carved leaves on his curls and cradled a tortoise-shell lyre in one bare arm. Like Rheia, his shoulders were draped in the elegant folds of a *himation*; unlike Rheia, he was otherwise naked. The sculptor had made the god beautiful, with a flat stomach and strong, lean legs: a runner's build.

Rheia frowned. It was definitely Appelon—as well as healing, the god's love for music was well known. But why wasn't it Areus, here in his son's lair?

Tearing her eyes away from the god, she spoke in a

tentative voice. "H-hello?" Dora had said the Beast knew she was coming, and she'd expected him to be waiting for her. But this room was empty.

"Through here." The reply was masculine and deep, with a strange, muffled reverberation to it.

Slowly, her feet stumbling with fear, Rheia crossed the room, heading through a set of pillars into another room. This one was warmer than the last; a fire snapped at wood in a hearth on the right-hand wall, replacing the damp air with a tangy smell of juniper smoke that pervaded the room despite the chimney sucking it away, emptying somewhere far above in the evening air. Before the fire, a figure dressed in a simple black *chiton* had his back to her. He removed a heavy clay bowl from the flames, his hands swathed in protective cloth. Rheia stared, mouth agape.

Below the shoulders, the man seemed perfectly normal. Perfectly human. He wore sandals whose straps curved around and emphasised his shapely calves, and she caught a glimpse of a strong thigh under the swinging hem of his knee-length *chiton* before averting her eyes. The line of his back, visible through the tunic's fabric, was as muscled as a soldier's, as were his bare arms. His skin was a lighter brown than Rheia's, as though he hadn't seen the sun for a while and was losing his tan.

But above the shoulders...

From behind, all Rheia could see was an unnaturally rounded head; a pair of curved, decorative ears; and those sweeping bull's horns, which were so tall he'd have difficulty walking through a door without ducking his head. In the firelight, everything gleamed the golden brown of bronze except for the horns, which were a brighter gold.

It's a mask? She gasped, her hand flying to her mouth.

From a distance, at the one sacrifice she'd attended, his head had looked like an animal's. Certainly the Beast in her dreams had an actual bull's head. But this? Up close, this was clearly a fake—albeit a convincing one. The metal, she saw now, was notched in a fur pattern, shaped by some master blacksmith in years gone by.

As the Beast turned, Rheia glimpsed hair, long and brown, curling out from under the back of the mask. Unlike a real bull's, the mask's hollow eyes were set to the front of the face. Their interior was lost to shadow as he faced her—and froze, as still as the statue of Appelon in the previous room. His hands, gone slack, dropped the clay bowl. She startled as it shattered into *ostras*. Toasted grains of wheat spilled everywhere. She stared back at the Beast. This avatar of Areus didn't just have the body of a man. He *was* a man. "Kore?" he choked out finally. The name echoed inside the mask's long muzzle.

She blinked, feeling stupid. He stepped towards her and she recoiled. "Kore?" he said again.

"M-my name is Rheia," she stammered. When he didn't reply, she added, "I'm the Orearean sacrifice."

For the space of a half-dozen heartbeats, the Beast stood motionless. Then, bellowing, he turned from her, smashing his hand into the wall. His head followed, the golden horns gouging the stone. Rheia screamed. Then she covered her mouth with both hands, stumbling backwards. Her eyes were fixed on the roaring man as he lunged to the side, tearing a tapestry down, trampling it beneath his shoes.

He might be a man under that mask, but he was still

a monster.

When she reached the entrance to Appelon's room, she turned and fled, sobbing with fear. Her terror propelled her up the stairs, her breath gasping in her lungs and her calves burning. She waited for the Beast to grab the hem of her *chiton*, to drag her back down. For his sword to plunge between her shoulder blades. But neither thing happened. The sound of his incoherent bellows grew fainter. As she reached the second lantern, they faded away altogether.

Dora saw her and hurried down. The fingers of the caregiver's good hand gripped Rheia's upper arm so tightly it hurt. "What is it? What happened?"

"H-he went insane." Rheia sobbed. "He asked if I was called Kore and then went insane. Who's Kore?"

Dora thrust Rheia to the side, stepping past her. "Do you know the way back to the *gynaikon*?" she demanded, her voice tight with urgency.

"Yes." Rheia swiped at her eyes with the back of her hand. "I think so."

"Good. Go straight there." Dora turned away.

"You can't go down there." Rheia grabbed the woman's shoulder. "He'll *kill* you."

"He needs me," Dora insisted, shrugging Rheia's hand off. "This is my fault. Now *go*."

Her bones so cold they felt like shards of ice, chilling her from the inside out, Rheia climbed the last dozen stairs to the top. She paused, looking at the heavy door. Every instinct urged her to shove it closed and block it but, even if she could figure out how, that would mean Dora couldn't escape.

Then again, Dora didn't *want* to escape. The woman

was mad. This whole place was mad.

"Excuse me?" a voice said, and Rheia whirled so fast she stumbled into the wall, bruising her shoulder. That same male caregiver she'd seen earlier, an older man with a frown crumpling his forehead, stood a few feet away. "You're the *thysia*. Where is Dora?"

Rheia pointed to the dark doorway with a shaking hand. "Down there. He went insane. You need to help her."

He stepped forward, his gait uneven. One of his legs was longer than the other. Rheia didn't care. "I need to get you back to the *gynaikon*. Before someone sees you."

"But what about Dora?"

The man shrugged. "I've known that woman my whole life. She's formidable. If she can't handle him, no one can." He reached out a hand as though to steady Rheia, but drew back. "Please. Come with me." His eyes, small and dark in a square face, were serious. "If the temple finds out you were out here, unescorted..." He trailed off.

Rheia felt sick, an image of Draconaidas's cold-eyed face flashing across her thoughts. Her virtue was so important to the temple that she'd been corralled away from the male *thysies* and caregivers. The high priest would be livid. In his eyes, her primary value was in her purity, and what that meant to the upcoming ritual.

Maybe that would be a good thing? For a wild moment she considered seducing this man, who was old enough to be her grandfather, but the wariness in his stance told her the attempt would be futile. He'd run before he'd let her touch him.

So instead, she nodded. The man led her back to the *gynaikon*, moving so rapidly despite his hobbling gait that she had to jog to keep up. He muttered a curse as

he regarded the locked door, pounding on it. After what seemed like an age, the bolt clicked and slid across and the door swung open. Erika's eyes were so wide Rheia could see white all around the irises; the hunchbacked woman held her pruning shears in a white-knuckled grip that spoke of a readiness to use them. She looked from Rheia to the man with an open-mouthed stare. "Dora is with the master," the man said gruffly, shoving Rheia through the door. It was the first and only time he'd touched her, and her shoulders ached with the impact. "I found the girl at the top of the stairs. Best we keep this between us, eh?"

Erika grunted her agreement, securing Rheia's trembling hand in her callused grip. She gave the man a grim smile and shut the door in his face, locking it and then hiding the key inside the folds of her *chiton*. The shears she hung from her belt.

Loose-limbed, Rheia slid down the inside of the door, leaning her head back against the smooth timber. Erika sat beside her, her frown conveying the question.

"Dora's with the Beast," Rheia whispered. "He went mad and he's going to kill her."

And then, in nine days, he's going to kill me, too.

CHAPTER FOURTEEN

"**A**re you in there?"

The young woman looked up at the familiar voice, although her hands kept moving as she ground the glossy, dark green nightsleep leaves. The smooth rock grated against the bottom of the curved stone bowl in time with her slow, measured breathing, and the cool tang of the herb lifted her senses. "Yes," she said between breaths. "In the adyton."

The priest stood in the doorway, his knuckles gripping the stone doorframe. He wore a simple white chiton, and his head was crowned with a circlet woven from a fresh bay laurel branch. The glossy, green leaves were bright against his golden-brown hair, even in the temple's artificial light.

"You shouldn't be here." Meditation forgotten, her hand dropped the pestle into the crushed herbs. She turned, her bare feet padding against the cold floor as she crossed the small room. The adyton of Eidoneus's temple wasn't large, and she reached him swiftly.

"I know," the man said, stepping forward to take her hands as she reached for him. His fingers were warm around hers. "I hope Eidoneus will forgive me, just this once."

She looked up at him coyly, but sobered when she saw there was no flirtatious look in his bronze-coloured eyes. His jaw was clenched with concern. Dread stole over her. "What is it?"

"There's a fire high on the mountain," he said.

Her pulse quickened. The foothills were tinder-dry, baked by the long summer, and the idea of a forest fire in the olive groves left her cold. "Does the army know? They will need to bring water up from the harbour."

"I—" He hesitated. "I'm not sure it's that sort of fire. Come. Please. I need you." His ears reddened. "Your counsel, I mean."

She turned to hide the soft smile that tugged at her lips. "One moment." Striding back to the adyton's far wall, she performed a quick obeisance to the small statue of Eidoneus that stood there. The statuette was no taller than her forearm was long, but the temple's priests held it in far higher regard than they did the bone-coloured sculpture that towered in the cella beyond. The verde antique marble, a dark green streaked with white, was rare on the island—that alone would have made the statuette priceless. Bending, she kissed the little Eidoneus on the head; the stone was cool against her lips and the top of the dagger he held scratched her cheek lightly. Saying a quick prayer, she draped a fold of cloth over the little god, concealing him from view. Then she tucked the bowl of nightsleep underneath the fabric so it was hidden from the casual observer.

Not that any would dare enter the adyton *of the god of death.*

"Now we can go."

The man took her hand in his own and hurried her through the temple, out into the heat of the noonday sun—

"Wake up!" A rough voice dragged Rheia from sleep. The hand on her shoulder was rougher. With a cry, the girl scooted back along the bed until her spine pressed against the cold wall. She stared, her heart racing as she shook off the disorienting blanket of sleep. The thin pre-dawn light barely outlined the shadows in her room.

A figure loomed before her. Rheia opened her mouth to scream and the dark shape shot out a hand, covering her mouth. "Shh!"

Rheia bit down, hard. The figure cried out, drawing back, and a sliver of dawn light glinted off a hint of silver, a rope flowing over a shadowy shoulder. "*Dora?*" she gasped, rubbing her eyes.

"Who else would it be?" the caregiver growled. She cradled her hand to her chest, curling her other arm around it protectively.

"Oh, I don't know. Perhaps a temple assassin?" Rheia wiped her mouth on the back of her hand and glared at the old woman. Then her memory of the night before returned in a wave and she gasped. "You're alive!"

"Assuming you don't chew me to death, yes." Rheia heard Dora take a deep breath as if to steady herself. Her voice was usually husky but now it rasped with fatigue. "I've just come from the master's rooms."

"You've been there all night?"

"Yes. He finally fell asleep."

Rheia's eyes widened as she imagined how terrifying

that must have been for Dora: trapped so far underground with only one exit, until the Beast passed out and she was able to slip away. But the caregiver's next words brought her up short.

"I need you to come back down there with me."

Rheia shivered, clutching her sheet over her knees as if for protection. "What? No! He's a monster."

"He's not a monster. That's what I wanted you to see." The bed sagged as Dora sat on the edge of the soft cushion. "It didn't work out the way I had planned."

Rheia bit her lip to avoid saying something sarcastic. What *had* the woman planned? That Rheia and her future murderer would sit down for tea? She was now able to see the dim outline of the woman's lined features, Dora's worried eyes and furrowed brow, and she realised with surprise that Dora wasn't wearing her golden circlet. Had she ever seen the old woman bare-headed before?

As if sensing her puzzled gaze, Dora spoke again. "I want to tell you something. But it's the caregivers' greatest secret. If I do, you can't tell anyone." Her voice was soft, barely a whisper.

"Who would I tell?" Rheia laughed bitterly.

"You can't tell the other caregivers I told you. And you can't tell Parthenia."

"That's not fair. Who would *she* tell?"

"She's Carmean," Dora said, as though that were explanation enough.

Rheia folded her arms and scowled, but the caregiver didn't relent. Finally, the girl nodded, reluctant. "Fine. I won't tell her. But you're doing her a disservice. She isn't a bad person. She's better than some Oreareans I know."

"Promise me."

"I promise." Rheia sighed.

"It's about the Beast. Something you need to understand. He's not an animal or a monster. He's just a man."

"I know. The bull head is a mask. But even men can be monsters. I saw the way he behaved. Aias throwing a tantrum is more civilised than that."

"What you saw was a man in pain." Dora's voice was tight with emotion, but her gaze was fixed on the window, so Rheia couldn't see her face. "Pain resulting from more than a hundred years of captivity and torture."

Rheia gaped, feeling as though she'd been kicked in the sternum. "Torture? *What*?"

"Despite what has been done to him, he's a good man. And when he saw you were the latest sacrifice, he snapped. I shouldn't have sent you down there ... but it would've been far worse if he'd seen you for the first time during the festival. What was I to *do*?" Dora twisted the end of her braid through her fingers.

"You're not making sense..."

Dora took Rheia's hand, tugging when the girl didn't move. "Come with me. I want to show you something."

"No." She snatched her hand away.

"Please, Rheia. More than you know depends on it."

"If you want me to trust you, then you need to trust *me*," Rheia pointed out. "Why is it so important that I go back down there? Beast or man, it's not like he was pleased to see me. If he wakes and I'm down there, what then?"

"He won't hurt you." Rheia made a small sound of disbelief, and Dora sighed. "Do you remember how I told you that, if the Beast died, Typhein would be freed?" The caregiver's voice was still soft, but her whisper carried a hard edge that sliced across the room, sharp as an

iron sword fresh from the whetstone.

"Yes."

"The reason I was down there so long is that once he calmed, he declared he would kill himself before he'd put you to the sword." Rheia's heart leapt, but before she could say anything Dora continued, "I have spent the entire night keeping him alive." The caregiver's voice broke on the last word. Was Dora ... crying?

"Maybe that would be a good thing," Rheia said, her voice gentle despite the harsh words. "Not him dying, but Typhein getting out. The army has fire-throwers now, and iron weapons. Maybe they could defeat the demon." She found the idea didn't excite her as much as it had when she'd suggested it to her grandmother.

Dora's distress blunted her enthusiasm. "Typhein is a fire demon himself," the caregiver said, rubbing her watering eyes. "Fire-throwers won't help against him."

"Oh." Rheia remembered Draconaidas describing the demon as appearing wreathed in fire. She should've realised that for herself. "Still—"

"Rheia, please. Come downstairs with me. I won't leave you alone with him. You'll be safe."

Rheia regarded the caregiver, hugging her knees to her chest. She didn't want to go back down those stairs. The idea made her feel like she couldn't breathe. But Dora would be there. And she seemed so adamant.

Besides, what was the worst that could happen? *The Beast will kill me early and the demon will get free.* If that were the case, Rheia thought, her lips tightening, at least Parthenia and the two male Carmean *thysies* would survive. For a while.

"As you wish," she sighed. "I will go."

CHAPTER FIFTEEN

Rheia chased Dora out of the room so she could wash up and get dressed in peace, which gave her time to muster her nerves. Her hands trembled as she fastened the brooches at her shoulder, trying not to dwell on that huge staircase into the mountain's bowels and the man— or monster—who lurked within.

Once she'd brushed her hair out, she wound herself in the same *himation* she'd worn the night before. The dark grey fabric was stark against the honey-coloured *chiton*, like the bare stone of the mountainside against the dry grass of the foothills beneath, but the *chiton* was freshly laundered and smelled of summer and the ocean. She held a fold to her nose and breathed deeply, closing her eyes as she imagined herself on the beach, wiggling her toes in the hot sand. Steadied by the thought, she squared her shoulders and marched from her room as though going to war.

Dora waited in the courtyard, which was awash in pale dawn light. Her good hand was clasped around the

elbow of her other arm and she bit her lip, frowning as she stared at the date-plum as though not seeing it. Rheia's sandals scuffed on the paving stone and the caregiver turned, a relieved smile washing away her grim look.

The only other sign of life was a faint rustle of sound from the dining hall, where Rheia guessed someone was setting up breakfast. The date-palm stood as motionless as a statue of a god, not even a leaf twitching in the still morning air.

"Are you ready?" Dora said.

No. "Yes."

Glancing towards the curtain-covered entrance to Parthenia's room, Rheia followed the caregiver towards the doors. Had the other girl noticed her absence the night before? Did she feel left out, given Rheia was being allowed out of the women's wing? Rheia doubted the Carmean girl would be jealous if she knew where Rheia had been, where she was going. Rheia would've given a great deal to still be in her room rather than being dragged out to see the Beast before she'd even eaten.

Her stomach rumbled, underscoring the thought. "Do I have time to get some food?"

Dora hesitated, looking between Rheia and the doors. Was her heart already at the bottom of that long flight of stairs? "Something you can eat as we walk?" she said, anxiety seeping into her voice.

Rheia nodded, darting into the dining hall before Dora could change her mind.

Erika looked up from arranging the plates on the table, her eyes widening with surprise. "You're up early."

"Dora is taking me back," Rheia said, picking up a

thick slice of fragrant, fresh-baked bread. It warmed her fingers.

"Back? Where?" The caregiver stood up as straight as she could with her crooked spine and studied Rheia's expression with fierce eyes. "You mean to see *him*?"

"Yes." Dipping the bread in an open dish of herb-speckled olive oil to moisten it, Rheia popped it in her mouth. Erika shuffled from the room, and the girl heard a muttered conversation between her and Dora outside. She did her best not to listen, taking advantage of the delay to eat several more pieces of bread, washing them down with some well-watered wine from the beautifully painted *amphora* at the end of the table. But she could see the two women through the open side of the room. Erika's hands moved in an animated way, movements sharp and angry. Dora shook her head, her eyes narrowed and her lips pressed together in a firm line.

Fortified and unable to delay any longer, Rheia returned to the courtyard and the conversation fell silent, although Erika gave Dora a flinty look. The older caregiver ignored it, her hand reaching to adjust her circlet and then dropping as she seemed to recall it wasn't there. She held her fingers out to Rheia. "Better?" she asked.

"A little." Rheia let Dora loop their arms together, although she could feel Erika's disapproving stare as they crossed to the doors and Dora unlocked them. What was the caregiver worried about—Rheia's safety, or the Beast's? The thought was chilling.

The cool of early morning clung to the corridors. Rheia hurried to keep pace with Dora's long strides, but slowed when they reached the pillared hallway that ended in the heavy stone door. The bread she'd eaten settled in a

sour lump in her stomach as Dora urged her towards the door with a gentle tug.

"I won't let him hurt you," the old woman promised, releasing Rheia's arm so she could drag the door open. For a moment, Rheia considered turning, fleeing back the way she'd come. Or trying to find her way out into the city. The knowledge that the citizens of Oreareus would march her right back to the house again stilled her feet. She couldn't bear the humiliation.

It didn't take Rheia as long to descend the stairs this time as it had the night before. Dora kept up a steady pace, not pausing at each landing as Rheia had. Soon they were at the bottom. With her heart in her throat, Rheia stayed so close to the caregiver's side that the fabric of their skirts swirled together as they walked.

The first difference she noticed as they crossed Appelon's room was that the air smelled of familiar flowers: chamomile and lavender, sweetly intertwined around the smell of juniper smoke to fill the air with a heady, soothing aroma. The last time she'd smelled those flowers had been the night before last, when Yalee had calmed her with them after Charis's visit—so she wasn't surprised to see the caregiver girl seated cross-legged on a cushion in the second room, her back to the smouldering coals of the fire. The girl's face was tired and drawn, dark smudges under her eyes as though she'd had a long night, and she didn't glance at Rheia and Dora as they entered. A blackened clay bowl sat amidst the coals, filled with steaming liquid that Rheia was sure was the source of the fragrance.

Breathing deep to slow her racing heart, Rheia took a moment to study the room; last night's visit had left her with only a fleeting impression of warmth and spilled grains. A table almost filled the far wall. One end of it was covered by a rectangle of leather, lined with bronze tools that glittered, wickedly sharp. A lump of wood, stripped of bark, sat beside the leather, covered in rough chisel marks. White wood shavings tangled together in a neat pile next to it. Beside the table was an open door-way, beyond which she could see the same pale blue tiles that were in the main bathhouse upstairs.

The hearth fire was set in the wall to Rheia's right; the wall on one side of it was hung with a simple, heavy tapestry, while the other was bare, revealing a closed door. She remembered the Beast tearing down the tapestry that had hung there; the huge swathe of fabric was folded in the corner, waiting to be rehung. The rail above the door was bent like a broken limb, one end trailing towards the ground.

On the other wall... Rheia followed Yalee's gaze. The first thing she laid eyes on was a low table—and sitting on the table was the Beast's heavy bronze mask. Its hollow eyes stared at her as she flinched back behind Dora's shoulder, her mouth turning acid with fear as her efforts to calm herself were forgotten. After a moment of nothing happening, she glared back at the mask, stiffening her spine. It was motionless. Empty.

That was when she saw the Beast.

He lay curled on his side on a low, cushioned bed. She couldn't see his face, which was turned to the tapestry-covered wall, but the long, golden-brown hair tangled around his head was the same as that she'd seen peeking from beneath the mask. And the black *chiton* he wore looked to be the same one she'd seen him in. The dim firelight caressed one bare arm, lending his skin more

colour than it'd had the night before.

He looked so harmless, his breath slow and even. Dora crept towards him, her sandals silent on the thick rug, and leaned forward to peer down at his face for a long moment. Rheia hung back near the door, her hands twisted together, and waited for him to leap up with a roar.

He didn't. Instead, Dora turned back, catching Yalee's gaze with a wave of her hand and then pointing to a little jar sitting on the mantel above the fire. Yalee nodded, holding up a single finger, but didn't speak. Rheia peered at the jar. It was painted with a familiar leaf. Nightsleep.

She frowned, unsure what to think. The man who'd terrified her so badly had been drugged to help him sleep. Pity unfurled in her heart as she regarded his hunched shoulders, and she looked at Dora. Was this what the caregiver had wanted her to see?

"He shouldn't wake," Dora whispered, coming to Rheia's side. "But still, we'd best be quick. I'm not sure how he'll react, seeing you here." She leaned over the hearth, blowing on the coals to coax a small flame to life. Plucking a piece of kindling from a basket against the wall, she lit its tip in the flame, sheltering it as she strode towards the closed door on the bare stretch of wall.

Rheia hurried after Dora. She liked Yalee well enough, but she didn't trust the slight girl to be able to stop the Beast if he attacked. Although Dora's protection wasn't much better.

"Would you?" Dora indicated the door with a wave of her fingerless hand. Rheia reached past her to grip the handle and pull it open.

The door opened into a huge, unlit space, and Dora strode inside. She turned to a table near the door, touching the flaming taper to a grey wick protruding from the nozzle of an oil lamp. It spat and sizzled as the fat-soaked flax caught alight. As the caregiver moved around the room, lighting several other lamps, Rheia stared at the slowly unveiled scene.

The room was long and rectangular, lined with pillars. It reminded her of the *cella* she'd seen at the temple of Areus, with votive offerings spaced at regular intervals along the walls. Most of the offerings were bunches of flowers that released a strong, dusty perfume as they withered, although unlit candles and clusters of incense sat artfully arranged in bowls. The stone wall was carved with markings, each arranged in a short column with a number at the top and four lines underneath. Frowning, Rheia, drifted to the closest column, peering at the neat, elegant script in the dim light. The first number read, "One". Underneath were four names.

Hippias, son of Achaeus.

Lysis, son of Lysias.

Artemisia, daughter of Menander.

Cynisca, daughter of Harpalus.

Rheia's eyes widened. Were these the names of the first four sacrifices? With her heart in her throat, and each of her hands clutching the opposite elbow through her *himation*, she looked along the wall. Each column was a new list. Four names. Four dead innocents. Four more lives spent to bind the demon, buying another year of safety for the island.

Dora stood at the far end of the room. When Rheia's eyes lit on her, the caregiver beckoned. But Rheia kept turning, her eyes finding the spot where the columns ended. Beyond them, blank stone waited to be filled with

more names. The last four names were lined up under the number "one hundred and eleven".

One hundred and twelve had been carved into the wall in that same hand, but the space for the names was empty. *One hundred and twelve years ago, a demon called Typhein came to the island of Cretea.* Rheia remembered Draconaidas's words with a shudder that seemed to pull the cool, damp air into her soul. That space was for her name: Rheia, daughter of Loukios. Also Parthenia, daughter of... Rheia's breath hitched as she realised she didn't know the name of Parthenia's father, or even the given names of the two male *thysies*. Fingers splayed and trembling, she touched the smooth, blank wall—a wall that had been cut from the earth beneath the mountain by some long-ago mason. Breathing fast, with tears stinging her eyes, she pressed her forehead to the stone. She wished she could sink into it, into the arms of Gaea, mother of the gods.

"Come," Dora said, wrapping her arm around Rheia and guiding her away from that blank space. "I know this is hard for you." The caregiver's voice was gentle and Rheia bowed her head to hide her tears, stumbling along. "Do you see now that every death pains him? He carves every name into the wall with his own hand, and has us bring fresh offerings once a week to remember them by. He lays the offerings out himself. He won't let us do it. He even cleans this hall himself."

"Why are you telling me this? Why do you care what I think of him?"

Dora didn't answer. Was the woman's love for the Beast such that she couldn't bear to have others think poorly of him? The girl grimaced, swiping at her eyes.

Too late.

"I wanted to show you this," the caregiver said, indicating a niche in the far wall of the *cella*.

The alcove was square, about as tall and wide as Rheia's arm. She peered into it, seeing the outline of a torso and head. A wooden bust. The dim lamplight gleamed off the polished timber.

"Wait here." Dora lifted the nearest oil lamp, carrying it back to where Rheia stood. The older woman's eyes were focused on Rheia's face, and the girl glanced down at the old woman's hand. Even though the lamp had a cover, the hot oil could still spill through the nozzle or filling hole. Still, the flame barely flickered with each of Dora's steps. "Look now."

Rheia turned back to the bust and forgot all about the candle.

She almost forgot to breathe.

A bust of a woman stared back at her, life-sized and carved from golden timber. The statue had slender shoulders. A graceful neck rose from the carved folds of the *chiton*, surrounded by a wealth of wavy hair that looked so soft Rheia wondered that it didn't stir with their movements. The face was oval-shaped, with plump lips curved in a smile beneath a long, straight nose. Carefully detailed lashes fringed almond eyes.

Rheia recognised the face. She'd seen it in the water at the fountain, in the shining bronze serving platter in the dining room, in the polished sheen of her father's iron sword. "Is it me?" she breathed.

"No." There was an odd note in Dora's voice.

With her heart stuttering in her chest, Rheia peered closer, seeing that the carved woman's face was more

mature than hers, a woman grown rather than a sixteen-year-old girl. "Then who is it? She could be my older sister. Or me in another five years."

"That," Dora said, "is Kore."

CHAPTER SIXTEEN

She drew her veil over her dark hair. The thin white fabric did a little to block the sun's hammer blows—not enough, but it was better than leaving her head bare.

The Appelonian priest led her up the paved street away from the agora and the row of temples lining one side of it, each door open to the public. Eidoneus's temple stood apart from the others, less because the god of death liked his privacy and more because his presence—and that of his servants—made some people uncomfortable. Most people, if she were honest with herself.

When they reached a broad intersection with a fountain burbling at its centre, the priest gestured to the left, leading her down a side street that smelled of stewing meat, of woodsmoke from someone's cooking fire and, faintly, of decomposing food scraps and other, less savoury aromas. A few more turns and they came to the place where the city gave way to foothills. Only the richest villas and the king's palace squatted above them, dwarfed in turn by the looming mountain. A winding dirt track meandered

away, disappearing over a distant slope. On one side of the track olive trees clustered, and on the other was a field surrounded by weathered wooden fences. Goats nosed at several low-growing shrubs, stripping the branches bare.

Beneath the olive tree, leaning against the gnarled grey bark, sat a boy. Not yet old enough to grow a beard, he lounged on the brittle grass, staring at the looming mountain—but sat up straight at their approach. His eyes leapt to the symbol that hung on a chain at her throat, resembling the head of a two-pronged spear forged from silver. He bounced to his feet and wiped his dusty hands on his even dustier chiton.

"All is well, Hippias," the priest beside her said. "This is Kore, priestess of Eidoneus." A vague sense of disquiet shadowed her spirit at his words, but, like a bird's silhouette before the sun, it was easily overlooked and soon forgotten.

The boy shifted uneasily at the priest's words. Like most of the gods, Eidoneus had his light and dark sides. But since his dark side included keeping the realm of the dead, people tended to overlook his other position as god of wealth and fortune, master of the precious metals stolen from Gaea's breast.

"Tell her what you told me," the priest coaxed.

"Th-there's a cave," the boy Hippias began, avoiding Kore's gaze. "It's halfway up the mountainside. It's hard to reach, and you have to climb like a goat to get up there." Behind her, one of the animals bleated as if in agreement. She hid a smile behind her hand, her eyes twinkling. "But there's a small spring in the mouth of the cave, before it slants down into darkness. The water there is always fresh and so cold it makes your teeth ache." He licked his

lips, gaze distant. "I climbed up there to refill my water skin, and that's when I saw it."

"Saw what?"

"Fire. In the cave."

"A cooking fire, perhaps?" she suggested, her voice gentle.

"No. Not a cooking fire." Hippias hesitated, staring at bare feet so dirty they were almost black. "It's better if I show you."

Kore frowned up at the priest. She had tasks to complete and, although acolytes minded the temple and tended to supplicants in her absence, they weren't permitted to finish making the nightsleep draughts. The herb was toxic in strong doses. "Is this necessary, Alexandros?" she asked him.

"Yes," he said, brushing a strand of hair from her cheek to tuck it beneath her veil. Her forehead tingled where the pad of his finger touched her skin. "I believe it is."

"Then let us be quick about it," she said briskly, trying to conceal her reaction to his touch. But the glint in his eye told her it was too late for that.

"Am I right to leave my goats here, Priest?" Hippias asked, his eyes flitting to the grazing creatures.

"This is Appelon's field," the priest, Alexandros, replied. "He shall not mind. Besides, we wanted to clear those shrubs. Your goats will do it for us. Still, let us be quick, as the good priestess says, before they run out of fodder. Those fences won't slow them down if they decide to stray."

They strode along the winding track. The boy trotted before them, clearly keen to have this task done.

Normally Kore enjoyed escaping the city's confines, stretching her legs and filling her lungs with fresh,

flower-scented air. But the sun was so hot her head began to ache, and beads of perspiration prickled the back of her neck, under the weight of her hair. She longed for the cool confines of her stone temple. A warm sip of diluted wine from Alexandros's hip flask wet her lips but did little to relieve the heat.

Finally, Hippias said, "There," and pointed up the mountainside.

At first she thought the speck of light was the sun, reflecting off a piece of exposed quartz. But then her gaze picked out the tendril of smoke creeping from the cave, trailing towards a sky so blue her eyes ached to see it. "That does look like a cook fire," she said, although the doubt was clear in her voice. Most Creteans didn't like to climb the mountain. At greater heights, the air grew thin and greedy, stealing the energy from a person's limbs. That this boy had scaled even so high as that cave said much for his constitution.

Alexandros shook his head, one hand shading his eyes as he frowned up at the fire. "For us to be able to see it down here, it would have to be as big as a bonfire. And that pillar of smoke must be as thick around as the agora."

"Oh." Her mouth felt dry, the wine sour on her tongue. She looked at Hippias. "You said you climbed up there. What did you see?"

"I didn't reach the cave, lady," the boy whispered, his face pale. "As soon as I saw it, I decided I wasn't so thirsty after all."

"Saw what?"

Hippias lifted his gaze to stare at her, his eyes wide and bright with urgency. "The entire mouth of the cave is aflame."

Rheia cracked open her eyes and squinted as bright light rushed in to stab at her brain. Her room never got this bright ... and why were the cushions so hard against her spine? Something itched the back of her neck, and she reached back to pluck up a blade of grass. "Huh?" Eyes adjusting, she sat up and looked around, rubbing her stiff shoulder. She'd fallen asleep under the shade of the date-plum tree in the *gynaikon's* courtyard.

"You must have been tired," Parthenia commented. She sat nearby, her expression pensive as she leaned over a thin timber panel propped on her knees. "You've been asleep since lunch." Was that a question in the other *thysia's* voice? Rheia frowned at her, but Parthenia seemed focused on what she was doing. She had a brush in her hand; her fingers gripped it close to the fibrous tip, which glistened black, pigment-dyed egg yolk clinging to each strand.

"I wasn't even sleepy," Rheia murmured. With her eyes narrowing with suspicion, she ran her fingers across each of her temples and then sniffed for the telltale aroma of nightsleep. Nothing. Still, just in case, she washed her face and throat at the fountain before scooping several mouthfuls of water from the basin and drinking them greedily. Sleeping during the heat of the day had left her mouth feeling gluggy and dry. Or maybe it had been her dream of walking under a hot sun, staring at a distant inferno?

Her hand froze, dripping water, partway to her mouth.

She'd always had vivid dreams, and since her *ostra* had been drawn they'd taken a darker turn. But the dream last night, and the one now—they weren't just figments of her imagination. She was sure of it. The details were too consistent between one dream and the next, and they lacked dreams' usual, disjointed nature.

And the priest in her dream had called her Kore.

Maybe it's just because I heard her name from Dora and then fell asleep? But she didn't believe it. And falling asleep the way she had... She frowned up at the sky, wondering whether some god was looking down at her, waiting for her to figure out what he or she was trying to convey. "Maybe send me a divine parchment next time? I don't have time for riddles," she muttered under her breath. Then she glanced up again to make sure a bolt of Diktaios Skyfather's lightning wasn't arcing down towards her to punish her for her insolence.

Above the waving branches, the sky was clear.

The forgotten sip of water had drained from her palm, and she wiped her hand dry on the hem of her *chiton*, walking back to sit in the grass beside Parthenia.

The other girl didn't speak, concentrating on her painting. The tip of her tongue poked out the corner of her mouth. But soon the silence became too much and Rheia blurted, "So I guess you're wondering where I disappeared to this morning."

"Not really," Parthenia said. "I assume you receive privileges that I don't. Like your grandmother's visit." She sighed, sounding resigned.

"You're not jealous?"

"Why should I be?" Her wide-set eyes regarded Rheia for a long moment before she looked back down at her task. "You'll be just as dead as me in another eight days."

Rheia winced at the brutal honesty in those words. Still, the need to talk about what was happening drove her to speak again. "You know those carvings in the dining hall?" She hated the tentative note in her voice, but couldn't help it.

"They're beautiful, aren't they?" Parthenia sighed. "They were what made me think maybe I could spend my life—what's left of it—painting. I used to love it. And maybe the caregivers will look at my panels after I'm gone and remember my name, instead of me being just another *thysia*."

Rheia thought of that wall of carved names and her throat tightened. Did the Beast know all of them by heart—there were more than four hundred—or were they there to jog his memory? Did all the faces stay with him too, or just Kore's because he had carved it when his recollection of her was fresh? And who was Kore, if not a sacrifice? Rheia hadn't seen her name on the wall … but she hadn't read every name, either.

Still, Rheia was sure, after what she'd seen, that the Beast was the unknown sculptor. "This morning Dora took me to see one of the carvings," Rheia said. "It was made over a century ago. And it looks exactly like me." Parthenia's brow furrowed, the only sign she was listening. "I think that's why she's been looking at me so strangely since I got here. She recognised me from that old sculpture."

And I know what I need to do next. Rheia swallowed, staring down at her hands. *I just need to find the courage to do it.*

"Excuse me," a loud voice said, making them both jump. Parthenia swore quietly, dabbing at an errant

smear of paint with her thumb.

Rheia looked up and saw Yalee. The caregiver girl looked refreshed since the last time Rheia had seen her; at least, the dark bruises of fatigue under her eyes were gone. Maybe she'd had a midday nap, too. "I have this for you."

At least she wouldn't have overheard what I told Parthenia, Rheia thought ruefully, taking the rolled parchment with a smile at the girl. Yalee looked away politely, hands behind her back, as Rheia unrolled the hide. It was a much finer quality than any she'd seen before: soft vellum, calf or kid skin. And it was new, without the telltale signs of having been scraped to be reused. Who would write to her on such beautiful material?

Her mouth went dry again as she realised she knew the elegant handwriting. She'd last seen it carved into a wall.

I know you have no reason to trust me, given how I behaved when last we met. I am sorry I frightened you.

I need to see you. Please come.

The letter was unsigned, but at the bottom he had drawn a symbol. A pair of bull's horns. The Beast.

It looked like the gods weren't going to wait for Rheia to find her courage.

CHAPTER SEVENTEEN

Rheia was already tired of climbing up and down these stairs. She wondered how the caregivers did it, bringing the Beast food and water every day. Yalee bounded ahead of her like a goat scampering down a cliff face, pausing to wait at each landing. Rheia followed more cautiously, trailing one hand on the cool wall for support as she picked her way down the stairs. Yalee barely concealed her impatience but Rheia didn't hurry, unable to shake the thought of what a fall would do to her. A broken bone was fatal if poison from the wound got into the blood.

As they neared the bottom, the younger girl dropped back, slipping her hand into Rheia's as though afraid she might flee.

Rheia's jaw hardened. She wasn't going to run. Even though she really, really wanted to.

Her eyes widened as music reached her, the warm sounds of a *lyra* rising up from below as though the earth itself was trying to soothe her nerves. The music pulled

her forward as insistently as the small hand in hers did. The sound was … beautiful. A cascade of notes, each one precise, some a single, plaintive sound while others formed a lilting harmony.

Beautiful and sad.

When she crept through Appelon's room and laid eyes on the *lyra* and the man playing it, her breath caught in her throat.

He was magnificent. The folds of his black *chiton* draped around his muscled frame as he sat on the side of his bed, the *lyra* resting on his knee. One hand held the bone plectrum with which he strummed while the other curled around the frame, pressing against the other side of the strings to silence unwanted notes: a dextrous dance she'd never been able to master. His hair fell around his face and shoulders, the firelight picking out golden highlights in the cascade of warm brown.

The bull's head mask on the table beside him—the mask that had terrified her so recently—barely registered in Rheia's thoughts as she stared. The Beast was most assuredly a man.

"Master," Yalee said, her voice as loud and flat as always, and the notes fell silent. For a moment, the only sound was the fire snapping at the logs in the hearth. The man looked up, bronze eyes meeting Rheia's.

She knew those eyes. Dizziness overwhelmed her and she gasped, her breath ragged in her throat; her hand clutched Yalee's so tightly the girl paled, staring up at her.

"You're here," he said softly, setting the instrument down on the cushion. He stood. She staggered backwards a step, and he froze. "I deserve your fear," he said, his voice rasping with shame and something else. Desperation?

"But please believe me when I say I don't want to harm you, Rheia. I wanted to apologise." He looked down at his sandalled feet. "You remind me of someone I knew long ago. Her name was Kore. I ... I lost her. When I saw you, I thought she'd come back to me. But you can't be her. I have earned no such miracle."

"Is your name...?" Rheia's voice sounded strange to her own ears. She swallowed and forced herself to release Yalee's hand before she crushed the girl's bones. *How can it be?* He didn't look that much older than her. She took a deep breath, as though preparing to plunge off a cliff into the ocean. "Are you Alexandros?"

The Beast's eyes widened so much she could see the white all around, startling against the fringe of dark lashes. His mouth fell open. Emotions flashed across his face: shock, fear and a despair so deep her heart ached for him. Finally, he whispered, "How do you know that?"

"The gods have been sending me dreams these past few nights," she said, twisting her hands in the folds of her *chiton*. "Since you called me her name. I've dreamed of her ... and you. And of fire on the mountain."

He stepped back as though she'd punched him in the gut, all the colour draining from his face. "Master?" Yalee said. She cast a rebuking look at Rheia and darted over to the Beast's side, placing her hand on his arm.

He waved her away. "I'm fine. Please, Yalee, wait out there." He gestured to the room where Appelon stood. Yalee narrowed her eyes and shook her head, reminding Rheia of Dora. But he gave the girl a pleading look, handing her the *lyra* with one hand and brushing her cheek with the other. The gesture melted her stubbornness and she relented, cradling the instrument in her arms as she

turned towards the outer room. The glare she gave Rheia as she stalked away was dark and full of warning. *Don't hurt him.*

Hurt him? *What about* me? Rheia wondered incredulously. But her fear had faded with his shock and his tenderness towards the caregiver girl. Those emotions made him seem more human, less like the terrifying monster of her nightmares.

"Why do you speak to her when she can't hear you?" The question fell from her lips unbidden, and she silently cursed the thoughtlessness of it.

"She understands more than you might think. Besides, it is better than the silence," he murmured. Colour was returning to his cheeks, the waxy shock fading. He stared at her as if he was unable to stop himself, running his gaze over her face like he couldn't credit what he was seeing. Like he wanted to touch her with his fingers, to confirm she was real, but didn't dare.

Seeing his face in the flesh before her, one she'd dreamt of, made her stomach flutter with nerves—and the intensity of his regard didn't help. He hardly seemed to have aged. Uncomfortable, she took a step back. "How can you be real?"

The words startled a laugh from him, showing her a flash of white teeth as the sound burst forth, warm and delighted. She smiled faintly in return, tipping her head to the side. "Did I say something funny?"

"No and yes," he said, the laughter dying. "Because I was just thinking the same thing about you. It's uncanny. I thought I had remembered wrong, not seen you properly when you came here last night. But you do look just like her. And it makes me wonder, how can you be dreaming

151

of me? How do you know about her?"

"I suspect dreaming of you isn't so unique," she murmured, eyes straying to that bronze mask. A shiver trailed a chill finger across the nape of her neck. "Of that thing, anyway."

"Yes. I'm the stuff of children's nightmares," he said. Rheia heard the self-loathing in his voice. Telling him she'd had those nightmares too didn't seem wise. He shook his head and continued, a question in his voice. "Still, you knew my name. This wasn't just some generic nightmare of the Beast."

"No, it wasn't."

He reached behind his back without looking, snagging one of the cushions from his bed. "Will you sit with me? Tell me about your dream?"

"If you like." She took the cushion gingerly, clutching it to her chest. The fabric was no different than the cushions on her own bed, but as well as the musty wool stuffing it smelled of woodsmoke and faintly, of dill flowers and the refreshingly spicy scent of cypress oil. His soap? Flustered at the warmth creeping over her cheeks, she dropped the pillow on the rug before the low-burning fire and sat. From there she could see Yalee, watching them from the entrance to the next room. The girl hadn't gone far.

As though not wanting to startle Rheia, the man eased himself onto the floor out of arm's reach, crossing his legs. The firelight illuminated one side of his face, his straight nose and strong jaw, while casting the other into shadow. Like Appelon whose statue was in the foyer, he was fashioned of light and darkness.

"You were a priest of Appelon once, weren't you?" she said. "That's why you have his statue? Why you play the

lyra?"

"Lots of people play the *lyra*," he replied, folding his hands on his knees. He had strong hands, and she wondered how he managed to stay fit trapped down here, rather than growing round as a lazy noble on the good food the caregivers provided. "But yes, I was a priest of Appelon. We were encouraged to learn music."

"Not born from Areus's thigh then?" She arched her eyebrows.

He smiled, shaking his head. "No. That's a priest's fancy. Will you tell me about your dream?"

So she did, speaking slowly as she tried to recall the details. His gaze was unblinking, unnerving. Those bronze eyes brimmed with the same speculation she'd seen in Dora's so many times—but underlying that was a great sadness as he looked at her and saw she wasn't his Kore, his priestess of Eidoneus. Had they been lovers? She recalled the way Kore had flown into his arms. How would those arms feel around *her*? The thought made her blush and look away, and she realised she'd stopped speaking, the flow of words trickling to a halt.

"Your dreams are true ones." His statement fell into the room like a pebble into a still pool: so small, but casting ripples that danced up her spine. "I don't know how it is, but they are true. Perhaps you are an oracle." He leaned forward, reaching out as though to stroke her cheek the way he had Yalee's. She froze, and he withdrew, his hand falling limp in his lap. He hung his head, long hair curtaining his face. "I'm sorry. I don't mean to do it, but I keep frightening you."

"It's not entirely your fault," she said, trying to keep her voice light despite the way her heart raced, fluttering in her throat. "Under the circumstances, anyone would have trouble setting a guest at ease."

He raised his head slowly, a frown between his brows. "Yes, you are my guest, and I have been a poor host. Can I offer you bread or wine?"

"No, sir. Thank you. I had lunch not so long ago." She bent her knees under the long skirt of her *chiton*, hugging her *himation* around her arms. The room was warm, the fire keeping the dampness at bay, but she still felt cold.

"Please, call me Alexandros."

"Alexandros," she said, savouring the sound. She liked the way the name felt in her mouth when she said it. "So those things truly happened?" she asked. He nodded. "What was in the cave on the mountainside?"

"It was Typhein. How he got there I don't know. Legends claim he'd been trapped in Eidoneus's underworld, far beneath the realm of the dead, but we—that is, Kore and I—never had the chance to figure out how he escaped, or came to be on Cretea. Oreareus, I mean. That is what the island used to be called, before the cult of Areus grew strong. Still, we had less than a day between seeing that fiery cave for the first time and the demon's emergence. There wasn't enough time."

"Oh." Rheia bit her lip. She recalled hearing the word *Cretea* before, during Draconaidas's speech before the lottery. That reminded her of something else. "Can I ask you a question?" What she really wanted to know was whether she could ask him a question without him flying into a rage. She didn't say it, but he seemed to divine her meaning, pressing his lips together for a moment before answering.

"Go ahead."

"Draconaidas, the high priest of Areus—"

"I know who he is." Alexandros's voice was flinty, and she gulped.

"Of course you do. Right. Well, he said a priestess was sacrificed to appease Areus, and that's how Typhein was defeated. Was..." She hesitated. "Was that priestess Kore?"

He nodded, his jaw clenching, and didn't say anything. His nostrils flared as though each breath pained him, made him want to tear down the mountain itself, the sky above. His gaze fixed on some distant point, and she wondered if he was recalling his priestess's death. Had the memory faded after more than a century, or was it still burned onto his mind's eye? Was that something you could ever forget?

She took a trembling breath. "I'm sorry. I didn't mean to... I just had to know."

That bronze gaze flew back to fix on her face, and suddenly his tension was gone. As though her words had been a needle puncturing a wineskin, the anger drained away, revealing the grief beneath: rocks bared by the receding tide. Sorrow welled in his eyes so that they shimmered in the firelight. When he blinked, a tear ran down his cheek, and he buried his face in his hands. "I know you're not her," he said, his voice muffled, choked with grief. "But you look like her. It's no coincidence you're here. Typhein has sent you because he knows I can't do it. Not again."

The sound of his stifled sob cut Rheia to the core and she froze, wondering what to do. Her gaze met Yalee's and the girl gestured at Alexandros, her expression impatient. *Why do I have to do it?* Rheia thought plaintively, but Yalee didn't respond to her imploring look.

Slowly, with her hands trembling, Rheia inched across the rug to kneel beside Alexandros. Then she slipped her arm around his broad back. He stiffened at her touch, but the sobs grew hoarser. Not knowing what else to do, she drew his head down to lean on her shoulder like she would do for Aias when he fell and grazed his knee bloody. Alexandros's silken hair was so close to her nose that she caught a hint of that distinctive scent, the soap smell that had lingered on the cushion. The skin of his arm was warm under her hand, heated by proximity to the fire.

Closing her eyes and thinking of her kid brother, she began to hum a lullaby—the same one she'd taught herself to play on the pan flute. The same one her mother had sung when she was little and afraid of monsters in the dark. Alexandros was such a riddle, so strong and terrifying, yet so tender towards his charges. He *was* the monster in the dark, with such a dreadful duty—and yet the weight of that duty had shattered him. She remembered the Alexandros in her dream, quick to smile despite his concern about the goat herder's discovery. This was a different man. A broken man.

This, she realised with sudden conviction. This was what Dora had wanted her to see.

Alexandros's crying eased and he fell silent, his body stilling as though suddenly aware of her closeness. When he lifted his head, his face was so near she could feel his breath on her cheek. Mortified, she leapt back like a startled hare. Her face flamed as she settled herself on her cushion, smoothing her skirt. What had she been thinking, getting so close to a strange man, a man who wasn't part of her family? So close she could smell his scent? Her mother would die of shame.

Of course, this was a strange man with a vested interest in keeping her pure. And Yalee was watching. Remembering the girl, Rheia looked up again. She was still in the doorway, one hand resting against the stone frame as she met Rheia's gaze. Her smile was gentle. Rheia barely noticed the curved lip of her deformity anymore.

Alexandros cleared his throat, and Rheia looked back at him. "Thank you," he said. His eyes were still magnificent, even reddened with grief: a warm, green-tinged brown. "I don't deserve your compassion. Especially under the circumstances."

"Oh, I don't know," Rheia said, laughing a little to hide her embarrassment. "Knowing you don't *want* to kill me earns you at least a little compassion. I think it's something we can both agree on. But..." She sighed. "If you don't do it, won't Typhein get free?"

He nodded, turning away from her as though he couldn't bear her gaze. He picked up a piece of tinder from the basket and poked it into the flames, watching as its tip caught alight.

"And there's no way we could defeat him? The army, I mean, not you and me."

"No. I don't think so. He's ... it's impossible."

Her heart sank. Here was a man who'd seen the demon the first time around, witnessed the damage it had done with his own eyes rather than only knowing about it from stories. Her dreams of the Oreareans rising up and defeating Typhein disintegrated like an incinerated log in the fireplace, crumbling to ash. "Then you must do it." Her voice rasped and she tensed so the fear wouldn't rattle her body until her bones flew apart. "You have to kill me."

"I can't," he whispered. "I won't."

"I want you to."

He glanced at her. "You can't mean that."

"I don't want to die," she said. Her voice trembled, but she thought about her family. Could she see Typhein freed, knowing her father would have to fight him? Knowing her brother, mother and grandmother lived in the city just below the mountain? Her next words were spoken with conviction. "I haven't given up on finding a way around this. But if there's no choice, if you have to choose between me and everyone else on this island—well, I'm just one girl."

Alexandros shook his head, turning to face her again. The light from the flaming tinder danced over his face. "I don't think you are *just* anything, Rheia, daughter of Loukios. I don't know if you're Kore, sent back to me by some gift of Eidoneus, or if you just look like her and Typhein has plucked you out of the masses to cause me pain for his own amusement. But I won't kill you. Not again."

Not again? It was the second time Alexandros had said it, but this time his words brought Rheia up short. Had he been the one to kill Kore, the one who'd laid the knife to her throat? Was that what he meant? If so, no wonder he'd been so upset to see Rheia walk into his home. She felt a sudden flash of annoyance at Dora for insisting they meet. The caregiver had to know what would happen. She knew about Kore. She'd seen the carving of the priestess.

Although what was it Dora had said? *It would've been far worse if he'd seen you for the first time on the day of the sacrifice.* Was the caregiver hoping to give him time to get used to the idea of killing his dead lover's lookalike? Rheia shivered—but, when she spoke, her tone was gentle. "I'm not Kore. I may be having dreams about things that

happened to her, but I don't remember being her." *I don't remember being with you. Or being killed by you.*

Alexandros dropped the tinder into the hearth before the flames nipped his fingers. "I know." Despite his words, there was a glimmer of hope in his eyes when he looked at her. A longing. "I know you don't remember, but what if you *are* Kore, and those dreams are your old memories, starting to come back?"

"I've never heard of someone coming back from the underworld," Rheia said. She could hear the scepticism in her voice and felt bad for Alexandros, but she didn't feel like she was a reincarnated priestess. She wasn't even sure what that *would* feel like. "Eidoneus keeps his charges secure. The old stories are brimming with heroes, even gods, trying to retrieve souls from the underworld. They all failed."

"If anyone could beg such favour from him, it would be her," Alexandros murmured, his gaze distant. "She was his high priestess, and he loved her well." He sighed, his shoulders sagging. "But there is no way to know for sure unless the god chooses to tell us. And no matter how it has come to pass, Typhein has taken advantage of it to place you here, to force my hand. Dora told me your theory that Draconaidas killed the other *thysia* girl and rigged the lottery."

"Yes, but that was Draconaidas, not..." Her eyes widened. "Are you saying Draconaidas is working for the demon?"

Alexandros grimaced, sitting back on the rug near her. "Yes. Typhein has usurped Areus and his influence has grown strong. He has glutted himself on death, and it's allowed him to spread his tendrils all across the island." His jaw was tight with self-recrimination.

"But you *had* to kill the sacrifices," Rheia protested. "Didn't you?"

He nodded. "I am the keystone. If I refuse to kill four sacrifices on the anniversary of the binding, it fails and the demon walks free." Alexandros clenched his hands into fists on his knees. "I loathe it. I loathe the fact I have become his slaughterer. But, Rheia, those are not the only deaths I'm talking about."

"What, then?"

"The fire weapons. The war with the Carmeans. So much blood."

Rheia gasped, thinking of Parthenia. Of her own father, such an accomplished captain. She felt ill. "Are you saying that was Typhein?"

"Yes. All of it. The cult of Areus, the minimising of the other gods to reduce their influence here—all of it is the demon, seeking to extend its power. I've seen it happening but could do nothing. After Kore... After the binding, I had some influence with the royal family. But I withdrew here, to the house, which was a gift from the king. I didn't want any part of politics. By the time I realised what was going on, I'd been reduced in the eyes of the city to a nameless animal, albeit a well-kept one, and forbidden to leave. My servants are shunned, cast out and reviled. I see but can do nothing."

"What about Areus himself? The real one, I mean, not the demon impersonating him."

"If the god of war knows, he has not acted. And now his temple is compromised." Alexandros unclenched his fists. When he spoke, his words were filled with despair. "Even Appelon doesn't respond to my prayers anymore. The gods have turned their backs on us."

CHAPTER EIGHTEEN

Rheia wasn't tired after dinner; her impromptu nap and the conversation with Alexandros had infused her limbs with restless energy. The night sweltered even after the sun dragged the worst of the day's heat below the horizon; the *gynaikon's* courtyard felt like the inside of a bowl set in a hearth fire. Normally, on a night like this, her father would take her and her brother down to the harbour, where the sea breeze made the air temperature more bearable. Aias would splash half-naked in the waves while his sister watched, envious but decorous, from the shore, waves rushing around her ankles and sucking the sand from beneath her toes. Even though the sand had itched and the occasional sand fly had hummed around like a tiny, gossamer-winged devil, Rheia wished she was there now.

Instead, she and Parthenia washed off the day's sweat in the courtyard fountain, Erika standing guard nearby. Rheia hadn't seen Dora since that morning, and she didn't want to risk running into the head caregiver by requesting a visit to the bathhouse. She wasn't sure whether the older woman would be at all pleased with her for going to see Alexandros with Yalee.

Rheia was still processing their conversation, her heart heavy with Alexandros's despair and her mind whirling with the implications of what he'd told her. She didn't feel like talking about it just yet—to Dora or to anyone. Parthenia didn't ask how her meeting with the Beast had gone, keeping her gaze lowered and leaving Rheia to her thoughtful silence. Rheia was glad; her fear of the Beast had been replaced by compassion, something she wasn't sure she could explain to the Carmean. She didn't want to see the incredulity in the other girl's eyes. She didn't want to wonder whether Parthenia was right.

Freeing the curtain so it fell across the doorway to her room, Rheia sighed with relief. She was alone. The air was marginally cooler inside the house's thick stone walls, despite the flames dancing on each lamp's wick. With her hair damp against her shoulder, she blew all but one of them out, the gloom settling around her.

She wasn't sure she could sleep, but she wanted to try. She wanted to see whether the gods would send her another dream. She didn't share Alexandros's conviction that they had turned their back on Oreareus; her dreams meant something, surely. Sitting on the edge of her bed, she began to brush the knots out of her long, tangled hair before it dried completely. Could she be a priestess of Eidoneus, returned from his underworld to … what? That was the question, wasn't it? The gods would no doubt approve if Typhein's grip on the island were loosened so they could return to their former position at the top. But surely they didn't expect so much of her?

Perhaps it's intended as a kindness. Rheia divided her hair into three, twining the strands together into a long braid. *A chance for Kore to forgive her lover for killing her all those years ago.* She snorted. Not even Eidoneus, who was a loner except for his wife, who only dwelled with him in the winter months, would be so naive as to think that bringing Kore back from the dead to forgive her killer, just in time to be killed again, was an act of compassion.

And, her fondness for her father's little statue of the god aside, she didn't feel anything like a priestess of Eidoneus. She wasn't special. She was just ... Rheia.

Alright, Eidoneus, she thought, changing into a light shift that still felt too heavy in the dry air, *this is your chance to prove Alexandros wrong. Prove you haven't turned your back on us.*

She waited, holding her breath. But she received no answer. Not that she'd expected one. Who was she to make demands of the gods?

The evening was too hot to bother with a sheet, so she lay on the cushions of the bed, her eyes fixed on the screened window as though by will alone she could coax a breeze through the holes. The breeze didn't come.

Neither did sleep. Rheia tried to relax her body, to take deep breaths. It didn't work. She tried to imagine being back in her bed at home, her mother singing her a lullaby and stroking her hair. All that did was bring tears to burn her eyes as she recalled her mother's gentle touch, the smell of her perfume.

Sighing, Rheia rolled over to stare at the heavy shadows on the far wall. Her mind turned to Alexandros, to humming that same lullaby to him as he cried in her arms before the fire. Closing her eyes, she recalled the scent of him. Flowers and cypress. His skin had been so warm beneath her fingers.

Her thoughts full of him, she finally fell asleep.

With a terrible sense of loneliness pressing down on her shoulders like a wet himation, Rheia stumbled through her parents' villa. She was looking for something. For someone. But the building stood empty, as though the inhabitants had left in the middle of lunch. Her father's sword, wrapped in its stiff leather sheath, leaned against the dining table. A crudely carved wooden soldier, one of Aias's toys, lay discarded in the middle of the courtyard. Her mother's folded shawl sat on a side table in the gynaikon.

But her mother wouldn't go out without her shawl, or her father without his sword. And the fire had gone out in the kitchen. They never let the fire go out. Where was her family? She picked up the toy soldier, turning it over as though looking for some clue.

"Mammidon? Father? Aias?" Her voice fell flat in the silent air, and she clutched a hand over her mouth to silence a panicked squeak, looking around the courtyard. Her heart kicked in her chest. What if someone heard her? That was what she'd wanted, but drawing attention to herself suddenly seemed like a bad idea. A very bad idea. "Tethe? Grandmother?" she whispered.

Outside the villa walls, from the direction of a nearby grove of olives, she heard a sound like a tree exploding. The sky above the courtyard hung low and dark, starless

and churning. She put the soldier down gently. Its tiny
round eyes faced the main door like a sentinel. "What is
happening? Tethe?"

"In here, Rheia." Her grandmother's voice, thready and
distant, came from her father's andron. What was she
doing in there? Loukios would be angry. The women of
the house could go in—to bring food and drink to guests—
but not uninvited.

"Tethe?" Rheia asked again, a little louder.

"Come here." Charis sounded impatient, and Rheia
scurried across the courtyard. The sky crept towards the
ground, inch by inch. A ceiling of heavy smoke. As soon
as she realised that was what it was, she smelled the
stink of it: burning trees and cooking flesh. Her stomach
roiled, a hand flying to cover her mouth and nose in an
attempt to filter out the stench.

Her grandmother stood against the far wall of the
andron, by the little shelf set into the wall. She was looking at Loukios's statue of Eidoneus. The sight of the god's
calm expression gave Rheia a moment of serenity, stilled
the trembling in her hands.

Just a moment, though.

Charis picked up the statue and held it out to her
granddaughter, cradled in both hands. "Here," she said,
her voice dry as the ashes from a funeral pyre, her eyes
empty. "This belongs to you now."

Rheia stared. "What? I can't. It's Father's. Where is he?"

"Gone to fight the demon like the good toy soldier he
is. You need this more than he does."

Rheia's fingers closed around the cool marble of the
statue. A jolt ran up them to her chest. Pain. Such terrible
pain, as if her heart might burst.

Charis crumpled to the ground.
Someone was screaming. Someone was—

Rheia sat upright in her bed, gasping. One hand clutched the air as though gripping the statue, tears slicked her cheeks, and sweat drenched her thin shift. Her nose tickled with the scent of burning oil, almost choking her. Panic rose to wrap a stifling hand around her throat. Her wide-eyed gaze raked the room. The flame in her lamp sputtered, olive oil almost consumed. That was what she could smell, she told herself, taking a deep, trembling breath. Not Oreareus burning.

As the pulse jumping in her throat slowed, her lips twisted wryly. Even though they made her uncomfortable for other reasons, she preferred the dreams Eidoneus sent about Kore to the twisted nightmares her subconscious offered as an alternative. And she wouldn't have minded another dream about the handsome, carefree Alexandros of a century ago.

The air had cooled, and she reached to pull the sheet up over her bare legs. Laughing at herself, she lay back against the pillow as the lamp finally sputtered and died, plunging her into inky darkness. She knew it was foolish, but she couldn't shake the longing to experience romance— even vicariously through dreams about Kore and that other, happier Alexandros.

Her amusement faded when she recalled the nightmare's final moments: her grandmother handing her the statue and then collapsing as though from a mortal wound.

Rheia's fingertips tingled as she recalled the smooth feel of it, the god's calm expression as he regarded her, scroll and dagger held aloft. So patient. So similar to the statuette in the previous day's dream of Kore. They were even made of the same green marble, streaked with white.

Verde marble. So rare on the island. Rheia bit her lip, recalling Kore's thoughts. Her eyes widened. Could it be the same statue? Surely not—why would her father have an artefact from the long-forgotten Eidonesian temple? No, it must be a coincidence. It had only featured in her nightmare because she'd been thinking of it before she fell asleep. Right?

Still, she couldn't shake the growing conviction that the statues were one and the same, and that they were—it was—important. Had Eidoneus sent her the nightmare to jog her memory, to point that fact out to her—the dreaming equivalent of a slap across the cheek to gain her attention? She shivered in the dark, suddenly cold as she wondered what else that abandoned villa might have meant. She needed to write to her family, to make sure they were well.

She needed to get that statue.

Rheia didn't sleep again, rising as soon as the grey light of pre-dawn tinged the sky outside her window. Dressing quickly, she found the piece of soft vellum Yalee had delivered the day before, with Alexandros's message written across it. With a pang she told herself was for ruining the beautiful material, she scraped it clean with the hard edge of a bracelet, swearing under her breath when she tore it near a corner. Still, there was enough space to write what she needed to.

Message complete and ink blown dry, Rheia rolled the

parchment and carried it out into the cool morning, looking for Dora. She hated to beg another favour, but she had no choice.

Dora wasn't in the dining room. Instead, Rheia found the pregnant caregiver she'd seen several times before. The woman must be close to her time, if the round swelling of her belly was any indication. She sat on a couch pulled up to the table, humming as her hands moved dextrously, weaving bare, slender willow branches to form a basket. Rheia paused, her eyes wide as she regarded the woman, the almost finished basket. "You haven't been sitting here all night, have you?" she blurted, and then clenched her jaw, feeling her ears warm with embarrassment at the awkward outburst.

The woman looked up. A serene smile lit her broad face, made it lovely despite the pockmarks scarring her cheeks, perhaps from some childhood illness. Seated as the caregiver was, with her skirts falling to the floor, Rheia couldn't see the club foot that had earned her a place among the Beast's attendants. "For several hours, but not all night. The baby was kicking and keeping me awake. And I was keeping my husband awake." Her voice conveyed her amusement. "He is grouchy when he doesn't get enough sleep, so I took over watch here. Can I get you something? Breakfast won't be here for another hour, but I could send for bread from the kitchen, or for some wine."

Husband? Rheia's eyebrows rose with surprise. But it made sense that the caregivers would find partners within their small group. Just because they couldn't find a mate among the general populace, that didn't mean they could never marry. Her gaze dropped to the woman's round belly as she wondered whether the babe would

inherit one or both of its parents' maladies. What would happen to it if it didn't? Would it be allowed to stay?

"Rheia? Are you hungry?" The woman's voice pierced her reverie.

She forced her gaze up from the woman's belly to meet her eyes. "No, thank you. Forgive me, but what should I call you?"

"My name is Polymede."

Rheia nodded and sat opposite Polymede, placing the rolled parchment before her on the table. She watched as Polymede's hands moved back and forth. The willow branches were fresh cut, not yet stiff with age. "I was hoping to speak to Dora. I haven't seen her since yesterday morning."

The other woman paused, studying Rheia over the top of the basket. "Since she took you to the master's rooms?"

Rheia nodded, looking down at her own hands. "Yes. I hope she's not in trouble or anything."

The caregiver laughed softly, starting to weave again. "No. Dora is first among the caregivers. Who would she get in trouble with?"

"Draconaidas?" Rheia suggested, peering through her eyelashes to watch Polymede's reaction.

The woman's jaw clenched and she took a breath before replying. "I'm sure Draconaidas wouldn't approve of your visits, but he has no dominion here."

"That's what Dora said," Rheia replied, a grin spreading across her face. She felt a little like she was talking with Aias, conspiring to steal honey from the pot in the kitchen. The thought of her brother made her throat tighten, and she felt her grin falter.

"I'm sure she did." Polymede pushed the end of her

last willow branch into the weave. She retrieved a small length of twine from her pouch and knotted it around the branch to keep it in place, cutting off the loose ends with her knife. "Dora had deliveries to manage yesterday afternoon. But she should be free this morning. Would you like me to request she come here?"

"Yes. Please," Rheia said. Polymede grunted as she stood, and the girl reached out a hand to steady her, hesitating before letting it drop. "But please don't wake her on my account."

"The sun's rising. She'll be awake. That woman never truly rests." Polymede's gaze dropped to the rolled parchment and then back up to Rheia's face. Her eyes filled with a compassion that made Rheia ache inside. "I won't be long."

CHAPTER NINETEEN

A s she waited for Polymede to return, Rheia watched dawn slowly outline the mountain in light and paint the courtyard in soft orange and gold. It wasn't long before she heard the clank of a key in the lock, but it was Dora rather than Polymede that came through the door. The early morning light was gentle, giving the girl a glimpse of how beautiful the older woman remained beneath the worry lines around her eyes and mouth, and the exhaustion smudged underneath each eyelid. She walked with pride straightening her spine and determination in her step as she entered the courtyard, smiling as she spotted Rheia studying her from the dining table.

"Polymede is bringing fresh bread from the kitchen," the older woman said as she sat on Parthenia's couch. Her gaze flicked to the parchment and back to Rheia's face. "I hear you went to see the master after lunch yesterday."

"Is that okay? He invited me," Rheia said, a little defensively. Perhaps she shouldn't have been so quick to erase Alexandros's message.

"Of course it is," Dora said with a shrug, and the girl exhaled with relief. "I would have preferred to be there, just in case, but the gods know as well as anyone that the master knows his own mind. And it ended well enough. He is happier than he was, and you are whole." Her voice was calm … but Rheia thought she heard the faintest tightness in her tone. Jealousy? She remembered again Parthenia's claim that Dora loved Alexandros, and felt the tug of a frown between her brows. If she wasn't careful, the head caregiver could make her life much harder than it was.

It was time to change the subject.

"I know I have no right to ask this, but I want to write to my family again." Rheia nudged the parchment with a fingertip so it rolled across the table to Dora. "They have a statue of Eidoneus. I wish to ask my father if I can borrow it, just until the … the festival." She let the despair that sat heavy on her chest, an aching constant in her life since the night before the lottery, show on her face. How pathetic she must look. "It would provide me with a lot of comfort."

Dora's eyes narrowed as she studied Rheia. Then she picked up the parchment and read it, presumably making sure there wasn't anything that would get the house in trouble if the temple intercepted it. There wasn't. Rheia had been careful. She hadn't even named the statue; she knew asking for the one in the *andron* would be clear enough that her parents would understand. "Would you like me to have it returned to them afterwards?" Dora's voice was soft with sympathy, and some of the anxiety drained from Rheia's limbs.

"Yes. Please. The statue is an important family heirloom," Rheia said, not knowing whether she spoke the truth or a lie—but she didn't want to mention how valuable it was. "My parents will want it back when I no longer … need it."

The lock *thunked* again, and Polymede came through, steadying a platter of bread on top of her head with one hand while she locked the door behind her with the other. Rheia's stomach awoke with a growl as the fresh-baked aroma drifted across to her. "Thank you," she said, squeezing Dora's hand as Polymede set the tray down. "It means a lot to me."

As Polymede cut the loaf into slices, assuring them a proper breakfast would follow soon, Rheia fought to keep the surge of exhilaration off her face. She wasn't sure having the statue would make any difference, or whether Eidoneus was really trying to tell her something, but the fact she was doing something—anything—to try and stave off her fate lifted her spirits. It gave her hope, something she craved.

Seeing that speculation back on Dora's face, she suspected the older caregiver understood all too well.

Rheia's breath caught in her throat when she saw Aias follow Dora through the double doors and into the *gynaikon*. Shock he'd been allowed into the women's wing gave way to giddy joy, and she launched herself at him with a choked cry, wrapping him in her arms and hugging his head to her chest. His tousled curls, flattened on top as though he'd been wearing a hat, tickled her nose. They smelled of soap and dusty sunshine. His wiry, nut-brown arms wrapped around her waist, hugging her as tightly as she hugged him. They trembled, and that was when she realised he was crying.

Rheia stepped back and looked down at him. "Were you this tall when I left?" Her smile was soft as she tipped his chin up to face her. Aias wiped his tears away with the back of his arm and nodded, staring at her face with wide, bloodshot eyes as though she might disappear if he so much as blinked. The skin around them was puffy, and her heart ached for her usually lighthearted little brother. "Do you have time to sit with me? We have lunch, if you haven't eaten."

Aias hesitated before nodding. "Are they treating you well here?" He followed her across the courtyard to the open-sided dining hall. The table was covered with food, and his face went slack with shock as he took in the feast—far too much food for just two girls. "Do you get meat at *every meal*?" His tone was incredulous. Other than fish, at home they were lucky if they got meat once a month.

"Not breakfast," she said, smiling. "This is Parthenia. She's ... Carmean." Rheia had almost called her "the other *thysia*", but the words had stuck in her throat. She was sure Parthenia would prefer to be defined by who she was rather than by her fate. Rheia felt the same way. "Parthenia, this is my little brother, Aias."

"Pleased to meet you," the Carmean girl said, her pale brown eyes meeting Aias's darker ones and crinkling with a soft smile. He stared back, stunned into silence. "I once had a brother much like you." The bracelets at her wrist jingled as she brushed a strand of long, dark

hair back from her forehead. The Carmean looked lovely in a *chiton* the colour of rose petals, her lips full and plump, stained red with the juice of the berries she'd been nibbling. No wonder Aias had been struck dumb.

Rheia nudged him with her elbow and indicated he should sit at the foot of her reclining couch. He jerked into motion as Dora came into the room, fetching an empty plate from a sideboard. The caregiver set it before him, but Rheia, sitting beside him on the padded cushion, was the one who speared a slice of fresh-roasted goat haunch and set it on his plate. "I want to do this," she told Dora in a low voice, adding a side of steamed vegetables and a hunk of bread. Dora nodded and stepped back, standing against the wall like a slave. Rheia sighed, knowing it was too much to expect she'd have any privacy while her brother was there. He might be nine, but he was still male. Aias hadn't even been allowed into her mother's *gynaikon* at the family villa—although that was more for their mother's and grandmother's peace than anything else.

Aias unhooked a bag from his shoulder and handed it to Rheia. Then he turned, attacking the food with a single-minded focus.

Holding her breath, Rheia pulled a fabric-wrapped bundle from the bag. It was heavy with the weight of stone. *The statue.* She pushed the cloth aside and regarded Eidoneus's placid face, her breath sighing out from between parted lips. It truly did look the same as the statue in her dream of Eidoneus's temple. The little god had his head at the same angle, slightly downturned as though looking at a kneeling supplicant, and the scroll in his hand was carved with the same faint indentations, meant to represent writing. She ran her finger along them, feeling the familiar bumps. The stone was cool under her fingertip. "Thank you," she murmured, not knowing to whom she was speaking: Aias, Dora, her absent parents, or the god himself.

With a pang of regret, she re-wrapped the statuette and set the bundle beside her on the table, out of range of her brother's clumsy elbows. "How is everything at home?"

Aias's shoulders went stiff and the pace of his chewing slowed as he glanced at her. "Fine," he mumbled around a mouthful. But his voice was flat, and after that quick glance he avoided looking at her.

"You're lying." Rheia folded her arms across her chest and frowned at him. A slow cold crept over her, making the hairs on the backs of her arms prickle a warning. Why was he lying? "What's going on?"

He swallowed, busying himself by picking up a thin stick of leaf celery and biting the end off with a snap of his teeth. He didn't even like leaf celery.

"Aias?" she pressed. "Is everything well at home?"

"They told me I shouldn't—" He stopped, staring at her. His voice dropped to a whisper. "I'm not supposed to upset you. I don't *want* to upset you. You've got enough to be upset about already, what with being here." He pierced Dora with a look. The caregiver pretended not to notice.

Rheia's stomach roiled as though she'd eaten bad meat, and her mouth went dry even as her palms grew damp. "Tell me."

"It's *Tethe*," he said, discarding the half-eaten celery as though all the energy had gone out of him. "She's dying."

Rheia clutched at the edge of the table with white-knuckled fingers as a wave of dizziness rolled over her. "No, she isn't," she whispered. Her voice sounded like it

was coming from the other side of the courtyard rather than from her own lips. "I saw her only days ago. She was fine. She *can't* be."

"She is." Aias was crying again, his face blotchy with new grief. "She w-went to the *agora* yesterday to buy some salt. Someone attacked her. H-hit her on the back of the head. The bone there isn't … it …" He shuddered, swallowed hard. "The guards found her in an a-alley. Discarded like gar—" Aias ground to a halt, his chest moving like a bellows as he gasped for breath. "I wasn't meant to tell you," he whispered, as if that were the most important thing, not the fact that their grandmother had been assaulted, her skull shattered.

Rheia forced her limbs to move, although they felt as heavy as stone. She wrapped her arms around her brother. His curls grew damp with her silent tears, tears she hadn't known she was crying. "You did the right thing. I'm glad you told me. I… You should take the statue back. If she is…" She couldn't bring herself to say the word. "Father will want it. So he can pray to Eidoneus, beg him to take her swiftly to the Asphodel Meadows. So she doesn't suffer or get lost." The meadows were one of the planes of the underworld, where those who were neither heroes nor villains spent their afterlife. It was a good end, and the best most people could hope for.

Charis had always loved the white asphodel flowers that grew in the fields around Oreareus city, their flowers pointing like spears at the heavens. The thought made Rheia's heart burn as though someone had set a fire to it.

Aias shook his head, pulling back a little. Rheia dropped her arms and met his gaze. "He said to bring it to you. He knows she's dying but he said to bring it anyway. Said it's what *Tethe* would want."

"Then I will use the statue to pray for her."

"Good," he mumbled.

"Did they catch who did it?"

"No." His voice was fierce, barely more than a snarl.

"Then I will pray for that too," Rheia replied, her voice just as fierce as her brother's. Vengeance wasn't Eidoneus's usual area, but it couldn't hurt. And the idea of turning her will towards achieving divine retribution made her feel a little better, since she couldn't stalk the streets the way she wished, her father's gleaming fire-thrower in hand as she hunted down the thief who had attacked her grandmother to steal a handful of silver. She met Dora's gaze over Aias's curls, and a sudden, desperate hope filled her thoughts. "Dora, could I go and see her?"

The caregiver's face was full of compassion, but her answer was uncompromising. "No."

"But—"

"The caregivers' duty was given to them by the royal house. If the king found out we'd let one of the *thysies* leave, we'd be put to death. And your parents' house is exactly where they'd expect you to go. The risk is too great."

"But I could sneak out. I promise I'd come back," Rheia insisted. Parthenia made a soft sound of disbelief and Rheia glanced at her. She'd almost forgotten the other girl was there. "I *would*. I just want to say goodbye."

"Everyone knows you're the Orearean sacrifice. You can't pass anonymously among the masses anymore—the entire city knows your face."

Rheia's shoulders sagged as she felt all the hope drain from her, leaving only that aching despair. "You're right." Her voice sounded flat to her own ears.

"About that. There's something else," Aias said slowly, lowering his voice. "I overheard Father and *Mammidon* speaking about it last night, after they brought her home. She had been in his ear about talking to the king. *Tethe*, I mean. Said that you believed the lottery was fixed, and that Draconaidas was a blasphemer."

Cold shivered up Rheia's spine like ice cracking from a blow. She had the sudden sense she knew where Aias's words were going. She did not want to hear this.

"Father went to the palace yesterday, asked for an audience with the king." Aias's voice was quiet. "He didn't get one; they gave him an *appointment*. But Father thinks word got back to Draconaidas. That the attack on *Tethe* wasn't a mugging. He thinks it was intended to silence her. And as a warning to him."

Not a mugging? Rheia stared at her brother, that chill numbness creeping out to encompass her limbs. Aias's face grew blurry. Then it tipped sideways and vanished into darkness as oblivion claimed her.

CHAPTER TWENTY

Rheia's head ached. Her knees were sore from kneeling on the cold stone. But neither discomfort matched the pain of the guilt, fury and despair burning in her chest. Her gaze was fixed on the small statue of Eidoneus, which she'd placed on top of the small jewellery chest in her room. A candle burned at its foot, sending a thin tendril of smoke to curl in front of the god's carved face. The dancing flame was the brightest light in the room, the early afternoon sunlight almost completely blocked by the blanket she'd draped over the window.

Footsteps behind her barely penetrated her focus. "You should be resting," Dora said, her voice gentle as she came up to the little shrine. "You hit your head quite hard when you fell."

"I'm fine," Rheia said, looking at the dagger in Eidoneus's hand. The god of the dead had a sharp side. "Do you have them?"

"Here." Dora pressed a small glass phial into her hands. It reminded Rheia of the bottle holding Charis's

rose perfume. "Attar of narcissus flower, as requested."

She looked up at the older woman. "What about the nightsleep oil?"

"I won't leave that with you, but you may have a drop for your offering." The girl heard the unsaid words in Dora's statement: too much narcissus oil could make a person throw up, or break out in a rash. But too much nightsleep oil was fatal. Rheia didn't have the energy to argue with the caregiver, to explain that she didn't plan to kill herself. Her lips twisted as she reflected that keeping her and Parthenia alive—for another week, at least— was Dora's primary duty.

Rheia used the longer taper to light the small, stubby candle in the fat clay pot Yalee had loaned her. It seemed to be the same one the younger girl had used to burn lavender and chamomile oil, first for Rheia and then for Alexandros—but although the inside of the hollow pot was black with char, the clay bowl that sat on top had been scoured clean. With a steady hand, Rheia poured an offering of unwatered golden wine into the bowl. The heady scent of fermented grape, sweet and fragrant with a hint of oregano and thyme, tickled her nose.

Dora uncapped the small clay pot she kept at her belt and tipped it, allowing a glimmering drop of nightsleep oil to dimple the surface of the wine. The oil's cool tang prickled Rheia's nose. She met the caregiver's gaze and, with a quiet sigh, the older woman let a second drop fall after the first. "Will you be needing anything else from me?" she said, her voice hushed out of respect—for Eidoneus, for the ritual, or perhaps for Rheia herself.

"No. Thank you. Please close the curtain on your way out."

Once the caregiver was gone and the fabric had rustled shut across the entryway to her room, Rheia let her shoulders drop for a moment. They ached with tension, one source of pain among many. The guilt she felt at the attack on her grandmother surged in her chest, threatening to overwhelm her. She struggled against it, pushing it back down into her belly, where it roiled ceaselessly. Yes, she was the one who'd urged Charis to speak out against what Draconaidas had done, but she hadn't caved in her grandmother's skull. She hadn't killed the other *thysia* in the first place. Or worked with a demon.

Rheia steeled her spine again, studying Eidoneus's shrouded face.

"Forgive me if this isn't what you're used to," she murmured, uncapping the little phial. The intoxicatingly sweet aroma of narcissus flowers twined among the other fragrances, heady and somehow smoky as she tipped several drops into the wine. "But I know narcissus flowers are Despoina's perfume. I dreamt of Kore making a nightsleep draft. And what god doesn't like wine?" Her lips twitched with amusement, and she willed them to stillness. She didn't know much about worshipping Eidoneus—these days, people barely even spoke his name, either from fear or neglect—but she was sure making jokes wasn't appropriate.

She'd considered also offering an animal sacrifice, but her heart had rebelled at the thought. Too many had already died as a result of Typhein's corruption. She wouldn't add another life. Even a rat's ... and she hated them.

Taking a breath, she resealed the phial and laid it on the floor beside the chest. Then she sat more comfortably,

her legs crossed, and focused her gaze on the statue and that twisting strand of smoke winding past the little god. It snaked towards the ceiling as it began to disperse, merging with the clear air to leave nothing of itself but a trace of scent amidst the heady aromas of evaporating wine and oil. Her breathing slowed and her hands curled on her knees as she began to relax. Her aches began to fade—even the pain in her heart eased somewhat, leaving determination in its place.

"I beg you, Eidoneus, Ruler of Many." Her voice came slowly, rough with pain. "Look after my *tethe*, she who is called Charis, daughter of Eugenios, when she comes to your halls. Let her not suffer on this side of life or the other." The words fell into a rhythm both unfamiliar and natural. She let them float up to the ceiling, riding on that curl of smoke like sailors standing on the deck of a trireme, carried away on the wind and the sea.

"Most beloved god of my heart, lend your all-seeing eyes to my father, Loukios, who has kept your sacred statue so well all these years, who makes offerings to you when others forget." Her voice dropped to a hiss. "Let him find the ones who harmed my *tethe* and bring them to justice. And when they do come to you, Lord of the Deep Earth, either by his hand or at the end of their lives, I beg that you cast them into Tartarus, the deep abyss, to suffer for all eternity."

The statue's serene face loomed large before her eyes. Her soul filled with fragrance until she felt as light as a downy feather, carried high on the breeze. Wine and narcissus, candle smoke and burning oil evoked a memory of a dream: crackling, blazing forests on the hillside. The room grew warm, then hot. Sweat beaded on her brow, trickled down her temple, but she persisted. "And Eidoneus, true god of the people of Oreareus—no, Cretea—lend me your wisdom. Let me know what I must do to free our people of the influence of the demon Typhein. To free our island of his tyranny once and for all."

As though ignited by the demon's name, the sound of exploding olive trees filled her thoughts; they detonated like the huge cannons that protected the harbour. The crackling grew to a deafening roar. Her hands clutched at her ears, covering them, but the sound was within her mind, as loud as ever.

A thought came to her, serene. It cut through the din, reverberating in her like the peal of a gong. *Kore.*

The terrible noise continued, but it was a storm raging outside heavy stone walls: it didn't touch her. "Eidoneus?" she whispered, her voice distant.

Kore.

"I am Rheia."

Yes.

Somewhere, someone was crying, sobbing with relief like a drowning child plucked from the sea. "He said you'd turned your backs on us."

Never. But on Cretea we are hindered.

The sound of flame redoubled, breaching the temporary sanctity with a crack she felt as much as heard. The stench of burning forests intensified, heavy with ashes and another stink, one that coated her tongue and turned her stomach to acid. Cooking flesh, like saccharine, metal-soaked charcoal, so heavy it blocked out the gentler scents of flowers and grapes. Her tongue curled against the roof of her mouth as if to deny the stench, and she huddled before the statue, burying her face in the skirts of her

chiton. Screams reached her ears, not all of them her own.

"What can I do?" she gasped between cries, her voice muffled by the fabric.

The reply came back to her, faint over the tumult.

Look for my brother's seal ring.

And then the noise and stench overwhelmed her. She wrapped the darkness and silence around herself like a cloak, and slept.

"She's awake. I'll fetch Dora." A familiar voice, usually surly but now coloured with relief.

Erika? Footsteps retreating, echoing strangely.

"Thank you," another voice replied, and this one jarred Rheia awake. It was male. Her eyes flew open, staring at an unfamiliar ceiling. No, not unfamiliar—she'd seen it before. But this wasn't her room. Why was she sleeping in the *bathhouse*? Frowning, she turned her head, her hair floating around her. Yalee sat to one side of her, the girl wearing a light grey *chiton* stained dark by the water that rose midway up her torso. As Rheia stared at her, the girl reached out a steadying hand. "You are fine. I have you," that other voice said as a warm arm slid under Rheia's back, holding her afloat. Startled, she whipped her head around, closing her eyes briefly as a wave of dizziness overcame her.

When she opened them, her heart stumbled, forgetting for a moment how to beat. Alexandros, the Beast, was in the pool, on her other side. His chest was bare, glistening in the slanted afternoon light pouring in the high window, although his shoulders and hair were dry. His bronze eyes gazed down at her, soft with concern.

Panic overcame her and her arms flew across her body. Her fingers tangled in wet fabric and she clutched it gratefully. She was clothed. The idea of being naked in front of a man made a blush heat her cheeks. She swallowed hard, willing the embarrassment away, before returning her gaze to Alexandros's face. "What happened?"

"You were overcome by fumes from the nightsleep and narcissus plants. You shouldn't use so much oil next time." His tone was gentle despite the chastisement in his words, and his gaze ran over her face so intently she could almost feel it as a caress on her skin.

"Two drops of nightsleep oil. Four drops of narcissus oil," she murmured, staring back at him. "Not so much."

"Then why were you feverish and unconscious?"

"I prayed to Eidoneus. I think T—" She stopped herself from saying the name, wincing as she remembered what had happened the last time she did. It may have just been in her vision, but it had felt real. And she didn't want to see what Typhein was capable of in the flesh. Her shudder at the thought made the water ripple around her. "I think the demon tried to stop him from reaching me. It was awful."

Alexandros nodded, the corners of his lips tightening briefly before drifting back down with worry. "Your fever has dropped. Would you like to sit up?"

She nodded, and together Alexandros and Yalee eased her upright in the water. Her hair fell around her shoulders in tangled strands, water streaming down her brow and cheeks. Alexandros's arm stayed behind her, around her waist, until she was steady. Then he withdrew. Her twinge

of disappointment as the contact ended surprised her.

Conscious of the wet fabric and how it clung to her curves, Rheia folded her arms in front of her chest. "Why are you here?"

"I am—was—a priest of Appelon. He may not respond to my prayers anymore, but I still know healing lore."

"Oh." Rheia remembered her mother using cool water compresses to bring down Aias's fever last winter. That the caregivers would take her to the bathhouse and immerse her in the cooler pool made sense. "I didn't think you were allowed to leave your la—" She stopped abruptly.

"My lair?" Alexandros's eyes crinkled with amusement. "You wouldn't be the first to call it that."

"It's a very nice lair," she said weakly. He laughed, and she smiled back. On her other side, Yalee climbed from the pool, droplets pattering down on the tiles like spring rain. "Still, I didn't think you were allowed. To leave it."

He looked away, studying the mosaic of tiles on the far wall as though he'd never seen it before. The picture wavered through the steam from the adjacent hot pool.

She dared a glance downwards, seeing with relief that Alexandros was wearing a cloth around his waist. He wasn't completely naked. "I can go anywhere in the house. I am the house's healer as well as its master and prisoner. I stay out of the *gynaikon* out of respect, and mostly stay in my lair when we have sacrifices here." Rheia's heart ached for him. Of course he wouldn't want to know the sacrifices. That would make it much harder for him to do what he had to.

With a brush in her hand, Yalee knelt on the edge of the pool, behind Rheia's head. She lifted Rheia's hair, which was heavy with water, and draped it across her already-soaked knees. Then, her fingers gentle, she began to work the brush through the tangles. Rheia sighed, leaning back a little. Her hands dropped down into the water by her sides.

Alexandros turned back to Rheia, his gaze running across her face, taking in the mass of her hair. His lips parted for a moment before he pressed them shut. "I should go. Leave you to the women's care."

"Don't." The word fell from Rheia's lips before she even registered her disappointment. His eyes widened and her cheeks burned. "I, ah. I still feel lightheaded." It wasn't entirely a lie. The sight of the beads of water across the bare skin of the priest's arms made her a little giddy. She drew her gaze back up to his face, wondering if he could guess the cause of her ailment. "And I want to talk to you about something."

Her heart did a little flip as Alexandros reached out, placing a warm hand on her forehead. He turned to Yalee. "Tea?" he said, making a drinking gesture with his other hand. Then he traced a word with a finger on the tile beside the pool.

Yalee glanced at it and nodded. "Now?" she said, her loud voice echoing off the walls.

"Yes. Please." He nodded as he spoke, and the girl stood, handing Rheia the brush. Rheia began to run it through her locks, more roughly—but effectively—than the girl had done. "Peppermint tea will help settle your stomach and keep the fever at bay," Alexandros continued, watching her movements. "Is your head aching?"

"A little," Rheia said, conscious that Yalee's departure meant she was alone with a man for the second time in

as many days. But she wasn't scared of the Beast anymore. Being with him made her feel … fluttery. Warm inside. "My father would be horrified if he could see me now," she said, and then bit her lip. What was it about this man that she couldn't stop herself from saying what she was thinking? "But I suppose you have an interest in keeping me pure."

"You mean for the ritual?" Alexandros said, staying at an arm's distance. She nodded. "Purity is the temple's fixation. The binding ritual requires four human lives, virgin or no. The stipulation of purity is something the demon added later." His voice grew as bitter as raw wine. "It guarantees I am a murderer of babies, children, maidens and boys. Those who haven't yet had a chance to experience life or to earn their fate. Not murderers or criminals, who I could kill with less guilt."

"That's awful," she gasped, her hand stilling on the brush.

"Yes. As I said yesterday, the demon causes me pain for its own amusement." His voice was rough with emotion, although no tears fell. The pain was a century old, too deep for tears.

With sympathy driving her, she reached out a hand to touch his arm. As soon as her fingertips brushed that smooth skin, she drew back in confusion, her gaze dropping to her lap. The light fabric of her *chiton* swirled beneath the water's surface. "I heard him, you know," she said, studying the material through the wavering surface of the water. "Before the demon stopped me. I heard Eidoneus."

"You did?" The tumult of emotion in Alexandros's voice drew Rheia to look back at him; shock, hope and a terrible sense of abandonment resonated there. "What did he say?"

"He—" Her words caught in her throat as she stared at the priest. When she spoke again, they came out as a whisper. "He called me Kore."

Alexandros's mouth fell open as he stared at her, his eyes widening and his muscles tensing as though he wanted to move towards her, to sweep her up in his arms. Instead, he held himself still. "I knew it," he whispered. "I knew you were her. Reborn."

"I still don't remember being her," she said, her voice as soft as his. She set the brush down on the edge of the pool. The bone handle clicked faintly against the tile. "Not really." Even as she said it, she wondered if it were true. Her mind didn't remember Kore's life, but she recalled the way her hand had reached out to him, wanting to touch him, wanting to ease his pain. Her body, her heart: they remembered.

"I've wanted Kore back for so long." Alexandros ran a wet hand through his hair, leaving damp furrows in its wake. His face showed the signs of his struggle: a creased brow, white lips, pained eyes. "And now you're here, I can't decide whether it's a gift or a curse."

The truth in his words resonated, making her chest ache. "It may be both," she said. The water rippled around her as she slid across the pool towards him. He stared at her, frozen as she stopped in front of him, tiny waves splashing against the bare skin of his stomach. One of Rheia's hands settled on his calf for balance, and she pulled it away as though scalded. Her heart flew into her throat. What was she thinking? "A lure and a goad, to get us to do what the gods want." She was so close she could see his pupils dilate.

"And what do they want?" he said, his breath warm on her cheeks.

"They want us to stop accepting things as they are and fight back. Rid ourselves of the demon." She knew with every fibre of her being that it was true.

"Me, you mean. They want me to fight back." Shame dragged his gaze down, and then he stiffened as he seemed to realise how close she was to him, how thin the fabric of her summer-weight *chiton* was. His hands curled into fists at his sides. Was he fighting the urge to touch her?

"You're not doing this on your own," she said, taking those hands in hers. They were bigger than her own, and her smaller fingers stretched to curl around them. Slowly, the fists relaxed and his fingers twined with hers. The sensation—the rightness of it—sent a shiver down her spine. "Eidoneus said we need to find his brother's seal ring. He said that's the key. And I'm going to help you do it."

Feeling brazen, nothing like her usual self, Rheia leaned forward and pressed her lips to Alexandros's. They were warm and smooth, surrounded by a delicious rasp of stubble, and for a moment they remained still against her, the former priest frozen in apparent shock. Then he growled softly in his throat, his lips parting and his tongue brushing against her closed mouth in a way that made her gasp. His tongue slid between her lips, tentative, and ran along her teeth. She touched it with her own tongue, surprised and delighted at the silky heat of it, at the fire that ignited in her belly. "Kore," he groaned, his mouth against hers. Before she could speak, he added in a tone of wonder, as if reminding himself, "Rheia."

The sound of light footsteps in the corridor outside the room brought Rheia back to herself as though someone had dumped a bowl of snow melt over her head. She scooted back in the water, her face flaming, as Yalee came into the room. The girl held a steaming cup, which she offered to Rheia; the fresh scent of brewing mint tea filled the room. Rheia inhaled deeply, trying to still the fire in her blood, and thanked the girl. She was conscious of Alexandros's unwavering gaze on her face, the surprise and desire in it.

As Yalee turned to the wall to fetch a thick towel, he spoke. "You may be intended as a gift or a goad, Rheia. But you're more than that. You're a miracle."

CHAPTER TWENTY-ONE

Dry and dressed in a fresh *chiton* the colour of spring grass, Rheia sat across from Alexandros on a leather-clad stool, a low table between them. Yalee had done Rheia's hair up in intricate braids that wound around her head. The chamber was small, its walls carved with the image of a twin-masted trireme bearing down on a sinuous sea monster. The creature almost seemed to move in the wavering lamplight. The room wasn't in the *gynaikon*, and Rheia felt like she could breathe easier out here, out of her prison ... even as she knew the freedom was an illusion.

Dora sat to Rheia's right, her eyes down as she served their evening meal one-handed. Rheia's mouth watered and her stomach twisted at the scent of the melted goat cheese coating the baked fish fillets; cumin seeds and sea salt glittered across the browned surface. She hadn't eaten at lunch, too distraught by Aias's news. Grown used to regular, hearty meals, her stomach protested the lack even as shame at her hunger weighed on her chest. She shouldn't be feasting when her grandmother lay dying. When she might already be dead.

Not wanting to break down in front of Alexandros, Rheia splashed wine into the broad cups. She needed to keep herself together. She didn't have much time—there were less than seven days now until the sacrifice, and her vision of Eidoneus had left her with a sense of urgency that pushed her like a giant's hand between her shoulder blades, propelling her forward whether she was ready or not.

Dora dished up three plates from the platter on the small sideboard, not two, and Rheia felt a twinge of disappointment. She'd hoped the older woman would give Rheia and Alexandros the privacy to talk … and perhaps kiss some more. Still, the girl tried to keep a pleasant expression on her face.

In contrast, Alexandros seemed glad Dora was there, smiling at her when she handed him the most generous serving. Did he regret kissing Rheia? Was that why he was glad the caregiver was there—so it wouldn't happen again?

Suddenly, Rheia didn't feel quite so hungry. She picked up the wine cup, curling her fingers around the graceful handles on each side. Bowing her head, she inhaled the sweet, spicy aroma. "What do you think Eidoneus meant by his brother's seal ring?" she said, studying Alexandros. "*Which* brother?" The god had several; Gaea and Diktaios had borne many children.

Alexandros dug strong fingers into the crust of cheese coating his fish, pulling off a morsel and studying it for a moment before popping it into his mouth. His Adam's apple bobbed when he swallowed. "He meant Areus. I'm sure of it."

"That makes sense, given the demon is impersonating him," Rheia said. Dora's eyes widened slightly, but she began to eat rather than articulating the cause of her surprise. Had she not known Alexandros's theory that Typhein had usurped Areus? Or was she just surprised he'd told Rheia? The girl sipped her wine, feeling a little smug.

"It's not that. Or at least not just that." Alexandros, hesitated, taking another mouthful. Then he squared his shoulders as though preparing himself to face an enemy. "During the ritual to bind T—"

"Don't say its name." Rheia shook her head, her eyes widening.

"Very well." Alexandros frowned. "Before the ritual to bind the demon, a suitable statue had to be found. The statuette we used was fashioned from a lump of gold imported from across the sea. The army was doing its best just to survive by the time Leohareus, the Arean high priest, began the ritual. The demon sensed it and abandoned the army to attack the temple. It blasted the building with fire. It was awful." Alexandros's bronze eyes grew distant, his pupils narrowing as he stared at the lamp flame. "The walls shook and great stones fell from the ceiling, some of them glowing with heat."

"You were there," Rheia whispered. "Inside."

He nodded, his gaze not shifting. "The statue of Areus toppled, landing across the altar. The priest was crushed beneath its weight. His disciple was barely more than a lad. Hieron, his name was, or Hiero. I don't recall exactly." A frown marred Alexandros's forehead for a moment and then he shrugged. His hair gleamed in the lamplight, shifting with the movement of his shoulders. "With his dying breath, Leohareus entreated the boy to finish the ritual. But the gold statue had been crushed, and the acolyte—although sure of his faith—was untried."

Rheia could imagine it: the choking smoke, its underside lit orange by encroaching flame. The broken priest, reaching out from beneath the statue of the god he adored to take his acolyte's hand, laying a terrible burden on him. Alexandros, attempting to save the priest even as Kore, follower of Death himself, shook her head, drew him back, told him it was impossible...

The image was so strong she startled and would have dropped her cup if Dora hadn't reached out and plucked it from her suddenly nerveless fingers. "Kore was there with you, wasn't she?" Rheia said, her voice little more than a gasp. Alexandros nodded. When it met hers, his gaze was full of longing, grief and a terrible guilt.

But he didn't speak, stilled by Dora's quelling stare. The caregiver handed Rheia a piece of bread. "Eat before you pass out, girl." *Again.* The word hung unspoken in the air, and, chastised, Rheia took a bite. The bread was soft and faintly salty, rousing her appetite. She ate it quickly, her hands growing steadier with every bite.

When she started on the fish, the peppery, nutty flavour of the cumin a delicious counterpoint to the tart cheese, Dora nodded her permission at Alexandros to continue. He blurted out the question that had been burning in his eyes. "Do you remember it?"

"I'm not sure," Rheia said slowly. "Maybe. I saw you, using the hem of your *chiton* to try and staunch the flow of blood. And m—Kore pulling you away so Hieron could hear his master's last words. It was Hieron, not Hiero." Alexandros had called the acolyte a boy, but in her mind

the acolyte looked about sixteen. Rheia's age. Did Alexandros think she too was no more than a child? He looked only a few years older than her, and she was old enough to wed. Outrage stiffened her spine. *Now is not the time, Rheia,* she told herself. Squeezing her eyes shut to block out the distractions, she probed the image in her mind. "I think ... did the priest give something to Hieron?"

"Yes," Alexandros breathed, and when Rheia looked back at him his expression was suffused with a pleasure that warmed her all over. "Yes, he did. It was his ring. The seal of the Arean high priest. Made of gold and set with an orange intaglio carved from carnelian. Shaped like Areus himself."

"That's what Eidoneus was referring to." Relief coursed through Rheia; a smile lit her face. Opposite her, Alexandros looked stunned, while Dora's lips pressed together. "He wants us to find that stone. What happened to it?"

"I don't know." Alexandros's soft words deflated her like a punctured wineskin. "Hieron finished the ritual. He bound the demon into the carnelian. We didn't have anything else to hand, and there was no time left. The demon was at our door, tearing its way in." He looked down at his hands. "I sometimes wonder whether binding the monster into something bearing the image of Areus, something so central to his worship, was what created that first crack. Maybe that was what let it insinuate itself into the temple."

Dora leaned forward, her braid swinging, and patted Alexandros's knee, which was bare below the short edge of his *chiton.* "You couldn't have known."

Jealousy swelled in Rheia's chest, and she dragged her gaze down to her plate, the geometric pattern half-concealed by the cooling fish. She had just met Alexandros. Dora had known him her entire life. Of course they were close. Friends, even. And so what if Dora loved him, as Parthenia claimed? Rheia had no claim on the man, even though she felt like she might have, once. And even though her thoughts ran wild with wanting to do so again.

Frowning, she forced her mind away from her confused emotions and considered Alexandros's words. "Do you think using the carnelian might also be why the ritual went so wrong?"

"Isn't that what he just said?" Dora said, her tone even despite the gentle chastisement in her words.

Rheia shook her head. "No, I don't mean what happened to the temple afterwards. I mean the binding, and Alexandros being trapped in it. I know Areus is a god who doesn't shy from killing, but my father always said he preferred his sacrifices to be the enemies of his worshippers. Blood spilled on the battlefield, not babies in a time of peace. Draconaidas said Areus gave his followers the binding ritual, and if that part of his story is true, then it doesn't make sense."

"Your father is a wise man," Alexandros said with a small smile. "And you're right, it wasn't something Areus would demand. But the carnelian wasn't what caused that change. Binding the demon required an act of pure will. Leohareus was the strongest man I'd ever met. His spirit was like rock, unbreakable. His acolyte wasn't as strong. Although he was able to bind the demon, it was able to ... add some conditions. If he hadn't agreed, *we* hadn't agreed, the binding would have failed, because Hieron couldn't have forced the matter."

Her mind reeling, Rheia blew out her breath. "So the

annual sacrifices, your enslavement—it was all because of an accident? No one would have needed to die if the statue of Areus hadn't fallen?"

"No one else." Alexandros's voice was hoarse as he said the words. His shoulders slumped and his gaze drifted downwards, guilt seeming to settle over him like a second skin.

"You mean other than Kore," Rheia said, speaking before she considered the wisdom of her words. Dora's eyes narrowed, her jaw hardening, but Rheia refused to be cowed by the woman's appalled stare. Rheia of all people should be able to ask questions about what had happened to Kore that day—and she didn't think Alexandros would give into his despair as he had the first time he'd met her. He had hope now.

Alexandros swallowed, his nostrils flaring as he inhaled. "Yes." The word was barely a whisper. Then he looked up at her, his eyes pleading. "Kore wasn't meant to be the sacrifice. Leohareus didn't discuss it with us beforehand, but I think he intended to offer himself at the end of the ritual. Only he died too soon. The rite was incomplete. And Hieron lacked the courage."

I do not fear an eternity in Eidoneus's halls.

Rheia shivered, the fine hair on her arms and at the back of her neck standing on end. The silent words resonated—she'd never heard them before, and yet she knew she had said them. Once, a long time ago. "He also lacked the courage to do the deed." Her words slowed, her eyes distant with the shadow of memory. "To kill her. And you were the only other person there."

"Yes," Alexandros said again, and that word was too small to contain all the self-loathing he imbued it with.

Rheia's heart ached. An apology for causing him pain sprang to her lips, but she hesitated. That wasn't what he needed to hear. Words bubbled up in her mind, from that same deep part of herself from which the memories sprung. "Kore forgives you," she said, and her voice seemed somehow deeper, more mature. "You did as she insisted, and she loved you for it even as it pained her to leave you." Alexandros's hand flew to his mouth, unable to muffle the sob that slipped between his fingers. His eyes glistened like amber, bright with tears, as he stared at her. "*I* forgive you," Rheia added, and Alexandros blinked, a tear escaping to flow down his cheek. He wiped it away, embarrassed, and Dora handed him a square of linen. He dabbed his eyes.

The sensation of being the mouthpiece for another fled, leaving Rheia hollow. Wanting to keep busy, she finished her fish. It was almost cold—although not as cold as Dora's disapproving presence—and she ate mechanically, washing it down with the rest of her wine.

Finally, Alexandros spoke, sounding sheepish. "Forgive me?"

Feeling as though she were the one who needed forgiveness, she glanced up from her cup. His eyes were dry, his skin reddened. "For what?"

"I don't usually ... blubber."

Rheia couldn't help snorting, and his eyebrows shot up. "That wasn't blubbering," she said, her tongue loosened by the wine, even watered as it was, "and I don't judge anyone, man or woman, for crying when something bad happens. The notion men shouldn't cry is just foolish bravado. My father is one of the strongest men I know, and he isn't ashamed to cry." She raised a hand to run

it through her hair before remembering Yalee's braids and brushing her fingertips against them instead.

"You misunderstand me. I am not ashamed. My tears weren't from sadness," he said, a smile quirking his lips. "They were from relief. I've longed to hear Kore say that for almost one hundred and twelve years."

"Oh. Um." She curled her hands in the fabric of her *chiton*, feeling foolish. But she refused to show it, straightening her spine and gathering her dignity around herself like a *himation*. "You're welcome?"

He chuckled. The sound was warm, sliding through her body to pool like undiluted wine in her belly, sweet and heady.

Dora began stacking the empty plates into a pile, breaking Rheia's reverie. "So Eidoneus has told you to find the stone the demon is bound into," the woman said. "For what purpose? Can we destroy it?"

Alexandros paled. "No! That would free him in an instant."

"If we're going to free him, we might as well just wait until the day of the sacrifice and then not kill anyone." Rheia tipped her head to the side with a rueful smile. "It'd be much less effort."

Alexandros laughed, but Dora clattered the plates together so roughly Rheia worried they might shatter. "So what *do* we do with it then?"

"Reattempt the ritual with a new binding object, perhaps?" Alexandros suggested, his tone soothing. He refilled the cups of wine before Dora could do it. "If the demon lost access to the temple of Areus, it would deny him of much of his power."

"And then we could give the new statue to my father

and he could take it out to sea and throw it overboard," Rheia said fiercely, imagining a dull, nondescript rock sinking into the bottomless depths, beyond sunlight, where no mortal would ever find it.

"That's not a bad idea," Dora said, putting the stacked plates on the sideboard. Her movements were more graceful now, her ire seemingly appeased by them taking her question seriously. "Although if you're going to sink him to the bottom of the ocean, you could do that with the intaglio he is already bound into."

"That might not sever him from his powerbase here." Alexandros leaned back on his stool, its leather creaking. "I don't know. But I don't know the ritual either. I saw it done, but I can't recall the details..."

"Let's worry about that after we find the stone," Rheia said. Her fingers twitched with the urge to smooth the worried frown from Alexandros's brow. "It will probably be at the temple. And if the details of the ritual still exist, they would be there, too. Draconaidas will have both somewhere safe. They're the source of his influence on the island."

"What if they are not?" Dora murmured.

"Then I will pray to Eidoneus and hope he favours me with the secret of the ritual just as Areus favoured Leohareus long ago." Rheia kept her voice confident, ignoring the butterfly fluttering in her belly. Eidoneus had told her to find the seal ring. If she could do that, prove she was his faithful servant, he would smile on her.

Surely he would?

"So," Alexandros said. His eyes twinkled in the lamp-light and his face lit with mischief. "Are you up for a night-time expedition?"

CHAPTER TWENTY-TWO

A summer storm boomed overhead. Rheia paced around the *gynaikon's* courtyard, sticking to the walkway under the shelter of the roof as rain teemed down, huge droplets of water striking the hard earth and bouncing, splashing into her path and spraying her feet. Icy rivulets worked between her sandals' straps to dampen her skin. Still, nervous energy filled her, drove her to keep moving.

She had been keen to set out for the temple of Areus the night before, right after Alexandros had suggested it. But Dora had argued against it—at first against the entire idea, and then, when she saw he wouldn't be swayed, against an immediate voyage. "Draconaidas lives at the temple," she had said, wrapping her good hand around her other one in a wringing motion. "He will be there; he will catch you. But tomorrow night he is dining with the king, and the temple will be almost empty. Wait a day! Plan your strategy."

And, although he'd seemed reluctant, Alexandros had listened.

Dora had returned Rheia to the *gynaikon*, leaving the girl feeling like a child sent to her room, before meeting Alexandros to discuss the details. Fuming and disappointed in turns, Rheia had lain awake half the night.

It was now mid-afternoon, and she hadn't seen Dora all day. Erika and Polymede tended to the sacrifices; when Rheia asked where the older woman was, they gave vague answers. If Rheia heard "she's busy" one more time, she might explode like the sky overhead.

"Do you want to talk about it?" Parthenia's voice was quiet, barely audible over the rush of rain to her left, as she fell into step beside Rheia.

"I'm just frustrated." Rheia's voice grew louder with each word. "We've got six days left, and I have all this energy right now and I want to *do* something with it." She waved her arm, indicating the drenched courtyard. "Not pace like a wild animal in a pen, waiting for slaughter!" Lightning flashed, turning the date-plum into a looming silhouette. The thunder roared. Startled, Parthenia stopped, her hand to her throat and her eyes wide.

"Can we go inside? Please?" she begged when the thunder had faded to a low growl, like that of a starving cur. "Diktaios Skyfather is angry, and I don't want to be near that tree in case it falls."

The plaintive note in her voice swayed Rheia where shouting wouldn't have. She nodded, leading the other sacrifice into her room. Parthenia sat on the fur rug in the middle of the floor, but Rheia leaned against the cool stone doorframe, watching the rain. The fountain was still running, its spray almost hidden amidst the downpour. How close was it to overflowing? A gust of damp wind sprayed her with droplets, but she welcomed their

chill after weeks of stifling heat.

"What's going on?" Parthenia asked.

Rheia turned her head to study the other girl. "What makes you think something is going on?"

"I'm not stupid." Parthenia raised her eyebrows. "You were gone for all of yesterday afternoon and evening, and now you're as cranky as my grandmother after she ate too much cheese."

The mental image forced a reluctant laugh from Rheia, who let the curtain drop to block out the worst of the storm's noise. Her *chiton's* hem was wet, she realised with a grimace as she walked over to the rug. She spread it around her when she sat so it didn't stick to her calves.

"So what is it?" Parthenia prompted. The storm had cast a shadow over Rheia's room, as though it were twilight outside instead of mid-afternoon; the oil lamps hadn't yet been lit, and Parthenia's face was a lighter brown oval against the dark sea of her hair. The little altar to Eidoneus was a smudge of paler grey against one wall.

"We're trying to find a way to stop the ritual." The words came out as a sigh.

Parthenia smoothed the thick fur of the rug with one hand. "Not to sound callous, and please don't think I object, but you've been trying to do that since you got here."

"It's different now. Eidoneus sent me a vision, said we needed to find the stone the demon is bound into. Alexandros and Dora are planning something, and I'm worried they're going to act without me. But they can't. It was *my* vision!" Rheia wondered if she sounded as pathetic as she felt just then.

If she did, Parthenia didn't comment. Instead, she

frowned. "Who is Alexandros?"

"He's the Beast. Alexandros is his real name." It took several heartbeats for Parthenia's stunned silence to penetrate the welter of Rheia's thoughts. When it did, she tried to smile, belatedly remembering her earlier decision not to tell Parthenia about Alexandros. She hadn't wanted to face the incredulity that now turned the other girl's face pale. "He's not what you think," Rheia added lamely.

"You *like* him!" Parthenia's mouth fell open. Rheia recalled kissing Alexandros and a blush swept up her cheeks like flame up a grass-covered hill. "How can you like him?" Parthenia demanded. "He's going to *kill* us!"

"It's ... complicated." Rheia found herself telling Parthenia Kore's story, how the original binding had gone wrong and what Alexandros's role in it had been. "He's just a man, and he's been forced by the demon to kill *thysies* all these years. He's as bound as it is." Lightning flashed outside, casting distorted, flower-shaped shadows across the room as the bright illumination pierced the holes in the window panel. Rheia blinked in their aftermath, counting to three under her breath before the thunder rolled once more. The storm was moving away over the mountain and out to sea. Finally.

When Parthenia was able to speak, her voice was neutral. "But if you're Kore, come back from the underworld, then he's killed you before. Right?"

"Yes. But he didn't want to." The words sounded lame, even to Rheia.

"Still, I don't know how you could like a man who has killed you. No matter what the circumstances." Parthenia's arm moved as she ran a hand through her hair. Long

strands tickled Rheia's outer arm. "And he's going to do it again."

"He's not. He said he won't." The words were hot, but then Rheia's shoulders slumped and she murmured, "Although if we can't find a way out of this, he's going to have to. And I think it might kill him, too."

"Good." Parthenia's voice was hard, although she softened it a moment later by reaching through the dimness to take Rheia's hand. "Not that he's going to kill you, or us, but that he feels bad about it. He *should* feel bad. And I don't care how charming or handsome he is. He has the blood of dozens of my people on his hands. Almost a hundred. If he died of shame after killing you, it wouldn't be too soon."

Rheia snatched her hand away and stood, trembling, her *chiton* clinging to her ankles like a demanding and very wet child. "How can you say that? He's a good man."

"You've known him for two days, Rheia!" Parthenia shouted back, leaping to her feet.

"Two days and a lifetime," Rheia whispered, her cheeks hot with tears of confusion, of denial. She didn't want to listen to Parthenia—her potential condemnation was why she hadn't wanted to talk to the *thysia* girl about Alexandros in the first place.

But there was a cold part of Rheia's own mind that wondered. *What if Parthenia is right?*

The memory of the kiss surfaced, a silent, heated counterargument all its own. She had never kissed a man before; although she'd been kissed by the acolyte of Areus, he'd initiated it and, in a nightsleep stupor, she hadn't responded. The connection she felt to Alexandros—and yes, the attraction—had moved her to do something she'd have never contemplated before meeting him. She'd never even kissed Galen. When she'd offered herself to the trader's son, it had been out of panicked desperation, not the overwhelming desire she'd felt for Alexandros.

And then there was Alexandros's reaction. After yesterday's uncharacteristic forwardness, he hadn't taken advantage of her. She'd been alone with him, dressed in a wet *chiton* that had embraced her like a lover, letting him see all of her curves. Any other man would have ravaged her then and there—even Galen had accepted her offer, although he'd been too afraid to do anything when she'd needed him to. But Alexandros hadn't touched her at all, except with his lips and his gentle, probing tongue.

Who knows what he would have done if Yalee hadn't returned? the voice in her mind suggested. She suppressed it ruthlessly.

Pulling herself from her confused thoughts, Rheia put her hands on her hips. "He's trying to help me find a way to stop the sacrifice. I should think you'd be grateful."

Parthenia hesitated, and Rheia heard her inhale a soft, slow breath. When the other girl spoke, her voice was calm again. "And I will be, if he's successful. But I won't ever like him. And I don't understand how you can, either."

Rheia bit her lip, her eyes searching the dim room even as her mind searched for an answer. "Sometimes I wonder how much of my attraction to him is coming from Kore," she admitted finally, her voice quiet. "I feel like … like I'm a riverbank and she's a stream, heavy with rain, washing through me. I'm still me, but she's all through me, in every part of my being."

"You're mud?" Parthenia gasped, stifling a giggle behind her hand. "That's awful."

"The comparison made more sense in my head," Rheia said, laughing. "And it's not that bad. I'm just struggling to figure out what is me and what is her. Or maybe there's no difference and it's all just me."

"It sounds very confusing. I suppose you should just be glad Kore wasn't a man," Parthenia said. Rheia's eyes widened, but before she could splutter a reply, Parthenia gave her an awkward hug. "I'm sorry for yelling at you. I obviously support you and Alexandros trying to save our lives, and if there's anything I can do to help please let me know."

The curtain covering the door was whisked aside. Dora strode in, holding an oil lamp in her good hand. The gentle illumination pierced Rheia's light-starved eyes. "Why are you two standing here in the dark?" the caregiver demanded, setting the lamp down on the jewellery chest beside the statuette. Then she turned, taking in their closeness, and her silver eyebrows rose high. "Did I interrupt something?"

"We're just talking about boys and hiding from the rain," Rheia said blandly as Parthenia stepped back, her eyes crinkled with amusement. "Can we help you with something?"

"I was looking for you," Dora said. Her gaze slid to the Carmean girl and then flicked back to Rheia's face. "I have something I want to discuss. In private."

"She knows."

Dora's face paled and she grabbed Rheia's arm tightly, drawing her to one side of the room. "What?"

Rheia yanked her arm free, not bothering to lower her voice. "I told her Alexandros and I are working on a plan to stop the sacrifices from going ahead. We didn't go into details, but that's because I don't have any." She narrowed her eyes at the caregiver. "Where have you been all day?" The thunder rolled in the distance, the storm getting in a growled last word.

"Don't change the subject, Rheia. She's Carmean. You two are in the same position at the moment, and I understand why that makes you feel she's your kin, but her people wish us ill."

"Only because we declared war on them and demand they make *thysies* of their children!"

"It's fine," Parthenia said, her quiet voice cutting across their heated conversation. She walked to the door, pausing in the open entryway. "I don't want to know anything else, in case it raises my hopes. But don't fret, Besadora. After all, who would I tell?" Her eyes fixed on Rheia's. "Whatever they get you into, I wish you luck, Mud Girl."

CHAPTER TWENTY-THREE

Rheia followed Dora along the gloomy walkway, past the leaf-strewn fountain and towards the *gynaikon's* double doors. The caregiver's pace was hurried, her sandals slapping the wet pavers. Rheia wore a plain, unbleached *chiton* in a sturdy fabric that was coarse beneath her fingertips after a week of wearing only the finest clothing. It hung stiffly to her ankles, while the *himation* she wore over the top was heavy and reeked of dried lavender. The rain had passed, leaving a clinging humidity in its wake, and she sweltered, hot and itchy beneath the layers.

Yalee waited on the other side of the door, in the statue-lined corridor. A carved timber *amphora* loomed behind her, its fat base narrowing to a graceful neck with handles curving from it like ears. Rheia wondered whether the *amphora* would be hollow or a solid block of timber, but Dora didn't pause to give her a chance to check. Yalee's face split into a broad grin as Dora swept past; the girl gave Rheia a little wave before falling in behind them, a skip in her step. The older girl gave her a quizzical look and Yalee's grin widened, her hazel eyes shining with excitement.

Dora led them to a small chamber decorated with a mural of a dolphin. If the rich smell of roasting meat was anything to judge by, they were near the kitchen, a part of the house Rheia hadn't been to before.

Her breath caught when she saw Alexandros waiting by the door. Instead of his usual black *chiton*, he wore a short, dun-coloured tunic beneath a worn bronze breast-plate. A skirt of dark leather draped to his knees, and his sandal straps encircled his calves in a most distracting fashion. A cloak hung down his back. The soldier's garb was as different to his usual sombre attire as it was to the priest's robes she remembered him in. And it showed off his athletic physique.

His eyes almost seemed to glow in the lamplight, gleaming the same colour as his armour. They twinkled with amusement. With a start, Rheia realised he was watching her staring at him. Cheeks burning with a blush, she turned away—and groaned when Dora picked up a thick shawl from a stack of neatly folded fabric on a carved table in the corner. She hadn't had to cover her hair in almost a week, and the idea of wearing such a heavy shawl made her cringe. "I'll melt in that."

"If your head is bare, you will draw attention, and you are well known in the city." Dora's tone was clipped, and Rheia wondered if the woman was still offended that Rheia had talked to Parthenia. Avoiding Rheia's gaze, the caregiver draped the material over Rheia's hair, pinning it in place with the ease of practice.

"Won't I stand out more, dressed for winter?" Rheia

winced as the caregiver tugged a stray lock into place.

"Some men prefer their women be fully covered, no matter the discomfort."

Dora stepped back to reveal that Yalee was also draping herself in layers of thick fabric. "She's coming with us?" Rheia said.

"Yes."

Disappointment knotted in her stomach. The girl was accompanying them to be Dora's eyes—if not her ears—and to chaperone Rheia.

Alexandros picked up a plain bronze sword in a leather scabbard. He belted it on slowly, with a little frown between his brows, and Rheia hoped he wouldn't have to use the weapon. Used to her father's ease with his sword, she recognised Alexandros's discomfort and lack of familiarity. His callouses were from carving wood, not from sword drills. He might use a sword as the Beast, but there was a world of difference between executing a helpless child and battling a capable foe.

With acid rising in the back of her throat at the thought, Rheia looked away and licked lips gone dry. Yalee's sharp gaze caught the motion and her excited smile slipped away.

"Yalee will stand out as much as I do," Rheia murmured, feeling as though she was stating the obvious. She didn't want to seem rude—she didn't care anymore about the caregivers' various afflictions—but the girl's split lip was plainly visible, and Oreareans weren't used to seeing deformities, regarding them as a sign of the gods' displeasure. Yalee would be instantly recognisable as one of the Broken Ones, the keepers of the Beast.

"You'll both be wearing face veils," Dora said. She

lifted a flimsy square of fabric. "If you keep your faces down, no one will see your features. No one other than a caregiver has seen Alexandros's face in decades, so he will be fine."

Alexandros gave Rheia an apologetic smile that grew indistinct as Dora fastened the thin veil over Rheia's face.

"Be thankful we're letting you go at all," Dora chided in a quiet voice. Rheia blinked. Was that resentment in her tone? Did she wish she were coming too? Rheia's gaze drifted to the fingerless stump of Dora's left hand, and she bit her lip. The caregiver was deft with that hand, using it to hold the fabric in place while she threaded pins through folds of cloth with her right one, but the condition was obvious and not easily concealed. Even Yalee's split lip was more easily masked. If Dora were a man she could wear a *cestus*, a battle glove, with stuffing in the fingers ... but there was no such thing as a glove for women.

Feeling a surge of pity for Dora, Rheia meekly submitted to her final ministrations, and they were soon ready. Alexandros led them out of the chamber and around a corner, not to the wide main entrance to the house but to a narrow, solid door. His eyes widened and his hands trembled faintly as he reached for the bar. Rheia felt her heart lift; his excitement was contagious. He'd been a prisoner in the house longer than any of them, even Dora—and she'd spent her entire life there.

Dora thrust a pair of empty baskets at Rheia and Yalee. "The temple is on the *agora,* correct?" Rheia nodded. "You are a husband, wife and younger sister, going to the market late in the day. There's a purse in your basket. Buy something, then make as though to head back. By then the sun will have set, and you can slip

into the temple."

Rheia's stomach gave a little flip but she nodded again, breathing slowly to calm her nerves. Still, her voice was tight when she spoke. "And we're sure Draconaidas won't be there?" The cloth in front of her face fluttered with her words, tickling her nose.

"As sure as we can be," Alexandros said, leaning the bar against the adjacent wall.

Dora turned away as though unable to watch them go, but her words reached them as they stepped through the door and onto a damp alley, all traces of anger and frustration replaced by concern. "Be safe."

Rheia tried to hide her jump as the door thudded shut behind them, followed by the muffled *thunk* of the bar being dropped into its brackets. She looked around, already cursing the veil over her face; it rendered the street indistinct, as though seen through a fine mist. Beside Rheia, Yalee craned her neck to peer up at the mountain. Its shape loomed, pale in the subdued light of the setting sun.

"We should hurry," Alexandros muttered, glancing up and down the street. "We're assuming the house's main gate is watched, but the more we linger here, the more chance a temple spy will spot us."

Rheia looped her basket over one arm and took Yalee's arm with the other. The girl stiffened for a moment, turning her face to Rheia, but then she relaxed, nodding. She understood.

Alexandros led them out of the alley, tense beneath his armour, his spine stiff and his chin drawn in towards his chest as if to avoid a blow. "Try to walk more naturally," Rheia whispered, stepping up beside him so he could hear her over the sound of their shoes' hard leather soles crunching on the wet street. "Relax your shoulders. Maybe hook a thumb through your belt." He glanced at her, his eyes widening with surprise. "Trust me," she added. He took a deep breath, the breastplate rising and falling with the motion, and then his stride shifted, lengthened. The nerves appeared to drop away, replaced by an easy confidence. Rheia could still see his excitement in the faint tremble in his knuckles around his sword belt, the sparkle in his eyes, but those wouldn't be noticed by a casual observer.

At the end of the alley, they turned right, onto the main thoroughfare that speared through the heart of Oreareus City, leading from the palace at the top of the foothills down to the *agora* and then to the harbour. The streets weren't as busy as they'd been the last time Rheia had walked them, on the day of the lottery, but nor were they deserted. Serving women and slaves hurried along, carrying baskets of food or clothing on their heads. Farther along, three young boys played an elaborate chasing game involving a small dog and a knot of worn rope. An old man sat on a stoop, watching them as he made the most of the fading light to polish a pair of greaves with an oily cloth.

When they rounded a bend, Alexandros paused, his mouth falling open and his eyes widening as though to drink in every detail of the view. On Rheia's other side, Yalee gasped, the fabric of her veil rippling with her indrawn breath. Rheia peered through her own veil, irritated and wanting to tear it free as she wondered what they were staring at. What was she missing?

The sun was low on the horizon, indistinct behind the

thin sheet of cloud the storm had left behind. Its light was gentler, less fierce than was usual for summer, and it softened the city. Oreareus was laid out before them, the main road a pale thread trailing down the slope, weaving between buildings. The squares and fountains were like beads strung on a necklace, while at this distance the statue of Areus in the *agora* was a mere toy soldier, something Aias would play with. Beyond the harbour, the ocean loomed, flat and grey as a writing slate.

The fingers of Alexandros's right hand moved at his side, almost as though he were wielding a tool, and the memory of all those carvings flashed across Rheia's mind. He was memorising the view.

Rheia switched her basket to her other hand, looping her elbow through it so she could still hold Yalee's arm. Then she hooked her other arm through Alexandros's, tugging gently while keeping her face down in an effort to appear demure. "We should keep walking," she said in a whisper. "Before we attract attention. Or get run over by a cart."

He glanced at her, his lips curving into a smile. "Of course, Wife," he said gruffly, his voice carrying. Rheia's heart flipped in her chest. Alexandros started down the hill at a measured pace easy enough for Yalee to match. His voice dropped to a murmur. "I'm sorry. It's been so long since I've caught more than a glimpse of the ocean. I've missed it."

Rheia's fingertips tingled at the contact with the soft skin of Alexandros's inner arm. "Is that why your sculptures are of *things*?" she asked absently, and then realised how it sounded. "I mean, they aren't of athletes or gods or sacred animals," she added hastily. "The usual things sculptures are of."

He nodded, looking down at the pavers before them. Weeds sprouted between the stones, withered from the heat. Today's drenching might encourage them to grow again. "I taught myself to sculpt wood after ... well. After. One of the caregivers suggested it, as a diversion to keep me sane. But I didn't exactly get out to see athletes or animals of any kind, sacred or otherwise. So I carved what I could see and hold. It sort of got to be a habit."

"How long did it take you to get that good?" she wondered aloud.

"Maybe fifteen years. My earlier works were terrible. Formless blobs, misshapen fruit that looked diseased. I threw them in the fire." His smile was self-deprecating as he glanced at her and then back to the street, his bronze eyes tracking people as they moved past.

Rheia thought of the lifelike carving of Kore, the centrepiece of Alexandros's shrine. It was the only piece she'd seen of his that was of a person, and it was a masterwork, so he'd done it at least a decade and a half after Kore had died. From memory. Her head spun.

They walked in silence for a time. Rheia was jarred from her thoughts when she felt Alexandros's other hand close over the fingers she still had curled around his bicep, as gently as if he were cupping a butterfly in his palm. When she looked up, he was facing away from her, taking in the view again—but she was sure he was aware of her every movement. "I have missed this," he breathed.

"Walking under the sky?"

"Walking under the sky with you."

Rheia's heart didn't just flip in her chest then—it leapt like a startled hare. A blush ran across her cheeks, and

she was glad for the shield of a veil even as the embarrassment made her aware of how warm she was. The evening,
while not as hot as usual, was muggy; the pavers beneath
her feet were already dry in places. Not even a hint of a
breeze stirred the leaves of the trees, let alone making
it through her heavy winter fabrics.

Still, she was walking under the sky with Alexandros.
She would enjoy it while she could.

CHAPTER TWENTY-FOUR

The sun was touching the horizon by the time they reached the *agora*, painting the marketplace in red-gold hues and long shadows. A few merchants were already rolling their products up in oiled cloths or loading them into baskets, while many others, not wanting to carry the last of the day's stock home, hawked their wares in increasingly strident tones. After the quiet of the house's *gynaikon*, the noisy chaos took Rheia's breath away, and Yalee's trembling arm against Rheia's conveyed the girl's anxiety. Rheia squeezed her elbow and smiled, glimpsing a grateful flash of teeth behind Yalee's veil as the girl returned the expression.

Turning, Rheia's gaze lighted on Phidias's stall. Galen's father had his head bent as he talked with a dark-skinned older woman who gestured to a wooden crate containing what Rheia knew would be an exotic, imported fruit. Phidias didn't sell local produce.

Her heart sank into her sandals when she saw Galen standing on the other side of his father. He was partially

obscured by the older man's bulk, but she could see how his wrist glittered with several pieces of pretty silver jewellery, chains with beads shaped like beetles and sinuous animals with pricked ears and winding tails. A girl, the woman's daughter if her dark skin and laughing grey eyes were anything to go by, leaned over the treasures—although her gaze was locked on Galen's.

He moved on fast. Rheia glared as Galen placed a daring hand on the back of the smiling girl's wrist. The idea he might have been flirting with other girls before the lottery, when he was also flirting with her, made her throat tighten and her eyes burn. *I can't believe I offered myself to him.*

Alexandros, looking from Rheia's veiled face to the stall, regarded the imported wares. "Would you like to buy some honeyed dates?"

"No." Rheia swallowed hard to clear the hoarseness from her voice. "I can't stomach them. Shall we get salted nuts instead? Parthenia likes those."

"As you wish."

The three walked arm in arm through the marketplace, buying a wrapped packet of spices and a jar of dried figs for Yalee to put in her basket, as well as the nuts and a small pottery jar of quince jam for Rheia's. They kept their eye on the temple of Areus, looking for movement in or out, but the pillared building loomed silent at the edge of the *agora*, seeming to gather the remaining light around itself. The carvings around the edge of the roof seemed deeper, their images of war real enough that Rheia imagined the trireme would burst forth from the stone and sail across the *agora* in search of far-off seas. Although her memories of the temple from the day of the lottery were hazy and confused, recalling the look on Draconaidas's face as the viper had confronted her made her tongue stick to the roof of her mouth with fear.

It's fine. He will be at the palace by now. She swallowed. *Please, Eidoneus, let it be true.*

When their circuit of the *agora* brought them back around to Phidias's stall, Alexandros drew Rheia and Yalee into the alley that ran down the pillared side of the temple. With a pang, Rheia realised it was the same one she'd suggested she and Galen slip away into when she'd propositioned him. She shoved the thought from her mind, studying the side of Alexandros's face as he peered back towards the market for signs that their departure had been noticed, his strong jaw clenched and his eyes narrowed.

When he turned and saw her intent gaze, a grin lit up his face. But all he said was, "I don't think anyone saw us. Come on."

Rheia and Yalee followed Alexandros down the alley. Two-thirds of the way along the building's length, they climbed the stairs to settle between two of the thick pillars that sprouted from the top of the shallow stone stairs to support the overhanging roof. "We'll be harder to see here," Alexandros said in a quiet voice. "They'd have to walk right by to spot us."

Rheia nodded, sitting against the fluted pillar. As she straightened her skirts, she wiped her suddenly nervous palms dry against the coarse fabric.

Someone had left a small offering against the stone exterior of the building, and the aroma of wilted flowers and cheap wine tickled Rheia's nose. The pillar was bumpy against her spine, even through all the layers of her

clothes, and she took a deep breath, trying to suppress her racing heart.

"I'm right here," Alexandros said softly. He sat beside her, close but not quite touching. The warmth from his body spanned the gap, gentle as a caress. "You don't have to worry."

"I'm fine," she said. Yalee prised the seal from the jar of nuts and slid her hand under her veil to pop one in her mouth. The crunching made Rheia jump, her pulse hammering. "I'll be fine," she said, trying to convince herself. Alexandros said nothing, but his lips pursed. "Last time I was here, the temple was guarded by four men," she murmured, thinking of the orange-clad guards with their bulging muscles. "There were also three acolytes, as well as Draconaidas himself."

"Most of the guards will be with the high priest at the palace," Alexandros said. "As should the senior acolytes. If we are fortunate, all that will remain within are one or two junior priests, left to tend the god overnight. It is an uncomfortable job and not one that senior priests volunteer for." He smiled, his gaze distant with memory.

"We will have to be quiet. The priesthood owns the guest house beyond the temple, and the priests live there. Those that aren't at the palace will only be a shout away, as will the city guard."

Alexandros nodded. "We will be."

Eidoneus, watch over us and stay your hand this night.

The light leaked from the sky, dropping the alley into a gloom so deep that, through her veil, Rheia could see almost nothing. When Yalee made an irritated sound and folded the flimsy fabric up out of the way over the thicker veil covering her hair, Rheia was glad to copy her. The night air was cool by comparison, drying the nervous perspiration on her brow.

"We should go," Alexandros murmured, taking the half-empty jar of nuts from Yalee and handing them to Rheia to tuck into her basket. "Let's leave these here. We can come back for them afterwards."

Adrenaline spiked through Rheia and her hands trembled as she stood. Yalee's expression settled into determined lines as the two girls followed Alexandros's shadow towards the entrance. His back was straight, his steps so careful his cloak barely shifted as he walked between the plump inside edges of the pillars and the wall—but Rheia couldn't help noticing he kept one hand on the hilt of his sword.

At the corner of the long wall, Alexandros raised a hand, and Rheia and Yalee stopped, their skirts swishing around their ankles. He peered around the edge of the wall, which protruded from the main body of the temple to form a screen on one side of the porch. Rheia's gaze flicked to the huge stone foot of the statue standing sentinel beyond the outer pillars. Areus faced out to sea, his back to the temple, and she found herself praying silently that, if the demon were indeed able to perceive the world through the god's eyes, it was also focused outward, on the lands it wished to subjugate.

Alexandros eased around the wall on almost-silent feet. With her heart in her throat, Rheia followed.

The porch at the front of the temple was framed on the side facing the *agora* by two pillars, more slender than the ones running around the outer wall, and on the other sides by walls—the screening one they had just slipped around, its opposite number on the other side,

and the wall inset with a pair of doors that led into the temple's *cella*, the main room. On either side of the doors, oil lamps nestled in sconces, their flames steady and casting yellow light.

The doors were closed, and Rheia's breath escaped in a sigh. If they were barred from the inside, then this trip was for nothing. The temple had no windows or other means of entry. Alexandros placed his hands on the heavy timber. The muscles in his upper arms flexed as he pushed.

With a scrape of timber on stone that had Rheia glancing back at the empty *agora*, one of the doors swung inwards. Alexandros opened it just enough for the three of them to slip through.

"Quickly." Alexandros entered the temple. Feeling exposed, Rheia followed close on his heels, pulling Yalee behind her.

The smell of sandalwood incense, woodsy and sweet, struck her, evoking the memory of her trial, of being kissed by a snake and then stripped naked to be anointed. A shudder ran through her. She searched along the walls for slithering shadows.

The temple was much the same as it had been when she was there almost a week before. The fat oil lamps were all lit, and the statue at the far end of the *cella* looked just as angry as she remembered, its pendant of Arean fire lending a dusky orange glow to the pale stone. The malachite snake twisted around the god's free arm, its arrow-shaped head glaring at her where she hesitated near the door. It reminded her of something.

"Last time I was here, there was a viper that dwelled beneath the statue," she whispered, her voice echoing faintly back to her. "Be careful."

Alexandros grimaced, but Yalee frowned a question at her. Rheia pointed to the stone snake and then to the statue's feet, weaving her arm in mimicry of the viper's sinuous movement. "Snake," she mouthed. The girl's eyes widened and she nodded her understanding.

There were fewer offerings along the walls than there had been on the day of the lottery. The city's preventative gift-giving frenzy had tapered off, the gifts becoming less generous, more indicative of what most people could afford: sprigs of herbs rather than expensive perfumes; a folded *chiton* rather than an entire roll of cloth. She wrinkled her nose, wondering if lining his coffers had been one of the motivations behind Draconaidas's decision to hold a lottery. The thought made her feel cheap.

Alexandros and Yalee spread out and began to walk down the room, giving each offering at the foot of the long wall a cursory inspection. Rheia hurried after them, not wanting to be alone by the door in case Draconaidas returned.

They met in front of the towering Areus. Alexandros raised a mocking eyebrow when he saw how well-endowed the sculptor had made the statue's nethers, and a surge of almost-hysterical amusement rippled through Rheia. She covered her mouth to stop the laugh bursting forth and giving their presence away to any acolytes who might be in the room beyond: the *adyton*, the most-holy room where only the priests of the god could go.

Yalee stepped towards the statue, her gaze fixed on the ground as she slipped into the narrow space behind its leg. Rheia moved closer, holding her breath as she waited for a hiss, a scream of pain—but the only sound was the

faint rustle of fabric as Yalee ran her fingers around the back of the statue's legs. Looking for a catch? A hidden compartment? Equally intent, Alexandros examined the front of the statue. His narrowed eyes fixed on the snake's face, the orange chips of its eyes. Rheia's heart thumped when she realised what she was seeing. Could this be it? Was the intaglio hidden in plain sight?

"Lift me?" she whispered, moving to his side. He nodded and bent his knees, wrapping strong arms around her calves. His muscles bulged as he stood, tense with effort, but he didn't make a sound. Rheia stiffened her spine, trying not to sway as he raised her into the air.

Holding Areus's cold, smooth elbow to steady herself, Rheia examined the snake's face, which was now level with her eyes. It was the same size as her two hands laid flat, side by side. Scales textured its skin, its closed mouth. She felt a surge of disappointment. The eyes were uneven balls of glass, the surface of each polished so she could see the clouds within: some impurity in the making process gave the illusion of a sunset sky trapped in a sphere so small she could cup both eyes in one hand. "These are beads." Her voice was flat with disappointment.

"Are you sure?" Alexandros looked up at her, and she nodded, biting her lip. Grimacing, he began to lower her back to the floor.

Suddenly, Rheia felt the coarse fabric of her skirts slip, scraping the skin of her legs. She gasped as she dropped several inches. One outflung hand snatched at the statue, attempting to arrest her fall, meeting nothing but air. Alexandros tightened his grip, grunting as her balance shifted. She lurched forward, and something smacked into her forehead. Stars bloomed inside her skull, gone between one blink and the next to leave pain in their wake. She stared at the thing that had struck her: the carved tail of the snake, sharp as a spear tip.

If she'd been a little higher, she'd have lost an eye.

Muttering curses, Alexandros steadied himself, lowering Rheia. She almost wept with relief as her sandals touched the stone floor. "Are you hurt?" Alexandros demanded, brushing her forehead with the tip of a finger. His touch was gentle despite the tight self-recrimination in his gaze.

"Ow," she said, her breath hissing between her teeth.

"Thank Appelon you're not bleeding. I expect you'll have a bruise there tomorrow." His eyebrows drew together, pinched with shame. "I'm sorry. I don't know what happened."

Rheia opened her mouth to reply, but the sound of a heavy footstep to her right choked the words in her throat.

"What in Areus's name is going on here?" a voice demanded.

CHAPTER TWENTY-FIVE

Rheia spun, her hand flying to her forehead as the sudden movement sent a spike of pain through her skull.

An acolyte dressed in rumpled carmine robes stood at the back wall of the *cella*, in the open-doored entryway to the *adyton*. Rheia recognised the golden hair, the slender features. She remembered his cool mouth on hers, and licked lips gone dry.

"You!" the acolyte said.

Beside Rheia, Alexandros stiffened. "Yes," she said quickly, before he could speak and reveal who he was. She doubted the acolyte had recognised him. If she was wrong, they'd know soon enough. "This is the priest who anointed me after the lottery," she added to Alexandros, not taking her eyes off the acolyte. "He was kind to me."

The acolyte stepped into the twin glow of the lamps and the statue's Arean fire. He clutched something long and slender that ended in a flared muzzle. A fire-thrower. The smaller piece of Arean fire that powered the weapon pulsed within a cloudy glass tube suspended under the bronze barrel.

"I didn't think to see you again until the day of the feast," the acolyte said. Despite the casual words, his voice was tight with nerves, and the hands holding the weapon trembled. Fear settled in an icy lump in Rheia's stomach. Her father had always warned her and her brother not to touch his fire-thrower, cautioning them that the triggering mechanism was as unpredictable as the sea in a storm. The acolyte probably wouldn't mean to shoot her ... but he might do it anyway.

"Please put the weapon down," she said, slowly raising her hands to show him they were empty. "We're looking for something. Maybe you can help."

The acolyte's wide eyes flickered from her to Alexandros, who was dressed like a solder, with one hand curled into a fist and the other again resting on the hilt of his sword. The fire-thrower's wide muzzle shifted to target him. Panic wound tight coils around Rheia's lungs. "You've escaped the House of the Beast and come here to steal from the temple?" the acolyte asked.

"No!" she said, although there was some truth to his words. "We aren't here for gold or other temple treasures. We've uncovered a plot by the demon. Please, just listen to us." As she spoke she eased forward a step, and then sideways, so she partially blocked Alexandros. If the weapon triggered, they would both be hosed with a spray of flame. But the acolyte had a reason to keep her alive, whereas he didn't know Alexandros was the Beast.

Alexandros stiffened, placing a hand on her shoulder. "Move behind me."

She ignored him. "Please," she said again. When the acolyte shook his head, she took a slow breath. "What is

your name? Forgive me, but I didn't think to ask last time."

"Timotheus," he said, his posture easing slightly.

Alexandros's fingers squeezed her shoulders, and suddenly he thrust her towards the floor, throwing himself down on top of her. Her breath *wooshed* out of her at the press of his bronze breastplate into her back. The sound of pattering feet was eclipsed by the roar of the fire-thrower vomiting forth its deadly load. Light flashed and the air above Rheia's head warmed so that the exposed cheek on one side grew hot. Alexandros hissed. The sound tickled her ear.

Someone grunted with pain, and the fire-thrower fell silent. "Get off me!" Rheia demanded, thrashing. Alexandros pushed himself up in a swift motion and darted towards where Timotheus had been.

Groaning, Rheia sat up and stared, her mouth falling open in consternation.

Yalee sat atop the acolyte, one hand around the barrel of the fire-thrower as she sought to wrest it from him. He gathered himself to shove her away, but Alexandros was there, yanking the weapon free and throwing it across the room. It smacked into the far wall with a metallic clang and the sound of cracking glass, followed by the equally metallic slither of a sword being drawn.

Timotheus froze when the blade appeared at his throat. With a satisfied nod, Yalee stood and took a step back, running her hands down the front of her skirts to straighten them. The shawl covering the girl's hair was singed, Rheia saw; it must have been caught on the edge of the torrent of holy fire.

No, not holy fire. Not Arean fire. It was *demon* fire. She tasted acid at the back of her throat.

"You nearly burned the lady," Alexandros said, his voice hard and his temples throbbing with anger.

"It was an accident," the acolyte said, his face pale.

Gritting her teeth, Rheia stood, glancing back over her shoulder. The wall behind her was black with soot. The cracked bottom of an oil lamp burned merrily, dripping oil into flaming puddles on the bare stone beneath, and the air stank of singed olives. On the opposite wall, the fire-thrower's glass bulb was shivered with cracks that glowed brighter than the rest of the glass, distorting the light within. But it wasn't leaking, thank Eidoneus.

"I ought to skewer you." Alexandros's voice was a snarl.

"Don't," Rheia said, moving carefully so Alexandros wouldn't realise how sore she was. She didn't want him to take it out on the acolyte. "He isn't our enemy."

"How do you know? He's of the temple. He must know what the demon has done."

"I'm not so sure," Rheia disagreed, noting the way the acolyte's eyes widened and a frown marred his forehead. "Draconaidas may keep that information to himself. Otherwise there would be rumours. People like to gossip." That last sentence was something she'd heard Charis say many times, with a shake of her head, and the memory made her smile for a moment. Then she recalled that her grandmother might be dead by now, and her heart burned with a grief far worse than her bruises and scrapes. "Let him up," she said flatly.

"Rheia..."

"Let him up!"

Alexandros took a step back, indicating with a jerk of his head that Timotheus should stand. Trembling, the acolyte clambered to his feet. "What do you want?" he

said, his gaze fixed on the bared blade of the sword. It gleamed a golden brown, catching the light. "And what do you mean, 'what the demon has done'? It is as bound as it has ever been."

"Yes," Rheia said, "but that hasn't stopped it from infiltrating the temple and subverting your master."

"What?" Timotheus tore his gaze away from the sword to look at Rheia. "No. It can't be."

"It is. Take us to where the temple's most holy items are stored. We are looking for proof, and the demon's undoing."

"I ... I can't."

"Does Draconaidas not keep holy items in the *adyton*?" Alexandros's anger had burned away to leave hard determination in its wake—cooler, but just as deadly.

"He does, but I'm not permitted to—"

"Show us."

Timotheus drooped, turning to lead them past the statue and into the *adyton*.

Rheia hadn't been in the Arean temple's most holy room before; the closest she had come to an *adyton* was in her dream of Kore. That had been a simple chamber, with a small altar, a shelf for herbs, and the statuette of Eidoneus that now sat in her room in the House of the Beast. The Arean temple's *adyton* was grand by comparison, fully half the length of the outer *cella*. Rich tapestries in scarlet and orange blanketed stone walls; black, woven rugs covered the floors to stop the chill. The colours resembled what the inside of a fire must look like: flames around and coals below. The lighting heightened the resemblance as, instead of smoking oil lamps, the room was lit with nearly transparent balls of fine glass, each containing a piece of demon fire. A smaller statue of Areus sat on an ornate altar carved from a red-veined white stone. The altar's sides depicted images of war, wreathed in carved flame as though the world were ablaze.

Rheia examined the statue of Areus. The snake sat higher on the god's shoulder than it did on the larger statue outside, so its wedge-shaped head was level with the top of the helmet's horns. Above the god's face. If she'd had any doubt Typhein controlled the temple of Areus, his *adyton's* reverence of fire and minimisation of the god himself would have extinguished it in a moment.

Alexandros noticed it, too. "And you deny that the demon holds sway," he said, his eyes on the malachite snake. "How do you explain that symbology?"

"I..." Timotheus stared at the statue as if seeing it for the first time. Then he shook his head. "No. The snake is an extension of Areus himself, his animal to control. The fact it is higher is a sculptor's whimsy."

"A sculptor's whimsy that your high priest has elevated to Areus's *adyton*, his most sacred place?" Rheia said, pity softening her words.

"If you looked at records from before the demon was bound, you'd find your god was never associated with snakes or fire before that event." Alexandros gestured to a corner beside the altar. "Stand there."

As Timotheus moved to obey and Yalee began to search the room with quick efficiency, Rheia approached the altar. She wanted to turn the statue away, so the snake's eyes could no longer regard her, but instead she dropped to her knees to study the front of the altar. She'd noticed a series of fine lines in the carving, running around the edges and down the centre like the doors of her mother's

jewellery cabinet. A small hole punctured the chest of a dying hoplite, piercing the soldier's heart. "It has a lock," she said, thinking of the contraption securing the *gynaikon's* doors. Dora had said the temple had given the house its locks, so it made sense the temple would have them, too. "Where is the key?"

"Draconaidas has it," Timotheus said. But his eyes were fixed on Yalee, his jaw tight as he studied her face, her split lip. "You have a Broken One with you. Is the house a party to this?"

"No," Rheia said.

Timotheus's eyes narrowed at her quick denial, and he gave Alexandros a searching look. "What is your deformity then, Broken One?"

Alexandros's voice grew dark and his eyes shadowed with the pain of memory. "Only the wound to my spirit caused by too much death."

Rheia leapt to her feet, not wanting to give the quick-thinking acolyte time to ponder what *that* meant. If he knew the Beast was walking around the city, who knew what he'd do? "We need to get into that altar or all this is for naught."

"Ask Yalee," Alexandros said, not looking away from Timotheus. "She has keys for all the house locks. One may fit."

"Do you think so?" Timotheus said, although the muscles of his expressive face grew tense. "Do you know how many types of lock there are?"

"At least a dozen, I imagine," Alexandros replied, his breastplate clanking as he shrugged.

"Well, yes. But we kept the mysteries of our own lock a temple secret."

Rheia gestured to catch the girl's gaze, and then pointed at the lock. Yalee's eyes brightened with understanding and she crossed the room in a swish of skirts, pulling her bundle of keys from the folds of her *chiton*. With her tongue caught between her teeth, she kneeled, running a slender finger over and inside the hole, judging its dimensions. Then she examined the jagged metal shafts, separating two similar ones from the rest. She jabbed each of them into the hole, twisting them this way and that.

Nothing happened, and Timotheus sighed with relief.

But Yalee wasn't done. She felt inside the hole again, and then regarded the shafts. Pressing one of the jagged edges against the hard side of the altar, she bent the protruding metal into a new shape. This she compared to the hidden interior of the lock, making several adjustments before inserting the newly shaped key into the hole.

Rheia held her breath as the girl jiggled the key, twisting it and then pulling it slightly back before twisting it again. Her grin brightened with triumph. "Done!"

With a *thunk*, something shifted inside the altar, and the door swung open with the pleasant aroma of dried lavender and old leather.

Inside the small compartment a dozen scrolls nestled in a wooden rack, each one rolled and stuffed into a sturdy tube. Words marked the side of each tube, and Rheia pulled them out, reading them aloud for Alexandros's sake. "Fire-thrower. Steam engine. Cannon." She looked up at him. "These are designs for the temple's creations."

"Demon-gifted tools of war," Alexandros muttered.

"This one says 'lock'," Rheia said, popping the wax seal off the scroll and unrolling it to confirm that it was what the label claimed. The fine vellum was soft under

her fingers as she studied the lines and markings depicting the inner workings of the mechanism that had secured the altar. "Tools of war and secrecy, perhaps."

"Is there any sign of the ritual? Its case will be much older." Apparently deciding the acolyte was no threat, Alexandros lowered the sword. He didn't sheathe it, though.

Rerolling the parchment and sliding it away, Rheia ran her eye over the scroll cases, sitting back on her heels with a frown. "None of these seem that old."

"They are two or three decades old, at most," Timotheus said, his voice soft and his hands held low and open at his sides. "Draconaidas started receiving visions of the god's will, of these divine plans, when he was still an acolyte. No high priest till then had been so deserving of Areus's favour."

"What about the intaglio? A pouch or jar? A box in the far corner of the compartment?" Alexandros half-turned to face Rheia. Although he didn't leave his post, his muscles bunched as though with anxiety, the desire to do something.

Her mouth sour with disappointment, Rheia reached into the compartment to run her hands around its edges and into its dark corners. She already knew the answer. The ritual and intaglio weren't here. Draconaidas had hidden them somewhere else.

"What intaglio?" Timotheus asked.

"The centre stone of the signet ring that belonged to Leohareus," Alexandros replied, gaze on the altar.

"Leohareus?" Timotheus gasped. "You mean the priest who bound Typhein?"

"Yes. The last true high priest of Areus."

A sudden choking sound brought Rheia's attention back

to Timotheus. She leapt to her feet, rushing to Alexandros's side. The acolyte's face had flushed an unhealthy red, sweat beading his brow. His hands clawed at his throat as though seeking to tear away an obstruction.

"What happened?" she demanded.

"I don't know." Alexandros shoved the sword's hilt into her palm and darted to the acolyte's side, locking his hands around the younger man's wrists. Muscles bunching, Alexandros dragged Timotheus's hands away from his neck. Raw scratches marked the skin, oozing blood. Leaning forward, Alexandros sniffed the breath coming from the acolyte's gasping mouth, then checked his head for signs of an injury. "Maybe he is prone to fits?"

The sword was an unfamiliar weight in Rheia's hand, the blade trembling. As she stared at the acolyte, his eyes rolled back into his head, red-veined whites staring blindly. Guilt reared in her thoughts, black and heavy. Had they done this, subjecting Timotheus to a fear for his life, undermining his faith in the establishment he served?

I'm missing something. She recalled the conversation just prior to his fit. The acolyte's last word had been ... the demon's name. "Eidoneus save us. Get away from him!"

The acolyte's limbs became suddenly loose. Alexandros caught him before he fell, turning towards Rheia. "What?"

"Get away from him! Now!" She stumbled backwards, lifting the sword as she'd seen her father do so many times, beckoning with her free hand for Alexandros to follow.

Timotheus stiffened, straight as a pike. Alexandros glanced down—and then dropped him, eyes wide with horror as he backed away, towards the far wall of the *adyton.*

Rheia's heart gave a violent jerk against her ribcage

at his expression. "What's happening?"

Timotheus stood, his movements awkward, and turned to face Rheia.

The golden-haired, gentle spirit of the acolyte who had been so kind to Rheia was gone, torn away like rags. In its place, a monster stared out from eyes gone black. Where the veins had been were threads of orange heat, like the embers of a banked fire.

"Kore," the monster said. "You're out of your cage on the hill, little girl." It spoke with Timotheus's lips, but its voice was low and dangerous. Inhuman.

"I'm not Kore." Tears burned her eyes. Timotheus was dead, just like that. She was as sure of it as if the god of death had told her himself.

The monster stepped forward, and she took an equal step back, barely noticing as Yalee fled the room with a strangled cry of terror. "You might be wearing new skin, but that's Kore's soul in there. How did Eidoneus do it, trapped in his hole?" Those burning eyes narrowed, and Timotheus's long, elegant hands hooked into talons. As his gaze moved, she felt the heat of it like a candle held close to her cheeks, her throat—almost hot enough to blister. "If I tear the flesh from you to leave the spirit bare, maybe I can see how the trick was done."

Alexandros vaulted over the altar, landing at Rheia's side. The unbalanced statue of Areus rocked for a moment, and then crashed to the ground. One of the horns on the helmet snapped off with the force of impact. "You're Typhein, aren't you?" she said. Alexandros reached for the sword, and she let him take it.

The monster smiled, showing teeth gone black, as though he'd been eating soot. His skin was slowly growing red, she noticed, as though from an awful sunburn. Around the mouth and eyes, the faint spots of blisters began to swell.

The demon's presence was burning Timotheus's body up from the inside.

"Impossible," Alexandros said, clutching the sword in both hands, an inelegant pose. "The demon is bound."

"True," the monster crooned, "but this boy is part of my priesthood and has dedicated himself to me. He called me forth, used my name in my place of power. That means he is mine. For as long as he lasts."

"He dedicated himself to *Areus*." Rheia's hands clenched into fists so tight she could feel her fingernails bite into her palms. Maybe if they stalled for long enough, Timotheus's body would be destroyed, the demon unable to use it. "Not to you."

"Areus is dead."

Alexandros lunged forwards, swinging the sword with a grunt. It glinted as it swept downwards, and for a brief moment Rheia thought it might strike true. But the monster lifted an arm. Blood spurted scarlet as the blade lodged in meat and bone, but there was no wail of pain. With a sharp motion, the monster yanked the sword free of Alexandros's grip. It hung from the creature's limp forearm, and Typhein glanced down with as much concern as if it had been stuck by a splinter.

"Now look what you've done," Typhein said. Those hot eyes bore into to Alexandros. Rheia felt her skin cool slightly as its regard shifted. "You're looking for my prison, but no one living knows where it is hidden. Not even *Draconaidas*." The priest's name came out as a hiss. "I will tell you where it is, if you like? But you must swear

to shatter it right away beneath your heel."

"Never," Alexandros gasped, staggering back. He rubbed his palms together as though they stung.

"No? Oh well." The demon shrugged with a crackle of burned flesh, and Rheia covered her mouth, acid burning her throat as she struggled not to vomit. "You have been my most useful servant this last century, high priest of Appelon. But I grow tired of our game and of my tiny prison. Destroying the intaglio isn't the only way to free myself. Since you've stubbornly refused to kill yourself no matter how I provoke you, I shall destroy you with this body and then show the people of Oreareus what a true god looks like. Imagine how far their armies will go with me driving them. I'll be the flaming lash at their heels. It will be glorious."

Rheia had a brief, hysterical thought of the demon setting foot on a trireme and cremating itself as the ship's timbers exploded into flames.

But then again, once the demon was free, it would be immune to fire.

"Move!" Yalee yelled from the door.

As though the word leant her feet the wings of Diktaios Skyfather's messenger, Rheia darted to the opposite side of the *adyton*. Alexandros was right behind her. Typhein stepped forward ... not pursuing them but heading towards the door.

Yalee stood there, eyes narrowed and holding the fire-thrower. The weapon was huge in her grip, but her stare was hard and her jaw clenched tight. The demon fire churning in the heart of the fractured glass pulsed faster than it had before, as though sensing the nearness of its creator.

"You fool," Typhein said. "I'm a fire demon. You can't destroy me with flame."

"But she can destroy your flesh puppet and send you back to your prison," Alexandros snarled.

Yalee pulled the trigger.

Rheia covered her eyes as flame spewed forth, filling the air with the sulphur stink of burning hair and a nauseatingly sweet charcoal stench.

"Damn you!" the demon howled, and then the snarling voice disappeared and an all-too-human shriek rose, riding the billowing, black smoke to the high ceiling.

Breaking glass tinkled, a delicate sound. A second scream arose.

"Yalee!" Alexandros tore his cloak from his shoulders and swathed his hands in it as he ran towards the girl.

The already-weakened glass containing the demon fire had shattered, showering Yalee's hands and skirts in white-hot fragments and liquid flame. Alexandros plucked the fire-thrower from the girl's hands, throwing it aside, and wrapped them in the fabric, smothering the fire. Rheia unpinned her larger *himation*, reaching forward to blanket the flames eating at Yalee's skirts before they burned the skin underneath. "We need to get her back to the house."

Alexandros slid his arms under Yalee, gathering the folds of fabric, and swept her up. The girl whimpered, her face tight with pain. Tears stained her cheeks as he carried her from the *adyton*.

Rheia hesitated, staring back at the now-silent pyre that had been Timotheus. She'd thought he was gone, but that scream... He'd returned to his body when the demon abandoned it, just in time to feel his death. The

flames dancing on his corpse licked at a tapestry, adding the scent of burning wool to the stench already polluting the air. The room would soon be an inferno.

"Rheia!" Alexandros called from the *cella*. "I need you to open the door!"

Eidoneus, please take Timotheus into your halls, she prayed as she sprinted across the stones of the outer room to where Alexandros waited, bouncing on the balls of his feet as though wanting to run. Yalee cried out, and he stilled himself with a tightening jaw. *And spare Yalee, if you can.*

She yanked open the door and they hurried out into the night.

CHAPTER TWENTY-SIX

Rheia pounded on the house door, her balled fist thundering on the timber almost as loudly as her pulse did in her ears. When it didn't immediately swing open, she struck the door again, and Alexandros followed it up with a kick that probably hurt his sandalled toes.

The door cracked open, and an unfamiliar male caregiver peered out. Face paling, he stepped aside. Alexandros manoeuvred through the doorway, careful that Yalee's limp form didn't so much as brush against the frame. "What happened? Is she...?"

"She's unconscious," Rheia said breathlessly, hurrying along the hall after the rapidly disappearing Alexandros. The man dropped a bar into its groove to lock the door and then followed with an uneven gait. "Passed out after we stopped at a fountain to wet the cloth around her hands." It had been the fountain near her family's home, but Rheia hadn't had time to feel more than a fleeting pang that she couldn't go to them, seek comfort in her mother's arms.

Find out if her grandmother still lived.

"I'll fetch Dora," the caregiver said, peeling off at a side corridor.

Rheia followed Alexandros to the healing room she remembered waking up in on her first day in the house, after Timotheus had accidentally overdosed her on night-sleep. It turned out the room was one of a pair. The first she passed was empty and dark. Glowing oil lamps lit the second, the room Rheia remembered. A bed sat against one wall, its head under a window now spangled with stars. A table ran along another, inset with a deep, empty basin. A chest sat on the third wall, under a shelf stacked with clean, folded cloths and holding a large ceramic jug.

Alexandros lay Yalee on the bed as carefully as if she were a baby. She groaned, her eyelids fluttering as if trapped in some dream, but didn't awaken. Her face was flushed.

Snatching the jug down, Rheia found it empty. "I'll be back," she said, passing a startled-looking caregiver in the hall outside. She remembered the path Dora had taken to reach the bathhouse from here, and ran the entire way, relieved to find it empty at this time of night. She stopped at the bottom pool, the cooler one, dipping the jug into it so the water could flood in. Then she hurried back to Alexandros.

He stood before Yalee's bed, speaking in a soft voice to Dora as he unwound his cloak from the girl's hands and dropped it to the floor. Dora murmured in sympathy as she saw the wounds, which were mercifully screened from Rheia's eyes by Alexandros's armoured back.

"I have water," Rheia said, upending the jug's contents into the basin. "From the bathhouse."

"Gods bless you," Dora said, hurrying to the chest. She reached inside and handed Rheia a small glass phial filled with liquid, turning towards the bed even as she spoke. "Put a dozen drops in the basin. It will help to cleanse any impurities from the water, since we haven't the time to boil and then cool it for her."

"Is she badly hurt?" Rheia heard a waver in her voice, and swallowed. She wouldn't cry. She wanted to be useful. Wailing like a baby could wait until later.

We failed. We failed, Yalee is hurt, and Timotheus is dead. Blinking hard, she unbound the leather seal from the phial and tipped it carefully, counting the honey-coloured drops as they fell to splash on the surface of the water. The intertwined sweetness of yarrow blossoms and undiluted wine filled the air.

"It could be worse," Alexandros said, not turning. His shoulders moved as he worked. "Her pain is actually a good sign. It means the inner workings of her hands haven't been destroyed. And her skin is red and swelling, not damaged beyond repair. Our first task will be to make sure the wounds don't become putrid."

"But the pain...?"

"I already gave her nightsleep for it," Dora said, taking the bundle of cloths. "It's the kindest way. Now, stir the oil into the water. The fabric needs to soak."

Rheia reached past Dora to grab a wooden spoon from the chest, turning back to the water.

"Is there anything I can do?" the male caregiver said from the open doorway. His face was pinched with worry.

Dora glanced from him to Rheia, nodding sharply. "Take over from Rheia. This isn't appropriate work for a *thysia*."

"I don't mind," Rheia protested as the man came into the room, his expression apologetic. "I want to help." But he shouldered past her, taking the spoon from her hands.

Dora too ignored Rheia's protests. "I'll walk her back to the *gynaikon*," she told Alexandros.

"Pick some plantain on the way back. We need to make a poultice," he replied, and Rheia's shoulders drooped. Dora was sending her away and he didn't seem to care. But then she shook her head, disgusted at herself. He was busy, doing what Appelon had called him to do all those years ago. He didn't have time to worry about her, or her feelings.

As she turned to follow Dora out the door, Alexandros called her back. "Rheia?"

Her heart leaping, she turned to him. "Yes?"

"We'll talk tomorrow." His bronze eyes had lost their shimmer, the glint of hope she'd given him. Her shoulders sagging under the weight of grief, she nodded and turned away.

"What happened?" Dora asked as soon as they were in the dimly lit hall. The woman kept her voice low, but it still seemed overly loud. The building felt deserted, everyone in their beds.

"The temple was unguarded, except for an acolyte of Areus who I think was sleeping in the *adyton*. He said the demon's name while we were searching for the intaglio, and it came to possess him."

Dora stopped, staring at Rheia. Shock and shadows worked together to render her face gaunt, haggard. "The demon is free?"

"No." Rheia kept walking, and Dora jerked into motion. "Once the acolyte was killed, it was forced back into its prison. That's how Yalee got burned. Using a damaged fire-thrower."

"She killed the acolyte?" Dora's good hand grasped her braid in a white-knuckled grip.

"Yes." Rheia remembered the swelling blisters on Timotheus's face, and added, "Although he was already dying."

They turned into the hall filled with Alexandros's sculptures, and Dora's hands shook as she shoved her braid back over her shoulder and pulled her keys out. What had happened to Yalee's own keys? Had they been dropped in the temple? Dora had already said the caregivers didn't rely solely on the temple's locks, but... "The demon said it's going to kill Alexandros so it can be free. And I don't know where Yalee's keys are."

"I'll check her pouch when I head back."

"If they aren't there, you need to protect him."

"I always do," Dora said, taking two tries to insert her key into the lock. She paused, glancing at Rheia. The look of determination, forged to hardness in the fire of love, was one Rheia recognised. One she suspected she might also be wearing. "Do you think the demon will be able to get another body?" Dora asked. The lock hammered as it disengaged.

"I don't know," Rheia said, lowering her eyes. "It said it was entitled to Timotheus's because he belonged to the temple. But the demon may try to trick another acolyte into saying its name."

"I'd best not allow Draconaidas into the house again then," Dora muttered, swinging the door wide. "He's the demon's knowing servant."

Rheia took Dora's hand, pulling her down the stairs

into the *gynaikon's* courtyard. "I saw plantain over here," she said as they crossed the still-damp grass. "Dora, when the demon possessed Timotheus, it began to burn him up from within. So long as you don't admit any temple servants with burns, we will be safe." *Hopefully.*

"But if Draconaidas were to invoke his master's name once he was inside the house's walls...?"

Rheia shrugged. She didn't know if it would work— whether it had been the circumstance of the spoken name inside the *adyton* that had allowed Typhein to act, or whether the creature had merely decided to do so when it realised they were searching for the binding ritual as well as the intaglio. After all, Draconaidas had spoken its name on the day of the lottery and remained unaffected.

"Best not to risk it," Dora said, pulling a small blade from her belt. She bent to cut two handfuls of the veined, oval-shaped leaves before turning towards the door in a swirl of skirts. "Goodnight, Rheia."

Rheia sagged as the door thumped shut, but her head jerked back up again at a soft, scuffing movement.

Parthenia stood under the porch covering the walkway outside her room. The girl's dark eyes were wide and her mouth was agape with horror. "The demon possessed someone? It walks the city?" Her accent was stronger than usual, perhaps heightened by her distress.

Rheia hurried to the *thysia's* side, taking her hands. They trembled in Rheia's grip. "No. It's back in its prison, for now."

"But you said..." Her gaze flicked to the plantain bush.

"We're just taking precautions."

Parthenia looked back at Rheia, snatching her hands free and hugging her belly. "So now instead of fearing the

Beast's blade, we must fear burning to death, or becoming a demon's playthings?" she said, her fear turning to anger. "Were you at least successful in whatever mad scheme had you sneaking out at night with a strange man?"

"Alexandros isn't a stranger to me," Rheia said, breathing slowly to keep her voice even. She understood Parthenia's fear and was too weary to fight with her. Not again. "Kore knew him all her life."

Parthenia ignored that. "But you weren't successful, were you?"

Weariness and despair settled over Rheia, a too-tight *chiton* weighting her limbs and her soul alike. "No," she said, gaze dropping. "The demon came before we could finish our search."

There was a long pause—so long she thought Parthenia might have slipped away, bare feet silent on stone. But when the *thysia* spoke, her voice was gentle. "If the monster acted to stop you, then you must have been close to something it didn't want you to find."

"Maybe," Rheia mumbled.

"I'm sorry for yelling at you, Mud Girl."

The nickname pulled Rheia's head up, though she didn't have the energy to smile. Even the tiny candle flame of hope Parthenia offered wasn't enough to light the darkness.

CHAPTER TWENTY-SEVEN

Timotheus's burning face, his pained shriek, chased Rheia from sleep. Her oil lamp had burned out during the night, its wick exhausted, and a hot, still darkness smothered the room. Unable to face the thought of yet more tormented dreams, she slipped from her bed and felt her way across the room to the door, drawing aside the curtain to admit the weak light of the lamps in the hall. There was no sign of dawn greying the sky.

She paused in the doorway for a moment, gulping deep breaths. Then she crossed to where the statuette of Eidoneus stood, sitting before it cross-legged. His serene face was hidden in shadow, so she closed her eyes and called it up in her memory. She needed a piece of that tranquillity. *I have failed you, Eidoneus.* She bit her lip until the pain burned, welcome amidst the numbness of despair. *I've failed and I don't know what to do next.*

The god didn't answer, and she reached out to touch the statuette, her fingers instead brushing against Yalee's clay pot. The offerings in it had burned dry and she had no wine, nightsleep or narcissus perfume to refill it, but she pressed her fingers into the sticky residue that was left in the bowl and held it under her nose, catching the faded fragrance: sweet and spicy, hot and cold. She inhaled until her lungs ached and the trace of scent filled her.

You only fail if you surrender.

The thread was as faint as a fading dream, and she grasped after it, hoping for more. But silence filled her thoughts. If that was all she was going to get... Straightening her spine, she let the words cloak her battered spirit as if they were a *himation,* protection against her despair. She breathed. And she prayed.

Eidoneus hadn't given up on her. She wouldn't give up either.

"Rheia?"

Her eyes flew open and she blinked, surprised to see the soft light of morning filling the room. Had she fallen asleep?

"Are you coming to breakfast?" Parthenia said, standing in the doorway, one hand on the doorframe and a knee bent beneath her *chiton.* Her gaze drifted from Rheia, still seated on the floor, to the statuette. "Forgive me, I didn't mean to intrude."

"It's fine. I'll come." Rheia stood, muscles protesting. Last night, before bed, the thought of food had churned her stomach, but her appetite was back: clean, sharp and trying to gnaw through her spine. She dressed in a fresh *chiton* and then joined Parthenia in the hall.

"How long have you been sitting there?" The other girl gave her a sideways look.

"I'm not sure," Rheia admitted with a shrug. "I couldn't sleep."

They headed into the dining room and Rheia sat, quickly eating a fresh honey and sesame cake. She was licking her fingers clean when her attention was caught by the outer doors to the *gynaikon* swinging open. It wasn't Dora but Erika, whose usually dour expression was even darker than usual, her mouth turned down and her eyes narrowed. She held her gardening shears closed. At a distance, their gleaming shape looked like a long dagger, making the woman seem dangerous ... and a little unhinged.

She beckoned, and the girls came out of the hall to cross the grass, Parthenia eyeing the shears as she swallowed a last mouthful of bread.

"Good morning," Rheia said with a respectful nod of her head, stopping at the bottom of the stairs.

Erika grunted. "No, it isn't."

Rheia clenched her hands in the folds of her skirt, her cheeks growing cold as the flagstones seeming to waver beneath her feet. "Is Yalee well?"

"Yes." The hard lines of Erika's face softened slightly. "She woke this morning." Rheia exhaled with relief, but didn't get a chance to dwell on the feeling as the caregiver added, "Come with me."

"Where?"

"Dora has something she wants you to see."

Parthenia stepped forward, her arms crossed. "I want to come, too. This gilded cage gets lonely when I'm on my own all day. And maybe I can help."

Erika's frown returned. "Dora sent for Rheia."

Feeling a surge of pity for the Carmean girl, Rheia put an arm around her shoulder. "Let her come, Erika. Please. What harm can it do? The entire house is safe, isn't it?

Not just the *gynaikon* and *andron*?"

The woman's jaw tightened. "Very well. But stay close by me."

She led them out of the *gynaikon* and down an unfamiliar corridor off the main hall. It was still clean and well-appointed, but the decorations weren't as lavish as they were in other parts of the house. "This is the caregiver wing," Erika told them in response to Rheia's questioning look. They reached a flight of narrow stone stairs and headed up them. "We keep a watch from high rooms such as this. They let us see over the walls."

See what? Rheia wondered, lifting her skirts so she didn't trip.

At the top, Dora stood in a sun-drenched, bare-walled room already growing stuffy with heat despite the huge windows. The sky beyond was a blue so rich it hurt the eye, and the caregiver's white *chiton* seemed to glow as she turned at the sound of their footsteps.

Erika glanced back as Parthenia entered the room and opened her mouth to explain, but Dora waved her away. "It's fine," the woman said flatly, seeming too tired to argue. "Would you please return to the bottom of the stairs, Erika? I don't wish us to be disturbed."

"Yes." Lofting her shears, the hunchbacked woman bowed stiffly and then disappeared back the way they'd come.

"What's going on?" Rheia said. The woman had reacted as though she'd been told to guard them, and it made the hair on the back of Rheia's neck prickle.

"See for yourself." Dora gestured out the window.

Rheia and Parthenia crossed to the open window, squinting and shading their eyes as they peered out

and down.

The window faced the front of the house; although they couldn't see the double doors at the entrance, covered as they were by the terracotta tiles of a long porch, Rheia recognised the distinctive, weathered statue of a smiling discus thrower, posed awkwardly in the courtyard beyond. Mercifully, the dais and altar where the Beast killed the *thysies* were beyond the line of wall and out of sight. Had Dora chosen this particular room to meet Rheia in for that reason?

Rheia narrowed her gaze as a flash of colour caught her attention. Leaning against the statue's bent knee was a guard in orange livery, the ball hilt of his iron sword glittering like a diamond. She caught her breath.

"What is it?" Parthenia asked, turning.

"That's a temple guard. The man in the orange."

"I know," the Carmean girl said, exasperation threading her words. "I've had the misfortune to make their acquaintance. What I'm wondering is if it's abnormal for them to guard the house. You seem surprised."

"It's not normal, no," Dora said, coming to stand beside them. Smudges of fatigue were crescents beneath her eyes. "And he's not the only one. There are guards at every door, each with a sword and focused inwards, not out."

"Do they say why?" Rheia said, curling her fingers around the window's sill. A faint breeze danced across her knuckles and was gone.

"They are for our protection. Or so they say." Dora turned to the table in the centre of the room and retrieved a square of thin timber the size of a breadboard. "That was pinned to our outer door this morning, for the *public's* information." Her voice was as sour as rancid wine as she handed the board to Rheia.

Rheia scanned the words hastily, while Parthenia frowned over her shoulder. "What does it say?" the girl said. "I can't read Orearean script."

"'Due to last night's attack by criminals and murderers on the sacred temple of Most Holy Areus, which resulted in the death of an acolyte,'" Rheia read, "'High Priest Draconaidas has directed additional guards be set on the House of the Beast, to protect the god's avatar-child and the sacred *thysies*.' That's outrageous!" She set the timber down before she gave into the urge to fling it through the window at the guard. She'd never hit him at this distance—she doubted even the discus thrower given life could manage it. "For a start, protection of the city isn't the temple's job. It should be the city guard!"

"Draconaidas has only tenuous authority over us, at best. But the king is unlikely to dispute his claim. This way, he doesn't have to divert resources to protect us." Dora glared at the guard as though wishing to skewer him with her gaze.

"I gather, then, that they *aren't* there to protect us?" Parthenia drew back from the window to stand in the cooler shadow beside it, fanning her face with her hand.

Rheia shook her head. "The demon knows we're the ones who set fire to his *adyton* last night. Draconaidas is trying to stop us from leaving again. Me or Alexandros."

"I agree," Dora said.

"What does Alexandros say about this?"

"He is sleeping," the caregiver said, the lines of her face softening. "He was up most of the night with Yalee and I didn't want to wake him for this. After all, what could he do?"

Rheia shrugged. "I suppose not much." Her half-formed notion of returning to the temple that evening withered and died. Staring at that orange livery, she gritted her teeth and frowned. "I need to write to my father," she mused aloud, and Dora glanced at her.

"For what purpose? Even Loukios would not be able to bestir the king to remove the guards."

"Not that. If I can tell him what to look for, maybe he can find the intaglio and ritual for us."

Dora's eyes softened with sympathy. "Rheia—"

"Don't try and convince me not to do anything!" Rheia's nostrils flared as she took a deep breath before adding more calmly, "I've ... no, *we've* only got five days left. Me, Parthenia and the others. I have to try everything I can." Her voice dropped to a whisper. "And I don't want to put Alexandros in a position where he has to decide whether to kill me or free the demon."

Dora hung her head, wiping a weathered hand across her face. When she looked up, her expression was resolute. "Write your letter. I'll carry it to your father myself."

"But..." Rheia glanced at Dora's other hand.

"Just write it."

CHAPTER TWENTY-EIGHT

Rheia, Parthenia and Erika watched as Dora emerged from under the house's roofline, crossing the courtyard with a basket over one arm. The other was concealed by neat folds of cloth, as though she were carrying it to market. If Rheia hadn't been looking for her, she wouldn't have been able to identify the woman: her usually straight spine was bent almost as much as Erika's, and her face was shadowed by a hair shawl drawn forward as though to screen her face from the sun's bite.

The temple guard watched Dora, his face turning as he tracked her shuffling path. His indolent posture didn't shift to indicate he recognised her, and Rheia recalled Aias's indignation at the city guards they'd seen at the *agora*. Her brother would be incoherent with outrage at the temple guard's unprofessional demeanour, which went beyond boredom and into contempt.

Still, better lazy contempt than efficiency. Draconaidas knew Dora, and the caregiver hadn't been sure the guards wouldn't recognise her, even though the caregiver never

left the house—the priest might have circulated her description, or they may have accompanied him to the house in the past. Better that the guard think Dora was an old slave woman sent to market.

Rheia wondered if Dora would be able to stop anyone noticing the missing fingers on her hand. The folded cloth was a clumsy disguise—but then, Dora didn't have to go all the way to the *agora*, just to Rheia's house and back. It was barely a ten-minute walk.

Erika sighed with relief when Dora passed out the other side of the courtyard and disappeared from view. "I'd best be getting you girls back to the *gynaikon*," she said, turning towards the door.

"Can we go past the healing rooms first? I'd like to see Yalee," Rheia said.

"I already told you she was well," Erika said, but Rheia begged with her eyes until the woman relented. "You remind me of my daughter," she grumbled, clomping down the stairs. Rheia's eyes widened with surprise. She hadn't known Erika had children. "Always charming her way out of trouble, and yet causing more in the process."

Behind Rheia, Parthenia laughed softly. "That sounds like you, Mud Girl."

When they reached Yalee's room, Rheia's breath caught to see a familiar figure by the girl's bed. "Master!" Erika said, her face flushing with embarrassment. "I thought you were down below."

"I woke and decided to check on my patient," Alexandros said, a smile lighting his face when he saw Rheia hovering in the corridor. He looked tired, although not as tired as Dora had. Maybe he'd managed at least a few hours' sleep.

"How is she?" Rheia said, slipping past the caregiver

to stand by the bed. Yalee reclined on the cushions, her eyes closed and her chest rising and falling with gentle breaths.

"Her temperature is good, and the wounds are clean," Alexandros said, nodding at the damp cloths draped over the girl's hands. They smelled sharp and bright, of cleansing herbs. "As the wounds start to heal and the chance of blood poison reduces, we'll need to focus on keeping the new skin supple so she doesn't lose too much movement."

Rheia tightened her jaw as she regarded the sleeping girl's pretty face: the sweep of her long lashes, her high-boned cheeks, the glint of teeth between parted lips. The girl's nimble dexterity had been what allowed her to guess the correct shape of a key needed to open an unseen lock. Rheia was sure she'd have never been able to do that, even if her hands had been small enough to fit in the hole. She hoped Yalee didn't lose her quick-fingered grace.

Thinking of the lock reminded her of something. "Did you find her keys?"

He nodded. "She'd put them back in her pouch before... Well, before."

The sound of Parthenia's light step as the girl moved into the room drew their attention to her. The Carmean girl's eyes looked wider than usual as she stared at Alexandros. He turned, straightening his *chiton* as she looked him up and down in a frank way that made Rheia blush. "Forgive me. I didn't realise we had company," Alexandros said.

"I'm Parthenia," the girl said, her accent making her origins obvious. "You must be the Beast. Alexandros, I mean." He winced and nodded, and she glanced at Rheia.

"I can see why you're so enthralled by him, Mud Girl. He looks good for a man in his hundreds."

"Parthenia!" Rheia's hand flew to her mouth, shocked and amused in equal measure.

"Life's too short to waste time being proper," Parthenia said with a sniff. Then she glanced at Alexandros, who looked as though he'd swallowed a sand fly. "Rheia told me your story."

"She did?" He glanced at Rheia, a question in his eyes.

"Indeed. So I'll try not to hold it against you if you cut off my head, although I'd be much obliged if you found a way to avoid it." Parthenia's lips quirked in a smile at his stunned expression, and then she yawned dramatically, stretching so the brooches at her shoulders glittered with reflected light. "I grow weary, Erika. Will you take me back to the *gynaikon*?"

Erika looked between Alexandros and Rheia, shrugging her agreement when he nodded. "I'll find someone to escort Rheia back there in a while."

As she turned to leave the room, Parthenia winked at Rheia. "Don't rush, Mud Girl."

"Why does she call you that?" Alexandros asked, frowning. Was he wondering whether to be offended on Rheia's behalf?

"It's a pet name," Rheia said, turning back to Yalee to hide the way her cheeks flamed at what Parthenia seemed to be suggesting. "I don't mind."

"It's good that you found a friend here."

"I found several," Rheia said, fingers brushing the fabric of Yalee's bed cushion. "Is she going to be alright? Really?"

"We're not in the harbour yet, but it's clear sailing so

far." He sighed, shoulders drooping with exhaustion.

"You should sleep," Rheia said.

"I did sleep. You're just as bad as Dora. She mothers me terribly," he said, reminding Rheia of Aias's familiar complaint. "I think sometimes she forgets I'm more than twice her age!"

"Well, you *do* look good for a man in his hundreds." Rheia grinned.

"Not hundreds," Alexandros said, straightening his spine and sticking out his jaw. "I'm not even a hundred and forty!"

"A mere babe," Rheia said with a laugh. "Still, I don't know that Dora wants to be your mother." She bit her lip, wishing she could take back the words. Why had she said that?

He didn't notice her expression, shifting from foot to foot and avoiding her gaze. "Did she say something to you?"

"No." Rheia looked down at her hands. "Is there something I should know?" When he didn't answer, she added hesitantly, "Are you and she...? Have you ever...?"

"No." His voice was barely audible, and he still wouldn't look at her. Was he lying?

"It would be fine if you had," Rheia said, ignoring the pain that stabbed through her chest at the thought. She looked towards the door, tears prickling her eyes. "Kore has been dead a long time, and she wouldn't blame you for finding someone else. *I* wouldn't, I mean."

A warm finger under her chin turned her face back to his. His gaze caught hers, his eyes the colour of dark honey, shadowed with pain. "It's not that. I know Dora was interested in ... in me, when she was younger. Before she was elevated to her current position, she was put in

charge of tending to my needs, and she thought..."

A mental image of Dora as she must have been, tall, graceful and determined, offering herself to him, flashed across Rheia's mind. She shoved it away brutally.

"I said no." Alexandros's voice was hoarse and he drew his hand away from her face. "I'd be lying if I said I didn't consider it. It's been a long time and I..." He bit back his words, shaking his head. "But it felt wrong. Like I would have been taking advantage of her. Like I didn't deserve to be happy."

"Dora is one of the strongest women I've ever met. I don't think anyone could take advantage of her. I'm not saying I wish you two were a couple, because I think that would..." Rheia inhaled sharply, cheeks burning. "But you *do* deserve to be happy. You do. And Dora loves you." She pressed her lips together before any more rambling words came out, embarrassing her further.

"Do you know how many people I've killed?"

"More than four hundred," she said softly.

"Four hundred and forty-five," he told her, his face filled with horror. "Hundreds of *thysies*. And you. How anyone could love a soul so black is a mystery to me."

With her heart aching, Rheia stepped forward, wrapping her arms around him. His black *chiton* was thin under her fingers, allowing her to feel the shape of his sides, the curve of muscle, as she hugged him to her. The pine-and-flowers scent of his soap filled her senses as he froze, as though afraid she might break if he hugged her back.

"You deserve to be happy," she said again, looking up at him, determined he believe her. "You agreed to enforce the demon's bargain where Hieron couldn't. You saved the city from flame. The mystery isn't how Dora could love you. It's how everyone else who meets you doesn't."

Alexandros stared at her, a wondering smile slowly blooming on his lips, in his eyes. But, although the muscles of his back tensed under her hands, he still didn't move. "Is this real, or just a dream?" he whispered.

"It's real."

With her heart in her throat, Rheia slid one hand up his ribs and around to the nape of his neck, pulling his head down so his soft lips met hers. They were parted with surprise or anticipation, and, remembering their last kiss, she slid her tongue between them, darting it in and out to test his reaction.

He moaned softly, pressing their lips together as though he wanted to breathe her in. Or eat her up. His hands were on her back, tangled in the cascade of her hair, and he pulled her to him, closing the distance between their bodies. Her belly fluttered and a fire grew in her at the feel of his hard muscles against her chest, the rasp of his cheek against hers as their tongues tangled. His hands slid down to the curve of her waist, his strong fingers pressing against her hips. "Rheia," he breathed against her lips.

"Yes?" she said, taking a trembling breath. Her lips felt swollen from his kisses, and she wanted ... more. But she didn't know what. Her mother and Charis had explained what happens between a husband and wife, and that it could hurt or be marvellous. Rheia had found the notion intimidating, but now, wrapped in Alexandros's arms, she found a new courage within her. She was sure it would be marvellous. *He* would be marvellous.

And she wanted to know just how marvellous. Before

she died.

"We should stop," Alexandros said.

"I don't want to." She caught his lips with hers and he surrendered to her for several moments before pulling back. She growled, low in her throat, and he laughed softly. "Alexandros…"

"I won't tumble you in Yalee's sick room."

That thought cooled her ardour a little. She pulled back to peer past his shoulder at the still-sleeping girl. An impish smile turned Rheia's lips upwards as she remembered Yalee silently encouraging her to embrace Alexandros the first time they'd talked, when he was grieving. "I doubt she'd mind."

"No, but I would." He bent forward to kiss Rheia's nose, his hands sliding back up to the safer territory of her back. "You deserve better. A bed covered with flower petals." He kissed her cheek. "Wine and sweets." Her ear, the breath tickling her until she squirmed. "A wedding."

She pulled her head back to stare at him, blurting the first thing that crossed her mind. "Were you and Kore ever married?"

He shook his head. "Priests don't marry. Priestesses either. But…"

"But?"

"Under the old ways, all it took for a man and woman to become married was that they coupled, joined their bodies and fortunes together. Weddings, the marriage rituals, they came later, as a way to mark the union and because it pleased the priestesses of Gaea to be given a chance to bless new love. But before, all that was needed was that a man and woman were one. That he claimed her as his, and that her father consented."

Rheia snorted. "So she didn't get a say?"

Amusement brightened Alexandros's eyes. "That's what Kore said, too. She said she claimed me first."

"So under the old ways, were you and Kore wed?"

He nodded, his gaze hot on hers.

"Then, since I'm her, isn't the wedding irrelevant?"

He leaned forward as though drawn to her, nuzzling against her ear again, catching the lobe in his mouth and sucking it gently for several moments. She gasped into his hair. "No," he said, and there was regret in his voice—almost as much as she felt. "Because these days it's expected, and what they say of a woman who lays with a man not her husband..."

"Eidoneus take them and their disapproval. They forfeited any right to care about what I do with my body when they sent me here to die." Her hand tightened in his hair, holding his head against her when he stiffened in surprise.

"But your family...? Your father...?"

"He didn't fight for me," Rheia growled, speaking a truth she hadn't dared to until now. Part of her felt the words were unfair, disloyal. But another part of her, a raw, aching part, still felt aggrieved that her father hadn't tried to prise her from the temple's grasping hands that day in the *agora*, or at any point since.

"I'm sorry," Alexandros said, his sympathy dragging her back from her thoughts. She looked up at his warm eyes as he shifted to hug her. Wrapped up in him, her gaze drifted lower, to the curve of his neck, the flow of his hair, the place where his neck met his shoulder... Taking her lead from him, she leaned in to nibble the skin lightly. She felt other parts of him stiffen as he

gasped in turn, and a surge of triumph flooded her. "I haven't given up on finding the intaglio," she breathed against his hot skin, "but if we fail, I only have five days left. I owe this city nothing beyond my life's blood, and I refuse to deny myself what I desire because of judgemental strangers. And I ... I don't wish to die a virgin. So—" She looked up at him, a glint in her eye. "—since you're the master of the house, will you be a good host and oblige me?"

Alexandros stepped back, and the air that passed between them felt cold after the heat of his embrace. She missed it, and when he reached out to run a light finger along her jawline, she leaned into the caress. "I want this more than you can imagine," he said.

"Then what is stopping you?"

"You're so much younger than me—"

"*Everyone* is so much younger than you."

"—and I don't want to do you wrong."

"Alexandros?" She reached up to take his hand, slipping her fingers through his.

"Yes?"

"Shut up and take me to your lair."

Laughing, he surrendered, leading her into the hall.

CHAPTER TWENTY-NINE

A distant sound pulled Rheia from a blissfully dreamless sleep. She was more relaxed than she had ever been; cushions shifted under her as she stretched and yawned, her bare skin warm with the heat of a nearby fire.

Her bare skin...?

She bolted upright, memories flooding back as she saw Alexandros sprawled beside her in the nest of cushions and blankets they'd made, laughing as they pulled everything from his bed and piled it on the floor. The room had been cold, and they'd wanted to be near the low-burning fire that filled the air with the invigorating tang of juniper.

Also, his bed had been impossibly narrow.

Alexandros sprawled beside her, a corner of blanket covering his slender hips and muscled upper thighs. The firelight painted his skin in hues of gold and honey; just the thought of it made her mouth water, but when she shifted towards him, a wince tightened her face, her muscles protesting the recent unfamiliar activity.

Her mother and grandmother had been right. The first time had hurt, at least in the beginning, but Alexandros had been gentle and patient, and afterwards he'd bathed her like a queen in his blue-tiled bathroom, washing and brushing her hair out as though it was an act of worship.

The second time had been better, and she smiled at the memory, trailing a feather-light finger along Alexandros's bare arm. He didn't stir, sleeping the sleep of the truly exhausted.

Rheia hesitated, reverie broken, as she realised the distant sound she was hearing was sandals smacking on stone. Hard-soled shoes on the stone stairs. They grew louder as their owner approached. With her heart in her throat, Rheia leapt to her feet, scrambling for her discarded *chiton* and the brooches to secure it. She couldn't judge the echoes to guess how long she had.

Alexandros's eyes flew open as she darted for the bathroom to dress, and she heard his heavy sigh as he sat up, taking in the situation. He muttered something about "a few hours more", his tone plaintive, but his exact words were muffled by the rustle of fabric.

The bathroom was chilly, the bath pool filled with water that no longer steamed. Her feet splashed in a puddle and she winced, trying to hold the *chiton* out of the water as she shook it to flatten the fabric. Why must the things be so ungainly? As soon as the cloth was untangled, she began to wind it around herself.

The owner of the sandals arrived, panting. "Master," Erika's familiar voice said, and Rheia suppressed a groan, almost stabbing her finger as she jabbed the last brooch through the fabric at her shoulder. It had to be Erika, with her sour disapproval? It couldn't have been Polymede? But no, Polymede was so heavily pregnant the stairs would be a danger to her, and Yalee was ... well.

There was a pause, and then Alexandros spoke in a long-suffering tone. "You might as well come out, Rheia. She knows you're here."

"If you're clothed," Erika added, her voice so warm that for a moment Rheia didn't realise it was her who had spoken.

Blushing hotter than the red-streaked coals in the fireplace, Rheia realised her belt was still out in Alexandros's main room. Without it, the *chiton* hung too long; chin up, she gathered it up in her hands and strode out of the bathroom. Wordlessly, Alexandros handed her the length of corded fabric, a faint smile on his lips. Letting her sleep-mussed hair hang to hide her face, she slid the belt around her waist. How had he dressed so quickly? Of course, his *chiton* was knee-length. There was less fabric to untangle.

"I thought you'd want to know Dora is on her way back," Erika said. "I saw her coming up the hill and came to find you." There was laughter in her voice, and Rheia looked up from rucking the excess *chiton* fabric up over the belt so it fell in gentle ruffles around her waist. Her mouth fell open as she saw Erika's usually hard eyes were twinkling, creased around the corners. The caregiver wasn't scandalised or judgemental. She was pleased.

Rheia didn't know how to feel about that, and she raked a nervous hand through her hair, trying to smooth it against her skull. It bounced back, defiant. *I shouldn't have lain down with wet hair.* She sighed.

Alexandros slipped his hand into Rheia's, his fingers

warm. The gesture soothed her nerves. "Leave it be?" he said softly, his inflection making it into a request. "I love your hair." She remembered him murmuring the same thing to her earlier as his body had pressed down on her, filled her. Heat raced up her neck to again dye her cheeks scarlet. Would she never stop blushing?

Erika made a sound like she was clearing her throat, and Rheia squared her shoulders. "I want to go see Dora," she said, taking a single step towards Appelon's room before the fire-warmed stone beneath her feet drew her attention downwards. "Ah, do you know where my sandals are?"

The caregiver failed to hide a grin behind her hand as Alexandros found Rheia's shoes under his bed, beside his own. He must have stowed them there at some point, but she didn't remember it.

"Napping in the daytime?" Erika asked as they passed the statue of Appelon. She gave Alexandros a sly look.

"I didn't sleep much last night," he said simply.

"Neither did I," Rheia added, crossing her arms across her chest.

Erika huffed a laugh.

They were partway up the stairs, Rheia and Alexandros silent and Erika humming under her breath, when the sound of a commotion at the surface drifted down. The caregiver fell silent and they all paused as one to let the echoes settle and the faint sound reach them cleanly.

It was yelling, a man's voice frantic with worry. The words almost seemed to blur together. "Master! Erika, bring him quickly! It's Dora."

"Dora," Alexandros gasped. Dropping Rheia's hand, he ran.

She leapt after him. Erika cursed as she fell behind. The stairs had always seemed overly long to Rheia, but she hated them twice as much now as her thighs burned and her already-sore muscles complained at the extra exertion. Why did he need to live so far below the ground? Any of the rooms in the caregiver wing of the house would do, and be more convenient. Was he punishing himself? Still, she pushed herself to stay as close as she could and, despite her discomfort, she was only half a flight of stairs behind Alexandros when he reached the top, able to hear the caregiver's words over her panting breaths. "She's hurt," the man said, clutching Alexandros's arm and then releasing it as though realising what he'd done. "Some temple guards—"

"Where is she?" Alexandros demanded.

"The healing rooms."

Alexandros turned to go, but hesitated, glancing at Rheia. She was almost at the top of the stairs, panting. She kept her hand against the wall in case her legs gave way. "Go," she said between gasps. "I'll catch up."

He didn't need to be told twice, disappearing up the corridor at a run. Climbing the stairs was one way to keep fit, at least. Rheia grimaced.

The unfamiliar caregiver looked after him, face crumpled in a frown, before glancing back at her. Beneath the neatly trimmed beard, his jaw was misshapen. "Would you like me to walk with you?" he offered, speaking slowly as he enunciated his words. But his eyes were wide and afraid. Alexandros might scoff at the temple's instruction that the *thysies* maintain their virtue—and more than scoff, in her case—but clearly many of the caregivers took the threat of temple reprisals seriously. He was the second male

caregiver she'd met who was uneasy in her company.

Feeling sorry for the man, she shook her head. "I'll wait here for Erika." He nodded with relief, but before he could leave, she caught his elbow. "Is Dora...?" Her voice broke. She swallowed, trying again. "Will she live?"

Giving her hand on his bare arm a wide-eyed stare, he said, "They assaulted her. Broke her fingers."

Her fingers? Rheia gasped, and the man nodded, meeting her gaze without flinching this time. Had her understanding elevated her in his eyes, from a sacred *thysia* to be avoided to ... what? A friend of a friend?

"Go after your master. Help him, if you can."

Without a word, the man set off, heading the same way Alexandros had. Raking her fingers through her hair, Rheia leaned against one of the red limestone pillars, trying to slow her racing heart. She stared up at the huge bull's head carving hanging above the stone door. It had terrified her the first time she'd seen it, representing an unknown monster that it turned out didn't exist. Now it reminded her of the temple, its sweeping horns so like those on the Areus statue in the temple's *cella*, and she scowled at it. The demon was the real monster, and so was its puppet, Draconaidas, and whichever guards did his unsavoury work. Had that lazy temple guard been hiding his recognition of Dora all along? The idea that he'd broken her fingers—knowing she only had one good hand—filled Rheia's veins with rage that made her want to scream at the sky, call down the wrath of the gods on such evil. But the gods' wrath was a lacklustre thing these days.

Her own wrath would have to do.

When Erika reached the top of the stairs, Rheia told

her what she knew and together they hurried to the healing rooms, each caught up in her own thoughts. It wasn't until Rheia saw the discarded basket sitting in the hall, up against one wall so no one would trip on it, that realisation hit her. She froze, her sandals skidding to a stop. She stared at the basket as though it were a viper, coiled and ready to strike.

Erika looked from the basket to Rheia, realisation turning her features sympathetic. She leaned forward, opening the lid and peering inside. "Empty," she said softly. "Perhaps she delivered it."

A hiss of pain drew Rheia's head up. The drape over the door to Yalee's room was drawn, allowing her to rest despite the commotion next door. The other healing room was crowded, two male caregivers—including the bearded one—moving around Alexandros with quick efficiency. One lay out bandages and small lengths of straight-cut timber while the other crushed leaves into a poultice.

Alexandros was by the bed, much as he'd been when Rheia found him that morning. But Dora wasn't unconscious, dragged down by nightsleep and exhaustion. She sat up, leaning heavily on one hand—her fingerless one—while the other rested in her lap. Her face was as pale as milk, with bright spots of colour marring each cheek. Her eyes were glassy, and even from the door Rheia could see her breathing was rapid.

Dora spotted Rheia, standing by the door. Their gazes met and—slowly, as though every movement hurt her— Dora shook her head.

The floor swayed under Rheia, and she put one hand out, gripping the cool stone of the doorframe so hard the pads of her fingers burned. Her head swam and, despite

the pain, she wasn't courageous enough to let go.

Erika entered the room, moving to stand beside Alexandros and partially blocking Dora from view. "What happened?" Erika asked as Alexandros put a hand against Dora's forehead, frowning.

"Temple guards," Dora said, her voice breathy and faint. Alexandros began talking to one of the male caregivers, telling him to go to the kitchen to fetch grape juice and wine. Rheia craned her neck to look past him, straining to catch Dora's words. "They caught me halfway … to Loukios's house. Dragged me into an alley. Took the letter. Asked what we were planning. B-beat me. Broke my…"

When Dora trailed off, Erika leaned forward to put an arm around her shoulder. "Come on, now. Lie down so the master can set those bones. If anyone can save them, he can." Dora mumbled a protest, but let Erika ease her back on the cushions. "We'll get you some nightsleep."

Dora looked as though she wanted to object, but her movements must have sent a flare of pain through her mangled hand because she let out a small cry.

Rheia fell back as the sound struck her, carrying with it a terrible accusation. It was her fault Dora had left the safety of the house. It had been her letter Dora was carrying, and the guards, suspecting as much, had moved to intercept it.

Draconaidas had the letter. He knew they were looking for the intaglio; she'd had to describe it in detail, seeing no way to refer to it in code. And—worse—her father *didn't* know about it. The temple had trapped her in the house. There was nothing she could do, nothing anyone could do.

And in five days she would be dead.

Cold crept over Rheia like a thief, even as her forehead prickled with perspiration. She clenched her hands into fists, her nails biting her palms as she slumped against the wall. The empty basket scraped against her ankle. *I will not faint.*

"Rheia?" Alexandros's voice, from across the room.

"I'm fine," Rheia lied. Black-winged despair closed in, a dark bird fluttering at the periphery of Rheia's vision. *I will not faint.*

"I'll look after her," Erika said, her voice gruff. "You stay with Dora."

Alexandros mumbled something Rheia didn't hear over the rustle of those black feathers, and then Erika was before her, taking her hands and looking into her eyes. "Let's get you back to the *gynaikon*," the caregiver said, chaffing Rheia's fingers before turning to lead her like a child away from the healing rooms.

"I'm sorry," Rheia said, stumbling as the corridor swayed beneath her feet. "I don't feel so good."

"It's the shock," Erika said. "You need to rest."

But the words grew distant as Rheia spiralled down into blackness.

CHAPTER THIRTY

Sleep clung to Rheia, reluctant to release her. Her limbs were heavy, as though she lay under a pile of furs rather than a thin sheet, and her head felt as though it had been swaddled like an infant.

She prised open eyelids gummed with sleep, recognising the familiar slant of afternoon light across her ceiling in the *gynaikon*. She couldn't have been asleep long, if it was still afternoon, but her body said otherwise.

"Rheia," Parthenia said, and stepped across the room. "Thank Gaea you're awake. How do you feel?"

"Fuzzy," Rheia croaked, swallowing. Her throat was as dry as a summer pasture.

"Any pain yet?"

Yet? She shook her head.

"Here." Parthenia helped her sit and slipped a reed into her mouth. Strained grape juice slid across Rheia's tongue, the sweet, thick liquid revitalising the dry tissues of her mouth and throat as she swallowed.

The memory of Dora doing the same thing for Rheia

on her first day in the house surfaced and, recalling the muzzy sensation she'd felt that day, she touched her temple. It was slippery with oil, and she sniffed the tip of her finger. A familiar, cool tang filled her sinuses. "Nightsleep," Rheia said, her voice sounding dull to her ears. Her forehead felt tight, a dull pressure just shy of an ache, but the bruising headache she recalled after Dora had awakened her from her previous nightsleep fugue was mercifully absent.

Parthenia nodded. "There's no shame in it. Erika told me what happened."

"There's no way out," Rheia said, and the idea didn't strangle her like it had. Nightsleep truly was powerful. She spoke slowly, probing her thoughts for the stab of despair. "We're going to die in five days and there's nothing I can do to save us." *Nothing.*

Parthenia's face tightened in a wince. "Four days."

"Four days?" Rheia blinked.

"You slept for a long time."

"Oh." Erika must have given Rheia a larger dose of the herb than she should have, but the girl found she didn't care. She took another sip of juice. "Is Dora well?"

Leaving Rheia to hold the cup, Parthenia turned to look out the window, and Rheia saw the sheen of oil on the other girl's temple. She'd had nightsleep too, then. "She hasn't come here, but the others say the Beast, your Alexandros, has splinted her fingers," Parthenia said. "They try to sound positive, but I think it's for show."

Rheia's chest tightened at the thought of Alexandros, but it was a distant ache, like a bruise almost healed. "And Alexandros? How is he?"

Parthenia shrugged. "I haven't seen him either."

Disappointment was a brief sting, fading fast. Of course he hadn't come to see her. She was in the *gynaikon*. "I should go to him. He'll be upset."

Parthenia nodded, taking the empty cup so Rheia could push the sheet aside. Moving felt like wading through water, but she forced herself to stand.

"He might have another plan by now," the Carmean girl said, but her flat tone said she didn't believe it. "Let me help you dress."

Rheia nodded, grateful for the assistance. Parthenia laid out a *chiton* the pale blue of a winter sea while Rheia bathed at the bowl of clean water. Once she was dressed, Parthenia brushed her hair until it crackled. "Do you want me to braid it for you?" the girl asked, and Rheia shook her head, remembering Alexandros saying how much he loved it out.

The tightness in her skull flared into a sharper pain as the two girls emerged into the *gynaikon's* courtyard. The hot sun seemed to stab through Rheia's eyes and into her brain. Wincing, she shaded her eyes, drawing Parthenia's knowing look. "Is it wearing off?"

"I think so," Rheia said.

"Let's get you some more grape juice. The sweetness helps," Parthenia said, leading her to the dining hall.

Erika sat in the open-sided room, her face pensive, but as they entered her expression flickered with relief before dropping back into its usual, bland mask. "How are you feeling?" the caregiver asked, standing so the girls could claim their customary couches.

"Headache," Rheia said, dragging her couch so that, when she reclined, her back was to the bright courtyard.

"Is there more juice?" Parthenia added.

"We have normal grape juice here, or I can send to the kitchen to have some strained for you," Erika said, picking up a heavy jug.

"I like it pulpy." Rheia watched as Erika poured a cup of the thick purple grape juice, opaque with crushed skins and seeds. It made sense for them to strain it when it was to be drunk through a reed, but she wasn't an invalid. "You gave me the nightsleep?"

Erika nodded, handing Rheia the cup. Her eyes tightened with anxiety. "I know you've refused it before, but the shock of what happened to Dora—"

Rheia waved her explanation away with one hand, curling her other around the cool pottery cup. "It's fine."

Erika's shoulders eased, the only visible sign of her relief. "Would you like another dose? It will cure your headache."

"No. Thank you," Rheia added, lifting the cup to take a mouthful of the dark juice. It wasn't as cloyingly sweet as the honey-thickened drink she'd had before, and the texture was coarser, but she enjoyed it more. "How is Dora?"

"She will heal," Erika said firmly, as though unwilling to entertain any other outcome.

"And Yalee?"

"She will heal, too."

Rheia opened her mouth to ask if she could see Alexandros, but a clunk from the lock on the double doors caught her attention. She turned to see them flung aside as Polymede hurried in. The woman's pregnancy-swollen face was pale, her eyes wide. Rheia stood, but before she could take more than a step, Erika pushed passed her, shuffling across the courtyard as fast as she

could. "Is it the baby?" she demanded.

Polymede's gaze flew to Rheia, and the girl took a step back, the table bumping into the back of her thigh. She knew the answer before the caregiver spoke. "No." Polymede ran a hand down her forehead, rubbing her eyes for a moment before continuing. "It... Draconaidas is here. To see *her*."

Adrenaline lanced through Rheia, dispelling her headache and the muzziness of nightsleep both. *Draconaidas?* Had he come to put a stop to her attempts to avoid her fate, once and for all? If he killed her, who would they sacrifice then?

"Does the master know?" Erika said.

Polymede shook her head. "The priest said he wants a private word with Rheia. That he doesn't intend her harm."

"And you believe him?" Erika said. Polymede's mouth turned down at the corners, and Erika sighed. "It doesn't matter. Where is he?"

"The trireme room."

"I will take her. You stay with Parthenia." Erika reached behind a pot, pulling out her familiar bronze shears and hanging them from her belt. "Rheia? Come along."

With her hands shaking and her heart in her throat, Rheia stepped forward. "You don't have to go," Parthenia said, her eyes wide and dark with fear as she reached out to grab Rheia's hand.

"He can't kill me," Rheia said, although her quavering voice revealed her doubt.

"Maybe not, but a sacrifice only needs to be alive, not whole," Parthenia said.

"Enough," Polymede said, her tone firm as she sat on Rheia's couch. "We won't let her be harmed."

Parthenia's eyes glittered, but she clenched her jaw shut, giving Rheia a stiff nod and releasing her hand. "Gods be with you, then."

Rheia nodded back. Erika's face was hard as she held the door open for Rheia to pass through. On the other side, two stern-faced male caregivers stood, each wearing leather armour and a bronze sword at his hip. "Good," Erika grunted, but Rheia noted the way the armour creaked with newness as the men closed the door so Erika could lock it. Could either man use his sword, or was it just for show?

More guards were in evidence along the main hall, standing in pairs, their gazes watchful. By the trireme room—the room where Rheia had shared a meal with Alexandros and Dora, she realised—a pair of orange-liveried temple guards stood, expressions contemptuous as they regarded the armed caregivers facing them from the opposite wall.

Rheia felt her spine stiffen at the sight of the temple guards. She didn't know whether either of these men was the one who had broken Dora's fingers, but they looked like the type of thugs who would take satisfaction in the task. Her fingers curled into claws, and she clenched her jaw to stop from shrieking her outrage.

"Bank your fire," Erika murmured as they approached and the temple guards turned to regard them. "Let it strengthen you, but remember who you're dealing with."

"Draconaidas is a snake," Rheia whispered back.

"Exactly. Don't goad him into biting."

Rheia nodded once, and Erika gave her a doubtful glance before pushing past her to enter the trireme room first. Rheia followed after.

Draconaidas was alone in the small dining room, sitting on the same stool Alexandros had occupied three days before, the carving of the rearing sea monster at his back reminding Rheia of Areus's viper. The high priest wore his customary *chiton* of scarlet threaded with gold, and the iron helm looked heavy, its sweeping horns in danger of chipping the wall behind him. His hard gaze ran over Rheia, taking her in, before he turned to Erika. "Fetch us refreshments," he said in his deep voice, and a thread of panic wove through Rheia at the idea of being alone with him.

Erika glanced at Rheia, taking in her suddenly stiff posture and wide eyes, before bowing towards the high priest. "I will send someone," she said, her expression bland. Draconaidas's eyes narrowed, and she continued, "With all due respect, it is my duty to ensure Rheia arrives at Areus's festival in the same state of purity as she entered our care."

Rheia admired the woman's ability to lie without flinching. She certainly hadn't taken any great care with Rheia's virtue

"That is my concern, too," Draconaidas said, his hands curling into fists on the tabletop. "Are you suggesting otherwise?"

"No, sir," Erika said. "But my duty is given to me by holy Areus himself, and I would not be foresworn."

Draconaidas regarded her for a long moment and then nodded, leaning back against the wall with a magnanimous wave. "Very well. Send for refreshments. We can wait." His gaze shifted to Rheia, and she clenched her hands in the folds of her *chiton*. "Will you sit, child?"

Rheia lowered herself onto the same stool she'd occupied

last time, so that she faced the high priest across the low, bare table. Erika finished her murmured conversation with one of the caregivers outside. Rheia glimpsed him as he passed the door, hurrying away with a hand on the sword sheath to keep it from swinging into his legs.

With her hands clasped before her, Erika stood by the door, her gaze watchful and her posture as straight as her curved spine would allow.

Remembering Erika's admonishment, Rheia tried to keep her voice polite when she spoke. "Why are you here?"

Draconaidas raised his eyebrows at her, and Rheia winced inwardly. "You want to charge straight in, then? Very well. Rheia, we have a problem."

Only one? "Oh?"

Draconaidas glanced at Erika, at the open doorway behind her. "You may not have heard, but two days ago the temple of Areus was attacked. The *adyton* was destroyed by fire and an acolyte murdered." His eyes widened, his expression softening. He looked earnest. Almost fatherly. "I have reason to believe the Beast was involved in the attack."

Rheia's mouth fell open. She was sure the high priest knew of her involvement in the incident at the temple, too. Typhein would have told him. But if he wasn't bringing it up, she wouldn't either. She closed her jaw so hard her teeth clicked together.

"Indeed," Draconaidas said, taking in her shock with an amused twitch of his lip that hardened her certainty. *He knows.* "You may not appreciate the religious significance of this, however. For the Beast to turn against its own divine father is a sign the creature is on the edge of madness. I spent all of yesterday fasting, praying to

Areus for a sign. This morning, I received one."

He reached down beside his stool, and when his hand reappeared he was holding a piece of rolled vellum. Rheia's belly skittered with nerves at its familiarity. It could have been cut from the same sheet as the piece Alexandros had used to invite her to speak with him. The same piece she'd scraped clean so she could write to her family, requesting they let her borrow the statue of Eidoneus.

Surely it was a coincidence? There couldn't be that many ways to tan vellum, after all.

But when Draconaidas placed the material in her trembling palm and she unrolled it, she recognised the elegant handwriting. The note was short.

I will not sacrifice Rheia, daughter of Loukios. Find another sacrifice, or in four days Typhein will be freed and the city will burn.

It was signed with the bull's horns. Alexandros's mark.

Tears prickled at Rheia's eyes and she blinked them away, swallowing hard. She would *not* cry in front of the high priest. Still, relief warmed her chest, and she found she was able to smile as she handed the vellum back to Draconaidas. He dropped it on the floor beside him as though it were a piece of trash.

With a scuffing of sandals, Erika moved to the side to admit two other caregivers. One carried a jug of wine and two cups, while the other held a tray of sweets. Draconaidas watched them as they laid the food out and filled the cups, the fingers tapping on his thigh indicating his impatience. As soon as they were gone he snatched up his cup to take a long drink. *He's afraid,*

Rheia realised with dawning wonder. She'd assumed Draconaidas wanted the demon to be freed, was doing the monster's bidding ... but what if that wasn't true?

"So are you going to do as he demands?" she asked, nodding at the vellum and folding her hands before her.

"We cannot," the high priest said, the base of his cup smacking against the tabletop so hard she feared it would dent the smooth timber. "Do you remember the ritual with the viper on the day of the lottery?" Rheia nodded. "That is when the—" His eyes darted to Erika, and he began again, changing what he'd been about to say. "That is when the sacrifices are confirmed by holy Areus. And that ritual cannot be performed within ten days of the feast."

He'd been going to say the demon. Rheia was sure of it. "So it wasn't a test of my virtue then?" she asked, her tone bitter as she remembered her terror, the way Draconaidas had seemed to enjoy it.

"That too," the high priest said, but his eyelid twitched. "However, the fact remains that you and the three *helot thysies* are the chosen sacrifices, and if the Beast acts on his threat, then the demon *will* be freed. The city *will* burn, and thousands will die."

Hope flared, tiny as a spark flying from a cookfire, in her chest. Could this man, this loathsome man, become an ally against Typhein? "The binding is flawed," she said slowly. "If we were to do it again, bind the demon properly, with no conditions, then the city could be rid of him. With your help—"

"No," Draconaidas snapped, snuffing the spark of hope. "The way things are has been decreed by Areus himself. Who are we to challenge it?" He paused, rubbing his

forehead, and then Rheia's eyes widened with surprise as he lifted the heavy iron helm from his head to place it on the floor beside his chair. His hair was cropped short and was as black as one of Alexandros's *chitons*. The skin at his brow where the helmet's rim had rested was an angry red. "Besides, it is too risky," he added more softly. "During the transfer, the demon would be free."

And the demon is the source of your political power. You don't want to lose that, Rheia thought sourly, sitting up straighter and folding her arms across her chest. "What do you want from me, then?"

"The Beast has clearly developed a … a fondness for you. The means by which it has done so are irrelevant now." The high priest's dark gaze flicked to Erika and back to Rheia; she was sure the caregivers would be made to pay for allowing their master to get to know her, so that he might develop that fondness. Didn't Draconaidas realise that was why Typhein had urged his priest to select her in the first place? To force Alexandros into refusing? "It—"

"He is not an *it*. As you well know. He is a man," Rheia said, her fingers digging into her forearms as she fought the urge to fling her wine into Draconaidas's face, cup and all.

"Very well." The high priest's eyes flashed and Erika cleared her throat, a soft warning. For Rheia, or for Draconaidas? "*He* has forgotten his loyalty to his divine master, and his vow to be the god's hand on the day of the sacrifice. *He* has forgotten that thousands of lives saved outweigh four lost."

"That may be so," Rheia said, lifting her chin. "But what do you want from *me*? Other than to die, I mean?"

The priest's top lip curled for a heartbeat, revealing a flash of teeth, before his expression shifted back to honest entreaty. "You must persuade him that, four days from now, he should spill your blood. That whatever feelings he may have for you are irrelevant in the face of the greater good. You must use whatever means are necessary. You are the only one who can save Oreareus from the Beast's threat." He leaned forward. "Rheia, you are the only one who can save your family."

Draconaidas's faint emphasis on the last two words made the threat clear. Rheia's blood turned to ice in her veins. She watched, suddenly numb, as Draconaidas reached into a pouch at his belt, pulling forth a lock of light brown hair bound with a piece of string. The hair curled in his outstretched palm, and Rheia stared at it, unable to move.

She knew that hair as well as she knew her own. The bouncy, unruly hair that took her mother half an hour to brush, its owner wiggling all the while. *Aias.*

Seeing her recognition, Draconaidas dropped the lock onto the table. It landed on a plate of honey and sesame cakes, the fine threads sticking to the glazed surface.

"What have you done to him?" Rheia whispered.

"He's safe. For now," Draconaidas said, wiping his hand against the front of his *chiton* as though Aias's hair had sullied it. When he spoke again, his voice was as quiet as hers had been. "But unless you do your very best to ensure *Alexandros's* obedience, he won't remain that way."

She clutched the edge of the table, her nails aching as they dug into it. "But I've already told Alexandros he has to!"

"Then tell him again. Find another way." Draconaidas picked up his helm and stood, placing it back on his head and stalking from the room. The helmet reminded her of Alexandros's heavy bronze bull mask, and fear clutched at her.

Alexandros wasn't insane, but if he had to kill her a second time...

Aias.

Rheia put her head down on the table and wept.

CHAPTER THIRTY-ONE

Rheia didn't know how long she stayed there, her head bowed and crying ugly, jagged tears until her eyes burned and her face felt puffy and raw. Finally, her grief subsided to sniffling, hiccoughing breaths, and she became aware of Erika's hand stroking her hair as the woman murmured for her to hush, that everything would work out in the end. Everything would be fine.

But it wouldn't be fine. Never again.

"What are you going to do?" the caregiver asked when Rheia fell silent.

"I don't know." She took a wobbly breath. "If I don't talk to Alexandros, Draconaidas will find out. I know he will. He'll hurt my brother." Her gaze fell on the lock of Aias's hair, now sitting before her on the table, brushed clean. She picked it up, running it against her cheek. It was smooth as a baby chick's feathers, and smelled of honey and temple incense. *Aias.*

"Then you must talk to him. To Alexandros," Erika said, saying her master's name slowly, as though doing

so required great daring.

"But he's already told me he won't do it. He won't kill me." The feeling of helplessness was a gaping chasm inside Rheia, one she could fall into, drown in.

Erika stood, walking around the table to pick something up off the floor. The piece of vellum. She held it out to Rheia. "Do you love him?"

Her fingers curled around the fine kid skin. "I ... yes. I do." In one hand, Aias's life. In the other, Alexandros's heart.

"Then you will find a way." She slid an arm around Rheia's back, helping her to her feet. "Let's get you cleaned up."

Erika led Rheia to the bathhouse, taking the vellum and lock of hair from her and putting them on a high shelf where they wouldn't get wet. The blue tiles were soothing, gentle on the girl's eyes as she lay impassively in the water, letting the caregiver wash her hair, scrub her skin till it glowed, and trim her nails with a tiny, sharp dagger. With her expression solemn, Erika helped Rheia to dress, and braided her damp hair so it hung in a heavy rope over her shoulder. Rheia touched the end of the braid, frowning. Alexandros loved her hair.

"Will you cut it off for me?" she said in a whisper, and Erika's eyes widened. "My hair. Cut it off."

"But it's so beautiful," Erika protested, stepping back, her hands raised in protest.

"That's the point." Rheia snatched the tiny dagger up from atop a chest of bath oils, holding the hair taut in her other hand. Gritting her teeth, she sawed at the braid, just behind her ear. The hairs popped and gave way.

Erika tensed, her eyes following the blade's path, so close to Rheia's throat. "Give me the knife, Rheia," she said in a calm voice Rheia had heard shepherds use when they didn't want to startle their flock.

"Will you finish it for me?"

"I suppose I must, now," the woman said, and Rheia surrendered the knife. Erika sighed, the tension flowing out of her posture as she pulled the half-severed braid around to Rheia's back so she could finish the job. "I can't stick it back on. Foolish girl."

"Long hair is for brides. Mothers. Girls with a future," Rheia said.

Erika sighed heavily, laying the length of hair on the chest where the knife had been. She combed what was left of Rheia's hair straight with her fingers. Rheia tried not to wince at the gentle tugging as Erika snicked at her hair with the dagger, trying to even the cut.

"There," Erika said finally, giving the girl a pat on the cheek before tucking the dagger away at her belt where Rheia couldn't reach it. "Dora will be very unhappy with me."

"I'm sorry," Rheia said. The ends of her hair brushed her shoulders, tickling them when she moved. Her head felt lighter. Untethered. Grief closed her throat as she regarded the severed braid, a tangible sign of her hope, sacrificed on the altar of Draconaidas's demands. Tears burned eyes already weary, and she clenched her jaw. *I won't cry again. He needs to see me calm. He needs to believe this is what I want.* "Can I have some nightsleep before I see him? Please?"

Erika nodded, her lips pressed together into a hard line. "Follow me."

Rheia retrieved the braid of hair and the note, tucking them into her *chiton*, before she followed.

The caregiver led her down the now-familiar corridor between the bathhouse and the healing chambers. When Rheia realised that was where they were headed, she grabbed Erika's arm. "I can't see him yet." Panic fluttered like moths in her throat. "Not until I've had the night-sleep. I—"

"He's down below," Erika said, gently prying Rheia's fingers loose. "It's fine."

"Oh." Feeling foolish, Rheia nodded that they should continue.

The healing chambers were flooded with golden afternoon sunlight. They reached Yalee's first, and Erika poked her head through the entryway, nodding once before gesturing that Rheia should follow. Her steps were quiet, and Rheia wondered if she was hoping to defer a confrontation with Dora.

Yalee sat, propped up by a mound of cushions, her hands covered in wet linen and resting on a bronze tray so her *chiton* wouldn't get soaked. A hint of green at the linen's edges told Rheia the material was there to hold a poultice in place. The girl's eyes shimmered like the surface of a still pool and nightsleep oil sheened her temples, but her colour was good—not flushed with fever or overly pale. Relief surged through Rheia. Yalee would heal.

Yalee's eyes widened for a moment before a wide grin split her face. "I love your hair," she said in her loud, flat voice.

"Thank you," Rheia said, her own smile fading when Erika took the jar of nightsleep oil from a high shelf, well out of the bed-bound girl's reach. Yalee's delight slipped away, her mouth turning down at the corners.

Erika picked up a twist of cloth no bigger than Rheia's

little finger. She unstoppered the oil, allowing the cool, sharp scent of snow on a pine-covered mountain to fill the room. Pure nightsleep oil: unblended, undiluted. Erika dipped the tip of the fabric into the oil, dragging it across the jar's brim to rid it of any excess.

Rheia closed her eyes when Erika swiped each of her temples with the oil. Her pores seemed to expand, drinking it in, and she breathed deeply of the cleansing aroma even as a single tear tracked down her cheek to drop from her jaw.

"Erika?" Yalee said, her voice tight. "Can I have another dose?" Erika shuffled to the bed, and the girl sighed with relief. "Thank you."

The ache in Rheia's chest began to fade, the knot in her throat to dissolve, as the cool scent filled her senses, numbed her emotions and eased her pain … just like snow numbed bare hands in the wintertime. Like frostbite.

"Erika?" Dora's voice came from the next room, tight with suspicion. "What are you doing in there?"

"Stay here," Erika said softly, patting Rheia on the shoulder. "I'll be back in a minute."

Rheia nodded, moving to Yalee's side so the girl could meet her gaze without having to strain. Neither of them spoke, and Rheia was able to hear snatches of the conversation next door. Draconaidas had come. Rheia had agreed to be sacrificed. Rheia had asked for nightsleep, and would speak to the master about her decision.

"He will be devastated." Dora's voice was hoarse with grief and frustration. Erika's reply was too soft to hear, but then Dora said, "Afterwards, please ask him to come to me. I want to make sure he's looked after."

"As you wish."

"Appelon take it, why do I have to be injured *now*? When he needs me the most?" There were frustrated tears in Dora's voice, and Rheia hung her head. Her newly shorn hair fell about her face, the ends tickling her jaw, her chin. *My fault.* Yalee stirred beside her, her hands moving on the tray as though she wanted to reach out to Rheia. A breath hissed between the girl's teeth and she paled, subsiding against the cushions.

"Shh," Rheia said softly, leaning forward to kiss Yalee on the forehead. "I just wanted to say I'm sorry for what happened to you. You're the bravest person I know."

The words had been too fast for Yalee to interpret, and worry tightened the girl's eyes, lined her face in a way that made her look older than her years.

"Goodbye," Rheia said slowly.

Yalee's gaze fixed on her lips. Sadness shadowed her face, the emotion softened and made hazy by nightsleep. "Goodbye."

When Rheia turned, Erika was standing in the doorway, watching with shimmering eyes. But all she said was, "Do you want me to take you to him now?"

A memory surfaced, of lying with Alexandros in the cushions before his fire, the warm light glowing off his skin, tracing the hard lines of his muscles and dancing in his hair. "Not down there," she said. "Can you please ask him to attend me up here?"

Rheia was in the trireme room again, but this time she'd arrived first and chosen the seat that put her back to the sea serpent. She didn't want to look at it. Erika had left a pair of armed caregivers at the door before going to find Alexandros, and the girl felt lonelier than ever as she struggled to recapture a sense of resignation to her fate. She was sure she'd felt it once. Before she'd been given hope.

The nightsleep helped. It let her see things logically. Who was she, to risk the lives of thousands—the lives of her family—for the chance to save herself? Those scales weren't balanced.

Distant footsteps and a raised voice caught her attention. She raised her gaze to the doorway, unsurprised when Alexandros skidded to a stop there. His hair was in disarray, and his *chiton* hung longer than usual, unbelted.

He was magnificent.

"Are you well, Rheia?" he demanded, coming into the room and crossing to her side of the table. His gaze ran over her face as though looking for signs of injury, hesitating for a moment at the corners of her eyes. He'd seen the nightsleep oil, then. "Erika told me—" He stopped, staring at her hair. "What happened?"

"Draconaidas came to speak to me," she said, ignoring the question about her hair. She moved her hands away so he couldn't catch them in his own. "Please sit down. We need to talk."

She'd hoped he'd take the seat opposite, but instead he sat at a right angle to her. The heat of his bare leg was warm beside hers, only inches between them under the table.

"What did he say?" Alexandros said. His bronze-coloured eyes were shadowed, his jaw clenching until she could hear his teeth grind together.

"He brought me these," Rheia said, not even blushing as she reached down the front of her *chiton* to remove the lock of hair, the vellum note. Alexandros had seen her naked, after all; the barest flash of skin was nothing compared to that. "The hair belongs to my brother," she added when his gaze fell on it.

"He's threatening to harm your family?"

"Yes," Rheia said, and before she could pull away he reached out to take one of her hands in his. His fingers felt unnaturally warm in hers—or was it that she had turned to ice on the outside as well as in? The sight of their hands together captivated her. They looked so right. A dull ache started in her middle.

"To stop us from trying to properly bind the demon?" Alexandros guessed.

"Yes. He doesn't want it to get free, and he doesn't want to lose his source of power by having us bind it properly." Rheia forced her gaze from their intertwined fingers to look at Alexandros's face. She wanted to smother it in kisses, even as she wished they had never met. It would be easier for both of them that way. "He's scared you'll make good on your threat and the demon will escape. I am to persuade you to fulfil your duty. Cut our throats and see the demon bound for another year."

Alexandros dropped her hand and sat back, the gesture so sudden that she jumped. "I will *not*," he snarled, his nostrils flaring.

"Alexandros," she said gently, "you must. As I told you when we first met, if you have to choose between me and everyone else on this island, I'm just one girl."

"You also told me you didn't want to die." His hands clenched into fists as though he wanted to fight a way free of this trap, a way for both of them.

Rheia took a breath, lifted her chin and said, "I've changed my mind. I want to go home to Eidoneus."

"You don't mean that. It's the nightsleep talking." His eyes welled with grief, but his gaze stayed unblinking on hers and his tears did not spill. "Rheia, please don't ask me to do this. I can't."

Beneath the icy numbness, a part of Rheia was screaming. But when she spoke her voice was calm. "I'm asking you to do this."

He slid from his stool to kneel before her; the stools were low, and his head was almost at the same height as hers. He wrapped his arms around her waist, pulling her to him, so their foreheads pressed together. His fiery gaze bore into her. His dill flower and cypress scent flooded her senses, mingling with the cool aroma of nightsleep until she thought she might burst. "You are not and will never be just a girl," he declared. "You are my wife." And he kissed her, his lips almost bruising hers. He seemed to be seeking to lose himself in her, to show her the strength of his defiance for those that would separate them. Separate them again, after they'd just found each other.

The heat that raced through her melted the ice, letting her love for him blaze forth. She curled her hands in his hair and their tongues tangled together. His lips were salty with tears, and she didn't know whether they were his or hers.

When they pulled apart, the anguish in his face sent a spike of regret through her, making her yearn for the nightsleep fugue to return. She shouldn't have let him kiss her. She'd just made it harder for him to hear what

she had to say next. "Yes, I am your wife," she said, her hands still wrapped in the fabric of his *chiton* as though they too never wanted to let go. "And I'm asking you to do this, as your last gift to me. We will be together in Eidoneus's fields, where the asphodel grows. I will wait for you there, no matter how long it takes. I swear it."

When she prised her fingers loose and stood, straightening her *chiton*, he began to sob. The sound was heartbroken, like a child crying after a nightmare. His grief tore through her, and she touched his bowed head one last time, her hand trembling, before striding around the other side of the table, towards the door. Her nightsleep blanket was in tatters; she had to get out of there before her resolve crumbled entirely. "I love you, Alexandros."

Erika was waiting in the hallway, her face blotchy, as though she too had been crying. The caregiver guards had been sent away. "Look after him," Rheia rasped. "And please, when you can, bring me more nightsleep."

Then, blind with tears, Rheia fled back to the *gynaikon*.

She wouldn't leave it again before the sacrifice. She wouldn't risk seeing him again.

CHAPTER THIRTY-TWO

Rheia wished that the sacrifice took place first thing in the morning, rather than at sunset. The waiting would have been over already. That would be better than her, Parthenia and the two male *thysies* she'd still not met having to wait all day to meet their deaths.

The sounds of the festival drifted over the house's walls and into the courtyard: cheering as athletes completed in feats of strength and speed; the clash of arms as warriors fought for honour and prizes; voices raised in prayer, songs to Areus and to the king. The air smelled faintly of roasting meats and spilled wine—and, more closely, of nightsleep oil, bright and sharp. Both girls had elected to have a double dose that morning with breakfast.

"It sounds like they're having quite the party," Parthenia remarked, sitting in front of another thin wooden panel. Her painting of a field of red poppies, done by memory, was only half complete. The sun was already descending from its zenith; she was running out of time to get it done, and her strokes were hasty, the tip of her brush glistening

scarlet with paint made from madder root.

"People give thanks to Areus for allowing us to prosper," Rheia said, staring up at the date-plum tree. The last of its blossoms had been washed away by the storm almost a week before, leaving it bereft. "My father used to take us down to the harbour rather than up here. He said it was because down there you sometimes got a breeze off the water, but he didn't want us to see the sacrifice, I think."

Parthenia laughed softly, bitterly. "And now you shall have a seat in the front row."

"Yes."

They fell silent for a time. Rheia thought of Alexandros, of his laugh, his bronze-coloured eyes, his gentle touch. The nightsleep kept the memories from paining her too badly. She hoped today would not destroy him. She prayed that, although she had failed to stop the ritual, Eidoneus would forgive her and find another way to see Alexandros freed from his duty so she would be able to keep her oath to him. Otherwise she'd be waiting forever.

When the door clicked open, her heart leapt, her hands curling in the grass beneath her. Parthenia sighed, leaning her painting against the trunk of the tree. "Is it time?" she said, regarding Erika and three other caregivers as they shut the door behind them and came down the stairs.

"Almost," Erika said. "Would you bathe first?"

Parthenia nodded, regarding the spots of paint on her hands, but Rheia shook her head. "I don't want to leave the *gynaikon*." Was avoiding Alexandros courage, she wondered, or cowardice? He'd sent her a dozen notes in the last four days, but she'd returned them all unopened. She knew that, if she read them, her resolve would waver.

"We will have water brought then," Erika said, nodding

at one of the other women, who left the way she'd come. The other women escorted Parthenia to the bathhouse.

Rheia stood, beckoning for Erika to follow her back to her room. The statue of Eidoneus stood on her jewellery chest, its feet covered with withered herbs she had cut in the garden. Rheia bent to kiss its cool brow, then picked it up and lay it in the centre of a square of fabric she'd spread across her bed that morning. "Can you get this back to my father?" she asked, folding the corners in to wrap the statue tight. "I told my family I'd see it returned to them, and after I'm dead the temple guards outside the gate should let you send messengers again."

"I will," Erika said, her voice soft and her face lined with a terrible grief and guilt that made her look decades older. "Have you eaten? Is there anything I can get for you?"

Rheia shook her head. The idea of food made her stomach churn and her mouth go dry. "I wouldn't mind some more nightsleep, though. So I can face him without weeping."

Erika must have anticipated that request, because she had the small jar in a pouch at her hip. She applied a dab of oil to each of Rheia's temples and then, after a brief hesitation, behind each of her ears as well. Rheia inhaled deeply, feeling the calmness seep into her, and waited in silence for what came next.

Soon the other caregiver returned with a steaming bowl of water and a fold of cloth, and Erika took them, dismissing her with a shake of her head. "I'll do this," she said softly, before turning to Rheia and saying in a louder voice, "Let me help you wash and dress."

"Alright," Rheia said.

"Polymede had her baby," Erika said with false brightness as she unpinned the brooches at Rheia's shoulders,

setting them aside. The *chiton* slipped down Rheia's body to puddle at her ankles. "A healthy little boy."

"That's good news," Rheia murmured as she stepped from the fabric.

"Yes. He's got the lungs to be a bard, that one." Erika picked up the cloth and dipped it in the water, washing Rheia with a gentle efficiency that reminded her of Charis on the morning of the lottery. *Charis.* Her grandmother was dead by now, she was sure of it, and the idea that Rheia would see her this evening in Eidoneus's realm drew a tiny smile to her lips.

The sacrifice *chiton* was a brilliant white, with small bulls' heads stitched along its hem in bloody splotches. The brooches Erika produced from a pouch were the same ones Rheia had worn when she'd come to the house: golden discs embossed with the horns of a bull. Rheia ran a finger over the raised arcs, thinking of Alexandros. He'd be getting ready now too, donning that heavy bronze mask. Had he also taken nightsleep to get him through this? She hoped he had.

Erika brushed Rheia's hair out, making a dissatisfied sound in the back of her throat. "I'm supposed to braid it down your back," she said. "But it's not long enough."

Rheia reached back, pulling the hair together like a horse's tail. "Just tie it with a ribbon. It doesn't matter."

"It does matter," Erika said hotly, brushing Rheia's hands aside so the tail fell loose against the nape of her neck. "I will make you beautiful, Rheia, daughter of Loukios. The citizens of this city will see what they are losing due to their cowardice. Sit."

Rheia sat on the fur rug, her fingers caressing its softness. How many *thysies* had sat here before her, done the same thing as their hair was tugged and woven, anointed with oil and twisted into an elaborate style fit for a wedding? Was the idea to keep the girls' hair out of the way, so Alexandros could make a clean cut? She decided not to ask, not wanting to further upset the caregiver.

Twice Erika left her side, first to rummage through her jewellery chest and then, when she was unsatisfied, Parthenia's. She returned from the Carmean girl's room with a pleased smile, holding a golden circlet made to look like a woven branch from a bay laurel tree. It reminded Rheia of the one she'd seen in Kore's dream of Alexandros as a young man ... although his had been an actual branch, not made from metal. She sighed at the memory, and Erika smiled. "Yes, it is lovely," the woman said, slipping the ends into Rheia's hair. "And now you look like a queen."

There were no adequate reflective surfaces in Rheia's room—the water bowl was empty and the scattered jewellery too small—so she contented herself with running light fingers over her hair while Erika watched with wide eyes and lips pressed together. The locks around her face had been pulled back so tightly against her skull that they ached. The circlet sat back a little from her forehead; behind it, her tresses were a mass of delicate braids and gentle curls that looped and swirled like waves. Beads were a round hardness, cool against her fingertips.

Erika held out several bracelets and Rheia slipped her hands into them. There wasn't a necklace, though; the long sweep of her neck was bare, lending credence to her theory that this was about a clean kill rather than

fashion. Still, she opened her eyes wide so Erika could trace them with charcoal, and then her mouth so the woman could paint it with red vegetable dye.

Erika stepped back to admire her handiwork, her hands clasped together and her eyes bright with unshed tears. "Perhaps you also need some nightsleep?" Rheia suggested dryly, and a surprised laugh burst from the older woman before she covered her mouth with a hand. "I'm serious."

Erika's mirth dropped away. "You have definitely made life interesting." She leaned forward to kiss Rheia's cheek. "Eidoneus keep you, little one."

"You won't be coming?" Rheia said, a thin thread of anxiety uncurling in her stomach. *I won't show fear. I won't!*

"As far as the house's doors," Erika said. "But the halls will be crowded, and I wanted to say it now."

"Please tell Yalee and Dora I'm sorry about their hands," Rheia said, her gaze dropping to her bare feet. The sacrifices didn't wear sandals.

"It wasn't your fault."

"Tell them anyway. And tell Alexandros…" She stopped. What could she ask the woman to say? What would sum up her love, give him the best chance of recovering from the hurt? "Tell him I forgive him, after this is done. And remind him I will be waiting on the other side, as I promised."

"I will. Come on," Erika said, her voice rough. Rheia glanced up to see the caregiver angrily swiping her eyes with the back of her hand. "Let's go see if Parthenia is ready."

Parthenia waited by the stairs leading up to the

gynaikon's double doors. Her *chiton* and brooches were identical to Rheia's, but her longer hair had been twisted into an elegant braid down her back. A silver clip shaped like an open asphodel flower sat at the top of the braid, and her wrists clinked with bracelets. She also wore no necklace.

The Carmean's eyes were wide, despite the clinging nightsleep aroma. When she slipped her hand into Rheia's, her grip was clammy.

"You will see your family soon," Rheia said, squeezing her hand. "Think of your brothers and the mischief they will cause."

Parthenia smiled, and together they turned to the door. "It's like you've met them."

"Orearean or Carmean, brothers are all the same."

Erika stepped forward to bang on the inside of the door three times with her clenched fist. On the other side, Rheia heard the scrape of a key in the lock, and then the doors swung open.

"We're going to the house's main doors?" Rheia asked. When Erika nodded, Rheia set out, Parthenia at her side. She wouldn't follow meekly on this last walk. She would lift her head and stride forth.

Caregivers lined the walls, some faces familiar and others she'd never seen before. They nodded as the girls passed, but the only sound was the rustle of fabric. The air was stuffy with the press of bodies. Somewhere deep in the house, a tiny baby screamed its outrage at the world, and outside the walls the city gathered as the sun sank down to the horizon—but here, in this hall, was a brief moment of peace.

I can do this, Rheia told herself as the girls reached

the main hall. Waiting there were the two male Carmean *thysies*, one Rheia's age and one perhaps twelve, dressed in knee-length versions of the *chitons* the girls wore. They nodded at Parthenia, who smiled faintly back at them, and then turned dark eyes on Rheia. She nodded, and the younger one returned the gesture. The older boy lifted his chin and turned his back on her.

"Don't be rude," Parthenia chided as the boys set off, following a pair of heavily armed caregivers, and the girls fell in behind. Rheia clenched her free hand, resisting the urge to push past them. "She is in the same storm-swamped, gods-damned trireme as the rest of us."

The older boy didn't reply, and Rheia shrugged, telling Parthenia not to worry about it.

The noise of the crowd grew until it became almost painful, individual shouts merging into a din. Dora waited by the house's main doors, her hand wrapped in linen and strapped to her chest so it couldn't be moved. Her face was pale, her brow beaded with perspiration. Her golden circlet was back on her head, her *chiton* was a rich burgundy the colour of wine, and her face was pinched with a worry that seemed to grow when she met Rheia's gaze. "You have done too good a job," she said, looking over the girl's shoulder.

"What else would you have had me do?" Erika retorted from behind Rheia, her voice almost a growl.

Dora didn't reply, but her gaze narrowed as she breathed in the heady scent of nightsleep oil that hung around all four sacrifices. She nodded.

As Draconaidas's booming voice rang out across the square outside and the crowd began to settle, Dora reached past the two boys to slip her fingerless hand behind Rheia's shoulder, nudging her forward. Rheia moved obligingly. "The master has requested the girls be first this year."

"Is that allowed?" Erika said, her eyes widening with something akin to panic.

She should have taken the nightsleep like I suggested.

"Draconaidas says yes."

The other woman muttered something Rheia was sure was blasphemous, but the words were lost under Draconaidas's speech about the demon and his named swords, and how Areus had answered the city's prayers with a binding and a Beast. Unlike on the day of the lottery, she noticed he didn't use Typhein's name. Was he afraid the demon might take over his body, burn it from the inside for the sin of working to ensure Alexandros did his duty? Remembering Timotheus's eyes, coated with blackness and threaded with fire, she thought Draconaidas was right to be worried. But she couldn't feel any pity for him. Not when ensuring the status quo was so personally beneficial to him that he could ignore the total corruption of the Arean priesthood.

Not when he'd had her grandmother beaten to death, and her brother kidnapped.

Dora's head cocked as she listened to the cadence of Draconaidas's speech. "It's time." The arm around Rheia's back tightened in a brief squeeze.

"Look after him when I'm gone," Rheia said. "Don't let him hurt himself."

"Always," Dora said, and Rheia walked out of the house.

For a moment she was blinded by late afternoon sunlight glaring off white-painted stone. She lifted her arm to shade her eyes as the crowd seemed to speak with

one voice, her father's name on everyone's lips. She heard hers, too, a fainter thread—and the sound of it made her drop her hands to her sides and lift her head high as her eyes adjusted. Flashes of movement to either side of her drew her gaze, and she saw that temple guards had fallen in beside her. Their watchful, wary gazes alternated between her and the crowd, kept distant behind a line of city guards.

A temple guard gestured to her left, and she saw a shaded path made by awnings fixed to the house's outer wall. *Are they worried the sun will burn my skin?* The thought was incredulous. But no, her feet were bare and the pavers, beneath all those scuffing sandals, would be hot from the sun. Beneath the awning they were merely warm, and she took slow, measured steps, enjoying the feel of grit on stone beneath her toes and the hot air that filled her lungs, a pleasant counterpoint to the night-sleep's chill.

At the end of the wall, the path turned right, marked out by heavy rugs, and she followed it up to the dais.

Draconaidas, dressed in his usual chiton and iron helm, stood on the platform before a heavy altar of stone that was carved with bulls and snakes and grooved with channels to funnel liquids down the front and into a hole in the ground. Slaves scrubbed the altar clean after each festival, but up close she could see the lines and indentations were stained a faint, rusty red. Some things no scrubbing brush could erase.

"I did as you asked," Rheia murmured, her hands clasped before her as Draconaidas held his arms up to the crowd, fingers spread in a mute call for silence. "Is my brother safe?"

The priest nodded faintly to his left. Rheia leaned forward to peer past him.

In the front row of the crowd, maybe ten paces away from her—but behind a wall of city guards—stood Antheia, Loukios and Aias. Her grandmother's absence confirmed what she suspected, and a pang of grief stabbed through her, even as her hungry gaze absorbed the features of her loved ones for the last time. Her mother's expression was desperate, her cheeks riven with tears. She wore the black of mourning, a dark veil covering her hair, and her hands clasped withered asphodel flowers, brown and past their time. Loukios stood beside her in his gleaming trierarch armour, holding Aias at his hip as though the boy were a toddler, not a lad nine summers old. Aias seemed unharmed, although the lock that used to fall so charmingly across his forehead was gone. The boy's eyes swam and his jaw was tight, as though he wanted to leap to the stage and kick Draconaidas in the shins. Her father's face was bruised, his knuckles split as though he'd been in a fight. His hard eyes softened and his lips parted as he took in his daughter's appearance, pride flaring only to be chased away by despair.

He mouthed two words, and she read them on his lips. *I'm sorry...*

Loukios had fought—maybe to save Aias, or maybe for her. It didn't matter anymore. She held her hand over her chest and then extended it to her family, as though throwing them her love to hold once she was gone.

Aias made a catching gesture, and the grief that surged through Rheia threatened to dispel the nightsleep's calm. *Not yet!* Panic rose on grief's heels, and Rheia dropped her gaze and stepped back beside Draconaidas as the

crowd sighed. A few snuffled with tears.

Just breathe. It will be over soon.

The gasp of several hundred breaths all caught at once made her look up, and for a moment her heart stopped in her chest.

Alexandros stood at the other end of the dais, wearing the ornate bronze bull mask. She felt his stare, even though his eyes were hidden by shadows in the mask's interior; it ran over her, taking in her appearance as though he'd been starved of the sight of her. She knew how he felt. Her gaze traced the bare expanse of his chest and arms; the leather, bronze-studded skirt that hung from his narrow waist most of the way down his thigh; the sandals whose straps wrapped around his calves. She knew that body, had explored it with her hands.

He clutched a sword in his grip—not the plain bronze sword he'd worn during their abortive trip to the temple of Areus, but a long iron one, its blade ornate and heavy with gold embossing. The light of the setting sun caught on the sharpened length of the sword, and Rheia struggled to tear her gaze free as she imagined that sharp line of metal slicing through her spine, the meat of her neck. Her breath came faster, and she struggled to slow it, to rein in the panic. To force her expression back to calm acceptance. Alexandros couldn't know. He had to believe she wanted this.

But she didn't want this. *I don't want to die.*

Draconaidas's arm fell on her shoulder, propelling her towards the altar, and Alexandros's knuckles tightened on the sword's hilt as though he was entertaining visions of beheading the high priest where he stood.

As she lay her head down on the sun-baked rock of

the altar, she felt a pang of sympathy for the other *thysies*. When they were brought up here, the stone would already be covered in her blood. It would stick to their hair and skin as they were splayed like a goat for slaughter. At least, by being first, she only had to contend with the sharp press of the altar's edge into her belly and the discomfort of a temple guard grabbing her wrists and pulling them taut so she couldn't yank free.

Footsteps came closer. She knew she shouldn't look, that it would be easier if she didn't, but she couldn't help it. The golden circlet scraped on the altar's surface as she turned her head. Draconaidas stood close by, taking in her posture, his tongue flickering out as it had done that day in the temple. A shudder ran over her, and she was suddenly glad for the watching crowd. "Alexandros?" she whispered, and he came closer, his presence forcing the high priest to take a step back.

Alexandros dropped his free hand to her hair, running it down the loops and curls to trace the back of her bare neck. A faint sound reached her, muffled and echoing. He was struggling not to cry.

Ignoring Draconaidas's warning look, she rolled her eyes up to meet the black holes in the mask, imagining Alexandros's bronze eyes behind them. "You must do this," she said, keeping her voice soft so he wouldn't hear the rising panic in it, only the love. "I forgive you. Remember what I said last time. I do not fear an eternity in Eidoneus's halls."

Choking back a sob, Alexandros lifted the sword. It reflected the sun like fire and she closed her eyes, feeling a tear leak out to make a wet spot beneath her cheek. "Please, Alexandros," she whispered, "make it quick."

The sword cut through the air.

Metal clanged on stone.

Voices roared.

"*I will not!*" Alexandros bellowed, and she opened her eyes in time to see him strip off the helmet and throw it to the ground. It rolled from the dais and stopped with a gong like a tolling bell. He hurled the sword after it. "She is my wife. I will not murder her for any man, god *or* demon!"

"No!" Draconaidas's voice was a snarl, filled with panic and rage in equal measure. He bent from view, standing with the sword in his hand. "Seize him. We will bind the blade to his hand, force him to swing it. Quickly! Before it's too late!" There was the smack of flesh on flesh, and the crowd screamed with outrage and confusion.

"Alexandros!" Rheia arched her back, tugging against the grip that held her like shackles against the altar. Her bare toes scrabbled against the stone, struggling for purchase. Adrenaline speared through her at the sounds of a beating. "Don't hurt him!"

"*Let go of my daughter.*" A fist thudded into flesh and Rheia was free. She yanked her arms under her and pushed up, scurrying back to the edge of the dais as a temple guard grabbed for her. Her father drew his sword with a slither and pointed it at the guard's face. "Leave her be." Loukios was used to yelling over the ruckus of battle, over a trireme engine at full steam, and his hard words carried to the edges of the square. "If the Beast, holy son of Areus himself, declares he will not kill her, then who are we mortals to question him?"

Rheia's eyes found Alexandros, surrounded by orange-liveried guards on the other side of the dais. Some had drawn their swords, and their blades swayed between Alexandros and Loukios.

"Are you mad?" Spit flew from Draconaidas's lips as he screamed, his face as scarlet as his robes. "Would you burn the city for ... for *love*?"

"There is no finer thing to burn for," Alexandros said. Some in the crowd sighed, a whisper of breath. Other voices rose in panic. Somewhere, a child began to wail. A fist struck Alexandros's stomach and he doubled over. His hair hung around his face. A sword was raised, pommel first, aimed at his skull—

—Rheia screamed—

—and halfway down the hill, with a crack and a roar of falling stone, the statue outside the temple of Areus exploded.

CHAPTER THIRTY-THREE

Everyone turned to stare as the cloud of grey dust rose to cover the sun, an imperfect disc as it crawled below the horizon. Several people climbed onto the statue of the discus thrower to get a better look. The guard with his sword raised to knock Alexandros unconscious lowered his arm slightly, his eyes so wide they seemed to bulge out of his head.

The grey dust turned as black as the smoke from an oil fire, coalescing into a vaguely humanoid shape. The crowd screamed, parents gathering their children and fleeing up the street, towards the palace, the only building that sat higher—or had higher walls—than the House of the Beast.

"It's Typhein! You've freed him," a temple guard snarled, raising his sword. Rheia backpedalled, and Loukios darted in front of her, knocking the guard's blow aside before running the man through with casual grace. With a gurgle, the guard toppled backwards from the dais, clutching at his stomach. His *chiton* was stained as red as Draconaidas's. Loukios's sword dripped onto the hot stones as he glared at the rest of the guards, daring them to come closer.

Behind them, Alexandros grunted with pain, and Rheia's eyes met her father's. "Please," she whispered.

"Stay close," he said, turning towards the mass of guards. He stepped forward, a threatening swipe through the air spraying drops of blood. One guard broke and ran. After a scared look at Loukios's murderous expression, the others followed after.

Alexandros knelt on the pavers. His torso and arms were covered in red welts. Rheia ran to him, brushing his hair back from his face. His cheek was already beginning to swell, and tears flooded her face. "You foolish man," she sobbed, kissing his forehead, his eyelids. But she couldn't stop smiling.

Loukios offered Alexandros a hand, hefting him to his feet. "This is my father," Rheia said.

The trierarch nodded at Alexandros before running his gaze over the departing crowd. When he saw Antheia and Aias approach, the tightness in his shoulders eased. "And if we survive this, you and I will be having words about you ... marrying my daughter?" He shook his head, incredulous, before turning to regard the distant *agora*. People scurried away from the oily cloud that gathered where the statue had stood. They were no larger than insects at this distance. "For now, we have larger problems."

Rheia clenched her jaw, her relief swallowed by a terrible guilt. The black smoke over the lower city flickered with orange flame, beating like a lightning pulse in a distant storm cloud. Slowly, it rotated until a pair of blazing eyes

and a jagged, smiling mouth were visible. Even from here, Rheia could smell the stink of burnt meat and ashes, and her face went cold with fear.

"The intaglio must have been in the statue outside the temple," she said, her voice sounding distant to her own ears. A memory surfaced through the haze of her shock, of hiding behind the statue's great stone foot, of the weathered maker's mark on a giant, carved heel. The monolith was at least sixty years old. "Draconaidas never had it."

Alexandros nodded, his gaze fixed on the distant sky. "Well, it's dust now. And we have perhaps five minutes before the demon finishes coalescing and has true form."

"Right." Loukios seemed to shake off the shock, wiping the blood from his sword with the hem of his *chiton*. Coming up beside him, Antheia winced but didn't protest. "Get yourself and Aias inside," he told her, raising a hand to forestall the boy's protest. Aias had gathered the dying guard's sword, holding it with both hands so its tip hovered just above the ground. "Somewhere made of stone, not timber."

"The palace?" Antheia looked up the street.

The crowd pressed thick around the palace walls, calling up with increasingly frantic pleas for shelter. Loukios shook his head, his brow creasing and his lip curling with disgust. "The king won't open the gates."

"The House of the Beast will shelter you," Rheia said. "There are even some underground rooms. They should be safe."

"Shelter *us*," Antheia said, reaching for her daughter. "You're coming too."

Rheia wrapped her arm around Alexandros and lifted

her chin. "No, I'm not. We freed him. We will see him bound again. And I won't leave Alexandros to handle it alone." *Never again.*

"But—"

"Please, *Mammidon.* Don't argue."

"Where is Draconaidas?" Alexandros said, frowning as he looked around the courtyard. Only a dozen city soldiers remained, one of them arguing with the others, his hand jabbing towards the flaming pillar of smoke. Seeing them, Loukios gave his wife a darting kiss on the cheek and strode over. His words were sharp, and the guards' shoulders slumped with relief.

"He went that way," Aias said, pointing down the hill with one hand. The sword's tip smacked into the ground with a ting. "Gathered up his skirts and ran. He had your fancy sword, too." The boy's eyes were wide as he stared up at Alexandros.

"To the temple?" Rheia guessed.

"That's right where the demon is," Alexandros said, rubbing a bruise on his arm and wincing. "He's fled back to his master."

Rheia shook her head. "Draconaidas was actively working to ensure that the demon stay bound. It will want to turn his skull into a wine cup for trying to ensure you killed me. It wanted you to refuse so it would be freed. But..." She tipped her head to the side, mind working furiously. "If he *does* have Leohareus's binding ritual, it will be either there or at his quarters. The ritual is the only way for him to preserve his hide." Movement at the house's entryway caught Rheia's eye. Erika leaned out one of the double doors, white-faced and beckoning. Dora stood at her shoulder. The other door had already been

closed. Rheia nodded to indicate she'd seen the caregivers, and then turned back to her mother. "Please go to the house. They will look after you."

Antheia nodded, her eyes wide. "I certainly don't want to be on the street."

"Here," Aias said, handing the bronze sword to Alexandros. Its tip was dented from striking the pavers, but the sides still gleamed, sharp-edged and dangerous. "Protect my sister."

"With my life," Alexandros vowed.

To Rheia's surprise, her mother bent to unlace her sandals. "What are you doing?" the girl squeaked.

"No child of mine is running barefoot through the city," Antheia snapped, thrusting first one sandal then the other at her daughter. With her lips trembling, the older woman snatched up Aias's hand and cut across the square towards the house. Her *chiton* trailed behind her like a black flag.

Rheia slipped on the shoes, her fingers fumbling in her haste to secure them. Alexandros held the sword, his gaze watchful and his muscles tense.

"I can't believe you did that," Rheia muttered, tying a knot with a jerk as she tried to sound cross with him.

"Not kill you?" She nodded, and he sighed. "I tried to. But I couldn't do it. That was why Dora had you brought out first. I didn't want to kill those boys or your friend if the demon was going to get free anyway." His voice became gently teasing. "I'd think you'd be grateful." Rheia glanced up. His smile made her heart ache with joy.

"But the city...?"

"I've had the blood of innocents on my hands for more than a hundred years," Alexandros said as Rheia stood, wiping her palms on her skirts. "Draconaidas was a fool if he believed that would stop me. At least now there's the hope of putting an end to it."

Loukios's voice rang out. The city guards marched in a line towards the sloping hill, facing the harbour. One of them had a horn and, at the trierarch's sharp gesture, the man raised it to his lips. A flat note rang out over the chaos, sounding three times, pausing, and then repeating. Over and over.

A call to arms.

The city was going to fight. Dread uncoiled in Rheia's stomach like that smoky form below, and she grabbed Alexandros's arm, tugging him into motion. Humans couldn't stand against the demon, not for long. "Let's go."

Her mother and brother entered the house and, as the door inched shut, her gaze met Dora's. The woman had her free hand raised, as if in protest. Rheia smiled but stayed at Alexandros's side. She was done with being cloistered.

"Remember," Alexandros called as they ran passed Loukios and the guards, their sandals slapping on pavers, "he's a fire demon. Your fire-throwers will do no good."

"But the cannons might," Rheia added. Her father's eyes widened, and then Rheia passed him. *Please don't take him, Eidoneus. Not today.*

The sun had slipped below the horizon, but enough light remained that Rheia could see the spout of smoke had grown two arms. Lines of fire flashed from their ends, their heat making the sky beyond tremble as if with fear. Typhein's twin swords, *Miaiphonos* and *Thouros*.

"Gods save us," she gasped between breaths, struggling to keep pace with Alexandros's longer stride as they

barrelled down the hill at a run, sticking to the side of the road, out of the way of the tide of people fleeing in the other direction. A stitch burned at her side, but she refused to ask him to slow, instead scowling and grabbing her skirts, hauling them up to her knees so she wouldn't trip. Her lungs ached and the bracelets jingled until she grew frustrated and tore them off, throwing them into the street to be scooped up by a keen-eyed stranger. She'd apologise to Erika later. If they both survived this.

Their pace slowed as they neared the *agora*. Over the distant wails of children and voices raised in frightened conversation, they could hear that trumpet sound growing nearer, and the marching of thick-soled boots on stone.

The army was assembling.

Typhein heard it too, the demon's gaze fixed on the crowd fleeing towards the palace. Behind it, other Oreareans ran down the slope towards the harbour, but they didn't seem to interest the demon, at least not yet. Its head and shoulders had grown terrifyingly solid, the smoke closing in on itself to form a hard skin the colour of soot, banded like the leathery underbelly of a snake. The creature was as tall as the statue had been, its face higher than the temple's roofline. That face was an unholy combination of a great lizard and a bull, huge horns sweeping away from either side of a round, stocky head whose eyes and flaring nostrils leaked droplets of fire. Molten tears. Already a pile of timber stacked beside a stone wall was ablaze, and an abandoned cart smouldered. The smoke stung Rheia's eyes and tickled her nose.

The demon's torso hadn't yet coalesced; Rheia could see the temple's roofline between flaming ribs. The swords looked solid enough, though, and Typhein reached down to wedge the tip of one under a market stall, flipping it in a cascade of burning fabric, honeyed dates and melted bracelets. The demon's laugh was like rocks grinding together, sending a shudder to race up her spine and prickle the hairs on the back of her neck.

"How do we get in the temple?" she whispered as they scrambled into the lee of a smithy's stone wall, peering at the demon as it flexed its muscles and glowered down its body at the column of smoke. It appeared to be tethered to the base of the statue of Areus ... or where the statue had been, at least. All that remained was half of one carved sandal, the bare toes covered with gently falling soot.

"We wait." Alexandros slipped his fingers into hers, kissing the back of her hand.

"But the people—"

"It's right at the entrance and there's no other way in. If we go out into the *agora* while it's there, it'll kill us."

In a rippling wave, Typhein's body turned inch by inch from smoke to armoured flesh: a torso borne not by legs but by a huge, sinuous tail that bulged and flexed as it supported the demon's weight. It was as large around as the trunk of a huge tree, gathering in on itself, muscles bunching as it prepared to lunge...

Rheia shoved Alexandros back so they both tumbled through the wide smithy door. She landed on top of him, and he grunted as his bare back scraped against sand floor—but his pained expression froze at a deafening snap followed by the sound of tiles crashing to stone. The distant trumpet sounded a different note, and she heard a voice roaring a command. *Take shelter.*

But it was too late. With a laugh that made Rheia's blood pound with terror, the demon began to move. The ground

trembled beneath her and Alexandros as it barrelled past, moving as fast as an athlete in a footrace. Its tail smacked against walls with terrible crunching thuds, like a runaway cart heading up the hill rather than down. She closed her eyes, praying they wouldn't be crushed by a falling ceiling ... but the trembling subsided as the demon moved further away.

Her relief was short-lived as the distant sounds of screams grew shriller. She scrambled off Alexandros, peering out the door to see the cracks that shivered through the wall of the villa opposite, and the spray of shattered tiles Typhein had swept from the temple's roof. "Merciful gods, save us," she breathed.

Close behind her, Alexandros spoke. "There he is." At first, she thought he meant the demon and she whirled, her eyes wide, but when she followed his gaze she saw the familiar scarlet and gold *chiton* she'd come to hate. Draconaidas had lost his helm somewhere, but his right hand clutched the Beast's ceremonial sword as though that would save him from the colossal monster.

In his left hand he held a scroll case and a bundle of cloth, and Rheia's heart leapt.

They watched as the high priest reached the temple's porch. One of the great pillars was cracked, and in one corner the roof leaned drunkenly, threatening to collapse. Draconaidas skirted around it, shoving on the temple's double doors. When they didn't budge, he pounded on one with the flat of the sword.

"Let's move," Alexandros whispered. "If he gets in and bars the door behind him..."

Rheia gritted her teeth, nodding.

Together, they slipped out of the smithy, trying to

move as quietly as possible across the shattered *agora*. Typhein had taken obvious delight in causing as much destruction as possible on his departure, and many of the tables had been crushed or set ablaze by gouts of flaming saliva. Timber crackled and popped, sending new columns of smoke towards the skies and covering the sounds of their sandals crunching through grit.

As they reached the stairs leading up to the porch, the door cracked open, a frightened young face peering out. Draconaidas shoved forward, knocking the child aside. Alexandros charged, his sword held defensively. The boy's eyes widened. Draconaidas turned in the doorway, but before he could raise the Beast's sword, Alexandros slammed into him, their bodies meeting with the thudding of flesh. Together they fell to the stone floor. Draconaidas struck out with the cloth bundle, tangling Alexandros's sword in the material. Cloth and blade went flying, the scroll case skittering after them. But the snarling high priest kept hold of the Beast's sword, and the muscles in Alexandros's shoulders bulged as he knelt over the priest, holding him down as he thrashed, spitting curses.

Gritting her teeth and lifting the skirts of her *chiton*, Rheia stepped around the waving blade and stomped hard on the priest's wrist. There was a snap and he screamed, the sword clanging from his grip. She kicked it out of reach.

In the open doorway, an acolyte—a pale-faced boy around Aias's age—watched with horror. "M-master?"

"Your master is a servant of the demon," Rheia said, scooping up the lighter bronze sword and pointing it at Draconaidas's eye. "Be still." She glared at the high priest,

her voice low and dangerous.

"Me?" Draconaidas said. His forehead beaded with sweat and he stank of fear. But he did as she'd demanded. "It's this maniac atop me that freed the demon, not I."

Alexandros's mouth opened, but Rheia spoke first. "Because you wouldn't agree to let us bind it so we didn't need to sacrifice anyone else."

"Well, then, congratulations. You win," Draconaidas snarled. "I'm here to bind the demon."

"Excellent," Rheia said, taking a step back. She bared her teeth in a smile, her gaze boring into him. "We'll just keep watch and make sure you do it properly this time. No requirement for *thysies*; no hole that lets the demon keep control of the temple and drive your war effort. Agreed?"

The high priest regarded her, his dark eyes narrow as he took in her dirt-stained *chiton*; her charcoal-stained, tear-tracked face. In the distance, Rheia heard a rumble as a building collapsed, and she struggled not to shuffle from foot to foot with anxiety. "Agreed," Draconaidas said finally. "Although I think you broke my wrist."

"Sorry about that," she said, not at all sorry as she collected the Beast's iron sword from among the offerings and handed it to Alexandros. "You're more familiar with the ritual than I am," she said softly, leaning in so her lips brushed his ear. "How about you make sure he doesn't try anything stupid? I'll stand watch at the door. At some point the demon will figure out where we are..." Rheia wasn't sure what she could do at that point, what any of them could do. But she felt a terrible responsibility for what was happening to the city, and refused to stand by and do nothing.

Alexandros nodded, hauling Draconaidas to his feet when the high priest took too long. "Don't set up right before the statue," he said when Draconaidas had collected his scroll and cloth bundle. "I won't have the ritual disrupted if it falls."

"Is that what happened last time?" Draconaidas asked as the two of them made their way to the centre of the *cella*. Alexandros growled a reply, and the high priest fell silent, unpicking the knot on the cloth-wrapped bundle and spreading it open on the stones. It contained a number of objects that were vaguely familiar to Rheia, stirring memories from Kore's days: a length of thin bronze wire wound into a ring, a small dagger, a glittering pile of bronze nails, a heavy wooden mallet. There was another item she'd never seen before: a crudely formed statue as long as her forearm, like a snake with arms. *Typhein*. A replacement for the shattered intaglio? She shuddered, pulling her eyes away from the dull grey lump of metal.

An effort had been made to clean up the temple after the fire had destroyed the *adyton*, but the floor and walls around the far door were black with soot, as though a giant had reached through to smear them with grasping fingers. The room beyond was dark. A bucket sat in the doorway, a stained cloth hanging over the side, and Rheia glanced at the acolyte still by the door, taking in his reddened hands, the nails torn and broken. He flinched at her regard, and pity moved her to approach him, her sword held low and unthreatening.

"We're not here to harm you," she said. "We came to make sure the demon is bound again."

He nodded, gaze taking in the clothing that marked

her as one of the sacrifices. His hair was the colour of dark, strong honey, falling loose on the brooches securing his carmine *chiton* to his wiry frame. He looked familiar. Had he been one of the boys at the lottery that day, one of the ones who had brought out the rigged jar of *ostras*?

"But you freed him," the boy said softly, his hands shaking as he sidled away from her. "Why do you want him bound again?"

"We didn't want him free," Rheia said, guilt bitter on her tongue. "But the gods wanted the sacrifices to stop, and they sent me to make sure they did." Even as she said it, she knew it was true. Eidoneus had sent Kore back to goad Alexandros into rejecting the demon's enslavement. The entrance to the underworld would be crowded tonight, and she wondered if the god considered it worth the cost.

What if the gods have decided Oreareus is too corrupt to survive? The thought insinuated itself like a tendril of noxious smoke. She didn't believe Eidoneus would send her back to the world to condemn her entire people ... did she?

"Then we must trust that this is the right thing. Areus will protect us," the boy said simply, and she gave him a wavering smile in return. His faith shone beacon-like from his eyes. How had Draconaidas managed to surround himself with those who still believed? Timotheus too had been a true believer in Areus, even as his soul belonged to Typhein.

"I hope you're right," Rheia said, sighing as she leaned against the open door to peer into the smoke-choked gloom. The only sign of life was a thin dog skirting the edge of the square, its tail drawn up to hug its belly. The fires were spreading, growing louder; on the opposite side of the *agora*, flames licked at the walls of a two-storey timber wine house. A spark danced on a column of hot air, riding it through the window of the villa next door. A flare of light inside said something had caught alight.

Even if we are successful, the city will be gutted.

The dog skittered sideways before bolting down the hill towards the harbour. Rheia's eyes narrowed as she saw movement at the mouth of an alleyway, one that paralleled the main road up the hill. A figure emerged from the smoke, dressed in a familiar burgundy *chiton...*

"Dora?" The gasp tore from her throat and she stared as the caregiver hurried across the burning *agora*, dirt-stained and pale-faced. "What are you doing here?" she said as Dora reached the broken temple porch, hurrying inside.

"You could have waited for me," the old woman grumbled, her shoulders slumping with relief when she saw Alexandros standing over Draconaidas. Alexandros's mouth dropped open when he saw the caregiver, but he recovered quickly, his gaze returning to the high priest.

"I didn't realise you wanted to come. Your injuries—"

"Gods take my injuries," the caregiver snapped. The acolyte boy stared at her, biting his lip. A smear of dirt on the side of his nose looked like a bruise. "I'm sworn into the master's service, and if he's here then I am, too."

A distant boom shook the air like thunder. A cannon? Rheia's lips curved as she realised her father had listened to her, but the expression faded at the demon's indignant shriek and the sound of tearing metal.

"Bring the boy here." Draconaidas's low order sent dread crawling up Rheia's spine to settle in her throat.

"I will not," Alexandros said, the iron sword steady in

his grip as he stood, his legs spread and immovable.

"The ritual requires a sacrifice. A life's blood to carry the prayer to the gods' ears and make it truth." The high priest sat back on his haunches, his right arm cradled against his chest in a posture that mirrored Dora's bandaged hand, and glowered up at Alexandros. "If you wish to save the *helots* and that girl, someone must die."

"I know," Alexandros replied simply.

Rheia was moving before she thought about it, running to Alexandros's side. He looked down at her, a sad smile shadowing his bronze eyes. "You will *not* sacrifice yourself!" she demanded, clutching his free arm. The lamplight flickered, covering him in orange shadows, and her voice dropped to a pained whisper. "I just found you."

"Who deserves death more?" Alexandros said, his eyes returning to Draconaidas. The priest hadn't moved, but his self-satisfied smirk made Rheia want to run him through. "An innocent—a child—or one who has more blood on his hands than any soldier alive today?"

"No. Not you." Rheia stepped backwards, shaking her head so vigorously one of the thin braids fell free of its pin, falling to scratch the back of her neck. When she blinked, tears ran down her cheeks like rain. "Draconaidas should do it."

"The sacrifice has to be willing," Alexandros disagreed softly.

"And I most certainly am not. It should be your Beast, but if not him then the boy. Or Besadora, perhaps? She's so old she's practically dead anyway." Draconaidas sneered, his yellowing teeth catching the light. "Either way, I don't care. Shall we get on with it?"

"You should leave, child." Dora's voice was soft, but

Rheia turned in time to see her pushing the acolyte towards the door with her good arm. "This isn't the place for you tonight."

Another cannon blast echoed across the city. The boy's face paled and, with a soft cry, he slipped from the temple, the patter of his sandals growing faint as he fled.

"Don't let him do anything stupid," Dora told Rheia. "I will return." Then she too disappeared into the night, following on the boy's heels.

"Oh dear. Alexandros it is, then." Draconaidas sounded smug. "As he said, he has *so* much blood on his hands. Will Eidoneus send him to Tartarus, do you think?"

"Shut up!" Rheia screamed, turning on the priest. Her blood pounded in her ears, noisy with the force of her loathing. "Every Carmean who died during the war you had us pursue is on *your* head. Every Carmean who has died at Alexandros's hand since you became high priest is on *your* head. Because you knew how to fix this and you did nothing. *Nothing.* Instead, you fattened yourself on the misery of others. You allowed Typhein into your head, to whisper his secrets of war, and you—"

Alexandros's indrawn breath brought Rheia up short, and she paled as she realised what she had said. The demon's name, in his place of power. She wasn't his acolyte; he couldn't claim her body, but she could still draw his attention to them. Her hand flew to her mouth. "I didn't mean it," she whispered.

A distant, rage-filled bellow made the ceiling shake until dust pattered down.

"You fool," Draconaidas said, scuttling away from the entrance and that terrible cry. "You've told it where we are. It will crush us all. It will—"

None of them saw the viper emerge from its hole beneath the statue, but Rheia gasped as the shape sped across the floor like a cast spear towards Draconaidas's left hand. The reptile's eyes were full of fire. Horror dawned on the high priest's face as fangs stabbed into the tender flesh between his thumb and first finger. He drew his hand back and the snake attacked again, this time striking his elbow. His shoulder. His throat.

Draaaaaacoonaaiiiiiidasssssss. The distant scream was full of triumph. *Diiiieeeeeee.*

Alexandros brought his sword down with a wordless cry, severing the snake's head with a single stroke. It spun away in a spray of blood, the demon fire in its eyes fading.

But it was too late. Draconaidas threw himself back with a choked cry, his heels drumming on the stones as a white foam bubbled from his gasping mouth, his nostrils, to coat his cheeks and chin.

Outside the temple walls, Typhein bellowed.

It was coming.

CHAPTER THIRTY-FOUR

Gasping, Rheia stared at Alexandros. He stood over Draconaidas, his eyes narrowed as he regarded the dying priest. "How long does he have?" she asked.

"Not long," Alexandros said. "Minutes, maybe."

Typhein bellowed again, and Rheia threw her sword to the ground. The sound made Alexandros jump. "That is more time than we have, if we don't get this ritual done." She moved to where Draconaidas had sat, ignoring the choked sounds from behind her. The scroll case had been opened, and a delicate parchment unrolled, its ends held down with bronze nails. Leaning over to read it, she bit her lip. "This seems straightforward enough."

"But the sacrifice...?"

Her gaze slid to Alexandros's and away. "That happens at the end. Let's worry about it then."

"I won't let you die." His words echoed from the *cella's* walls as he stepped over Draconaidas to kneel beside her, clutching her hands. "I would rather see the demon freed and the whole city destroyed than let you offer

yourself again." His voice broke, and he swallowed hard, reaching out to take the parchment. "Agree you won't sacrifice yourself, or I throw this into the fire." She lunged for him, but he stepped back, still nimble despite his bruises.

"Alexandros, no!" She leapt to her feet and stepped towards him, her hands out. "My family is on that mountain. And yours."

"My family died a century ago."

"The caregivers are your family. They love you; you know they do. Don't condemn them to the flames." *Where did Dora go? She wouldn't let him do this.*

"*Promise me.*" His eyes were narrow and his jaw clenched as he stared down at her, already halfway to the nearest oil lamp. But she could see the panic there, trembling on his lips, through his fingers.

"You would have me kill you?" she rasped, tears choking her.

"As I killed you, yes." The hint of a smile crossed his lips and was gone. "It's only fair."

"What about Draconaidas? He's not dead yet."

"He's not willing," Alexandros reminded her, his tone gentle. "Promise me."

The rumble of Typhein's approach grew nearer, and she nodded, her shoulders slumping in defeat. "I promise."

"Good." Alexandros handed her the parchment, moving to kneel on the cloth's other side. His hands shook as he flattened his leather skirt, its studs gleaming. "Let's get this done quickly, before Typhein brings the roof down on us."

Rheia knelt, handing Alexandros the mallet. "Strike a nail when I say." He nodded, and she picked up the lump of dark grey metal. It was lead, she saw, fashioned to represent the demon. Draconaidas had prepared this one, just in case—the perfect vessel—and she hated him all the more, knowing he'd had the tools to do this ready but had declined to use them until forced.

"Areus Katokhos, lend me your spear!" She hesitated. The ritual had been provided by Areus all those years ago, but calling to him and not the god of her heart felt wrong to her. So, placing her hand on the lead doll's head, she added, "Eidoneus Katokhos, lend me your dagger!" Alexandros's eyes widened in surprise before he gave her an approving nod.

Gritting her teeth, Rheia twisted the doll's head. It moved easily; the neck was thin and the lead soft. "As this lead is cold and helpless, also cold and helpless is Typhein. Cold in wisdom, thought, memory! Let his fire be dampened and his mind confused; let all these things be twisted around!"

"*Noooooooooooooooooo!*" The pained scream was followed by a crash, like a drunk stumbling into a wall. But the sounds were closer than they had been. Much closer. Another minute and the demon would be on them.

With her hand trembling, Rheia lay the lead doll on the pavers and picked up a bronze nail. She placed the tip on the doll's blank face, pressing it in slightly so it sat on its own, and pulled her hand away. She nodded to Alexandros.

As the mallet descended, she said, "May Typhein be made blind." With a clang, the nail drove through the lead to scrape on the stone beneath. The nail's head was bent, the lead face of the doll dinged. She affixed the next nail to the centre of its chest. "May Typhein be made

weak." *Clang*. The third nail went through the doll's trailing tail. "May Typhein be made lame." *Clang*.

The crash of falling stone outside was so close that more dust sifted down from the ceiling. "Hurry," Alexandros said, picking up the dagger.

Breathing fast, Rheia took up the length of bronze wire and the doll, winding the wire around its head as quickly as she could. "I bind Typhein, demon of Tartarus, in your presence, Areus Katokhos, and in your presence, Eidoneus Katokhos." The wire covered its head and she worked it around the body, moving so fast her fingers stung, the wire biting them. "May Typhein be restrained in hand and tail and body. May he be trapped in this doll, able to trouble the living no more. As the dead are powerless and still, just as powerless and still will Typhein be, in hands and tail and body!"

A splintering crash from the *agora* made Rheia jump, the bronze-bound doll tumbling to the ground before her. It sounded as though Typhein had swept headfirst into the remaining stalls outside, thrashing and bellowing. The smoky glow coming through the doorway grew brighter, and the temple roof shook as something heavy landed atop it with the scrape of vast scales over stone.

Alexandros picked up the bound lead doll and placed it in his lap. His eyes met Rheia's across the scattered objects. He placed the dagger to his throat.

"No," Rheia moaned, her chest aching so fiercely she thought she might die on the spot.

A huge, fiery blade plunged through the ceiling in one corner of the room, its edge scoring the statue of Areus. One of the horns fell free and clanged to the ground as a wave of heat rolled over them.

"I have always loved you," Alexandros told Rheia as smoke curled around him, tender as a lover.

"*Stop!*"

The voice carried such a weight of command that they did, Rheia's mouth hanging open and Alexandros's eyes bulging.

Dora ran into the *cella*, her lungs heaving and her face white. Her *chiton* was torn and a new line of scratches marked her brow, as though she had fallen. "You will not be the sacrifice to bind the demon, Master."

"But—"

"*I* will." She crossed to kneel before Alexandros, sliding her fingerless hand into the crook of his elbow to lever the dagger away from his throat. A thin line of blood welled on his skin where the sharp blade had nicked it. "Let me do this last thing for you."

"Dora, no." His voice was a whisper, almost lost in the roar of noise as another blade pierced the ceiling, this one at the other end of the *cella*. The gold circlet in Dora's hair flickered and danced, reflecting the flame.

With a terrible grinding sound, Typhein began to draw the two swords together. He would cut open the roof as if it were a crate and pluck them out, to crush them or eat them. Rheia shuddered.

"Yes, Master," Dora said. "Let me give you a life with the woman you love." Her gaze found Rheia's amidst the smoke and falling debris. "Can you help me wield the knife?" she asked. "I can't…"

This is so wrong. Rheia felt sick to her stomach. Dora had been kind to her in the house, had recognised that Rheia might be Kore and had brought her and Alexandros together. And now Rheia had to kill her?

But what was the alternative? Rheia had promised it wouldn't be her. And it couldn't be Alexandros. It just couldn't.

Heart aching, she nodded, reaching forward to pluck the dagger from Alexandros's hand, the doll from his lap. "Move back," she told him, her voice gentle. A flaming sword swept overhead and they all ducked, the heat scorching. Bits of hot terracotta rained down. "Hurry."

Weeping, Alexandros leaned forward to kiss Dora on the cheek. Her eyes fluttered closed, her love for him clear on her features, burning brighter than the sword sawing through the roof above them. "I'm sorry," he choked out.

And then, half-blind with tears, he stumbled to the far wall, pressing himself against it as though holding himself back.

"Lean forward," Rheia murmured, and Dora knelt, leaning on her one good hand. Her other arm was still bound to her chest, her broken fingers helpless. "That's it."

"I almost failed," the caregiver whispered, her face ashen but for two bright red circles on her cheeks, the scratches on her forehead. "I knew he would offer himself to save you. That's why I came. But I went out to make sure the boy got away safely, and then the demon was on top of the building. I almost didn't get back in before ... before ... I *told* you not to let him do anything stupid."

"I tried, but he doesn't listen." Rheia placed the lead doll on the ground in front of Dora's knees.

One corner of the caregiver's mouth turned up. "You've noticed that, too?" She glanced upwards. "The demon's almost through. You'd better do it. Just ... look after him. Love him."

"I already do," Rheia said, her eyes and throat and

lungs all burning.

"Bless you." The old woman closed her eyes, craning her neck so Rheia could see the jumping vein at her throat. With her hands trembling, the girl raised the sharp little dagger, placing it next to Dora's skin.

"Do it," Dora commanded.

Clenching her jaw, Rheia drove the blade into the woman's throat.

Hot blood poured out in an iron-scented flood, drenching the dagger, Rheia and the lead doll. For a second, Rheia was too stunned and horrified to speak; then she remembered she wasn't done. The parchment was illegible, splattered with scarlet, but she closed her eyes and turned her face to the heavens, her voice thundering out over the shattering ceiling and the demon's snarl.

"Typhein! By these words, you are bound. By the blood of a willing sacrifice, you are bound. By the grace of Areus and Eidoneus, you are bound. *Walk our world no more, demon.*"

Typhein's shriek of defiance flooded into Rheia, crawling up her nostrils, into her mouth, until she burned from lack of air. She tumbled backwards, clawing at her throat as her head struck the hard stone. Lights flashed before her eyes. Pain blossomed.

Free me. The voice bypassed the noises flooding her ears—Alexandros's despairing cry, Dora choking her last—its wheedling tendrils slithering into her mind. *Kore, free me and I will leave this island be. I'll go across the sea and crush your enemies to dust.*

Trapped in a smoke-filled darkness inside her mind, Rheia was blind. The demon's enormous, malevolent presence was all around her, constricting her until she

thought her bones would shatter and her flesh would turn to pulp from the creature's weight. Typhein burned her, tasting her inside and out.

The pain was as bright as molten iron.

But the memory of Parthenia's gentle accent and wide-set, laughing eyes danced to the surface of Rheia's thoughts. Painting so that she'd leave beauty behind her. Sitting by Rheia's bedside so she wouldn't be alone as she despaired. *I wish you luck, Mud Girl.* "No," Rheia gasped, the word tearing from her throat. She would not unleash the demon on Carmea to save herself.

Then let me keep this temple, the demon cajoled, *that I may strengthen your army and power your weapons. I am what has made your people great. You would be nothing without me.*

"No." Her voice was stronger this time, and she became aware that someone was cradling her head, wiping her face clean with a gentle hand. The demon's constriction eased a little and she took a trembling breath. Even filled with smoke, the air was sweet on her tongue.

You cannot bind me, weak-willed girl child. You are an inconsequential speck! Where is your god now?

"I am a priestess of Eidoneus," Rheia snarled, "and he is keeping a special space in Tartarus, in the deepest, blackest abyss, just for you." She struggled to sit, swaying. Alexandros slipped an arm behind her back to steady her. "Typhein, I reject you." Her voice grew stronger, the demon forced farther from her with each word, leaving her thoughts clear at last. "As lead is cold and helpless, also cold and helpless is Typhein. Let his fire be dampened and his mind confused. Let his devil's tongue fall silent forever more. As the dead are powerless and still, just as powerless and still will Typhein be. No priests, no sacrifices, no control. By these words, you are bound. By the blood of a willing sacrifice, you are bound. *By the grace of Eidoneus, Ruler of Many, god of my heart, you are bound.*"

The sizzle and stink of burning blood drew Rheia's gaze to the lead doll, its shape distinct despite being coated with blood. The tail end of a black, gritty cloud poured into it, swirling and strobing with fire as it was sucked down like a fishing boat into a whirlpool. The bronze wire glowed white hot for a moment, burning the lead doll clean. Then it darkened, leaving the doll looking perfectly normal, despite lying in a sea of blood in a shattered temple. Rheia shuddered.

"I thought he had you for a minute there. That smoke..." Alexandros shook his head, as though trying to cast off the memory. "How do you feel?" He reached out to run a hand over her skull, his fingers probing the mass of her hair, where her head had struck the ground. It felt bruised but entire. Erika's ornate hairstyle had saved her. The bay leaf circlet had stayed fixed in her hair, Rheia realised with wonder as Alexandros's fingers scraped against it. "Rheia?"

"I'm as well as you would expect." Rheia tested her thoughts, relieved to find she was alone in her mind. Her gaze went first to Draconaidas, who had breathed his last unnoticed some time during the confrontation with the demon, and then to Dora.

Dora...

The older woman had fallen on her side, the lower half of her silver braid soaked with blood. Her circlet had rolled away to stop at the foot of the statue of Areus. Her eyes were closed and her face was peaceful.

"Eidoneus preserve and keep you, Besadora," Rheia whispered, tears gathering on her lashes to fall when she blinked. Alexandros's arms went around her and she let him hold her, too weary and heartsore to move.

Armour jingled and voices called in the *agora*, shouting back and forth as they discovered half the square ablaze and the demon gone. A trumpet blasted close by, a call for a bucket brigade to bring water from the fountains, the harbour. They'd be lucky if any citizens were close enough to help, though. Every able-bodied soul had fled.

"Rheia? Rheia!"

The sound of her father's voice made Rheia exhale with relief. He was alive.

"In here," Alexandros called. "We're in here."

Loukios appeared in the doorway, his breath escaping in a hiss as he took in the scene. "Rheia!"

"I'm well," she insisted as he pulled her to her feet, embracing her. She winced at the smear of blood she left on his shiny breastplate, but he didn't seem to care. "Really. I'm just bruised."

Alexandros stood, folding his arms across his bare chest in a way that made him look like a child expecting a reprimand. "The demon is bound, sir."

Sir? Rheia raised her eyebrows, and Alexandros smiled ruefully.

"Into what?" Loukios said, reaching back to his shoulders to unpin his cloak. When the heavy fabric fell loose he draped it around Rheia, covering the blood-soaked, clinging *chiton*.

Alexandros bent and, hesitating, lifted the corners of Draconaidas's original cloth bundle, which still lay underneath everything. The lead doll tumbled to the centre as he knotted the fabric into a tight ball. "Into this."

"Well done," Loukios told him, not extending a hand to take the gruesome bundle.

"It wasn't me," Alexandros said. "It was your daughter. She is a wonder."

Loukios looked at Rheia, as though seeing her for the first time. "You?"

Rheia lifted her chin. "It turns out I was a priestess of Eidoneus in a past life," she said, drawing the cloak around her and heading for the door. The two men trailed in her wake, and she smiled.

Charis would have been proud.

CHAPTER THIRTY-FIVE

G ulls wheeled overhead, yellow eyes scanning the waves and grey-plumed wings spread wide to catch the sea breeze. The air coming off the ocean was cool, heady with the tang of brine as it drove the pall of old smoke away from the docks and back towards the island's heart. Rheia watched the birds wheel and listened to their piercing cries, which carried over the murmur of the people who had come to see the trireme off.

The difference between this loosely gathered crowd and the packed, cheering one that had welcomed the triremes home more than two weeks before was stark: faces once florid with heat and enthusiasm were now solemn in the cool of dawn, raw eyes and bruised cheeks speaking of recent losses. Worry creased some faces, those wearing expensive dyed *chitons* and glittering jewellery—those more likely to have relied on the flow of *helot* plunder to make their living.

The demon fire powering the bathhouses and hearths of the rich had stopped working the instant the demon was bound and, although weaponsmiths had turned their attention to adjusting the fire-throwers' and cannons' designs so they might run on normal flame, they weren't optimistic. The Orearean army was more vulnerable than it had been in decades, and Rheia could almost smell the anxiety on the air as rich traders contemplated the consequences of angering neighbouring nations and then being rendered helpless by the gods.

Or maybe what she could smell was some households' new lack of bathing facilities.

The heavy tread of armoured men approaching along the planks drew Rheia's gaze, and she smiled when she saw her father leading his greatly expanded crew towards his trireme, his bronze armour glowing warm in the golden light of the early sun. From the outside, the vessel looked much the same—even the figurehead of Areus remained, although someone had painted over the fiery gems in the carving's eyes, for which she was grateful. She knew the interior was changed, though; Loukios's ship was the first to have had the engine removed and the rowers' planks restored. Men had been hired, and Rheia wondered how they would fare, this first time out of the protective lagoon of the Orearean harbour. A week didn't seem like enough practice, and anxiety knotted her stomach as she regarded the fresh-faced young men trailing behind the soldiers.

"We'll be fine," a warm voice said from her shoulder, and she whirled to find Alexandros had approached, his soft step hidden by the sounds of the march. The muscles in his arm bulged as he cradled a rectangular bundle wrapped in sailcloth at his side. Her gaze dropped to it, her eyebrows raised, and he nodded. Typhein's lead doll

was contained within, bound by all the protections they had been able to devise. It nestled in an iron-banded, hardwood chest whose interior was lined with lead and stuffed with dried aconite and nightsleep leaves. A wax tablet sat beside the doll, its surface etched with Typhein's binding. Eventually the sailcloth would rot and the iron would rust, but Rheia prayed the ocean and the gods would take the demon to Tartarus before then.

"I will be glad when you're home," she said in a quiet voice that was husky with overuse. "The city is uneasy, with the palace razed and the army weakened."

"I know," he said, leaning to kiss her hair. In memory of her grandmother and Dora, she'd elected not to wear a shawl, instead weaving the golden laurel bay circlet into her locks. The laurel bay was sacred to Appelon, but she was sure Eidoneus wouldn't mind. "Try to get some rest while we're gone. It should only be a day or two out past the islands to deeper waters to drop off this fellow—" he glanced at the sailcloth bundle "—and then we'll be back."

"Do I look so tired, then?" she said, pouting, and he hesitated before seeing her teasing smile.

"You're as lovely as a spring flower," he said, bronze eyes glowing almost golden in the sun as his free hand slipped around her waist to draw her to him. "But, although it was kind of you to lead the dirge at so many funerals, perhaps you ask too much of yourself."

"Eidoneus would have wanted it." She shrugged aching shoulders, knowing it was true. More than two-score people had died during Typhein's attack, most of them at the palace as the demon tore it down in his search for Draconaidas. Each evening, after a day spent leading processions to the cemetery, Rheia had returned to the house, accepting Erika's fussing and honey-infused teas before falling into a dreamless sleep in Alexandros's arms. "Besides," she added, bumping him with her hip, "you've worked just as hard." The line of injured people outside the house had often gone clear across the courtyard.

It was a different kind of pain each of them tended, but it was pain nonetheless.

"Ah, but now I'll get to relax on an ocean voyage, away from the city's demands," Alexandros said.

"That's unlikely," she said, her eyes crinkling with amusement. "Have you *met* my father? He'll have you scrubbing the decks to test your worth."

As if he'd heard them, Loukios shaded his eyes and turned from watching the crew board the ship to regard his daughter and the man beside her. His expression tightened, and Rheia stood up straighter, hiding her smile behind her hand as he came towards them. "We are almost ready to depart," Loukios told Alexandros, his voice gruff and his shoulders squared.

"Very good, sir." Alexandros withdrew his arm from Rheia's waist, but his gaze didn't drop from her father's. Rheia was pleased he didn't let Loukios cow him. Alexandros claiming her as his wife without her father's consent was grounds for a challenge, but as she and Alexandros were regarded by most of the city as heroes for their role in freeing the island from the demon, Loukios had declared him a suitable match. Rheia suspected her mother's hand in that, although Antheia had only smiled when asked.

"When we get back, perhaps we could see about organis-ing you two a proper wedding," Loukios said gruffly. Rheia opened her mouth to object that it wasn't necessary,